TSUNAMI

STEPHEN BARLAY

TSUNAMI

tsunami: series of monumental sea waves, caused by
disturbance of ocean floor or seismic movement,
capable of swallowing the largest ships

HAMISH HAMILTON

London

For Judith and Alan Young

First published in Great Britain 1986
by Hamish Hamilton Ltd
Garden House 57–59 Long Acre London WC2E 9JZ

Copyright © 1986 by Stephen Barlay

British Library Cataloguing in Publication Data

Barlay, Stephen
  Tsunami.
  I. Title
  823′.914[F]   PR6052.A654

  ISBN 0-241-11721-6

Typeset by Computape (Pickering) Ltd, North Yorkshire
Printed and bound in Great Britain
by Billing & Sons Ltd, Worcester

CONTENTS

I

A HITCH IN MACAO

Survivors of the South China Sea disaster had some horrific tales to tell. Initial news flashes had already dubbed their ordeal *Tsunami Terror*, and now everybody in the port of Macao agreed that those who *Escaped From The Clutches Of Freak Waves* must have been lucky, incredibly lucky.

'A miracle,' declared the Panamanian consul under whose flag the late *Alida II* had sailed. 'A true miracle,' he repeated, turning his vacant eyes of piety towards the skies and beyond. 'The Madonna herself must have kept the modrefokkers' balls afloat,' he concluded with a joyous sigh, and sucked the last of the whisky from his hip-flask. The owners' agent in Bermuda, the managing agent in Piraeus, the insurers in London, the charterers in Florida, and relatives of the dead, had already been notified, so all that remained to be done was to take statements from the survivors before they went on an inevitable binge and drank holes into their godless guts.

The consul was expected to interview the crew one by one, but they were in an understandable state of shock – why else would they insist on togetherness at all times? – and he felt it would be uncharitable to break up the party. Besides, their account of the tragic events was unanimous and quite straight forward.

On her way from San Francisco via Yokohama to Manila, the 8,000-ton dwt *Alida II* sailed head-on into Typhoon Louise at a point some fifty miles equidistant from Batan Island and the southern tip of Taiwan. Within minutes, the ship began to take water, and list critically to starboard. Captain Fraser ordered the radio officer to put out the Mayday call. For the following ten minutes, the *Alida II* hogged Channel 16, the wavelength reserved for emergencies. The raving seas swallowed the horizon. There was no sign, no hope of assistance – anybody who could would only run from Typhoon Louise.

The crew put up a brave fight to keep the ship afloat, but their efforts were doomed. The men were full of praise for each other and the captain. When freak, cork-screwing waves curled up in her path,

1

the *Alida II* took an uncontrollable nose-dive, and probably broke
her back. There was an explosion in the engine room (the consul
noted that the timing of this added mishap had not been unanimous)
and the crew were ordered to abandon ship. The second explosion
came only seconds after the lifeboats had been launched. The captain
and eight of the men went down with the ship. But then a miracle.
Within five minutes or less, the Greek freighter *Minerva Blue*
appeared from out of nowhere to mount a heroic rescue operation.
One lifeboat overturned. Bosun Tom Chung broke his ankle as he
was fished out of the sea and hoisted aboard. Donkeyman Hiller suffered severe shock: he had been plucked virtually from the jaws of a
shark. He now listened to the proceedings in sullen silence, but
agreed with Second Mate Ting-Chao, the surviving senior officer,
that he would not need hospitalisation and would prefer to stay with
the crew.

At three in the afternoon, the six survivors had a meal, copious
enough for twice their number, and met the world press – two local
stringers and a breathless girl reporter from Hongkong. The crew
recounted their experiences and, under keen questioning, admitted
that the *Alida II* must have been exceptionally unlucky: Typhoon
Louise had not created such severe conditions anywhere else in its
path and so, in fact, the ship must have been the victim of a tsunami,
a freakish combination of giant waves that would dig big enough hell-
holes to gulp down a fleet.

The girl from Hongkong was anxious to hear more about Donkeyman Hiller's encounter with the shark, but he was not in a talkative
mood, and Ting-Chao put an end to the press conference. By then,
nobody could begrudge them a bit of fun and relaxation. Keeping
together faithfully, they took two taxis to the Palace of Unbounded
Heavenly Happiness – arguably the best value-for-money establishment afloat north of the tenth parallel – where they chose partners
in their late ship's pecking order of seniority. Donkeyman Hiller
paired off with a docile Malayan girl and followed her to cubicle No.
9. The two of them reappeared in the 'display room' in the record
time of three minutes. Hiller paid a deposit for her, planning to take
her on a bar-crawl first. He seemed to have eyes only for his own
shoes, hurriedly dragging the girl along, smoothing his recalcitrant
blond curls with his free hand, and never noticing what a close interest a swaying drunkard paid to his departure.

Bucken, call Bucken, call him now, his instinct told him, but Hiller
refused to listen. *Stick to routine*, he urged himself. *Wasn't it Bucken
who taught you that, in a panic, Mother Routine is your best friend?
Damn you, Bucken. You'd improvise, wouldn't you? Or, perhaps, you*

2

wouldn't panic, would you? Am I panicky? Yes. Hiller was sober and cool enough to recognise the symptoms.

On the seventh floor of Scotland Yard, a red light flashed on a miniature switchboard. The operator answered at once: the call from Macao had come in on an unlisted priority line, and the time had been automatically logged. The conversation was recorded.

'This is MLX Donkey. Give me Greenfingers.'

'Not yet in. He's on his way.'

'Shit. What's the time there?'

'Zero-eight-fifty-six precisely. Any message?'

'It's an emergency, dammit.'

'I'll try to connect you with his car.'

'Okay . . . No . . . I'll call him in five minutes.'

The voice was subdued. On the recording, music could be heard in the background. Sergeant Ron Spire, alias the Donkey, Code MLX, alias Hiller, donkeyman of the *Alida II*, had resorted to the emergency routine reserved for moments of utter despair. Assistant Commissioner 'Greenfingers' Dodd sat by the phone, waiting for that second call, all day and half the night. He dined on soggy, pre-packed sandwiches that brought back youthful memories. Cops on the beat had not been so well paid, not in those days. When I was a sergeant . . . his brain began to churn out well-rehearsed lines, but he stopped himself. He felt sorry for Detective Sergeant Spire. It had shown real bravery to volunteer for such unorthodox undercover work. It would be a lonely job – and the lad knew it. Even the emergency procedure would promise more hope than help. And if that failed . . . where would he run? Bucken? Bucken used to have him under his wing, trained him well . . . but no, Bucken would not even know about Spire's secret assignment. On the other hand, he might guess how Spire's mind worked in a panic. Dodd reached for the telephone. Only now did he realise that he had squashed the last of his cheese-and-pickle into a disgusting ball of goo. Wiping his hands gave him time to think and change his mind. He dialled Lord Ashenbury's private number instead.

The butler promised to get his master promptly. 'Would you care to hold, sir?'

As if I had a choice, thought Dodd. He knew the score only too well. He would never make Commissioner. He would have to retire in a year or two, but at the age of fifty-eight there would still be rich pickings outside the force if he had Ashenbury and the City on his side.

3

'Dodd?' the voice was sleepy.

'Yes, sir.'

'Is it about the *Alida*?'

'Yes, sir. I wasn't sure if you'd heard.'

'I did. What about the Donkey?'

'Survived, but . . . er . . . there seems to be a hitch . . . He's missing, just now.'

'Oh . . . It won't be easy to replace him, will it, Dodd?'

'We'll have to try.'

'*You* will have to try . . . And, Dodd . . . do let me know if you have some *good* news.'

Dodd rang off. He could not blame the man: the City cherished bearers of good news. Until only the day before, Greenfingers Dodd had been just such a man. Anything that was good news to the City would be good for Britain, even for the big wide world of finance, and above all for an Assistant Commissioner about to retire. So now he felt angry with Spire. And there was nothing he could do for him. Dodd's thoughts returned to Bucken. Yes, the Chief Superintendent was in a class of his own. He might have some ideas but no, it would not be politic to ask for his advice just now. For, once again, Bucken had proved himself a bloody pain. He ought to know that some special considerations were called for when his suspect happened to be a junior minister's titled daughter. No favouritism, of course, but a certain degree of leniency. Compassion. Now he would have to learn the hard way that there was more to policing at a high level than merely catching villains irrespective of . . . of anything. The problem was that, if Bucken was to be taught a lesson, Dodd could not ask for his advice about Spire. Not without losing face.

At two in the morning, Dodd decided to call it a day. He went home and shared his pillow with his radio bleeper. At the Yard, the emergency line remained manned and free at all times throughout the night. But that second call from Macao never came.

In the Moon and Monkey, a Macao honky-tonk, a girl's scream could be heard clearly over blaring music, singing, yelling, laughter, and the clicking of mah-jong tiles. Bouncers moved in fast to cut out excessive horse-play with the ladies, but the screaming hostess sat unaccompanied and unmolested at a table near the edge of the dance floor. Blood was dripping on her hand from a crack in the ceiling. The bouncers told her to shut up and behave herself if she wished to continue working in a civilised establishment.

The music was turned up a little louder, free drinks were offered to shocked witnesses, and, while the police were being summoned, hostesses were urged to keep the party going.

Upstairs, in a room rented by the hour, a naked mutilated body was found swimming face down in a pool of blood. It was noted that the victim was 'a male foreign devil' (meaning white, without malice, in Chinese police vernacular), and that he must have been there for several hours, certainly long enough for the blood to seep through the floor into the bar below.

The victim's clothes were on the bed. The pockets were empty, offering no immediate means of identification. His severed hands and index fingers were laid out neatly on a bedside table. Inspector Poon radioed Police HQ to report yet 'another case of thousand slashes'.

The doorbell did not work. The brass frigate knocker looked much too grand for the rickety door of the flat in London's Bayswater. It produced thunder on the plywood. The woman at the door smiled: Bucken had always run away from possessions. When they had divorced for the second time, he insisted that she should keep the house but he would take the brass frigate, his only souvenir from his parents' burnt-out home.

She knocked again. This time the random noise became a rhythm of twos and threes that would tell him who was at the door. She paused. Silence. She had phoned earlier and there had been no answer, but she knew it meant nothing. He might or might not be in.

His morning paper was still on the floor, outside the door. *Tsunami Swallows Ship In South China Sea*. Tsunami? To her it sounded like a Japanese whisky. Heatwave, silly season and news starvation were the alchemy of lukewarm, asinine and lean headlines, Bucken had once said. He loved heatwaves. She abhorred them. Now even the slight effort of picking up the paper made her flimsy, low-cut dress cling. Perhaps I ought to have dressed more modestly, she thought. Too late. She heard the approach of bare feet padding on the naked boards of the hallway.

The door creaked reluctantly. 'Sarah!' Chief Superintendent Bucken sported a polychromatic bath-towel, tucked in round the waist, sarong-style. 'What's wrong, Sarah?'

'Wrong?' She would never admit how much it pleased her that he looked so concerned. 'Is my visit bad news?'

'Not at all.' He was ogling her from top to toe. 'Just a little unexpected.' At forty-two, she looked more delicious to him than ever. A sprinkle of forget-me-nots around her nipples seemed to grow three-dimensional under his gaze. But perhaps he was only imagining it.

'Don't be silly.' She held up the headline to cover herself.

Her embarrassment amused him. A warm smile reduced the weight of his chin: a film of sweat smoothed over the furrows and softened the craggy face. Yet he felt puzzled and worried. She would not come here without some pressing reason.

'I tried to call first.' She read his thoughts.

'The phone didn't ring.'

'Didn't it? She rose on her tiptoes and caught a glimpse of the living room over his bare shoulder. An almost empty Bacardi bottle stood on the floor just beyond the open door. Behind it, a telephone extension cable snaked across the room. She looked at him and they both suppressed a chuckle. He knew that she knew that when he wanted to sleep or had a visitor, he would stuff the phone and a cushion into a chest of drawers: better than having the receiver off the hook because that would only reveal to callers that he was at home.

'May I come in?' she asked and, sensing his hesitation, added hurriedly 'It's urgent. And I . . . I mean Jeff and I are going away for a fortnight.'

He led her into the kitchen and poured her some iced orange juice. 'Congratulations, Sarah. I would have written to you. I'm sure you'll be very happy.'

'I hoped to tell you myself.'

'Too late.' He made it sound like a joke. He had heard only the day before that Sarah was to marry Jeff Reed, a retired Commander of London's E Division, who now had some very cushy job in airline security. It was most annoying that Bucken could not fault him in any way. Reed was a suave, greying widower, and a first-rate cop. Had Bucken accepted a desk-job like his in or outside the police, Sarah would have never divorced him. 'Lucky Jeff.'

'Lucky me.'

'Do you love him?' He knew it was a question he should not have asked, but it was irresistible.

'He's a nice man.'

'That's not what I asked.'

'That's what matters. And now the good news.'

'You're pregnant, too.'

'Very funny.'

'I'm sorry. I apologise.'

'Accepted. Because I know that you're under a lot of pressure.'

'Am I?' He wondered how much she knew. She had always had friends everywhere in the police, even in the Big House. People would ply her with gossip and secrets, open up to her, use her as an emotional dustbin.

'Are you still fed up with the job?'

'Now and then.'

'Then here is your chance to get out in a big way. I've brought you an offer, well, tentatively. But it's still very hush-hush.' She heard footsteps and stopped.

Bucken got up but he was too late. The door opened and a girl appeared. Dressed in a brief smile she said 'Sorry. Didn't know you had a visitor.' She was twenty, and had been signed up to advertise some 'bread-free bread' on television as the 'winner of the inch-war'. She crossed the kitchen with the confidence that made her look over-dressed, and ran the tap.

'Sarah, this is Helen,' said Bucken and felt like an idiot. But what else can you say? 'Helen, this is my wife.'

'Hi,' said Helen without turning.

'Ex-wife. Twice removed,' snapped Sarah.

'It's all right, I had an auntie like that,' Helen assured her, balancing an overfilled glass of water as she kicked the door gently shut behind her.

'Bitch.' Sarah managed a smile.

'It's . . it's just that I seem to have another of those spells,' Bucken fumbled for words. 'You know. The younger generation seems to have decided that I'm an educational institution. Can get very boring.'

'You could have fooled me.'

'And what's your offer?'

'A top job. A new international security firm is being set up.'

'I've heard about it.'

'They want you as chief executive.'

'Who want me?'

'The boss? The shareholders? I don't know.'

'Who told you about this?'

'My uncle. You know, the one on the Stock Exchange.'

'What has he got to do with the new company?'

'I don't know.'

'Who asked him to ask you to get to me?'

'I don't know. It was very hush-hush. But serious. They'd pay you a lot of money.'

Damn them, thought Bucken, now they want to buy me off. The timing of the offer could not be a coincidence. In connection with a drug racket investigation, Bucken had discovered the involvement of Lady Carolyn, fifteen-year old wayward daughter of a junior minister tipped to graduate soon to the Cabinet. Wheels within wheels had begun to turn, veiled and not so sophisticated requests had been

7

made to 'those concerned with the investigation' not to lean too heavily on the 'child', but Bucken would have none of it: he claimed she had been instrumental in making new contacts among kids for the pushers, developing clients, some of them in their early teens, supplying them with free samples, and turning some experimenters of the 'one must try everything at least once' brigade into confirmed heroin addicts. Full evidence was still eluding him, but he was determined to get it. 'Did you say a *lot* of money?'

'Yes.'

'Pity.'

'You mean you won't even consider it?'

'I will. Most carefully. But only if you can tell me who's made the offer to your uncle.'

'I don't know.'

'As I said – pity.'

Sarah looked around. 'Not much has changed around here.'

'No.'

'And still no carpet in the hall.'

'No.'

'Lack of time?'

'Partly.'

She stared at him straight, in defiance of what she was about to do – hit him below the belt. 'And partly money. Lack of funds. You haven't changed.'

'True.'

His salary could have guaranteed him a good life with easy access to everything material within reason and a little beyond, except that money seemed to be dripping away from his fingertips. He refused to discuss it, even in the good days with Sarah, but she saw enough to have a fair guess where the money had gone: an incessant pilgrimage of social flotsam and jetsam would find its way to Bucken's door and go away richer. Sarah knew some of them: ex-cops who looked as unsavoury as their ex-con sharers of Bucken's favours; a gin-sodden prostitute; a recidivist gambler; some post office hero whose broken spine had earned him the Queen's medal for gallantry.

He always said that he was no do-gooder, and Sarah took his word for it. She knew that being charitable embarrassed him. Yet he would not clarify what he overspent on. So was it some form of guilt that drove him to pay up and make up for all the underhand methods and unfairness perpetrated in the name of – what? The law? His ambition? Self-aggrandisement?

'Well,' she said at last, 'I know that now and then you get a kick out of power. I mean the power to punish and the power to help. So

8

why not take this job? It could keep your menagerie in the style they're accustomed to.'

'That was unkind.'

'I know. It was you who taught me to fight dirty.'

'You were a good pupil.'

'I only mentioned your cripples because . . . ' She stopped.

'Because you wanted to help me?'

Her face said it all: here we go again, same old story, you'll never leave the Yard, no matter what, not even if I married you for the third time in the hope of a real home life, like before our second marriage.

He looked equally sad. It hurt that she might be a party to some conspiracy. They would remove him from the drug case, buy him off with cash and pay him off with Sarah. No, she would not help anyone to bribe him. So he had no hard feelings. But the warmth of the moment, the pleasure of seeing her, all that was gone. And, probably, the best chapter of his life was now closed. Wiped out. He felt cold, devoid of happy memories.

'I'm sorry I had to drag you in, Bucken.' Greenfingers Dodd paused and stared at the two neat stacks of papers on his desk.

Bucken knew he was expected to say it did not matter, he was only too pleased to answer the Assistant Commissioner's urgent call, but he was not in a charitable mood. His week off had been long overdue. Besides, he hated the heavy scent of some prize-winning exotic greenery that had earned the AC's nickname and turned the room into a jungle.

'I mean it couldn't be helped. A couple of things have come up.' Another pause. 'Not very pleasant ones, I'm afraid.' And, when Bucken still refused to help him with questions, Dodd began to fiddle with the delicate thorns of a flowering cactus. 'When did you see that girl last?'

'What girl?'

'You know . . . what's her name? That minister's daughter.'

'Lady Carolyn? Oh . . . a couple of days ago.'

'In connection with your investigation, I presume.' It sounded casual enough to put Bucken on his guard.

'No. I mean yes, but accidentally.'

'Oh?'

'I was having a hamburger in a caff down Queensway. She came in, spotted me, and asked if she could join. I had a feeling she might have grabbed the opportunity to talk to me on my own.'

'Why?'

'She was more apologetic than usual. So I advised her to make it easier for herself and cooperate. She said she'd think about it.'

'That's all?'

'Yes.' Bucken felt like yelling, *Out with it, you sly bastard*, but his voice remained mildly bored and uninterested. 'It's all in my diary. You wish to see the entry, sir?'

'She now says you summoned her to that café.'

'Bullshit . . '. if you'll pardon the expression, sir.'

'She said you made advances. You suggested a cruise down the Nile at her expense – and all would be forgiven and forgotten.'

'And you take that seriously?'

'Of course not.' Dodd was at his jovial best. 'We get these things all the time, don't we?'

'But?'

'But, of course, this is a little more difficult. I mean she complained to her father who, in turn, mentioned it to someone at the Home Office. You know how it goes.'

'You mean it's now an official complaint against me?'

'Oh no, not at all, I wouldn't be talking to you on my own if it was, my boy, but . . . well, you know how it is . . . it was mentioned, it's not on record, but it can't be ignored.'

'I understand, sir.'

'Do you?'

'Yes. You want to hand it over to A10 and, before they start rubber-heeling me, you want to warn me. I appreciate it.'

'I intend to follow no such course. I don't believe the girl's version, not a word of it. I want no scandal. We'll keep it in the family, shall we?'

'Thank you, sir. But no thank you.' Bucken stood up. 'If you pay any attention to it at all, you've got to suspend me and hand it over to A10.'

'I have nothing to hand over to them.' Dodd began to lose his patience at last. 'I can't name my source and he wouldn't back me anyway. I thought I could help you with a friendly warning to hand over the whole thing to the drug squad, where it belongs. You were a fool to talk to her at all on your own.'

'I could always deny it. Not that I'd want to.'

'Not that you could. You two were seen together by her friends. If she wanted to set you up, she seems to have done it well.'

'All right, I'll ask for an investigation against myself.'

'And it'll lead to nothing except a scandal that could ruin her father as well as you. We're under attack, Bucken. If we're not *seen* to be beyond any reproach, the fucking civil liberty gangs will have multiple orgasms all over the bloody place.'

'Quite right too, sir. It's their job to watch our ass.'

'You were not so understanding towards them when you were in Special Branch, Bucken.'

'Then it was my job to watch their ass both for kicks and for national security.'

'Well, we'll leave it at that, shall we?' Dodd quickly drafted a few sentences in his mind for Bucken's annual assessment. Lack of political sensitivity. Limited sense of diplomacy . . . He decided to file a note on the whole affair with the comment: allegation cannot be substantiated: no further action at this stage.

'Anything else, sir?'

'Yes. Do sit down. Some bad news, I'm afraid. Sergeant Spire is dead.'

'Dead?' Bucken leaned forward, seeking support from the edge of the table. He's too young, he meant to say, but he had no breath to say it with.

'He was killed.' Dodd shifted the cactus and pulled a dozen scene-of-the-crime photographs out of an envelope 'Murdered, to be precise. I'm sorry. I know you were friends.'

Bucken stared at the pictures. He was used to gory scenes. These made his stomach turn. 'That's . . . that's no plain murder . . . that's an execution.'

'Yes, you're probably right.'

'Where? I mean what happened?'

'Can't tell you much, I'm afraid. He's been doing some undercover job. This happened in Macao.'

'Macao? How come? And why?' He was stunned. His brain refused to deal with the message. He shook his head as if that would help to clear his thoughts. Theirs was a peculiar friendship. Bucken had trained the young policeman who, in turn, idolised him. Bucken had never had any children. Ron's friendship used to give him a whiff of experiencing parenthood.

'It's very sad. He was a good man.' Dodd turned and took a slim folder out of his personal safe. 'Because of the peculiar circumstances and the risk we'd anticipated, he left his will with me. You and I are named as executors. You're also one of the child's guardians. I suppose he discussed that with you.'

'Yes.' But, of course, it was a joke. Over a few jars in the Wellington Arms. 'Does his wife know?'

'Yes. It wasn't easy to reach you. And I thought I could, well, spare you . . . '

11

'So what are we doing about this?' Bucken cut in, decapitating the cactus as he flung the pictures on the desk. 'I'm sorry.'

'Sorry?' Dodd was in shock. He picked up the flower and held it to the stem as if contemplating how to glue it back. 'Do? What can we do about it? We can't do a thing, and you know it.'

'But . . .'

'It's outside our jurisdiction, Bucken. We can't run an investigation in Macao. The local police is doing everything possible, I'm sure.'

'Is that good enough?'

'No. But we have no alternative. We can't even admit, I mean fully, that he was doing an undercover job.'

Fury welled up in Bucken's throat. He wanted justice, no, revenge for a young brave cop whose death seemed to be regarded by Dodd as just a hitch in some Far East operation. 'What was his job?'

'Something to do with maritime fraud. On a very big scale. That's all I can say. I'm just as concerned as you are. Believe me. But my hands are tied.'

'Can't I do something . . . as a friend . . . sort of privately?'

Dodd shrugged his shoulders.

'I have a great deal of holiday and accumulated time off. I'm willing to use it.'

'It's not that simple, Bucken.'

'I know.'

'Besides, you've got enough on your plate as it is.' Only the AC's tone suggested that Dodd might be ready to make a deal. If Bucken opted out and let somebody else handle the minister's daughter . . .

'I understand, sir.'

'Do you? I doubt it. And then there's the question of money. It would cost a fortune to go into it.'

It was Bucken's turn to shrug his shoulders. 'I have some savings.'

'Well, if you're that determined, I can't hold you back from using your own time, your own money and acting in a private capacity.'

'I'd have to know what he was up to.'

'Let me think about it. Perhaps I can find some way to help you a little. Under the counter, of course.'

'Thank you, sir.' Bucken felt like apologising. Greenfingers was a good man, after all, under that callous façade.

When the door closed behind Bucken, Dodd dialled Lord Ashenbury's number. 'I think we may be able to develop a new volunteer, sir,' he said.

'I knew you'd come here, Bucken,' her tongue tripped over his name, 'I just knew.' She was drunk, paralytic, in fact, from the potent mixture of grief and every drop of gin and sherry in the house. Empty bottles all over the place testified to that. Somewhere upstairs, a small child cried. 'His clothes are still here. What do I do with them? Look . . . I can't throw 'em away, can I? Look . . .' For some incomprehensible reason, she insisted that Bucken should inspect them.

'He used to call me Sugar. And he said you were the best.' She began to back away, leaning dangerously. Bucken gently steadied her. She did not seem to notice. 'He's been away for a year. A whole year. He said Ssssshugar . . . no holidays, nothin'. Ssh. It's too dangerous. Isn't that funny?' She suddenly threw her plump bare arms round Bucken's neck. 'Ron always said you were the best . . . you werrre the verrry verry best . . . Now show me how good you arrre . . .' She swayed and all her weight pulled on Bucken. 'He said Sssshugar . . . be good. And I was. But why? What for?'

Bucken peeled her arms away, led her to an armchair and let her collapse. 'Steady now,' he said, just to say something, put a blanket on her, and played baby-sitter through the night. By dawn he grew very angry with the world, Sugar and Dodd almost as much as with Ron Spire. He should not have died so young.

The perfectly matched graining of the oak panels created the impression that they had once wrapped just one monumental king of the forest. The champagne was Dom Perignon, fresh Pacific prawns formed a pink waterfall covering a miniature iceberg, slices of smoked salmon were dotted by segments of lemon in sterling silver squeezers, and Lord Ashenbury was most apologetic for the dull setting and simplicity of the lunch. 'I'm ready to own up, it was my personal choice, gentlemen, but,' he turned to Bucken, 'as Mr. Dodd knows, our boardroom is checked for bugs twice a week and may well offer the most confidential four walls outside the safe room of our Moscow embassy.' The pomposity of the speech was counter-balanced by the self-mocking undertone, and Bucken warmed to him instantly. It would have been difficult not to. Ashenbury was a perfect host and had already paid Bucken the compliment of knowing a great deal about his triumphs, varied exploits and sometimes questionable methods in the name of dedication. He was tall, even taller than Bucken, and his height was exaggerated by his slimness and slightly stooping posture. The twinkle in his blue eyes seemed a reflection of his silvery hair; well-toned muscles lent bounce to his gait; the casual fit of his clothes would have revealed the enormity of their price only to those already in the know; and his long fingers, though strong, denied any trace of physical labour for several generations. He was the epitome of the English aristocrat. But that he was not. Bucken, too, had done his homework.

Ashenbury had worked his way up from the humble hopelessness of a City insurance clerk's position, and achieved just about everything the square mile of money-making could offer. A prominent underwriter of risks at sea and in the air, with more fingers than anybody's fair share in the pie of shipping, he was an adviser of the State – 'governments come, governments go,' he liked to say, 'the minions who serve them stay on to advise.' It was he who had alerted the government and, in turn, Scotland Yard to 'some hanky-panky on a massive scale' and arranged, eventually, unofficial backing and finance for Spire's mission.

'I understand you're keen to uncover what happened to your protégé.' He had Bucken in his sights.

What the hell did he want? A declaration of faith? The detective kept silent and concentrated on the salmon.

'How much do you know about his work?'

'I know the punchline. He's dead. Now perhaps someone could tell me the joke.'

Ashenbury liked his abrasiveness and smiled. 'Well, I won't bore you with the details . . . '

'Please do.'

'All right.' Ashenbury spoke for thirty minutes without any interruption. He painted a bleak picture of world shipping; with the Western sea-powers tottering on the brink of extermination. 'Politicians are kidding themselves – or us – when they speak about the light at the end of the tunnel. It's rubbish. The recession is still with us, and nothing reflects it more than the state of shipping, where we have the most disastrous situation for at least fifty years, and probably ever. Mammoth shipping companies and multi-millionaire insurance syndicates are going under, and as a result, national economies suffer hardly bearable losses. Shipping thrives on wars even if the booms are followed by recession. But it appears that, now, the booms are shorter and recession periods stretch ever longer. We had a mini-boom in 1980. Since then – nothing.'

Bucken sipped his champagne, rested his gaze on the green, choppy seas of two priceless Turners, and wondered how much all this had to do with the cutting up of a good cop.

Ashenbury might have noted his wandering eyes, but paid no attention. 'With the world economy in dire straits, we have far too

14

many ships chasing precious little cargo. Despite rising costs, time charter and voyage freight rates are below even the 1975 level. Bulk carrier and tanker owners are only too keen to operate even at a loss. Heavy taxation of profits and the wages extracted by the unions force most ship-owners to escape and fly "funny flags" – you know, flags of convenience. But nothing helps: we have a ship glut. So entire fleets are mothballed. You know what it costs to have a ship laid up and preserved? Something between one and four thousand dollars a day'. No wonder people can't afford it. Hundreds of freighters are just rotting away. In Brunei, in one of the mothball bays, I saw three feet of grass growing on the decks of fine ships after a single year of neglect. In the Greek islands, it's like a tanker cemetery. In the beautiful bay of Elefsis near Piraeus, and for miles and miles off Delphi, you can't see the water for the tankers.' Ashenbury's voice faltered but, by the time he had refilled the glasses, he was again in full control.

'Much of this is, of course, our own fault. Miscalculation, you might say. We were too optimistic about industrial growth. But it's the classic case of what the Yanks call the Arkansas hog cycle. The farmers raise pigs for bacon and, because it's good business, more and more farmers jump on the bandwagon. Soon there's a bacon glut, supermarket prices fall – and a lot of farmers go bankrupt. Those who survive stop breeding, and suddenly there's a bacon shortage. So farmers begin to breed pigs for bacon.

'In our case, we built bigger and bigger ships because the profits were fantastic. New supertankers earned their building cost almost overnight. Bankers were falling over themselves to lend money. A medium-size cargo ship could easily earn seven thousand dollars a day, more in boom time. But, now, most owners are delighted if their fine huge oil tankers get loaded with water for the Middle East.

'The world fleet of big tankers is valued – and insured and mortgaged! – at some fifty billion dollars. You know what they're worth second-hand? Perhaps a third of that. If that. Because there're no buyers. Mind you, it's a sensitive business. I know a shrewd Lebanese who, at the first scent of the Iranian crisis, bought a tanker as it was loading oil for just under eight mill – dollars, that is – and sold it a week later for nine and a half. Not bad, is it? And such profits are just round every corner. Supertankers that were built in '75 for seventy mill are now selling at scrap value for under four. If we had some war, just a little one, almost anywhere, the same ship could fetch thirty mill overnight.

'Then, on top of it all, you have the Communist threat. The Soviet merchant fleet is enormous and growing every day. Like the Japanese shipyards, they undercut everybody. Our maritime might is dwindling. Britain lost some seven hundred ships in half a decade. A third of the Greek-owned ships are idle. Thousands and thousands of Western sailors are out of work. The owners who are still trading must hide more and more behind nameplate companies in the Bahamas, and use Philippine, Chinese, Polish and other cut-price labour with Korean blue certificates to beat the union trap. Everybody's on the fiddle, but don't blame them, Mr. Bucken, it's a matter of survival.'

'Fiddling is one thing. Killing cops is something else.' Bucken's voice was cold.

'True. But it's not that simple. When trade and maritime insurance revenue are down, when fewer ships are plying the seas, you'd expect claims, too, to decrease. But this is not the case. Claims are up. Disastrously. Fraud is not just an old weapon in the fight for survival, it's also grown into big business. The only boom industry we have right now. It attracts outright crooks as well as survivalists. Old-established houses, traders of impeccable reputation, even people like Oldman Savas are rumoured to be on the bandwagon. And why? Because the survivors of the slump will grow fat and wealthy on the corpses of the bankrupt. We estimate that last year the hundreds of fraudsters collected one and a half billion dollars by cheating banks, traders and ship-owners, sinking and burning ships and cargo, using all the tricks in the book.'

'Can't you stop the pay-out?'

'Not very often. To delay and ask too many questions without some hard evidence is bad business. Bad for banks, bad for the insurers' reputation. And to get the evidence? Well, almost impossible. Who should investigate? Which of the countries involved? The one where the owner is registered or the other under whose flag the ship is trading? Or where the ship was loaded or unloaded or where it disappeared or which nationality some of the crew were? In most cases it's impossible to discover who the real owner of a ship is and who really benefited from some fiddle.'

'So that's where Spire was brought in.' Bucken's eyes left Ashenbury and bore into Dodd who sat there, nodding politely, with the measured lack of interest of a casual spectator at the opening of a church bazaar. 'Did he know what he was up against?'

'There was very little time to brief him,' said Ashenbury.

'He knew he'd have to learn it all on the job,' added Dodd.

'So you dropped him in the shit without telling him whether he could swim or drink his way out of it. Is that what you call sound business practice?'

There was a long pause. Then Ashenbury said very quietly: 'It's not just business, Mr. Bucken. It's a matter of national survival.'

'Okay. Give me the details. And I mean facts.'

'You don't need details, Bucken,' Dodd rebuffed him brusquely. 'You're interested only in your friend's fate. So it'll suffice to say that we suspected the birth of a colossal fraudulent conspiracy, that could start a war or at least bankrupt Britain and some other countries, too. Spire managed to supply some evidence about the crime syndicate involving some of the most respected houses, but, beyond that, all we know is that he survived the last voyage of the *Alida II*, which might have been a rust bucket job.'

'It's the trade name for the classic trick,' volunteered Ashenbury. 'They over-insure a rusty old ship or, even more likely these days, they load valuable cargo and sink it all for insurance or, better still, sell the cargo secretly before they burn the bucket. If you wish to go to Macao to find out about your friend's fate, Mr. Dodd will be able to give you at least some guidance, I'm sure.'

'But no official backing. We can't sanction the breaking of international agreements. We can't investigate outside our jurisdiction. So you're on your own. And make no mistake about it: you're a marked man as soon as you make your first move. But – you volunteered.'

'I know my side of the bargain.'

Ashenbury sensed the rising waves of tension: instant mediation had earned him many boardroom victories. Ignoring Dodd completely, he leaned across the table towards Bucken. His voice was full of reassurance. 'Needless to say, unofficially, we'll back you to the hilt.'

'We? Who are *we*?'

'Myself, the City . . . ' he gestured vaguely towards the massive, crown-shaped chandelier, 'and above . . . '

Bucken sighed. It would not be the first time that he was invited to get himself burnt in the so-called national interest. Bloody sucker, he told himself. They know you. They knew Spire. But, unless you knew for sure that they were bluffing, how could you say 'no' to the bastards?

The Happy and Safe Barber shop did not quite live up to Bucken's expectations. Probably, it would have been more satisfying to replace his konked-out electric razor than to submit to a 'very close shave – galanteed'; to sleep a couple of hours instead of electing the 'hot towel rejuvenation special'; and to put his hands under a passing

17

lorry rather than allowing the barber to crack his neck and knuckles repeatedly, but he had no time – and, somehow, the overall effect was not all that bad. At least he could keep his appointment with Inspector Ricky Poon of the Macao Police Department, despite the late arrival of the hydrofoil from Hongkong. Posing as Donkeyman Hiller's cousin, Bucken carried a specially issued passport that described him as 'John Hiller, civil servant'. He had come with high-powered introductions from London and Hongkong, so Poon had to see him. But nothing could force the moon-faced inspector to make his visitor feel welcome. His initial answers tended to be mono-syllabic, as if his treble chin refused to handle a full workload.

'Do you have any details of my cousin's death?'

'No.'

'Any suspicion who might have killed him?'

'Not really.'

'Or why?'

'No.'

'How about the *Alida*? Can it be raised?'

'No. It's some 18,000 feet down.'

'But the US Navy can, I believe . . . '

A raised eyebrow cut Bucken short: this was not a Russian sub-marine or an atomic bomb – why would the US Navy bother?

Bucken understood. He nodded, accepting the unspoken answer, but having already seen the Panamanian consul, that pious drunk, he had to ask many more questions. 'Typhoon Louise was pretty nasty.'

'True.'

'But not all that nasty, I'm told. I hear that nobody apart from the survivors and the press spoke about a tsunami.'

'That's right.' Poon looked at his watch to indicate that he would not have all day to appease influential visitors.

'How come the Greek ship that picked up the survivors had been so near yet was untouched by those giant waves?'

'Luck, I guess.'

'Did any other ship hear the SOS?'

'You mean Mayday. I don't know.'

'And how come that none of the *Alida* crew was swept overboard in that huge dive the ship took?'

'Perhaps the nine victims were.'

'That's not what the survivors said to the consul.'

Poon stared at Bucken, then shrugged his shoulders. 'I know.'

'They said it was the captain who had ordered them to abandon ship. So he must have survived the big dive with the rest.'

'True. Unless somebody else gave the final order. The men were in shock. Memories get confused.'

'When can I collect my cousin's belongings?'

'This afternoon.'

'What about the girl he was with?'

'What about her?'

'I'd like to see her.'

'Not a good idea.'

'Why?'

'Could be dangerous.'

'Dangerous? Look, Inspector, you didn't know my cousin. He was such an innocuous fellow. He wouldn't mix with dubious or dangerous company. All right, he was a bit adventurous and he liked to get his end dipped in every port, but basically he was just an honest and clean-living young sailor.'

'Was he?' Poon pulled out his desk drawer and produced a small leather pouch. 'Then why did he carry this?'

Bucken recognised the pouch. It contained Spire alias Hiller's lock-picking instruments. Spire had been an expert at handling them. For appearances, Bucken had to pretend that he was not familiar with the contents of the pouch, but a single glance told him that something was missing. Oh yes, that slim metal box with the fine wax for taking impressions of locks. 'What are these?' he asked. 'Some sort of medical stuff?'

'Usually, it's burglars who'd carry them.' Poon stood up and looked at his watch once again. 'Anything else I can do for you, sir?'

Bucken found it difficult to adjust to his status of a mere citizen, with no right to ask any questions, and lacking the weight to impose his will. He was on the wrong side of the desk, and it made him feel uncomfortable. Is that how Spire must have felt?

'Anything else, sir?'

Was that the moment to try to grease Poon's palm? For once in his life, Bucken had substantial resources at his disposal to buy cooperation if necessary. The problem was he had no idea how to offer a bribe. A young woman brought in some papers for Poon to sign and it gave Bucken time to think how best to make use of his new-found, temporary wealth.

On his last night in London, he had wanted to give Helen a special treat. He bought her dinner and roses. Awaiting them on their return to the flat, he had laid on a bottle of bubbly, cheap and Italian but bubbly nevertheless, packed in a plastic bucket of ice. She looked at it – and laughed. 'Are we screwing goodbye?'

'For the time being, yes.'

19

Although theirs had never been a meaningful affair, it irritated him that she did not seem to mind too much. Life was just a big joke to Helen, and most things from funerals to sex made her laugh. Sometimes he'd find it most disconcerting to make love to her peals of laughter. On that last night, he had forgotten to lock the phone into the bottom drawer and, sure enough, it rang at what most women would have regarded as the worst possible moment. Not Helen. She laughed. And urged him to answer the phone. And found it exciting to try to keep him inside her while he spoke to Ashenbury.

'Hope you don't mind this late call, Mr. Bucken, but there are a couple of things I want to tell you myself.'

'I understand,' Bucken croaked.

'Are you all right?'

'Sure . . . go right ahead.'

Helen took it as an encouragement and grinned. She went into a bump and grind routine in slow motion and Bucken could not pin her down.

'With Mr. Dodd's approval, I've changed your ticket to first class. I hope you don't mind the interference. It's a long trek to Hongkong.'

'Thank you.'

'Don't mention it,' whispered Helen and made him laugh with her.

'On your arrival, an envelope will be waiting for you at the airport. It contains credit cards and details of the account we've opened for you at the Hang Seng Bank with twenty thousand dollars. U.S., that is. The bank has also been authorised to grant you generous overdraft facilities, no questions asked. Use it prudently, but use it freely if you feel that money can get you some answers.'

Bucken meant to say 'thank you' and ask what the catch was, but no sound except a suppressed little groan came out.

'Mm. Yes. Er, what else?' Ashenbury was somewhat thrown by Bucken's lack of conversation or even minimal politeness. 'Oh yes. Just one other thing. I'd consider it a personal favour if you could keep your eyes and ears open for any news about a chap called Donald Quincey.' He paused.

Helen climaxed, shaking with silent laughter that did nothing to alleviate Bucken's predicament, but he was past caring about being nice to Ashenbury.

'You must have heard of him, Mr. Bucken.'

'Sounds . . . familiar.'

'An American. Medium height, about forty, forty-two, soft features, but women find him very handsome. He was a sort of finan-

20

cial whizz-kid. He stormed the City with a hare-brained cut-price insurance scheme, and his crash was as swift and spectacular as his rise. But he's a decent fellow. He didn't deserve what he got.'

Bucken sighed with relief and rolled over, almost strangling himself with the telephone cord. 'Oh yes.' He remembered now. The crash had come about two years earlier. It made headlines for weeks: they dubbed him 'Don Quixote, the Freddie Laker of Lloyd's'

'I warned Don in good time,' Ashenbury continued, 'but he wouldn't listen. Still, I was sorry for him. I wanted to help him but he disappeared. He may be cracking up. Or crippled. Or both. I've now heard he might be in the Far East. If you found him, perhaps I could do something for him, before it's too late.'

The call had left Bucken wondering if the first class ticket and generosity of the City were repayable by the private favour of tracing Don Quincey.

Poon had finished with the papers and waited for his visitor to leave. Bucken was still undecided about the bribe. His instinct was against it. He had an idea. Let Poon reveal something about his own greed. 'I'm hungry, and I'd like to have a real good meal. What's the best place around here?'

'There're lots.' Poon seemed unimpressed by the flash of wealth.

'I tell you what. You have lunch with me, you choose the place, and whatever else would go with a real Macao treat.' He winked and found himself quite disgusting.

'Okay.'

Poon drove and hooted his way through bustling street markets, avenues of muted elegance, shadows of venerable mansions, newly raised heaps of concrete and ancient banyan trees, and then along the water front. As they approached a row of floating palaces, Bucken identified their destination by the gaudy colours, queueing limousines and uniformed chauffeurs jockeying for parking slots. He was wrong. Poon drove on. The scent of sandalwood that followed them everywhere began to mix with the stink of rotting fish and human waste. It was a peculiar sensation that, for once, Bucken saw no need to worry about the cost of the outing: nobody would ask him this time to justify his expenses.

Poon stopped the car in front of a hole in the wall adjoining a temple. He led Bucken through the hole, across a sea of dust studded with beggars in varying state of disease and disintegration, and stopped in front of a dump where spices and good food blended with the air of decay. 'You're in A-Ma-Kao,' said Poon. 'The Bay of A-Ma, the patron saint of seafarers. So eat where the seafarers eat.'

Bucken was pleased that he had trusted his instinct not to offer

21

money. The Orient was not inscrutable after all. Poon was a decent sort and would have been offended by a bribe. So halfway through an excellent meal – between the double boiled pig's tongue with whelk and the stewed garoupa fish – he said to Poon: 'Okay. Let's stop bull-shitting. You know that there's something rather odd about the loss of the *Alida*, and I know it, too. And now, to show you goodwill, I give you something for nothing. One piece is missing from that bur-glar's pouch . . . It's the tin in which my cousin used to keep his wax for imprints. Locks were his hobby.'

'Thank you.' Poon did not even look up from his rice bowl when he pulled a slip of paper out of his pocket. He handed it to Bucken. 'Any idea what this is?'

There was nothing but a list of meaningless four-, five- and six-figure numbers. 'Telephone numbers?' Bucken speculated. 'And if yes, whose and where?'

'Do you recognise your cousin's handwriting?'

'No, but I can get it verified. I'll need a copy. Where did yo find it?'

'It was hidden in his seaman's book.'

'How come that not all his belongings went down with the ship?'

Poon shrugged. 'When I give you his things, will you be looking for anything special?'

'No.' Bucken paused. 'I mean yes.' He decided to tell him half the truth. He hoped to find some secret notes Spire might have made. He also wanted to make sure that Sugar would not be exposed to unnecessary suffering. 'He was a young man. He liked women. If there're any pictures or letters from some girl somewhere, I want to remove them before his belongings go to his widow. Why should she remember him by the awful shock it would give her posthumously?'

It was a small hold-all that contained everything left of Sergeant Ron Spire. Bucken signed for it and, before taking it to his hotel room, reminded Poon not to forget to copy the list of numbers for him.

'I'll take it to your hotel. It'll cost you five hundred dollars. U.S. dollars.'

Bucken tried to look inscrutable. His hopes ever to gauge Orien-tals had just evaporated. He knew he was out of his depth here. But at least he had steered a correct course more by luck than design: to offer a bribe would have been an insult – to pay the price allowed Poon to keep face.

Back in his hotel, Bucken laid out the contents of the hold-all. Apart from the well-worn seaman's book (classy forgery, he pre-sumed) there were no documents of any significance. No letters, notes or smut, no girlie pictures either. Bucken knew that most of the survivors, including Spire, had bought some fresh clothes before the press conference. Spire died wearing his new outfit, most items in the morgue had Macao or Hongkong labels, so all the clothes in the hold-all must have been what he had worn aboard the *Alida*. Bucken checked the seams in case there was something concealed inside. He found nothing. A sudden urge made him lick the oily clothes here and there. They did not taste salty. He held Spire's old shirt to the light. There were no traces of dried salt anywhere. How come? Wasn't Spire in the sea for some time? Wasn't he pulled from the teeth of a shark? And if not . . .

Sharp pain from a blow on his neck blanked out the intriguing conclusion.

Some fifteen minutes later, the throbbing of his head was the first indication to Bucken that he was still alive. He came to in stages. His chest hurt. He found it difficult to breathe. Opening his eyes, he discovered the reason. A mass of muscle and fat of the Japanese sumo wrestling kind was seated on him, spreading all over his torso. Somebody was pouring water on his face. Voices spoke in Chinese. How many were there? One sounded strangely faltering. A foreign devil? Bucken's mind was still foggy. His hands and feet were tied.

'Mr. Hiller?' The voice was soft, almost gentle.

Hiller? Where is Hiller? Hiller is dead, Bucken thought.

'Don't try to be an actor, Mr. Hiller.'

Oh yes. That's me. Bucken began to connect. He had almost denied that he knew anyone named Hiller. 'What do you want? What's going on?' It was an effort to speak.

'Who gave you this hold-all?'

'The police.'

'Why?'

'Because I'm a relative.'

'Whose relative?'

'Hiller's. He's dead, you know.' He groaned as the big man shifted on his chest.

'And what's your interest in him?'

'He was . . . my cousin.'

'That's all?'

'What else?' Bucken's mind began to clear. It must have been a hell of a chop that put me out like that, he thought. He remembered now Spire's clothes and the absence of salt.

'What's your real name?'

'Hiller.'

'Occupation?'

'Civil servant.'

'I think you're a liar.'

'Check my passport.'

'I think your passport is a liar.'

Bucken looked up and could not see his inquisitor. The voice suggested that the man was just fishing. There was a rapid exchange in Chinese. Somebody said 'okay'. Then the soft voice said: 'This is a lying dog. Take his left eye.'

The fat man's hand dropped heavily on Bucken's face. Bucken felt as if his jaw had to support the whole man. He saw a broken fingernail as a massive thumb threw a shadow over his left eye. With a desperate groan he tried to move his head, but the weight only increased on his jaw. Fear paralysed him. Then the thumb touched his eyelid. But, instead of pressure, there was only a light, massaging movement. His eye burned. The thumb withdrew. But the heavy hand still held his face. Bucken saw half his field of vision cloud over. He was blinded in one eye. Only some blurred light filtered through on that side. He screamed and bit the hand, but the man did not even seem to feel it.

'Now. What's your name?'

'Hiller,' Bucken whispered.

'Your real name. And your real interest in sailor Hiller.' And after a pause: 'Do yourself a favour, foreign devil, answer truthfully and save your life.'

Bucken was on the brink of telling him the truth. What's the point in suffering when they're going to kill you anyway?

'We could make it a lot more painful to you.'

'I believe you. And I'd tell you anything if I knew what you wanted from me.'

The phone rang. Somebody whispered: 'Police.' After another rapid exchange in Chinese, the pressure lifted from Bucken's chest. The men left the room as noiselessly as they had entered. A few minutes later Inspector Poon arrived to deliver the list and pick up his five hundred. He freed Bucken and examined his eye.

'You'll be all right. They smeared liquid opium in your eye. It causes temporary blindness. They use it all the time to disable greyhound favourites. You've been lucky.' He led Bucken to the bathroom, and ran the tap. 'Rinse it thoroughly.'

The cold water seemed to hurt more than the smear. 'Get me a doctor.'

'Keep rinsing. Can you describe your assailants?'

'Only one.' Bucken groaned. 'I'll remember his weight as long as I live.'

'Two-ton Cheng. Professional frightener. One hundred dollars an hour for any job. Quite harmless.'

'He could have fooled me.'

'He can't stand the sight of blood. They say he's afraid to scratch his piles in case he draws blood. We'll pick him up.'

'We have no proof. Only my word against his.'

'Good enough for me. In my book, my customer is always right.' Poon pulled Hiller's mysterious list of numbers from his pocket. 'Lucky I didn't wait to give you a copy until tomorrow. I might have lost our deal.'

'I would have sent you manna from heaven.'

'I'd prefer cash.'

Bucken kept blinking. His left eye saw nothing but a milky blur. 'I may not have enough cash.'

'Don't worry. By the time we've cashed your cheque, had you seen by a doc, and got you to the airport, you'll feel a lot better.'

'It may shock you, Inspector, but I'm not ready to leave. I want to see the girl my cousin picked up at the brothel.'

'Why?'

'I want to know how he spent his last hour.'

'I've warned you before. It could be dangerous. Leave these things to the professionals.'

'What professionals?' Bucken meant to ask, but decided to trade rather than pick a fight with him. 'I agree, Inspector, of course I do, but sometimes an amateur will notice things even the best professionals can miss.' He paused, soaked a towel, put it over his face, squeezed more water into his eye, as if forgetting about Poon's presence. Even without looking he knew that the man must be fidgeting. Bucken enjoyed his little game of upmanship.

Poon resisted the urge to ask questions but, finally, curiosity got the better of him. 'What are you getting at?'

'There's no trace of salt in my dead cousin's clothes . . . It's as if they've never been in the sea . . .'

Poon viewed him with renewed interest. He would not stay indebted to a foreign devil. 'Okay. I'll find the girl and we'll talk to her together. But it might take a couple of days. It might be the shock, but she's gone to ground.'

The hydrofoil from Hongkong came to a rest with a sigh. Ting-chao, second mate of the ill-fated *Alida II*, was waiting at the quay-side. He was fed up with Macao and worried about the unexpected complications. Everything had gone so smoothly until that dammed don-

25

keyman tried to have some private fun. Couldn't foreign devils ever understand rules and orders? If Hiller was not already dead, Ting-chao would have killed him now in cold blood. And yet it was all so stupid. If only Hiller had not gone his own way, if only he had not died before he could tell what telephone number he had tried to call from that bar, Ting-chao would now be away in happy anonymity like the rest of the *Alida* crew and would not have to face Ruzicki and his probing eyes.

Disembarkation had begun. Johannes Ruzicki was easy to spot among the passengers. He was taller and thinner than the others, walked purposefully with a straight back, slicing through the crowd like a blade. Ting-chao watched him with a mixture of fear and respect, and greeted him with ill-fitting servility. He knew that *Johannes* was a German name, that Ruzicki had some thriving shipping business in Vienna, capital of a country with no sea, that his real name was *Jan* because he came from Czechoslovakia – a country Ting had once looked up on the map to convince himself that it did exist – and that Ruzicki stood no nonsense in business. But doing business with Ruzicki was good. Ting-chao knew that from years of experience.

The two men walked in silence to the hired car. Ting-chao took the wheel and drove through narrow alleyways towards the outer junk-harbour. Ruzicki stared ahead, saying nothing. Every unspoken word sounded like an accusation to Ting-chao. He tried to volunteer something about the voyage of the *Alida II* and the press. Ruzicki cut him short with a nod: 'I know.'

How come? Was there a spy among the crew? Did Ruzicki double-check everybody? Ting-chao was itching to find out but Ruzicki was not the man he would question.

'What about the rest of the crew?' Ruzicki asked.

'Dispersed. As you wished.'

'No problems?'

'No.'

'What about Donkeyman Hiller?'

'The men say it was an accident.'

'You mean he cut himself shaving.'

Ting-chao began to laugh but, when his eyes met Ruzicki's, he quickly controlled himself. 'He left the Palace of Unbounded Heavenly Happiness with a Malayan girl.'

'Why?'

'He bought her out. Wanted company for drinking.'

'And?'

'I had the place watched to keep nosey reporters and others away, just as you wanted it, and the men followed him from bar to bar.'

'So the girl might have seen them.'

'It's possible.'

When the car had stopped and the headlights had gone out, sea, sky and the narrow path melted into a massive inkwell. Ting-chao led Ruzicki by the hand, stepping gingerly from plank to junk to plank. Most of the boats were out by now, fishing; the remaining few, huddled like sheltering sheep, seemed deserted.

The cabin in the hold of the junk where the three men waited for Ruzicki would have been uncomfortable at the best of times, but with the presence of Two-ton Cheng it was definitely overcrowded. 'I've got you the money,' said Ruzicki and put his slimline briefcase on a beer crate, 'but first a few questions. You tailed the donkeyman. Why did you pick him up?'

'We don't have to tell you anything,' said Two-ton. 'We don't even know who you are. And we're not working for you.'

Almost before he had finished the sentence, something clicked. Ruzicki held a six-inch flick-knife to the lips of the big man. 'You're working for me now. Right?'

'Right.'

'Swear.'

'I swear.'

'Swear on the knife.'

'Now look . . . '

The blade flashed and drew blood. 'I'm looking.' Two-ton Cheng paled and began to sway. The blade moved with his face. 'Now kiss the knife and say thank you.' The thick lips pursed for a kiss but the blade sliced through them in a sweeping move only to return, as if on the rebound, and pierce the throat. The big man collapsed. Blood gushed, ceaseless gurgling accompanied the twitching of the body. 'Now you two. You're working for me, aren't you?'

The two men tried to look straight ahead, ignoring the long blade as well as the dying man on the floor. 'Why did you pick up the donkeyman?'

'He looked very worried when he made a phone call. To London. And he spoke in some sort of code.'

'What number did he call?'

'It began with 230. He said he'd call them again. So we picked him up to find out what he was up to.'

'We wanted to know what number he'd called in London, and why,' volunteered the second man, anxious to please and to keep his eyes from Two-ton Cheng's death throes. 'We thought you'd want us to find out.'

27

'And did you?'

'No. But the man said that Ting-chao would understand.'

'Man? What man?'

'The foreign devil.'

'What the hell are you talking about?'

'The foreign devil Ting-chao sent along to go with us and watch the sailor and the Malay whore.'

What an unholy mess, thought Ruzicki. He felt furious with Ting-chao. Why the hell did he involve some European? Weren't there enough Chinese crooks? He knocked on the low ceiling. Steps came running and Ting-chao's face appeared in the hatch above. His eyes noted but chose to ignore the corpse on the ground. 'Anything wrong?'

'Come down here.'

Ruzicki made the two men repeat what they had told him. He saw Ting-chao's face pale in anger. A violent outburst in Chinese followed

'Speak English.'

One man wanted to say something, but Ting-chao silenced him: 'These monkey-farts are liars. I never sent any foreign devil to go with them. I don't know what they're talking about.'

'No?' The man was frightened and unstoppable now. 'Then how did he know what we were up to? Why did he say that you'd sent him? Why was he the first to kick the sailor in his sacred sack?'

'Then why is it that you've never mentioned any foreign devil to me before?' Ting-chao retorted.

'Why should we? You sent him, you knew he was there!'

Ting-chao moved forward menacingly, but Ruzicki stopped him. 'What did the man look like?'

'He was a foreign devil, that's all. They all look alike.' The second man just shrugged his shoulders in support: how could anyone ask such a question? Wasn't the answer quite obvious?

'Was he taller or smaller than me?' Ruzicki asked patiently.

'Smaller.'

'Dark or blond?'

'What a question – he had hay for hair, of course.'

'What was he wearing?'

'A shirt.'

'What sort?'

'Just a shirt. But he behaved like a very important foreign devil. He gave orders. He told Two-ton to hit the sailor harder. That's how the accident happened. And, if it was up to him, we'd have killed the sailor's cousin, too.'

'Cousin? What cousin?' Ruzicki was stunned.

Ting-chao explained: 'I heard from a relative who is a cleaner at the police that a man called Hiller came to Macao. He is the donkeyman's cousin and he got the dead man's belongings from Inspector Poon. There was no time to reach you, so I told Two-ton to go along and talk to Hiller and have a look at the donkeyman's bag in case there was something that shouldn't be in there. But I sent no foreign devil with them.'

'No? You mean he just turned up?' One of the men shouted back at him, and the other added: 'And if you hadn't warned us to stop and get out of the hotel because the police were coming, that scarface would have made Two-ton kill the cousin, too.'

'Scarface?'

'Yes. The foreign devil had a scar on his face.'

'Then why didn't you say so right away when I asked you?' Ruzicki sounded almost avuncular. It was obvious that the men were lying, for some reason, perhaps to minimise their own contribution to the donkeyman's death, and now they had invented some characteristic, too, an easy and obvious one like having a scar, to make their story about the imaginary foreigner more credible. He decided that he had had enough of them. 'Come with me,' he said to Ting-chao. He noticed that the two men looked dangerous for the first time. But of course – the money. They're worried about their money. 'You wait here. The money is in there.' He opened the case to let them see the stacks of banknotes, then closed it again. 'I'll leave it with you, but don't touch it. Ting-chao will be back to share it out.' That reassured them. He started up the ladder.

On deck and out of earshot, Ruzicki took a deep breath to exhale all the stuffy air of the hold, but the smell of blood and fright lingered on in his nostrils and made him feel sick. He turned his anger on Ting-chao. 'What a fucking mess! There're witnesses all over the place.'

'I'm sorry. I'm very sorry.' He agreed that the thugs below had been turned into liars by fright. 'They could not guess what you'd blame them for. They must have tried to talk their way out of trouble. That's why they invented the foreign devil. And that's why they now blame Two-ton for everything.' He paused to wait for some reaction, but Ruzicki just stared right through him. 'What do you want me to do?'

'Clean up the mess.' Ruzicki thought for a few seconds. 'Yes, get these two to deal with the Malay girl. She must have seen them. And the donkeyman might have told her something.'

Ting-chao thanked his good fortune that he had not been present

29

at the killing. Otherwise he, too, would have to die. 'What about Hiller . . . I mean the cousin . . . '

'Yes, let them kill him,' Ruzicki nodded, but then frowned and changed his mind. 'No, somebody might suspect the connection.'

'He could be drowned in his bath.'

'No, it would still make two sudden deaths in the same family. Get your relative who works at the police to find out where Hiller lives and works. And I want to know when he leaves Macao.'

'Okay.'

'You play no part in the girl's accident. Once your men have done the job, get rid of them. Do it alone. I don't want anybody else involved in that. Do it here and burn the junk with the bodies.'

Ting-chao nodded obediently but his eyes were wide open now, waiting patiently for something that had not yet been mentioned.

Ruzicki understood. 'Oh yes, you may keep their share of the money.'

Garlic, ginger and frying onion permeated every hole, hut and cave that human misery had designated as homes for entire families. Bucken would have sworn that Poon had no idea where they were in that warren, but he was wrong. The inspector bribed, battered and threatened his way to the back of a laundry where the Malayan girl was hiding out. His sergeant then chased away countless relatives and, to the accompaniment of their distant wailing, went to work on her. He promised he would force her to make love to a dog and welcome 'the biggest, brightest new-year-day petard up in your sweetest orifice', but the girl swore that the donkeyman had never told her any secrets or given her any keepsakes, not even money. She said two men took her sailor away from the Moon and Monkey and she never saw him again.

'I don't think we'll get anything else out of her,' Poon whispered to Bucken, who then closed in on the girl.

'Listen. I believe you. I'm not police. I've lost my only cousin. His poor, poor parents will want to know how he died. Was he brave? Was he happy?' He took out a wad of crisp ten-dollar bills and flicked through them as if absentmindedly.

'Oh yes, yes,' she volunteered without much conviction. Her smile of hope and fear was sweet, whoring had not yet stamped out her innocence. She then repeated her story. Hiller had bought her out and taken her on a bar-crawl. 'From one bar he make little telephony call. From the next bar he make other little telephony call.'

'He made another call?'

'No. He very angry. And much afraid. But don't tell his mother. Tell her he brave.'

'How do you know he was afraid?'

'He . . . he . . . ' she rolled her eyes, raised her hands protectively to suggest fear and, unable to find the word, collapsed on the floor to complete her story.

'You mean he fainted?'

She said something in Chinese to Poon who, in turn, told Bucken: 'Sort of. Apparently, his legs gave way. Must have been drunk. Or dead scared.'

No, that's not Spire at all, thought Bucken, and shook his head.

'Believe me. Please.' The girl gripped his arm.

'Why would he be scared?'

'I don't know.'

'Perhaps he had seen an enemy.'

'I don't know.'

'Perhaps some big fat Chinaman . . . ' it was a shot in the dark.

'Oh yes. Two-ton Cheng always there. He work in Moon and Monkey.'

Bucken avoided Poon's eyes. 'Ah. Perhaps Two-ton Cheng frightened my cousin.'

'No, no. Two-ton very nice. He no frighten your cousin in other bar.'

'You mean you saw him in another bar *before* the Moon and Monkey?'

'Oh yes.'

'So what happened when he collapsed?'

She reverted to her original story. Two men, one with a knife, ordered the donkeyman and the girl to go with them. They locked her in a room upstairs. She heard loud music, and a lot of screaming by a man. So she screamed, too, but nobody heard her.

'Did Two-ton Cheng stay downstairs?'

'I don't know.'

Bucken counted out ten bills and, to the girl's horror, tore them into halves. 'I want you to show me where exactly my cousin collapsed. You get the half of each now, and the other half in the Moon and Monkey.'

All her muscles tensed as if she was having a seizure. Fear and greed vied for possession of her will.

'What are you getting at?' Poon whispered

What was the point in explaining to Poon that Sergeant Spire had been no coward? In all probability, Spire had spotted a tail, perhaps Two-ton Cheng himself, and, when he felt cornered, he would

31

pretend to be uncontrollably frightened, 'collapse' so as to dispose of or hide something precious. It was Bucken who had taught him the old trick petty criminals would use to fool a green cop, make him feel sorry for them – and dump incriminating evidence, drugs or stolen property in the gutter. 'Don't worry,' Bucken told her with a reassuring smile. 'Even if Two-ton is there, nothing can happen to you. I'll be with you. I'll be just another client who bought you out. And Inspector Poon and the sergeant will be right behind you.'

She snatched the halves of the mutilated notes from his hand. I must have overpriced her, thought Bucken, but then he saw tears in her eyes. As if she was entering a suicide pact made irresistible by the prize.

Judging from the volume of music, the Moon and Monkey should have been in full swing, but it was too early for that. A few sleepy girls and lazily scratching bouncers looked up when they saw the door open, but lost interest fast in the staggering drunk on the supporting arm of a Malayan girl. She led Bucken to the corner of a huge square-shaped bar, and he slipped her the other halves of the money. He ordered whisky as he swayed dangerously. It gave him sufficient angle to see the foot of the bar. There was a gap. Just wide enough to slip something in, something like a small metal box full of fine wax, the only item missing from Spire's burglar's kit. Bucken decided to pay the girl a bonus.

Two Irish sailors tried to compete desperately with the blaring music. Bucken joined in, yelling heartily. A waiter approached him offering the best table in the house. Another waiter snapped at the girl – something evidently unfriendly in Chinese.

'They want me to go away,' she whispered, 'they want you to drink with their girls.'

'Then go away!' shouted Bucken: he had noticed four eyes watching him from behind a bead curtain. 'Yeah! I'll have two of their girls.' He drank his whisky, staggering backwards, and collapsed, smashing some glasses as he seemingly tried to hang on to the bar. The sailors laughed, the girl was shoved towards the door, and a waiter summoned assistance for the customer. Bucken's fingers found their way into the small gap. It took only a little scratching to coax the slim box out of its hiding place. Two bouncers reached under his arms to help him up. As he rose, the street came into view. On the opposite side, enveloped in charcoal smoke, Poon and his sergeant were squatting at a stall, gobbling some satay from the tips of wooden pins. With her back to the Moon and Monkey stood the Malayan girl, about to cross the road. When a pick-up, laden high with melons, thundered down the street, the men's grip on Bucken tightened. At the same moment, another pair of thugs stepped forward through the bead curtain. Driven by instinct, with no time to work out what was happening, Bucken hit one bouncer and shook himself free from the other. The thugs might have been distracted momentarily by the crash outside, but a moment was all that Bucken needed as he dived through an open window to the side street and ran. From the corner, a tall thin European took a step backwards – similarly startled, perhaps, by the crash. His move was too sudden for Bucken to evade him. The impact knocked the man to the ground, where he lay face-down swearing in a language which sounded Slavic. The crunch of crowded consonants was still in Bucken's ears as he darted down the street, turned, twisted, doubled back, and finally leapt into a taxi with a sigh of relief: as well as his pursuers, he had certainly managed to lose himself in a maze of elbow-wide archways and passages.

Outside the Moon and Monkey, Poon and his sergeant had been caught off balance by the sudden approach of the seemingly out of control vehicle. The driver jumped out, rolling with the loose-muscled ease of a trained acrobat, while the pick-up crashed into the street stall, injuring the satay seller, and splashing the red juicy flesh of melons everywhere. By the time the two policemen regained their feet, the Malayan girl had disappeared from the far side of the street. They found her not more than five yards away. She lay among the smashed melons, half her skull gone. It could not have been the pick-up which had hit her: she had been bludgeoned savagely with something like a mallet or a brick. Somebody's timing must have been excellent. A couple of young women were screaming, other people stood and stared impassively. Most of them must have seen everything: the crash, the kill, the get-away. But Poon knew better than to nurture vain hopes of finding Chinese witnesses to help the police.

Bucken resigned himself to living with yet another painful memory. The blank trustful face of that nameless Malayan girl would haunt him as long as he lived. Excuses for himself he had aplenty: his own life had been at risk, he had had a job to do, it had been Poon's duty to protect her. But Bucken knew that it was he who had coaxed her out of hiding and tempted her with that half a fortune. Was the small metal box worth it? Could anything be worth it?

The wax impression in Spire's tin looked meaningless. It was a six-digit number following a sign that Poon recognised as something Japanese. A few hours later, the impression was identified as the

33

marking of a ship engine from Kobe, a Japanese yard. A telephone call to Kobe revealed that, according to the records of the yard, the engine had recently been supplied and fitted as a replacement for the old diesel of the *Lena*, a German-built 8,000-ton Russian freighter.

The Russians never used foreign crews. They would never permit unsupervised visits. How on earth and why had Spire taken an impression of the number that would clearly identify the engine of a Russian ship? And why would he protect it with his life? If he was tortured, he must have resisted telling them anything about the metal box. Bucken closed his eyes. Back came the photographs on Greenfinger Dodd's desk. The body on the floor . . . clothes on the bed . . . hands and index fingers on the bedside table. 'Did you say eight thousand ton deadweight?' he looked at Poon.

'That's right.'

'Isn't that . . . ?'

'Yes it is! Same size as the *Alida II*, come to think of it.' Another call to Kobe established that the ships would probably be of the same age, too. The shipyard also confirmed now that the mysterious numbers on Spire's list were identification markings of various replacement parts in the same Russian engine room, and that the job had been completed in May. So Spire must have been aboard the *Lena* within the last three months – during the period he was sailing in the *Alida II*. Impossible. Unless Spire served on the *Lena* and not the *Alida*, after all. Oh yes, the Russian ship might have been sold and renamed *Alida II*, except that the *Alida* documents showed a different history, and Macao shipping experts were quick to assure Poon that the Russians would sail their ships to smithereens rather than sell them in the second-hand market. It was the death-knell for another tempting theory.

The conclusion that there must be some connection between the two ships became inescapable. Spire was a survivor of the *Alida* sinking and attached vast importance to his Russian evidence. So what if it was the *Lena* that had sunk in the Tsunami? If so, where was the *Alida II*? Had she been repainted and renamed only to trade on under her new identity while the owners cashed in on the insurance? Why would the Russians be a party to that? They would use every trick in the book to undercut competitors and make a fast buck, but there had never been any evidence of their involvement in a rust bucket fraud.

'One or the other ship must be around,' Bucken thought aloud. 'If the *Alida* is now disguised, how can we eliminate the *Lena*?'

'If she's working coastal waters, nobody outside Russia might ever see her.'

34

'But if an official approach was made, the Russians wouldn't want to appear uncooperative. They'd tell us if she was alive and well and trading in Vladivostok.'

'They would give us an answer, yes, even if it's a lie. But it's worth a try.' Poon left the room to institute some inquiries.

Bucken stared at the little metal box. He could visualise Spire tumbling deliberately so as to slip it into the gap at the foot of the bar. He ached to revenge his young friend's wasted life. If only he had five minutes with the killer or the man who had ordered the kill, he would have no qualms about the interrogation. This was a personal matter. Whatever the risk to himself. But did revenge justify the risking of that Malayan girl's life? Could anything justify it? She would probably be alive if he had taken Sarah's advice, resigned and joined that security outfit. Too late.

Bucken tried to concentrate on the most crucial enigma: what was the extremely urgent message for Dodd that had persuaded Spire to resort to the perilous emergency procedure and put through a virtually open telephone call? If that ship had sunk, Spire would be in no hurry – there would be no evidence. But there would be both proof and urgency if the *Alida II* had not sunk! It would explain why there was no salt in Spire's clothes. It would not explain the Russian engine number.

Poon returned. 'I've given them some cock and bully story.' For once his English had faltered but Bucken did not smile. 'We'll get some sort of an answer, Mr. Hiller.' He said *we*. He put special emphasis on Hiller. By now he must have convinced himself that the donkeyman's cousin was a trained investigator. He would suspect Interpol or intelligence. Bucken did not care which.

'Can we trace the *Alida*?'

'Only by luck. Lots of patience and luck. I've already sent a request to every police force and port authority in the world. But there's no guarantee that they'll ever read it.' Poon's voice was coloured by the professional frustration Bucken knew so well.

'How about the crew? I mean the survivors.'

'They've dispersed. I doubt if you could ever find any of them. And if you did, somehow, you'd never even beat anything out of them – if they lied to me and the consul in the first place.'

The two men's eyes met. They both knew it was too easy and foolhardy to view suddenly everything from a suspicious angle. There was the question of the ship herself. The *Alida* was no rust bucket. The surviving documents and the charterers' statements agreed that she had recently been modernised. There was a Classification Society inspection report to substantiate the fact. Yes, the report

35

could have come from a corrupt inspector but nothing short of the reappearance of an unmodernised *Alida II* would induce him to admit anything. And why would anybody suspect the owners? The ship was profitable. And she did not even seem over-insured.

Ruzicki & Partners, the Viennese company that had just chartered the *Alida* for three years, had a great deal of work lined up for the ship. Their losses, too, might be more substantial than the insurance cover.

Some details of the ship's last movements could seem questionable in retrospect. But would they look suspicious if there had been no disaster? Apparently, after she had loaded in San Francisco, she did not sail right away. Unusual? Yes. An unwarranted delay could gnaw away at the owners' or charterers' profit. They would not allow that to happen. But there was a statement by the dead captain on record. It spoke about some 'unexpected technical hitch'. So soon after modernisation? Could it be sabotage? If yes, why? To make the ship wait for news about Typhoon Louise? For then there was a second inexplicable hold-up in Yokohama. Finally, the *Alida* sailed right into the path of that storm. And so did the *Minerva Blue*, the Greek ship that would eventually pick up the survivors. Carelessness by both captains? Pressure by the owners? There could be several valid explanations.

There was also the question of the 'mixed cargo' the *Alida* had loaded in San Francisco. There were containers holding four hundred tons of bourbon for Japan. Lead and zinc concentrates of great value. Sixty tons of electronic goods for Manila. A thousand tons of batteries, milk powder, and medicines, as well as twelve hundred tons of frozen fish to replace the same quantity lost at sea only a month earlier. (The original consignment of fish earned itself a place in the annals of naval mishaps when the ship carrying it had run aground near Honolulu, and an olfactory alert appeared in Lloyd's List: 'ship stranded, hatches leak, water in hold, fish going soft – all shipping to steer well upwind.')

'Could any of this be of special interest to the Russians?' Bucken asked.

Poon listened to the wail of passing fire engines. 'Must be another fire in the harbour,' he said. 'We get a lot of those. People are very careless.'

'Thanks for telling me. But I think I deserve a better answer. Without me, you wouldn't have the wax impression and wouldn't ever suspect a possible connection between the *Alida* and the *Lena*.'

Poon nodded. 'Are you intelligence?' he asked softly.

'I'm not. And if I was, I wouldn't tell you. So why bother to ask?'

'The CIA is interested.'

A man brought in a telex. Poon read it, then passed it to Bucken. The Russians seemed keen to oblige: they confirmed that the *Lena* had had a new engine installed but, apart from that trip to Japan, she had been plying 'Soviet coastal routes exclusively for the last two years'. To the two men this was the confirmation of a lie: Donkeyman Hiller/Spire could not have gained access to the ship and those identification numbers in Russian waters. Now it was even more imperative to prove the sinking or to trace the *Alida* wherever she was. Her appearance with her massive 250-ton Stülcken derricks, raised forecastle and a cruiser stern was distinctive enough to be remembered. If she was on the run, she would need fuel. Somebody in some port would have seen her unloading or taking on bunkers. Patience and luck – would they be enough to find her?

'What about the CIA?' Bucken reminded Poon.

The Chinese detective hesitated, then shrugged his shoulders. 'Those sixty tons of "electronic goods" bother them. Apparently, there were some essential parts of a . . . ' he consulted a note in his drawer 'of a VAX 782 series computer. It's worth a million and a half U.S., capable of guiding some missile systems, and very much the stuff the Russians would gladly go to any length to get.'

'If it's strategic high-tech under embargo laws, the Yanks wouldn't have sold it without proper end-user certification,' said Bucken. 'Who was the buyer?'

'The Saudis. The deal was negotiated by . . . ' another look into the drawer 'by Wetzel, some Cairo-based German trading company.'

The phone rang. While Poon listened, Bucken decided to send an urgent message via London to the CIA about Spire's investigation and the wax impression. If nothing else, they might be in the best position to trace the *Alida II*.

Poon's inscrutability had slipped: he looked pale and furious as he replaced the receiver. 'A junk caught fire in the harbour. By luck we had a fire-boat nearby, and with shore assistance they managed to put out the flames in time to find three bodies on board before they had been incinerated. Two had been shot, one had his face cut and throat pierced. The two haven't been identified yet. The third was easy. It's Two-ton Cheng.'

'Shit.' Bucken had had different designs on Two-ton.

Poon frowned and shook his head. 'It must be coincidence.'

'What?'

'A few years ago I had the misfortune of investigating a murder. The victim's throat was not cut but pierced like Two-ton's. The pathologist told me that it must have been a slow and painful death.

The man must have choked on his own blood. It happened in the upstairs room of a noisy bar so nobody would hear anything, but I had to interview all the potential witnesses who had been there at the time – among them, a gentleman from Vienna.'

'So where's the coincidence?'

'The same gentleman arrived here yesterday.'

'How do you know?'

'He called me. He's here to clear up some questions of insurance concerning the *Alida*. His name is Ruzicki.'

'Ruzicki? Sounds familiar.'

'You have a good memory, Mr. Hiller. You'd have seen the name among the *Alida* documents. Ruzicki and Partners of Vienna were the charterers.'

'The connection between the two murders and your man are a bit tenuous, wouldn't you say?'

'Sadly, yes.' Poon shrugged his shoulders and smiled apologetically. 'He just . . . well, sort of looks the part. We policemen must sometimes go by instinct, but a civil servant like yourself wouldn't agree with that, I suppose.'

'Quite.'

'I'm sorry. I shouldn't say things like that about a most reputable trader, particularly not to someone who was merely the bereaved cousin of a recent murder victim.'

Bucken ignored the tone of irony. Ruzicki. He rolled the name round his mouth, making the 'c' first sound like an 's' and then like 'ch'. 'Is he Russian or something?'

'Let's have a look.' Poon walked to a large filing cabinet that contained all his dormant cases. He returned to his desk with a thick file that was going yellow at the edges. He untied a ribbon and rummaged among the papers until he found what he was looking for. 'He lives in Vienna and New York, but he's Czech by birth.'

But Bucken hardly heard him. He was staring at a photograph in the file. 'It's him,' he mumbled 'I'd swear it's him. The tall man I bumped into on my run from the Moon and Monkey. He swore in a foreign language.' He moved to the edge of his seat. 'Can we pull him in and roast him?'

'We?' Poon smiled. He could hear a policeman's eagerness.

Bucken shrugged his shoulders. 'Think what you like.'

'Did he see you?'

'Don't think so.'

'You'd better keep your throat well wrapped. I've no grounds for "pulling" or even asking him in. We can, of course, look out for the murder weapon, but right now, we have a lot of problems with legality, and I can't even authorise a search of anybody's hotel room. What *you* do is none of my business. He's in room 522.'

That evening, Bucken watched Ruzicki order dinner in the hotel restaurant. Yes, he agreed with Poon: the man looked the part; his body was stiletto-shaped, and the long, strong fingers suggested a better fit for the knife than the gun. When Ruzicki cut into his tournedos, Bucken strolled across the busy lobby and took the lift to the fifth floor.

It gave him a pang of satisfaction to work with Spire's lock-picking kit. It felt as if the young man was still alive, watching his back, helping him. He had no idea what he could hope to find. If there was nothing suspicious to discover, he would know at least. It would be gratifying, of course, to come upon a stiletto with bloodstains on the blade or a brand-new similar weapon still in its original packing – in Bucken's experience, knife-men liked to have a spare – but the man downstairs looked anything but the fool who would pepper his room with self-incriminating evidence.

Bucken used a torch and worked methodically. He went through pockets and drawers, felt under the mattress and looked under the bed and the carpet. The shoes in the cupboard were stuffed full with fresh and half-soiled socks and underwear. Frowning, he picked them out to uncover some five thousand dollars in cash keeping the toes in shape. A small revelation for his labours, but it told him that Mr. Ruzicki was a cautious man who travelled well prepared for emergencies.

A plastic file, full of papers, left carelessly on top of the dressing table, could not contain any great secrets, but Bucken flicked through them just the same. They all dealt with the various claims arising from the *Alida II* disaster. One of the letters had come from D. Savas of Rotterdam, Piraeus and New York, and another from the ship owners' agent in Bermuda expressing hope that 'Ruzicki & Partners would clarify the position with Mssrs. Wetzel and the Saudis'. On the corner of the letter, a note was pencilled: 'Shepheards 26-28.' Mssrs. Wetzel were in Cairo. Wasn't Shepheards some legendary old hotel in the Egyptian capital?

Bucken dropped the papers, switched off his torch, and froze: he heard steps stopping outside the door. Metal tinkled. A click: a key entered the lock. Bucken moved fast. He would be behind the door once it opened. Ruzicki might be armed. With a lethal stiletto? Bucken reached for the handkerchief that was always stuffed with nonchalant flamboyance into his breast pocket. Tied to the bottom of the cloth was his bunch of keys. Taking advantage of the surprise it could cause, and swung with a flourish in a fiercely swiping arc, it was a formidable weapon even airlines would not suspect or confiscate.

The door opened and the lights came on. Why would Ruzicki leave his dinner half way through? Bucken's grip tightened on the handkerchief.

It was room service. Two chattering Chinese maids delivered some clean shirts, turned down the bed, pinched a handful of cigarettes, and left without ever looking behind the door.

In the beam of the torchlight, Bucken noticed Ruzicki's suitcase which stood leaning against the wall. It was locked, but easy to pick open. Yet it was empty. Why would Ruzicki lock it? Bucken ran his hands lightly along the lining. His fingers stopped on a small, raised surface. At the far end he could reach under the lining. He found a British passport. The photograph in it was Ruzicki's – the name was not. A fake. Poon could hold Ruzicki and ask some embarrassing questions. Ultimately, a charge would only alert Ruzicki. Bucken decided against doing anything about it. He slipped the passport back into its hiding place.

Wetzel in Cairo. Bucken re-examined the papers and copied out the address. Shepheards 26-28. If the figures were dates, they were only three days away. It would be interesting to see what sort of outfit Wetzel's was and whether Ruzicki would be visiting them with the fake passport. Yes, that could be useful.

In normal circumstances, Bucken would have to seek Dodd's approval before embarking on an additional, costly trip. He refused to admit even to himself how exhilarating it was to enjoy full independence and to be able to make snap decisions. Why not? He would fly first class to Cairo on other people's money with no questions asked, keep no meticulous notes, write no reports, give no account of his plans and movements in triplicate – just back a hunch with almost forgotten youthful irresponsibility.

On his way back to his hotel, he had a feeling that he was being followed. A couple of sudden U-turns convinced him that he was wrong but suddenly it struck him that the danger might be real. Ruzicki's appearance in Macao might be a questionable coincidence. But it could be no coincidence that so soon after the Malay girl's death Two-ton Cheng and another two men had been killed. Somebody was cleaning up the mess in the wake of Hiller's torture. What if they wanted to silence Hiller's nosy cousin, too? A strange alertness came over Bucken. He caught himself seeing dangers everywhere, listening to little sounds that might not fit the landscape. He diagnosed undercover jitters in his own tense behaviour. But why take unnecessary risks? He decided not to return to the hotel. He would leave all his clothes and belongings behind, buy replacements in Hongkong and charge everything to Ashenbury's account. A quick getaway would also spare him from Poon's questions. He merely wrote and posted a note of apologies to the Inspector:

'Sorry, had to rush. You'll understand. Visit to mutual friend's hotel negative. He's travelling with a great deal of cash and a reserve passport in the name of Eric Lang (hidden in suitcase lining). Thanks for everything, will be in touch.' And as an after-thought he added: 'Please collect and store my things left in the hotel.' The extravagance of throwing good clothes away without a care was not something lavish expense accounts could teach him overnight.

The chandeliers in the lobby glittered too brightly and, apart from the bellboy, nothing was old about Shepheards. On the way from the airport Bucken had already heard that the old Shepheards had been burnt out – though others quickly assured him that rats rather than flames had devoured it. It was disappointing not to sleep in a legend, but it had some compensations. Bucken's room overlooked a gently curving stretch of the Nile: the windows shut tightly enough to keep out the heat, the incessant hooting and honking below, and the omnipresent dust that attacked every opening with the persistence of the Cairo black-market money-changers. He slept better and longer than any night since the news about Spire's death.

After breakfast, guided by the headwaiter's invaluable admonition – 'in Cairo, wherever you go, sir, you must remember that even in banks and government offices tips, baksheesh and presents are *not* forbidden' – Bucken did not bother to dream up clever ways to approach the receptionist. He simply flashed a ten-dollar bill, and five minutes later was told that the hotel register contained no bookings for Mr. Ruzicki or Eric Lang, the name in the counterfeit passport. Bucken swore at himself: he had jumped to the wrong conclusion and acted too hastily, Ruzicki was not coming to Cairo after all. He decided to have a look, at least, at what sort of an outfit Wetzel – General Trading and Shipping Co. of Cairo, Piraeus and Marseilles was. Gambling life and limb on crossing the street, he bought a map and began to walk, because cars seemed to cover the roads like a magic carpet unable to move, let alone fly.

By the time he reached the Talaat Harb Square he had already acquired the elementary art of proceeding like a maniac without actually attempting to die. Ignoring the violent hooting that was not so much a warning as a key factor of local folklore, he turned into a narrow street. In No. 11, where Wetzel's was supposed to be, there was only a dark little shop with a window crammed full with semi-precious gems, rubber toys and a vast range of coloured ampoules and bottles, as if an army had brought specimens for laboratory tests. The door of the shop was similarly crowded, by a large gentleman sporting a shiny three-piece alpaca suit with total disregard for the heat. He smiled and Bucken smiled back. There was no sign of Wetzel's. It must be the wrong address.

Bucken walked on, to return a few minutes later. The man was still in the door. 'SprechensieDeutschParlezvousFrançaisDoyouspeak-English?' he rattled without pausing for breath and spotted the answer in Bucken's eyes like a true expert. 'What can I do for you, sir?'

'Nothing at all, thank you.'

'Ah, but you're wrong, sir. Something can be done for everybody. Are you a tourist? Are you here on business? We have the most beautiful gifts, spice scents and flower perfume concentrates, not like the cheap water they sell you in France but the real Secret of the Dasar, Nefertiti, Harem perfumes that will make you irresistible, Royal Amber paste that make you taste of the oriental magical charm, blends of opium, lotus flower, Christmas night and the scent of Araby, at twenty per cent off the price to you as a friend. Step inside, please. Please.' As the man shifted his bulk, Bucken noticed three small name-plates behind him. Wetzel's was just large enough to accommodate its long name and international list of branches. The man to his credit reacted instantly to Bucken's stare. 'To businessmen we can offer five-star service, telephone, messages, telex only five minutes away, tea, coffee, money-changing at the best rates in Cairo, and for you, as a special friend, a further twenty per cent off the price of Antique Amber, Frankincense, Omar Khayyam, Sweet Pea, Aida and oils that turn your office into a garden of magic flowers.'

That would certainly please Dodd, thought Bucken, and let the man usher him into the darkness of the shop. Seated in a throne-shaped gold chair, facing the photograph of his host shaking hands with a pilot ('The founder of the El Shukry Commercial Organisation greeted by the Air Force'), Bucken allowed himself to be talked into buying some small quantities of Black Narcissus, opium and Sheiks' Desire, and mentioned vaguely that a friend of his might be interested in obtaining a business address. The large man produced immediately a quarto-sized business card ('Shukry and Mozes, The Most Attractive Trading Company And Archaeology') with a full list of the available scents, and begged Bucken to tell his friend that service was five-star with coffee and telephone and best rates to special friends. References could be obtained by writing to existing clients.

While Bucken wrote down the clients' names, the founder of the organisation offered another facility: Mr. Wetzel himself would be here tomorrow, Bucken could come and ask him about the service and make perhaps some additional purchases at very special prices, available only to the very best, oldest friends and most favoured clients.

Bucken felt like kicking himself. He would have given hell to any young detective constable for overlooking the possibility that Ruzicki might come to Cairo using yet another passport. The hotel receptionist knew a crazy tourist when he saw one, and welcomed Bucken with the enthusiasm due to an old customer and a new ten-dollar bill. The man was busy, so this time Bucken's investment bought an opportunity to look through the register himself. And there it was, an advance booking for Mr. Wetzel for three nights from the 26th. As he was about to shut the register, a fresh entry among the day's arrivals caught his eyes: Mrs. P. Quincey, room 421. Bucken was stunned. Could it be another coincidence? Should he report it to Ashenbury right away and ask him about it? What was his interest in the Quinceys? Did he suspect that there might be a connection between the Quinceys and Spire's investigation? Where would Ruzicki fit into the picture? Where would Ashenbury fit into it? I must be turning into a right old paranoiac, thought Bucken, I'll soon suspect myself, too, if I don't watch it.

He decided to have a drink while thinking it over. The bar at Shepheards had a permanent midnight atmosphere. The pianist played nostalgic hits of the early fifties, and Islam seemed to be lenient at least towards its favoured sons who could afford the prices at such exquisite watering holes where the wells produced nothing but alcohol. Bucken felt quite certain that Ruzicki would arrive next morning with a passport in Wetzel's name. All that remained to be done was to witness his checking in and obtain a photocopy of his entry and signature. It would be a small reward for the dash to Cairo and Bucken could not yet see how to take full advantage of it, but if he was right, Ruzicki's status as a most reputable charterer would be dented a little. It would also give Dodd something if he needed to bargain with the FBI or CIA for information on the missing *Alida* and her cargo.

The question remained: what to do about Mrs. Quincey? Ashenbury was interested in her husband, but the register did not mention

Mr. Quincey. If Bucken found out where her husband was, it could do no harm to have Ashenbury in his debt. He chose a table from where he could watch the entrance of the hotel and part of the lobby, and asked the ancient bellboy to point out Mrs. Quincey to him when she came down from her room. He ordered a large Bacardi on the rocks and settled down for a long wait, trying to guess whether her looks would match the name. Elegant and in her forties? Over-age American air hostess with a plastic smile? A toothy aristocrat?

He was still on his first rum when a young woman caught his eyes. Behind her, the bellboy was busy signalling. He raised his hand and tapped his nose a couple of times. Bucken watched her as she walked along the miles of polished mahogany bar. Sad, black eyes in a thin, girlish face, short and dark blonde bobbing hair curling in a half moon towards the chin, a finely drawn nose with the nervous nostrils of a young deer, hardly any make-up, a quick dart of the tongue to wet thirsty lips. She was of medium height, she moved with light determination without hurrying, and the back of her tight-fitting skirt had the rhythm to suggest the barest acknowledgement of admiring glances that followed her right across the room.

The pianist adjusted his back-up synthesizer and began to hum the theme music of *A Man And A Woman*. Bucken had no doubt who the woman was. He waited to see if there was a man for her to meet. Just under the red egg-box ceiling, a huge tapestry banner ran the full length of the bar:

Unborn tomorrow and dead yesterday,
why fret about them if today be sweet.

Mrs. Quincey took one of the few free stools at the far end, under the word *fret*, and ordered a large Campari soda. Bucken guessed she was not expecting anyone. Her eyelids came down as her lips closed on the edge of the glass, and she swallowed her drink almost in a single gulp. She needed that, thought Bucken, and contemplated his strategy. He could go for an easy approach. Hello, you must be Mrs. Quincey – right? Sorry to intrude but I used to be a great admirer of your husband. How is he? What has become of him? I saw a very clever assessment of his career the other day. You think he might be interested? I'll send it to him. Where does he live these days?

He decided against it. A little flirtation and, if possible, a pick-up would be more fun. If it failed, he could fall back on the more direct routine. He walked up to the bar and took the last stool in the row, next to hers, under the *why*.

'May I join you? . . . I'm sorry, how stupid of me: I'm gambling on your English as it's the only language I speak.' His smile seemed to have no effect on her uninhibited gaze, so he repeated his question

44

a little more slowly and much more loudly, the way an Englishman would be expected to make himself understood.

'No,' she said at last but, seeing his open disappointment, a little laugh appeared in her eyes. 'No, you may not. But the seat is free and I wouldn't dream of preventing a gentleman from taking it. So if that's what you meant,' she gestured towards the stool 'feel free.'

'No, I must confess, that wasn't what I meant.'

'Oh?'

'What I was hoping for was that you'd say yes and ask me the time or ask for a light or drop a lace hanky that I could recover ever so gallantly or, better still, there would be a sudden conflagration from which I could rescue you so that you'd feel obliged to accept a drink from me – and then,' he paused for breath 'then I'd have someone to say "cheers" to when I had a drink.' His breathless delivery was intended to make it all sound the mockery of a slick pick-up but, somehow, a touch of truth had crept into his voice, adding some conviction to an empty opening.

'A most honourable intention. I mean if this time it's true that you had nothing else in mind but to alleviate your loneliness.'

'Caught out again. The story of my life,' he sighed theatrically. 'Because I also meant to ask you something.'

'My name, I suppose. How boring.'

No, I know your name, he meant to say, but the temptation was too great to keep talking to her. 'No,' he said and pointed at the banner above.'Just wanted to know if you liked that.'

She looked up but she could not read the words without leaning further and further back until the stool almost toppled. Protectively, Bucken held out his arm. 'The inferno!' he exclaimed 'I've saved you, after all.'

She ignored the contact and read the lines. Her lips moved but the words were almost inaudible: 'Why fret indeed?' Her eyelids were closing but the sadness Bucken had first noticed was seeping through.

With a gentle push he helped her and the stool regain their balance. She was not even conscious of it. She seemed mentally to float away, and he was anxious to bring her back. 'You think it's Omar Khayyam?'

'Maybe.'

If I walked away now, she would not even remember I was here. 'Would you . . . would you like a drink?'

She slowly shook her head. She might have been responding to someone else. Or herself. Then her eyes opened, a little surprised. The mocking sparkle returned, and she emerged from the trance as suddenly as she had sunk into it. 'No, thanks, but would *you* like a drink? I hope you haven't got strong principles against accepting drinks from strangers.'

'None whatsoever. Mine'll be rum, stranger. Neat. And white, if possible. On the rocks.'

'How virginal.'

'It's got to be. It's a new experience.'

'You mean you've never had it before?'

'That would be a lie, I'm afraid. But it's the first time I've realised what a lot there is to be said for women's equality.' He was putting off the moment to ask her about her husband. He was free until the morning.

His drink was poured before she could order it. He was about to raise his glass to her when she stood up. 'Enjoy it.'

'You're off?'

'The Sphinx is waiting.'

'A sightseeing tour?'

'How did you guess?'

'May I join you?'

'No.' She gave him another of those searching looks. 'But, if there's room for one more on the coach, I can't stop you, can I?'

He got a seat behind her, stared at the smoothness of her neck, her wind-blown hair, and wished she was looking at him from under her sleepy eyelids. Next to her, a keen German tourist made notes of everything being pointed out on the way, and when the guide had stopped talking, he translated lengthy passages for her from a massive tome of information he carried to elevate mere pleasure to the heights of spiritual enrichment. She listened patiently, but Bucken could tell she was miles away.

'Here we are. Please keep together.'

They stared up at the Pyramids, then strained their muscles to descend into a burial chamber that, bare of all its treasures, looked as inspiring as a housing estate after the football fans had finished with it. Bucken longed to stay near her. She could have allowed the whirling crowds to separate them, but she did not. She looked taller than her actual height because she was so slim, with tempting curves wrapping a fine bone structure. She was the only woman in the group wearing a skirt. He reckoned she was in her early thirties, younger than Sarah but light-years older than Helen and his other usual bed-warmers in the Bayswater flat. Moving from sight to sight, trying to guess what sort of nose the Sphinx used to have before centuries of stone-leprosy, their exchanges were small-talk and brief bouts of verbal sparring but somehow, they were in silent communication.

'How long are you staying in Cairo?'

'A few days. And you?'

He said 'until tomorrow', meaning it's up to you.

On the way back, he mentioned he would like to see the Al Azhar mosque and Khan el Khalili, the bazaar.

'Is it safe?'

'I guess so, stranger. Would you like to come?'

She meant to say no. It came out as yes. She would not go back on her word.

After showering at the hotel, they met in the lobby and took a cab. From the mosque, they had to cross the road to the bazaar. Compared to this place, the Talaat Harb would have seemed monastic. Dodging the viciously-crowding bumpers frightened her, and she reached for his hand. They were still holding hands like teenage lovers when they got lost in the maze of shops and stalls. They bargained for souvenirs, shared laughter and the moon, the thrill of dark corners and the dizzying effect of watching clouds passing the tip of a minaret. He gave her a long sales talk favouring the real Secret of the Dasar and a little Sheiks' Desire as opposed to the Scent of Araby at a very special price for very special friends. The samples she was forced to try on the back of her hand smelt better on her than in the bottle. It was as they were leaving the scent shop that he was hit by a sensation of imminent threat. Were they being followed? He led her playfully on a dash through winding alleyways, taking sudden turns and doubling back. No, there was nobody after them. He felt sure about that. And yet the threat remained. He knew he was right to put it down to his old paranoia: his work and dedication had robbed him of most things he really cared for. It would be a pity to lose this stranger.

Out of the bazaar, guided by his map, they walked along a deserted street where he could check and re-check that nobody was tailing them.

'Are you on the run?' she asked quite casually.

Chasing was the other, inherent part of being on the run. One could not exist without the other. So it was not quite a lie when he said 'yes, sort of', because it sounded more romantic than saying I'm a cop.

They dined in the lost splendour of the Ali Hassan El Hati, under half-lit chandeliers with single bulbs hanging from bare wires. The cheap plastic water jug on the even cheaper plastic table seemed to multiply into an endless production line in the fading magnificence of huge, arched mirrors that faced each other the length of both walls.

They ate quietly, their mood was subdued. By now he knew that it couldn't be just a quick affair.

'What's your name?'

Her question was unexpected. He almost said Hiller but checked the urge. 'Bucken.'

'Just Bucken?'

'That's what everybody calls me. Even in bed.'

'It's a lonely name.' She ignored his defensive flippancy. She was drinking most of the wine.

'Perhaps I deserve no more.'

'Are you a lonely man?'

'Far from it. Why?'

'You wanted someone to say "cheers" to in the bar. I knew how you felt.'

'Did you?'

'You didn't ask my name.'

'You said you'd find such questions boring.'

'It's Papeete.'

'That's not a name . . . that's an . . . island?'

'It's the port of Tahiti. My parents chose it because they were convinced that I'd been conceived on a cruise, just passing Papeete.' She finished the wine.

'You're drinking too fast.'

'Am I?' She saw his eyes caressing her neck, her breast and arms, piercing the table to reach for her thighs. She knew she ought to leave now, but refused to. She had not wanted a man, a particular man, like this for a long time. Too long, perhaps.

Back at the hotel she accepted one more drink at the bar. And another. Bucken kept looking towards the entrance. He would not have been surprised if Poon or a killer with a long stiletto or even Spire himself turned up to take away what was good in his life. He was back on rum. Doubles. It made him feel elated and depressed simultaneously.

'Yes, you do have that lonely look. Sort of hunted. Or is it haunted? By whom? A lover?' She asked for a large brandy. 'Talk to me and stop staring. Please. Talk.'

He wanted her to see him as a winner and a hero, but the moment was wrong for lies. Spire was dead and feeling a winner eluded Bucken. So he spoke about lost battles and lost causes, lost women and friends, and a blank-faced girl who had died because of him.

She leaned across to kiss him lightly on the cheek – goodnight and goodbye.

'Shall I see you again?'

She shook her head.

'Later?'

'No.'

'Tomorrow?'

'Unborn tomorrow?' She sounded sober and hurt.

'Yes. So why fret?'

She smiled. Her smile was sour. 'One more drink,' she said. She gulped it down, stood up, and her knees gave way. He caught her. 'I . . . I want to go to my room.' She gargled with the words. How had she got so drunk so suddenly? Bucken led her towards the lobby. She let him virtually carry her. The receptionist still on duty – didn't they ever sleep? – winked at Bucken and produced both their keys in a flash. Bucken felt like hitting him in those knowing eyes but could not let go of her.

In the lift and along the fourth floor corridor, she held on to his neck as he carried her. She let him open her door. When he put her down inside, he caught a glimpse of a sitting room: she had a suite. She waited, silent and swaying. He wanted her badly. But she was drunk. Too drunk to know what she was doing even if it had come about with such incredible suddenness. So it would be rape. He wanted her to want him in sobering daylight. So he said goodnight, and closed the door from the outside. He could have sworn that he saw tears in her eyes, but he knew, of course, that he must be wrong. He would give himself a chance to find out for sure during that unborn tomorrow.

In the morning, Bucken was up early. The travel desk was not yet manned, he would cancel his flight reservation after breakfast. He witnessed Ruzicki's arrival and heard the porter addressing him with 'welcome back, Mr. Wetzel'. Useful to know, though aliases were not the crime for which Bucken wanted to get him.

Bucken went for a walk. He planned to be first in the breakfast room so as to give Papeete the choice to join him or not. But the traffic along the Korneish, the riverside road, was even more murderous than usual. It delayed him. Before he could enter the breakfast room, he saw Papeete through the glass doors. She was in animated conversation, sharing a table with Ruzicki. Her presence was no coincidence. Bucken wanted time to think. But for that there was no need to cancel his flight.

The oak panelling of Ashenbury's office seemed to have lost its warmth, the seas in the Turners had grown more menacing. Bucken restricted his report on Macao to basics: Spire's fate, the killing of the Malay witness, theories about the *Alida*. Ashenbury was examining his finely manicured fingertips but Bucken knew he would not miss a

49

single detail. Dodd tried to pretend he was not even present. He would not have been if it was his choice.

'Let me ask you some questions, sir.' Bucken leaned a little closer to Ashenbury as if to emphasise that his searching gaze would record every flicker of reaction.

'Go ahead.'

'Have you ever come across a man called Ruzicki?'

'Yes. A strange man but respected in the trade. He's based somewhere in Europe.'

'Would it surprise you if he was involved in the *Alida* case?'

'Depends in what capacity.'

'He had the ship on charter.'

'Means nothing either way.'

'And if he came to Macao?'

'Wouldn't you if you had a lot of money riding on the ship?'

'Would it shock you utterly if he was implicated in some murders?'

Ashenbury studied the ceiling. 'It would *surprise* me, yes.'

'Why are you interested in Don Quincey?'

The smooth suddenness of the question jolted Ashenbury's imperturbability. He viewed Bucken with additional respect 'I've told you. I want to help him if I can.'

'What is he up to these days?'

'Nobody knows.'

'Do you know his wife?'

'Yes. A very beautiful young woman.'

'Are they still together?'

'I don't know. I imagine so . . . ' Ashenbury looked as if a separation had never occurred to him as a possibility. 'Why do you ask?'

'I met her in Cairo.'

'You . . . What the hell was she doing there?'

'Breakfasting with Ruzicki. You seem *surprised*.'

'It's just that I don't know what to make of it.'

'They could be lovers.' Bucken smiled.

'Could be.'

'Or in business together.'

'She wouldn't understand the first thing about business.'

Bucken told him about Ruzicki's passports and trading under the name of Wetzel. It was obvious that, with a tip-off, the Macao police as well as the Egyptians and even the Austrians might be able to prove that Ruzicki had committed various minor and not so minor offences, but no police force would have the authority to conduct and coordinate a full international investigation of the main problem, the disappearance of the *Alida*. Ashenbury sympathised with Bucken's

50

frustration. Dodd condescended with a smile of the 'I could have told you' variety.

'That's exactly why we needed a capable and brave volunteer like Spire,' said Ashenbury.

'And now we want to catch his killers,' Bucken snapped. 'It's none of our business what grand criminal designs somebody in some foreign land may hatch. If anything, the *Alida* is the Yanks' head-ache. Have you passed on my findings and suspicions to them?'

'Yes, we've tipped off both Interpol and the CIA,' Dodd announced with relish. He liked to be seen as an international oper-ator. 'They seemed interested and grateful, and I reckon they've mobilised worldwide resources. That means a search with thousands of agents and stringers and co-opted seamen looking out for the ship in every port, shipyard, pirate's and smuggler's cove.'

'But not at the bottom of the sea,' said Bucken, mostly to himself.

'And I agree,' Ashenbury nodded. 'That's where she is. Maybe not where she is said to have sunk, but down for sure. These are pros. And, if there's a Russian involvement, it's an even greater certainty that they won't risk having the *Alida* caught some day.'

'Why not?' It irked Dodd that Ashenbury had sided with Bucken. 'It's a great deal of extra profit to sink their ship and still have her.'

'The difference is peanuts.'

'We're talking about a million quid!'

'A million and a half, but dollars, Mr. Dodd, always dollars in this game.'

Annoyed by Ashenbury's pedantic, tutorial tone, Dodd was deter-mined to deliver his own lecture. 'Whatever the value, without the ship we'll never get a conviction. And as I expounded to you, sir, at the time, international policing has numerous pitfalls, including the greater potential of corruption and leaks. The more people there are involved, the greater the likelihood of more murders, just as it hap-pened in Macao. And why? Because, as you said, these are pros. So we're back to square one. Without somebody on the inside, we'll never avenge Spire's death. If anything, it's a one-man show,' he concluded with a sigh.

Bucken decided to tell him to go and find that one man and get himself stuffed on the way. But his lips changed the words. 'May I see Spire's reports, sir?'

'I'll have them ready for you in the morning.'

That evening, Bucken visited Spire's widow. He took her some presents, toys for the child, and cash, saying it was from the police benevolent fund. She was in tears and he had nothing to say to her, so he encouraged her to try out the scents on herself right away. The

51

fragrance of the Cairo bazaar rose from the bottles and reminded him of Papeete. It reminded Sugar of happier days. She broke down, crying, and Bucken had even less to say to her. He planned to stay for half an hour, no more, but she was in a state of complete disintegration with drink and despair. He could not leave her in a hurry.

'What do I do, Bucken? Who'll want a widow with nothin' but a kid to her name? I'd even lose these lousy married quarters if I shacked up with someone who wasn't a cop. I'm not cut out to be a single parent. I like men, I don't like to be on me own. I 'ave nothin' to prove. I don't want them to say "look, ain't she clever? ain't it somethin' how she's managing?" No, ta very much. I want a man to love, that's all. But who'd want me? Look at me? Look.'

He wanted to say, it's all your fault. You're a very pretty girl but you're letting yourself go, and this place is a dump. You ought to comb your hair and get out of this housecoat full of holes from cigarette ashes. He said nothing.

'I know what you'll say, Bucken. That it's all my fault. That I let meself go.'

So he lied to her. That any man would be only too glad to have her. That she had a smashing figure and a sweet face, and as soon as she combed her hair and wiped away her tears she'd look a million dollars, and fine men would just queue up at her door. 'And that's what Ron would want for you, believe me. Mourn him, yes, never forget him, but be your happy and beautiful self again.'

She began to believe him. But she needed proof that these were not just words. Bucken knew there was only one kind of proof and he would not make love for charity. His quota of drunken ladies for the year had been fulfilled. It was time to leave. He got up. 'Wait,' she said. Upstairs the child began to cry.

After a few minutes he heard the shower spewing water. When she returned, she was wet and naked.

'Don't be silly,' he said.

'Why not?' She pulled his jacket apart. Her taut nipples were wetting his shirt.

She was young and hungry, and he hated himself for suddenly wanting her, but he tried to tell himself, with some justification, that there was no way to retreat, even if he really wanted to, without shouting, 'I'm a liar and you're an undesirable slut.' Which she was not.

In the morning, she had started to tidy up the house before he woke up. More cheerful than the night before, she was unashamedly grateful. She promised him to pour all the gin down the sink. But he could not bring himself to promise that he would come and see her again. Not for quite a while anyway. He would be away on a job. She said she understood. But did she? He was afraid he might have done more harm than good in the long run if she ever figured out his motives, and he felt rotten about it. But at least he had helped her to face another day.

He drove straight to the Yard. Dodd took 'all the relevant papers' out of his safe, and handed them over with a grand gesture as if doing Bucken a favour. 'Incidentally,' he said casually 'your pending drugs case has been transferred to Narcotics. A temporary measure, of course, only to ensure the continuity of the investigation.'

'Against that little slut or me?'

Dodd laughed heartily. He liked to be known as a man who could appreciate a joke.

Spire's file was an obvious victim of gross malnutrition. There were hardly any names and 'susses' in it even though Bucken had trained him to record all his suspicions and delete them if they became untenable. Had Spire forgotten that 'during investigations everybody is guilty until proven innocent' or had someone removed all such leads? Oldman Savas, some Graeco-American big-shot in shipping, was the only character in whom Spire seemed to have any sustained interest. There were notes on his deals, financial upheavals, life-style, and offices in Rotterdam, New York and Piraeus. It appeared that Spire had been impressed by him: 'the man is larger than life, quite happy to carry responsibility for many people on both sides of the Atlantic, for entire villages in Greece. A Greek godfather of style?' There were several vague references to 'suspected frauds and fraudsters and business associates'. Ruzicki was not mentioned among them, but Don Quincey was. At some stage, Spire had asked for a run-down on Quincey's career. The file contained a few notes on that, and a photograph: Papeete's.

The operational notes revealed Spire's approach to the problem. He had gained some experience as a seaman, befriended a few underworld characters, and participated in some maritime fraud.

Bucken asked for details.

'Irrelevant,' said Dodd. 'He reported to me, only verbally, one to one. We kept no records. He picked up some apparently reliable information about a *club* that had been formed by several supposedly impeccable names and other great untouchables like this Savas. With some capital from . . . well, available to him, Spire was planning to get involved with that club one way or another, and build up a comprehensive list of suspects.'

Whatever else Spire might have achieved, he had left behind no such list to give Bucken a starter. 'How long did he spend on this?'

'Oh, on and off a year, I'd say.'

'With such an indirect approach he might have been at it for years. When did you see him for the last time, sir?'

'Before he joined the *Alida*. After that, there was only a phone call saying that he had picked up some scent and would report as soon as poss. And that was that.'

Dodd's operational notes and comments were attached – all in neat handwriting. So they didn't even trust the office typists, thought Bucken. Dodd explained: 'Poor Spire. Towards the end he saw threats from every quarter. His reports reeked of suspicion and fears that this... this club or whatever was immensely powerful with contacts everywhere, even here, inside the Big House.'

'If his death is anything to go by, he might have been right.'

'Quite. But we don't know, do we? And there couldn't have been a leak against him from here, because this is all that we had in writing, and it never left my safe. They must have killed him for whatever they found on his person.'

Bucken had doubts about that. For one thing, he knew, the killers had never found Spire's burglar kit.

According to Dodd, in a reference to further verbal reports, Spire had lately grown obsessed with threats to the national interest though he could not substantiate any of his theories. Spire referred to 'political undertones' of crimes and 'major swindles that might be a serious menace to the shipping and general economies of the West'. Therefore, he suggested, minor crimes that might be discovered 'should be ignored, at least temporarily, so that we get a chance to go for the jugular of the big swindlers'. Big words without evidence. Bucken was annoyed.

Most of the time, Spire had used a courier (not named in the file), and only in his last moments did he try to activate the emergency channel. Bucken saw that fact as evidence that Spire must have had some information of very great importance, something about the Russians or about 'the big swindle'.

Bucken shut the file, returned it to Dodd, and volunteered to take over Spire's job. He found it somewhat off-putting that Dodd did not look surprised or impressed. I've been taken for granted or tricked into this, thought Bucken, and disliked both possibilities, but he would not back off now. They arranged to have lunch with Ashenbury who promptly rejected their proposal: 'I thought that Mr. Bucken might direct the operation from now on, that's all. After Cairo, he's ruled out as an undercover man. If Ruzicki is a bad apple, as bad as you think, and hears about your visit there when he was doing business in Cairo, well . . . don't you agree?'

54

'No, sir. I could use Cairo to strengthen my hand by double bluff. If Mrs. Quincey and Ruzicki were connected, and I turned up on their doorstep, they'd convince themselves that only an amateur, a madman, would take chances like that.'

'Alternatively, they could keep you out of the way. Somehow.'

'That's a chance we'll have to take.'

'*You* will.'

'But I must hold as many trump cards as possible. We'll have to concoct some cover story. I must look like a real bad apple.'

'We'll work out something.' Dodd sounded a little too eager for Bucken's liking.

'Nothing for public consumption, of course,' Ashenbury stepped in, 'just enough to convince them if they really have the muscle to look inside Scotland Yard. After all, when this is over, Mr. Bucken will surely be reinstated with due honour and recognition.'

'Goes without saying, sir, we can't afford to lose people like him – or Spire for that matter.'

II

A NAKED GHOST IN ROTTERDAM

Rotterdam was at its morning worst. Near the port, thick haze shattered the sunlight into blinding particles to compound the drivers' plight: the surging, halting river of cars and coaches crept into the Maastunnel only to emerge and flood into a dead-end lake of traffic on the north side. Oldman Savas told the driver of his Daimler to drop him at the West Zee Dijk and pick him up at the office at half-past twelve. He cut across the park, enjoying a breath of fresh air with the never-absent hint of diesel, a smell he had learned to love with his mother's milk. His bodyguard, a swarthy young lout who wore his libido on his sleeve, swaggered three steps behind him.

Significantly, Savas met no one familiar. There had been a time when every other passer-by would seem to know and try to befriend him in every major port of the world. It had always been like that as far back as he could remember – at least until the day it was his turn to need friends. Then, he looked around, and saw himself standing in a desert. My fault, he told himself, only a fool like me would rely on goodwill and friendship. Tough. Things would have to be rectified.

He entered the building where his Rotterdam branch office occupied two of the best rooms on the third floor. Two rooms there were a luxury when shipping companies, agents, insurers and other punters in the sea game would gladly pay premium over the top to buy space enough for a brass name-plate or a desk-and-telex foothold. The Cypriot doorman greeted him in Greek – it was the Oldman who had recommended him for the job – but, absentmindedly, Savas answered him in pure Bronx. With his private key he opened the door of the smaller lift *For Tenants Only*, and tapped out a combination code that allowed him to ascend to the seemingly non-existent ninth floor of the eight-storey building. He re-programmed the lift to return it to the ground floor, then entered a cell a monk might have found cramped and bare except for the view of the port through a wall of bronze-tinted glass. He swivelled his armchair away from the tempting sights to face a control panel and a battery of six TV

screens. At the flick of a switch the private close-circuit network
flashed to life. He glanced at each, a face a screen – yes, they were all
there, his valued, tolerated and intolerable partners. He greeted each
in turn with a nod, and they nodded back. Seated in an array of
adjoining cubicles, they could see and hear him, but nobody else.
They had all known each other well for many years, but their debates
and key decision-making procedures were channelled through him.
That was why the system had worked smoothly for more than two
years now: each member of the syndicate could criticise any partner,
argue and vote freely without giving rise to hard feelings, personal
animosity among such financial primadonnas, because only Oldman
Savas would know who said what, and he would never tell anyone.
He was not the most influential among equals, but he was accepted as
the most trusted member.

Savas chose the case of the *Alida II* to be the first item on the
agenda simply to get it out of the way. He switched on the sound of
screen No. 5 and channelled it to all the cubicles so as to let Ruzicki
address the members directly. There was no point in playing games
of secrecy when everybody knew that the *Alida II* had been Ruzicki's
pigeon.

Ruzicki's report was brief. The insurance claims on cargo and ship
were lodged, the 'additional profits' would be distributed among the
members on completion of the second phase. The yield was expected
to be 4.75 million dollars to the syndicate alone. Savas knew that
Ruzicki would probably make three times as much. The question
was: how? Before the scheme went into operation, Ruzicki had
asked Savas to find him a wreck on any naval scrap heap in any part
of the world. Not just any wreck, it had to match very precise specifications regarding age, tonnage and lay-out. Why? When Ruzicki
gave Savas the requirements and told him that it would not matter
what state the wreck was in as long as it had full documentation, it
became obvious that this must be a truly extraordinary scheme. Even
if Ruzicki was vicious enough to pull it off, he was not clever enough
to devise it on his own. So he must have a partner. A member of the
syndicate? Who? Quincey? What a pity.

The question not only puzzled but pained Savas even though he
knew that the unwritten articles of the association were perfectly
simple and clear. Every member was free to pursue any profitable
scheme irrespective of its legitimacy. Every member was duty bound
to help all the others – no questions asked. The syndicate would take
a share from all transactions. The common goal was to amass a huge
'fighting fund'. With that they would finance some special deal of
unheard-of magnitude that would elevate all of them to the ranks of

the richest in the world, rich enough to become stalwarts of business ethics and legitimacy. It was a stirring thought that, by now, the final master stroke had begun to take definite shape. Quincey – or Savas himself, for that matter – would never again be at anyone's mercy. Yet, on some odd, emotional level, it hurt Savas that the Quinceys could be mixed up with the Ruzickis of this world.

'Any questions?' Savas put on ear-pads so as to resume his filtering role. Screen No. 2 wanted to know how the nine victims had died.

'Accidentally.'

Nos. 3 and 6 questioned the inevitability of the deaths. Ruzicki offered some explanations but, clearly, he was irritated. If he knew whose questions had implied the criticism, he would go gunning for the offender even if it caused the break-up of the syndicate.

'As old Savas will testify, and he's old enough to know,' hissed Ruzicki, allowing his Czech accent to slip through for once, 'we've taken every possible precaution.'

'As far as possible, no doubt,' said Savas, but did not believe Ruzicki any more than the rest of them. He despised them all, even himself, most of the time. Some of us have better motives for our actions than the rest, he thought, but does that make any difference? Do our motives lend us justification? Do we need any justification?

'What about that missing crew-man?' asked No. 3. Good point, Quincey, thought Savas as he conveyed the question to Ruzicki.

'Our associates *and* the police are looking for him. He may be dead but I guess he's probably holed up somewhere in an alcoholic coma with a whore.'

Savas turned a little to the right, enjoying the panorama from the corner of his eye. Beautiful, beautiful ships everywhere. He knew that everybody laughed at him for finding every ship, just about everything afloat, beautiful, very beautiful, but he had long ceased caring. He was a fourth-generation sale-and-purchase agent, trading in ships of all shapes and sizes, hating to part with any one of them. So let them laugh: the Savas family would still be trading when these punks clamoured to buy up Scottish castles and respectability with their ill-gotten gains. And if they found it funny that everybody, including he himself, called him Oldman Savas, then again let them laugh. No harm done. He had never been plain Savas. Until the age of six, almost sixty-four years ago, the Greek community of New York used to call him 'Savas Oneos', Young Savas. When his father died, he was dubbed Oldman Savas faster than the corpse could cool, because his brother was only two years old. He was then groomed to head an empire.

'It seems an accepted fact that a Tsunami was responsible for the misfortune of *Alida II*,' Ruzicki concluded. Screens 4 and 6 were amused by his indignation but only Savas would see them. Quincey on Screen 3 warned against complacency: 'Indubitably, Typhoon Louise must have been one of the nasties, but most reports failed to offer any support for the Tsunami theory.'

Ruzicki would not yield an inch: 'Tsunamis are rare and totally unpredictable. Only old sailors' tales and sometimes the remains of horrible destruction can testify to what happened. In this case, there's no wreck, no physical evidence. But the survivors have testified – and they were there!'

Noting with a sigh of relief that the *Alida II* was now out of the way, Savas proposed to deal briefly with another two, relatively minor points on the agenda. A vote was taken to appoint somebody to take charge of security and act against all outsiders as well as any partner who maliciously or negligently endangered the ultimate goal and raison d'être of the syndicate. The unanimous voting went just the way the old Greek had feared most: Ruzicki got the job. Savas would give him the code to a Bermuda account where half a million dollars had already been deposited as a security starter fund.

'Any questions, gentlemen?'

'Yes,' Screen 6 told Savas. 'Most of us need fresh faces to be used up front for our operations. Could our new security chief help us with recruitment and vetting?'

Savas put the question in his own words to the rest of the screens. They all agreed that this was a problem, and Ruzicki promised to look into it.

'But urgently, please,' pleaded Screen 6, 'we need more front men now!'

'You mean fall guys,' said No. 3, but Savas did not bother to convey the quip. He took a deep breath, and for a few seconds contemplated a prayer. He decided against it. It would not be appropriate. Not that he was particularly religious – only births, deaths, weddings and the January Blessing of The Waters in the port of Piraeus would ever bring him into a church – but he had what he termed his 'schizophrenic code of morality'. According to that, criminal acts, even in a good cause, would not qualify for divine assistance. But, everybody must start somewhere, he thought with uncompromising self-mockery, and this is where we start. He glanced at the three sheets of paper lying on the edge of the TV console, three summaries of grand designs for the potentially biggest financial killing on record. Not even Savas knew which members had submitted them. There were only single copies (the partners had studied them but always in the Oldman's presence) and after the vote they would be shredded. He looked up. 'Well, gentlemen, the moment has come. We must choose the big one.' He tried to make it sound light.

Two of the schemes were excellent, but the third was ingeniously simple in its enormity. It was that third option Savas hated most – the option he would select without any hesitation.

He held up the three sheets for everybody to see, and studied the faces on the screens. He noticed the tension: if they made the right choice and followed the plan to its every monstrous letter no matter what, the syndicate could dissolve at least a billion dollars richer within a year.

The voting was quick and no more emotional than ordering lunch in a junk-food take-away. The decision was almost unanimous. With the exception of Don Quincey on Screen 3, every partner voted for that third option, entitled Suez Closure. On this occasion, because of the weight of the problem, unanimity would be a must.

'The vote is five to one. The debate will be through me, as usual,' said Savas and turned to Screen 3.

'If we block the Canal and only we have advance information, huge fortunes could be made. So my vote was not intended to detract one iota from the tremendous potential of the Suez option. In fact, I hope that Oldman Savas will convey fully my greatest admiration for its originator whoever he is.' Quincey paused to allow Savas to turn his haughty Harvard into Bronx Greek for the partners' benefit. 'But aren't you playing down, perhaps even forgetting, the political implications? We're dealing with one of the most sensitive areas in the world. If we succeed, we may trigger off another war. Admittedly, a war would keep the Canal closed infinitely longer than we ourselves could, and that would double, even treble, our profit potential. But war is not our business, gentlemen, not at all.'

The consensus of opinion deemed the risk of war minimal and, in the light of the plan's profitability, quite acceptable. They were more concerned with the technical problems of a privately-engineered closure of the Canal than with the political implications. 'No important drug exists, none can be invented, to be truly efficacious without certain side-effects,' admitted Screen 6 and, like the others, hurried to pay some lip service to the undesirability of political upheavals and wholesale slaughter.

Hypocrites, thought Savas, goddam hypocrites. Political upheavals, uncertainties and wars had always meant rich pickings for the traders and speculators of the sea. He himself had been brought up to keep an eye on the world press, pay liberally for items of private intelligence, and never forget the family motto that 'bad news is good

60

news' for all Savas interests. Except that his father had never dabbled in actually making the news. Perhaps in those days, one had the choice. He noted that Ruzicki on Screen 5 was beaming. Was the Suez option his baby? Was he clever enough to dream it up?

'Nothing ventured, nothing gained,' Ruzicki cackled. Savas twitched but delivered the remark dutifully to the others. He knew instinctively how the partner on Screen 3 would feel. Yes, Don Quincey deserved more decent company but, surely, it had been his own choice to be here, perhaps because, like Savas himself, he had grown fed up with being the loser and the underdog. Then, suddenly, a disturbing thought occurred to the old man. Only Quincey would have the vision to come up with something as diabolical as the Suez option. Was Don objecting to it only to ensure that all partners would go into it with their eyes open? Savas guessed that Quincey would presently withdraw his objection and make the vote unanimous. Yet he felt weary and full of resentment when, after a moment's hesitation, the younger man proved his guess right.

'Before we break up,' said Savas, 'I'd like to wish you all luck with your individual schemes, but I must warn you that our main operation will demand more and more of your time and specialist knowledge. For simplicity of reference, we'd better code-name the plan. Any suggestions?'

'Tsunami,' blurted out Ruzicki. 'The Tsunami option. It will make waves and it could blow the biggest hole ever in the pocket of world finance.'

Oldman Savas scanned the screens. Six nods answered him. Code-names did not matter any more to the get-rich-quick artists than to those with scores to settle. People on the screens began to gather up papers and leave. They would meet in the office below to toast the 'Tsunami' with vintage carrot juice, Alka Seltzer, herbal cocktails, whatever their cursed diets permitted. As the screens went blank, only Quincey remained in his cubicle. His wife stood behind his wheelchair. During debates, Papeete would never speak or vote. She was not a member. Yet, possibly, it was she who had started it all. Or was it that news item, barely two years ago?

THE BEGINNING OF THE END
OF A DREAM

In the wake of the spectacular crash of the dreamer's empire, Don Quincey, 38, known as the Don Quixote or Freddie Laker of the insurance market, was rushed to Westminster Hospital last night. The nature of his illness has not been disclosed.

On September 9, 1981, the news item was tucked away on the financial pages of the London dailies: Don Quincey had failed for once to make the headlines. His wife refused to talk to the press. Two days later, she spirited her husband away by ambulance to an undisclosed destination.

On September 12, 1981, she telephoned a dingy taverna behind the seafront in Piraeus, where Oldman Savas liked to conduct seven-figure business transactions over a plate of feta cheese and salad.

'Have you heard?'

'More than that,' said Savas. 'I've already arranged for my Chinese stroke specialist to fly in for a consultation.'

'Thanks.'

'How is he?'

'No change. He can't move.'

'It's terrible. The end of the dream, I guess.'

'But not an accident.' She paused. 'They ruined him. You know that, don't you?'

'He's not the only victim.'

'That's why I'm calling you. Don once devised a scheme . . . a very special scheme . . . Do you know what I'm talking about?'

'Yes.'

'You remember it? I mean the subject.'

'Sure. We toyed with the idea and had a lot of fun with it.' Quincey had once asked him about certain aspects of maritime fraud and then suggested some ways to make a great deal of money in no time at all. He wanted to assemble a team of respectable specialists who could help each other and cash in on their expertise. The exercise would culminate in something truly stunning, something so big that it would be above all suspicion. That was about four years ago, Savas reckoned. Now that it had been brought up again, it embarrassed him because he had already been involved with some fraudulent deals for about a year. Surely, Quincey or his wife wouldn't know about that . . .

'Did you say fun?'

'Well, it was an intellectual exercise.'

'Some exercise,' she said. 'It could net several millions. Dollars, that is.'

'Or more.' He wondered what she was getting at.

'I believe you weren't interested at that time.' Her voice was probing.

'Neither was he . . . I mean not seriously . . . It was . . . a bit of a . . ' He let it hang in the air.

'It's no joke now. I hear you have problems.'

'Who hasn't?'

'That's just what I mean. Things have changed.'

'What things?'

'Circumstances.'

'Are you suggesting that Don has changed his mind?'

'I have. On his behalf.' She sounded desperate.

Savas understood: despair had already driven him a long way into uncharted territories. 'Is he well enough to work out the details of his scheme?'

'He will be. The doctors have promised. Are you interested?'

'Let's say I understand how you feel.'

'But are you interested?'

'Look, Papeete, if this is serious, I mean an actual business proposition, I'll have to talk to him.'

'You're talking to me. Don't you do business with women?'

'You mustn't be touchy. You're too beautiful to be a feminist.'

'You must be joking.'

'Perhaps. Perhaps not.'

She felt furious and ready to hurt him. 'I think your age is beginning to shine through.'

'You may be right. But, if it's business, I'd prefer it to be cold and businesslike rather than something . . . something emotional.'

'Why? What's wrong with feeling strongly about something? What's wrong with yearning for revenge?'

'Only that it could turn into a way of life. A pitiful and ugly way. I'll try to talk you out of it . . . And myself.'

They met, she listened, they fought and made peace, but he failed to talk her out of it. He respected her for it, but regretted his own feelings of respect – an unacceptable allowance for her predicament. It also shamed him that he himself was so attracted to Quincey's fraudulent ideas, but he would find all of it easier to live with if he kept her out of it. Savas belonged to a generation that expected its women to labour elbow-deep in muck and clean up all family muck – but never rake it in public. Yet she would not bend and the compromise he made brought him some rewards. She became something special to him. If he could start all over again . . . But he could not. And Don was just right for her. An ideal couple, he often thought. They could be his children. He sometimes wished he could swap them for his own. Working with the pair of them had given Savas a great deal of joy in the form of paternal, sometimes patronising, comradeship. Every time Quincey's health improved a little, every time the couple touched or kissed each other, Savas felt it was he who would soon make love to a wonderful woman by proxy.

Savas and Quincey now stared at each other through television cameras. 'So, it's settled,' said the old man.

'Quite.'

'How do you feel about it?'

'Rotten.'

'Don't be a hypocrite, Don,' Papeete slapped him down. 'You've always said that the Suez option would be the most profitable.'

Fury welled up in Quincey's eyes. She stood his hostile gaze. He turned back to the camera to face Savas. 'Papeete had a good time in Cairo,' he said with a stiff smile. 'She must have had time to think of my erring ways.'

'But it's true, isn't it?' she persisted. 'It was you who explained to me that we're, well, we three are in it for the money and revenge. So why start bellyaching now?'

'It's just that I sometimes wonder . . . '

'Okay,' said Savas, 'then let me say something I should have said long ago. You're a young man with a young wife. You have plenty of time to get well, start again and hit back in some legitimate way. So here's your opportunity. Get out. This may be your last chance.'

'And yours, Oldman. You don't like "Tsunami" any more than I do. So why don't *you* get out?'

'I'm too old to start again.'

'It's up to you, isn't it?'

'Is it really?' Savas thought about the hundreds of Greek and Greco-American families who depended on his success. Could he tell them that they would be ruined financially because their Oldman had suddenly grown squeamish?

'What are you afraid of, Oldman? That the partners would kill you?'

'They might.'

'It would take a unanimous vote, and I'd vote against it.'

'Thank you, Don, I know you would.'

Papeete was about to say something but Quincey silenced her with a jerky turn of his head.

A few minutes later, all the partners gathered in the Savas office below to drink to the success of 'Tsunami'. Quincey volunteered to carry out the basic feasibility study into the technical aspects of a complete closure of the Canal and the best ways of cashing in on it. The partners were grateful: the stroke had not stemmed Quincey's flow of bright ideas, and he retained the knack of pressing the right buttons for quick answers to any questions.

The doorbell still wouldn't work. The brass frigate knocker threatened to demolish the plywood door. Bang-bang. Pause. Bang-bang-bang. Pause. Sarah listened. She heard him come running on bare boards. There was still no carpet in the hall, and the door creaked when Bucken opened it. He was unshaven. His clothes were a mess. She had never seen him like that.

'We've got to talk.'

'Come in.'

'I'm not alone.'

'Then go away.' He looked alarmed.

'It's John Freemantle.' She stepped aside and an ageless, withered face with cold blue eyes appeared.

'Then piss off. Both of you.' Bucken knew him well. Freemantle was a crude, boozy but first-rate journalist. Bucken had once helped him a lot with hot tips, but right now friends could be as dangerous as enemies. 'Haven't you heard?' He grabbed the reporter by the throat.

'You're drunk,' Freemantle croaked.

'Yeah. Drunk. That'll be my defence for having kicked you all the way down the stairs.'

The journalist was hurt and frightened but stood his ground. Good man, thought Bucken, and gave him a little push.

'You're mad,' said Sarah.

'Yeah, mad and drunk.'

She turned to Freemantle: 'Will you wait for me in the pub round the corner?'

Reluctantly, Bucken let her come in after the journalist had gone. The living room looked even less lived in than she remembered. The heating was not on despite the October cold that oozed from the walls. Sarah's clothes smelt of rain and she felt shiverish. He offered her a drink and a seat. She turned both down. 'How was the wedding?' he asked.

'Fine.'

'Hope you'll be happy.'

'Thanks.'

'Doubt if Jeff would be pleased to find out that you came here.'

'He knows.'

'Oh.' Bucken felt a little pang of disappointment. She touched his arm. 'I wouldn't have come without a good reason.'

'I understand. What can I do for you?'

'The question is what I can do for you.' She reached for the bottle and sipped some rum. It made her cough. 'What's going on, Bucken?'

65

'What makes you ask?'

'Are you in trouble?' She noticed that he was avoiding her eyes. 'Look, I could still go back to that new security outfit and tell them you might be interested in a job after all.' She paused to let him sneer *no thanks, I have a job*, but he said nothing. 'Can't I help?'

'No.'

'What have you done?'

'Nothing.'

'Have you been framed or something?'

'Why do you ask?'

'You look really down and out.'

'That you didn't know until I opened the door. You were surprised.'

'Okay. I'm not here to argue.'

'Why are you here?'

She buried her face in her hands for a moment. It seemed to hurt her to say what she had in mind. 'A few days ago Freemantle came to see me. He said he was investigating a story that the best detectives of the Yard were being hounded and squeezed out in the name of some so-called cleaning up of the police. He said the top brass talked about efficiency and purity of methods, but all they really wanted was to replace cops with bureaucrats. He saw it as proof of his theory when he heard that you might have been given the push.'

'It's none of his bloody business.'

'Were you made to resign? . . . Why? . . . Did you do something?'

'What do you think?'

'It's rubbish. That's what I thought and Freemantle agreed. But then I talked to people, and I heard the rumours.'

'What rumours?'

'Something about bribes. Screwing a suspect for favours. Something that happened in . . . Have you been abroad, Bucken?'

He shrugged his shoulders.

'Cairo?'

'So?' At that moment, Bucken could have killed Greenfingers Dodd in cold blood. Hadn't he promised, hadn't he sworn there would be no leaks, no actual rumours, nothing beyond a dust cloud of doubts?

Sarah turned away from him. 'I'll never forget Freemantle's face when he talked about you. You know what a hard-nosed pro he is. But his eyes glazed over when he said you must have been fitted out because there's no other explanation.'

'Does it count what he thinks?'

'Yes, to me it does. Because I saw his eyes. He may be a rough and uncouth gutter-press snoop, and he may not know how to spell "tears" but I swear he knows how to shed them. "No. Not Bucken. He wouldn't be on the take. I know them all. He's the best. The best." He kept repeating it. And I agreed.'

'Bullshit,' said Bucken because he felt embarrassed.

'Pity,' she said, and turned to leave without another word, but she called back from the top of the stairs 'Goodbye, Bucken.'

He would have liked to run after her and tell her everything, but his secrets were not for sharing and he knew he had no right to burden her with them. He shut the door and paused in front of the speckled mirror of the hall: a spent face with bloodshot eyes stared back at him. In the last eight weeks, he had led a double life posing as a boozing, troubled cop on the slide at night – and a keen, overworked, investigative reporter in daytime.

His head was now swimming with newly-acquired facts and clichés. Warnings were ringing in his ears – whatever they were worth. *Never forget that the City is a more sensitive mechanism than a thermostat. The old-boy network is forged out of steel around here. Trust is the key. 'My word is my bond' is the motto of the Stock Exchange. Same goes for the Baltic Exchange where ships find cargoes and cargoes find ships wherever in the world they happen to be. Anybody can make money in the City: anybody with some expertise, readiness for hard graft and some luck, except that some need considerably more luck because they lack contacts. If you want to impress Savas and the like, you must speak their language.*

It was Ashenbury he had to thank for most of that. The aim was to give Bucken a crammer's course in the basics of the City and, particularly, the essentials of shipping. For that they invented Andrew Warman, an Australian journalist, who benefited from Ashenbury's invisible backing. In order to avoid revealing any connection between them, the introductions to open heavily-padded doors would always come through the friend of a friend of a friend. He visited the *House*, the floor where the Stock Exchange traded, Lloyd's *Room* for insurance deals, and spent long, hungry, lunch-hours mingling with the peripatetic congregation under the dome of the marble-clad Baltic Exchange.

Boothy-Graffoe, a cuddly old man, was Bucken's guide and mentor at the Baltic. Apart from his white mane and business acumen, everything about him was small – his hands, feet ('still wearing my prep school shoes'), pointed nose, glittering eyes full of humour, and always low voice ('this is a hysterical institution, Mr. Warman, if I start chartering on a slightly unexpected scale, the market may go haywire and people of *your* ilk may soon read crises or the threat of a major war into my modest doings').

Mostly they sat in the semi-darkness of one of the high-polished wooden boxes – reminiscent of the coffee-houses where the Exchange, like other City institutions, had been founded – and watched several hundred brokers milling among the marble columns, answering the Waiter's incessant calls for Members, handing out duplicated sheets that invited bids for cargoes to be carried from Rangoon or Durban or Pensacola, swapping vital intelligence, fixing ships for single voyages or months to come, and sanctioning deals worth half a million or more with a binding nod.

The Baltic, known as the most confusing promenade on earth, came to sudden life at about nineteen minutes past noon every day – when most major ports of the world were still awake or about to rise – and died a sudden death at two o'clock, long hours before the Superintendent struck the black bell of the *Ceres*, a tragic eighteenth-century sailing ship, and bellow through the yawning empty hall, 'The Exchange is closed, gentlemen, if you please.'

'By that time, everybody is away, of course, lubricating their throats with vigour,' said Boothy-Graffoe who never failed to joke that his name was an anomaly because he was, in fact, a teetotaller. 'You may find it strange, Mr. Warman, but I'm not proud of my abstinence. I don't regard that or even clean living as an essential of integrity. You see, ships and money are a game for people who live in the real world, warts and all. We can tolerate saints and crusaders no more than headlines and snoopers.'

'Yet you're here, talking to me, a potential snooper and headline-maker,' Bucken needled him.

The old financial wizard remained unperturbed. 'But of course I am talking to you. I must ensure that your articles will be kind to me, and a little chat is the cheapest form of bribing you.'

'People have tried it with cash and failed,' Bucken bragged in the manner he imagined a journalist from down under would. 'Once they offered me gold, a lump that size,' he held up his fist, 'would you believe it?'

'I would, of course, I would. You strike me as a man of integrity, Mr. Warman. But integrity only means that you can resist the lure of money or even a lump of gold. However, when we talk about real money, and I mean a lot of money, that's something different. Have you ever tried to resist a half a million, Mr. Warman? That wouldn't be a matter of integrity any more but realism, a question of foolishness.'

'Oh well,' Bucken sighed, 'no journalist, policeman or other ordinary person is worth that sort of money.'

'You never know.'

'But I do know. Those who have that sort of money to give away go to jail for a lot less than half a million.'

'Ah! But what if that half a million can make them another ten million?'

It was at the sudden-death hour of the Baltic that, one day, Bucken noticed Ruzicki towering at the centre of a group. Boothy-Graffoe followed Bucken's gaze by instinct: 'You have an eye for interesting characters, Mr. Warman. That bullet-head next to the tall man is Manny Berner, a prominent Member and the key broker in one of the biggest houses. His reputation is unblemished, I should say, but then . . . whose isn't?'

The fine tone of the innuendo deserved admiration. Even a good lawyer would fail to sue you successfully for hefty damages, thought Bucken. 'And the tall man?' he asked with measured lack of interest. 'Oh, some wheeler-dealer of reasonable standing. Quite decent fellow. Not very important to your research.'

Bucken wondered whether Ruzicki's credit would go up or down if those prominent Members knew that Ruzicki also traded as Herr Wetzel in Cairo.

Bucken learned about freight rates and Charter Party, Bills of Lading, Panamax, f.i.o. and f.o.b., Baltimore Form C and bareboat charter, until his head reeled as much as it cleared concerning his approach to the job: following Spire's hunch, he would really go for the jugular and try to ingratiate himself with Oldman Savas on whom he had built up a comprehensive dossier.

Ashenbury approved of his plan: 'Savas looks as if he was involved. If he is, and if you play your newly-acquired knowledge well, you might become useful to him in whatever he's up to. Take your time. Don't waste your main chance on trying to save the odd million for some insurance company or catching a petty thief.'

Lines of communication and emergency routines were agreed with Dodd who would handle Bucken's reports personally. As for cover, Bucken wanted the relative security of the double-bluff: he would use an alias; if Savas ever investigated his background, his real identity would probably come to light; they would then find out that he had left the Yard 'under a cloud' and that would explain his use of an alias.

By now, Bucken did not doubt Spire's assessment that Savas might have contacts even inside the Yard. All that remained to be done was to provide eventual investigators with a good lead to the 'dirt' on Bucken. Dodd's technique of creating that *tasty record* had been most annoying – if Sarah and Freemantle could get wind of it, anybody else would – but now it was too late to undo that damage without blowing the flimsy cover.

69

On their last evening together in the board room, Ashenbury was most apologetic about it all. Bucken hardly listened. He drank the champagne, gulped down some lobster, and then locked himself in Ashenbury's private suite behind the Turners to change into his 'sliding downhill fast' costume. Before he left through a back door he had used throughout his training period, Ashenbury offered him a warm handshake: 'Ask for whatever you need, contacts, influence, cash, whatever, and I guarantee you'll have it.' He also reminded Bucken of Don Quincey: 'I'd still be grateful for any news of his whereabouts. I'd really like to help him.'

That night, Bucken telephoned Freemantle and summoned him to the flat in Bayswater.

'Okay, wring my neck, guv.'

'I can't. I need you.'

'An old, nosey hack like me?'

'Yes, because you'll keep your mouth shut.'

'You mean you trust me?'

'Yepp.' And, before he might appear to be too soft, he quickly added: 'Because you know I'll gut you if you fail me.'

'Big words, Mr. Bigshot. What's the game?'

'What do you know about Ashenbury?'

'He's a scheming shit. But how else do you make it to the top? You don't.'

'Have you ever met Don Quincey?'

'Sure.' Freemantle was in his element. He regurgitated all the headlines and gossip about the crusading Don Quixote, darling of the insurance windmill, who had been vilified by them all at the first opportunity. 'Arse-licking shits they were, guv, but he was no better, of course. He cheated, the little darling, and he made the biggest mistake of them all: he let them find out.' He matched Bucken drink for drink, raved about Quincey's wife Papeete ('they dubbed her a society beauty but she was more, much more, she had real class and after the collapse she swore that her husband would be back'), and proved he had an inexhaustible capacity for smut.

Freemantle would have gone on all night, but Bucken stopped him at dawn. 'Listen. You've been trying to tail me for weeks. So here's your chance to get somewhere. I'll give you a scoop. Be at Bank Station at twelve forty-five tomorrow. Keep your eyes open and do an honest reporting job if you still remember how. Everything except my name or I gut you, got it?'

The journalist nodded. The cloud of alcohol lifted from his eyes. 'Is that all, chief?'

'No. One day, perhaps, somebody will want details of that little

70

story. I want you to remember and sell them. Get a good price, you mug.'

'You mean I sell your name, too?'

'Everything that was only hinted at in your story. Including my name, yes.'

'Okay, Bucken. I won't ask you what you're up to. Whatever it is, I wish you luck. You've just restored my faith in human nature. Well, almost.'

'Oh, piss off. Under that shit-coloured cynical lemon you wear for a face, you're just a sentimental ninny.'

'And what are you, you ugly hunk of meat? How on earth did they manage to get a mouse to mount a shark to produce you?'

'Here, drink up. You won't impress me with your zoological genealogy.'

'And you me with your rotten strongman act. Because, the day we run out of the likes of you, I chuck in my own high-wire act, and go into something profitable like writing morality plays for political campaign managers.'

In the lunch hour, pinstripes, brolly-bouncers, bowler-stalks and other varieties of the soldier ant infested the pavements of the City to gather their morsels, down their pints, drown their frustration and celebrate their survival. It was hard to move faster than the throng but Bucken's foul clothes and unsteady gait guaranteed passage even along the foot of the Old Lady as the Bank of England was affectionately known, and down Cornhill. Bucken noted that Freemantle was tailing him faithfully. Others, disgorged by massive edifices of status, paid him no attention: today's eccentrics might be the success stories of tomorrow, and success would make City folk forget and forgive everything. After all, most of those monuments of achievements, with their fine brass and mahogany bowels and ostentatious, stern façades, had been built by vulgar if industrious gamblers and eccentrics.

Bucken turned into Birchin Lane and became submerged in a labyrinth of dark passages where the uninitiated would hope to find nothing but the edge of this flat planet. The rain had stopped, and Bucken went through a tunnel to Ball Court. The man he sought would be drinking champagne in the little yard outside Simpson's Tavern or in the cellar bar of the Jamaica Wine House, the site of London's first seventeenth century coffee house.

He saw the man as soon as he had entered the Jamaica cellar. In turn he was noticed by Helen who was serving behind the bar. People

71

crowded her patch of beer pumps, and Bucken could not blame them: she looked stunning. On a long-gone hot day – was it really only eight weeks ago? – she had smiled but could not manage a laugh when Bucken told her that it was all over. She did not ask why or who else would take her place in his life. Since then, they had met only once, accidentally, when she confessed that her modelling job and the inch-war advertisement had become casualties of the tightening belts of commerce. Without telling her, Bucken arranged the temporary barmaid job for her in the Jamaica: *resting* models could lose their gaiety, basic Guccis and other tools of their trade at the drop of a plumed hat.

She was shocked to see him now in the state he seemed to be in, but poured a double Bacardi on ice first, and asked only afterwards: 'What the hell's hit you?'

Bucken leaned drunkenly across the bar and whispered 'Will you do me a favour?'

'You name it.'

'When they throw me out of here . . . '

'Why should they?'

'I might do something I shouldn't have done.'

'How about doing something to me you should have done every day?'

'Please.'

'It's your funeral.'

'That's right, and I want you to spit on the grave by saying loud and clear so that everybody can hear it: "And that man used to be some top cop, would you believe it?" Okay?'

'You're crazy.' She rubbed her eyes as she laughed. She had always suspected that there was something suicidal about the guy, and now she mourned him.

Another large rum later Bucken stumbled against the chairman of Seven Seas Shipping, and accused him of spilling his drink. The man, Hollywood's image of a boardroom demi-god, reacted indignantly. Bucken pushed rather than knocked him to the ground. Somebody shouted 'police!' but the younger generation needed no help. Bucken was shoved and chased all the way up the narrow stairs. His eyes registered Freemantle watching the scene in disgust, and he half-heard Helen shouting without any conviction, 'And a top cop at that, would you believe it?'

By the time the last edition of the evening paper carried the news item 'drunken ex-cop hits shipping supremo', Bucken was hitching a lift to the Harwich ferry and on to Rotterdam.

On paper, at least, Oldman Savas was still a multi-millionaire. His family lived in grand style, commuting regularly between New York, Rotterdam and Piraeus. In international shipping circles he commanded special respect: in Greece and America, his word was law to several thousand people. If he said 'no calls, no visitors', his devoted secretary would seal off his door, telephone and telex lines. Yet, that Tuesday afternoon, she broke the rule twice. First she put through a call from Papeete – the secretary knew that Oldman had a soft spot for her – and later came in to announce a visitor. There was no need to ask who it was: everybody but Ruzicki would be turned away. Savas realised that the old woman must have recognised that he was powerless to say no to Ruzicki, and her understanding was as humiliating as the fact itself. He nodded gravely, accepting the inevitable. She sensed his mood. 'I'm sorry. It must be hard to be Oldman, Mr. Savas, to carry everybody's burden.'

'Just show him in, will you?' He would not need or tolerate anybody's sympathy. Despite valid excuses, he had no one except himself to blame for the situation. His Ruzicki connection was older than the syndicate. When it began, Don Quincey was still a high flyer in London, and the Savas name was commercially gilt-edged, morally inviolate.

Traditionally, to be Oldman was more of a responsibility than a distinction. His great-grandfather, who had founded the shipping empire at the age of seventy-two, used to be known as Savas Oyeros, the ancient Savas, mainly because of the grandfatherly interest he took in everybody's fate around him. The nickname was inherited by his son, and it was he, the second Savas Oyeros, who emigrated to America. The role of a tribal elder followed him across the ocean. From then on, responsibility for the neighbours left behind and the scattered, village-sized Greek shipping community on the East Coast was to be handed down with the name that would soon be – as they put it – yankified.

When the worldwide recession hit the present Savas empire, something drastic had to be done for all the ageing work force, several smaller ship-owners, boat-builders, shipyard cooperatives, shareholders and their families whose livelihood was at stake. It was, in fact, the tribe's interest that persuaded Savas to take the plunge into unorthodox, speculative ventures. Yet even his most promising ideas seemed to bring nothing but a spate of disasters that drained his resources as well as credit, when it was credit that he and his groups needed most to survive.

It should have been ominous to him that, out of the bleakness of recession, Ruzicki, a superficial acquaintance, approached him with a double-barrelled offer: credit at extortionate interest, and some urgent work for which Savas or his associates would be allowed to charge double the going rate. There would be some highly profitable charter deals, and repair jobs for the shipyards. There was only one condition: 'Cash on the nail but no questions.' First the appearance of two coastal tramps had to be altered. Then a freighter had to be patched up. People at the yards were grateful to Savas but sought his advice when it turned out that the freighter had been damaged by shells and explosions. They suspected that all the ships from Ruzicki might have been engaged in gun- or drug-running. Savas swallowed his anger and advised them to go ahead without any questions.

Finally, Ruzicki asked Savas for a little help: 'Just a white lie, Oldman. I need some proof that the freighter had gone into drydock just two weeks before it actually arrived. In return, my clients could guarantee some extra credit facilities.' Savas agreed to help. He and his people were close to several lucrative completion dates. If they were paid promptly, as promised, he would sever his Ruzicki connection. His hopes were wrecked by inexplicable fires and petty, almost spiteful strikes. Ruzicki sympathised, and volunteered to put together an emergency package. His backers would salvage Savas and his various groups, accept various Greek assets as security, and take temporary directorships on the board of the Savas family holding company. Savas refused the offer though he knew that several hundred 'tribal' jobs were at risk because numerous businesses could face bankruptcy.

'Alternatively, we could offer one or two highly profitable voyages to your ships,' said Ruzicki, adding, almost casually, that the captains and crews would be granted temporary leave, that the cargo and destination would be unspecified, and that Savas would have to lend his good name to the deal. Before Savas could say 'no' to that, too, Ruzicki struck a tone of ingratiating warmth: 'I understand your dilemma only too well, Oldman. But do you have a choice? Your debts will soon be called in, I happen to know. And I'm trying to help . . . almost as a family friend.'

'How come?'

'You really must think about Greta. Poverty is not for her, you know that.'

Savas felt paralysed as if bitten by a poisonous snake. He could not react as fast as he wanted to. How did Ruzicki know his wife? How well did he know her? He called her Greta. Was he her lover?

'She's a distant relative of the Hohenzollerns, isn't she? Well, I happen to know some members of that family. The acceptance of some home truths and adjustment to lower standards have never been their forte.'

Savas showed him the door, but his gesture was weak, and they both knew that Ruzicki might be asked to return one day.

Marrying Greta was the greatest single error Savas had ever made. Yet he knew he would repeat the mistake every time. She had everything he sought in life: class, beauty, independent spirit. She was twenty-three years younger than her 'oily trader of a husband' and thrived on despising him. She took her first of many lovers on the second day of their honeymoon at St. Moritz, and would taunt Savas forever with their 'youth, style and good breeding'. His tragedy was that he loved her, and her affairs excited him. The more outrageously she behaved, the more he tried to please her.

His oldest Greek friend once plucked up courage to warn him that she would sleep with virtually anyone in sight.

'But for money – only with me,' Savas answered with a painful, self-deprecating smile.

To compound his error, he had been foolish enough to allow Greta to deal with the children's upbringing. They had grown into aristocrats without a title, without much substance but plenty of style, and the readiness to make no secret of their conviction that their father's role in the world could not be simpler: 'If your misfortune is to be a plain trader, you must have money at least.'

Oldman Savas was anxious to justify their attitudes and respect them for their outspoken independence. But it never ceased to hurt him that his dumb, hedonistic weakling of a son was just hanging on to the coat-tails of titled jetsetters, spending wildly to cover his father's unforgivable ancestry. Savas knew he would have to ensure the family's future by training someone else to be in charge. He imported a cousin from Greece to run his empire, but the young man died, to Greta's eternal amusement, 'a true prole's death' from a neglected toe-nail infection. Savas fought back with new plans, but the recession now threatened to ruin them all.

After Ruzicki's insulting proposition, Savas decided to mobilise his final resources: the family assets together with what Ruzicki had termed credibility and good standing. He had, after all, friends everywhere. They as well as the banks and business associates listened to his requests and proposals with sympathy. All promised him early answers, and all kept their word. Within a week, regretfully, all turned him down. There were hints of mysterious pressures brought upon some of them. Ruzicki was vaguely implicated, but Savas stopped caring. He would never ask for favours, go cap in hand, ever again. He summoned Ruzicki and agreed to capitalise on everything, his name, standing and expertise, in a big, fraudulent way.

Crime, more than just the rocketing profits, brought Savas an unexpected bonus. Those piratical ventures, charter party fraud and rust bucket jobs, began to affect his style and outlook on life. His children were quick to sense even the most subtle manifestations of the change. Somehow, he was not the 'petty little trader' any longer. He seemed to have attained a status even Greta could not classify. Savas wallowed in his glory, and treated his family with some new-found contempt. He kept his more sobering thoughts at bay – most of the time. In moments of doubt, he would arrange lunch with old business *friends* who had rejected him in his greatest need but envied and nobbled him blatantly these days. He knew that many of them must be on the brink of bankruptcy. Over his plate, he would study their faces that were encrusted with the pallor of long sleepless nights. He felt no pity for them.

When Savas had just about accepted that there would never be a way to turn back, the idea of the syndicate came along. He joined Quincey wholeheartedly, and by now he knew that his salvation was in sight. 'Tsunami' would make him so rich that all the dirt could be washed away. Including the compulsion to see Ruzicki at any time.

'Go on, show him in,' Savas repeated with a John Wayne smile of invincibility that revitalised the old Cerberus of his office door. She left the room jauntily: while Oldman was around, there would always be hope for everyone.

This time Ruzicki needed a new name-plate shipping company in Australia and a front in the Cayman Islands to arrange the 'delivery' of fifty thousand tons of non-existent maize to an African country. 'Do you think we could up the price?'

Savas shrugged his shoulders: 'If you up the kick-back, too, why not? I know the minister involved well enough.'

'Great. You pay him whatever he wants, Oldman. You won't regret it. Any news about a wreck?'

'I m working on it.'

'It's got to be six thousand tons deadweight with precisely the specifications I've asked for.'

'They were fairly common, you know. Does it matter in what state she is in?'

'Not at all. If she's good enough for the scrap heap, she's good enough for me.'

'I may have something in Abu Dhabi.'

'Fantastic! You're nothing if not the fastest gun in the business.'

'I wish you were, too. I wouldn't mind if the *Alida* business was over and done with.'

'Don't worry. It's in hand.'

'We had several deaths at sea. And then that donkeyman . . . what's his name? . . . Hiller?'

'That has nothing to do with us. He was killed in a very Chinese fashion. A thousand slashes . . . or is it a hundred?'

'What was it? A fight? Over some girl?'

'I've investigated it myself, Oldman, but nobody in Macao would tell me anything. The place is swarming with spies and foreign agents of all kinds. Perhaps he was involved with the Russians. Perhaps the Chinese didn't like that. Who knows?'

Like a naked ghost who had lost his shroud of invisibility, Bucken felt peculiarly exposed in Rotterdam: even ghosts prefer to haunt familiar grounds, he thought, as he began his wanderings without friends, allies, signposts, files and the other usual crutches of police-work. He divided his time between watching Savas and discovering in bar after bar that it made no difference whether he ordered a *jonge*, an *ouwe*, *jenever*, *bessen jenever* or *alstublieft*, because he would get a gin every time. So why not ask for a gin in the first place? Because I prefer rum, he thought, and stopped being adventurous.

As he did not want to risk tailing Savas singlehandedly, he spent many a 'drunken' hour on benches in parks from where he could watch Savas's hotel and office. On the second day, he struck gold: he saw Savas and Ruzicki leave the office building together. Gut reaction assured him that it could be no coincidence.

Bucken contemplated a break-in at the Savas office, but decided against it. He would stick to the original plan, and gamble on going directly for the jugular. He began to work on his cover and chose to make it ominously transparent. If Papeete was connected with the racketeers – a thought that depressed him beyond reason – his obvious amateurism would help, hopefully, to convince everyone that Cairo had been a coincidence, and that he was what he pretended to be, a falling angel, sliding downhill fast, a bar brawler, a disgraced cop escaping to sea, who would take any work as long as there were no questions asked on either side. In Rotterdam, the crossroads of the western hemisphere with its international labour pool, he was well placed to start his new life. The sailors' job supermarket catered for everyone: union stalwarts; experienced seamen who would command top rates when the industry thrived; the palookas who could not tell the fo'c'sle from the Monkey Island; the discards who had blotted their seaman's book by drinking, drugtaking, smuggling, raping young ratings or piloting the bosun's teeth down his throat; the medically and morally unfit as well as those who had fallen on hard times in the Philippines, Greenland, Scotland, Thailand, Tanzania or Tampa Bay – everybody who was ready to accept rotten food and accommodation with similarly attractive wages on rust buckets or something worse. The lack of a union card (lost accidentally or through disciplinary action) might be overlooked, but a seaman's book would be essential to most employers, so Bucken set out to get one. Unfortunately, the black market viewed newcomers with understandable caution.

Savas could help him easily, Bucken felt certain about that. The old man seemed to know everybody in the port where he conducted strange business transactions in the evenings. He dined frugally with his bodyguard and, over a glass of red wine, he made long-distance telephone calls that Bucken was dying to but could not overhear.

So Bucken, too, began to frequent Savas's favourite haunt, the *Melkweg* in the docks, where *melk* was the only liquid never served, even with coffee, and where he sought to establish an alcoholic reputation as well as some underworld contacts. In two days of hard drinking he failed on both counts: everybody drank hard in the Milky Way and nobody would tell him where he could buy a fake seaman's book. So, at midnight, he decided to go about it the hard way.

He listened patiently to some innocent banter about football in Dutch, French, Spanish, Chinese, Gujerati and mostly pidgin English, until an opportune moment arose for him to bellow that Johann Cruyff was a 'shitty player'. As expected, even the non-Dutch objected to such sacrilege, and a few uncomplimentary remarks were exchanged about their respective mothers' and fathers' mating habits. There were still no hard feelings among them, and it would have been left at that if Bucken did not insist on taking it further.

'He's not only shitty, he's a cheat!' he yelled drunkenly at a bearded native. 'All Dutch players are cheats!'

'Shut up or I'll break your arm!'

'Dear, oh dear! Fright will make me shit shot, nancyboy.'

Playing the average hooligan, he knew how to cash in on the ways British fans endeared themselves everywhere. By the time the police arrived, Bucken had obtained a bloody nose and a reputation for a devastating left hook. The night in the dock police cooler provided him with the basics of a criminal record as well as an essential contact. The Dutchman whose idol he had insulted turned out to be a good-humoured connoisseur of sailors' international battlegrounds, and highly recommended him the Player in Durban and the Navigator's Mate in Cape Town for a decent fight any night of the year. On their release in the morning, he also introduced Bucken 'to the right circles'. It was an imposing American, a white-haired Southern colonel type straight out of *Gone With The Wind* who, reputedly, had worked the pumps in the great vegetable oil swindle, and who could supply seamen's books according to taste.

'If you don't wish to make a prudent investment, sir,' he boomed, 'and if you choose to settle for the shoddy and cheap, look elsewhere and may God the merciful and promiscuous be with you. For you'll need all the help you can get if you go after jobs with a stolen article. That I could get you, sure as daylight, for five hundred Yankee dollars, but do you want that? Surely not. I can tell. For a second five hundred I could get the original name removed and your own imprinted, but that's still no way to build an honest to God career for your young life. No, siree, I wouldn't let you!'

'Cut the bullshit, will you?'

'Right. I like a man of action. And I'll get you what you really want. A genuine fake, right? It would cost you two grand on the open market. But, because you're the Dutchman's pal, you can have it for a thou, complete with a CDC. Now: Panamanian or Liberian, what will it be?'

'Makes no difference.'

'How right you are, sir. What matters is that it'll be an original, registered by a Panamanian consul, just don't ask me where, and it will show any name you choose including your own. Now what do you wanna be? First mate? Second mate? Third engineer? Chief engineer costs double.'

With uncharacteristic humility, Bucken settled for the designation of a mere greaser. The colonel took pity on this simpleton of a client, and knocked a hundred off the price. Twenty-four hours later, Bucken received his red seaman's book with a perfect embossed stamp confirming that his photograph on page four was a true likeness and that he had presented suitable evidence to satisfy the most stringent regulations concerning his entitlement to this internationally recognised passport. The book came complete with additional documentation, including a Continuous Discharge Certificate that proved beyond doubt that 'bearer' had served as a greaser for five years in all aboard various vessels, and that his conduct had been VG every time.

'Heartfelt congratulations,' said the American. 'It's a pleasure to do business with you, sir. Let me know if ever you have the funds and decide to look for further promotion.'

Bucken was ready to make his move and ingratiate himself thoroughly with Savas. He dialled his emergency number at the Yard. The call was answered without any delay.

'This is the Gardener from Bayswater. Give me Greenfingers.'

'Right away, Bayswater.'

A few seconds later Dodd was on the line. 'Any problems?'

'I need two burly fellows. Plain clothes and some sort of seafaring identities essential. They may end up in the nick for a day or two.'

'You know that we can't afford to get implicated in any shape or form.'

'You won't. As long as the men's papers stand up to superficial scrutiny. They may be fined, that's all.'

A few hours later, a sergeant and a PC arrived at Rotterdam. A suitably unsavoury pair, they looked the part, Bucken had to admit to Dodd's credit. He met them at the airport, briefed them, took them to the Melkweg, and told them how he would finger Savas there. 'Just do as I tell you, and under no circumstances will you come to my help, whatever happens. Is that clear?'

The following day, Bucken tailed Savas to the office. He noted that there were several cars entering the underground garage of the building: there must be a direct access from there to the offices. In one of the chauffeur-driven limousines, Ruzicki and a man Bucken had never seen before were the passengers. Behind the tinted windscreen of a pregnant custom-built vehicle, Bucken thought he had recognised Papeete. Was she driving her husband to Savas? The wide rear door would easily receive a wheelchair. Were people assembling for a conference? Bucken longed to know. The hunter's adrenalin began to flow and blurred all visions of the risk Bucken was about to take.

Savas sat at the console and switched on the closed-circuit TV system. He greeted each new arrival on the screens with a formal gesture. The Quinceys appeared on screen No. 6. Don nodded back without a word. He was squeezing the left arm of his wheelchair. His right hand was hanging lifelessly. He seemed agitated, even angry. Behind him, Papeete stood facing the camera, trying hard not to show how tense she was. Trouble between them? Savas hated to see her upset. They had been betrayed. Don had been ruined and crippled by the strain, they were right to seek revenge, but it hurt the old man that he could never make them quit.

Savas turned to stare out towards the port. He watched the

Liverpool Bay, a majestic third-generation container ship, sail past. The hull was white and virginal, the might of the engines irresistibly masculine, the wagon-sized containers on board colourful and, from this distance, toylike – a microcosm of Savas's world as it ought to be.

A few minor matters were dealt with swiftly. Savas conveyed some harsh, anonymous criticism towards two of the partners who had missed a couple of recent meetings. Fortunately, this time everybody was there. Savas switched the network to direct listening to Aldo Selli, an American who operated a small, lately unprofitable fleet of refrigerated ships and bulk carriers. Selli had helped to compile and was now asked to sum up Quincey's feasibility study on the closing of the Suez Canal, and the profit potential of 'Tsunami'.

'We have two preliminary reports and assessments, only one single copy of each and every one, which you can all read and study in Oldman's office if you wish or desire as undoubtedly, I'm sure, you will,' he began ponderously, taking every opportunity to use two, preferably three words where one would do, and making Savas wince every time.

The tedium of Aldo Selli's style failed to disguise the fact that, in the short available time, Quincey had done a good job. The first report dealt with some technical aspects of sabotage that could close the Canal. 'There will be, as we must accept, a certain as yet ill-defined risk of casualties as well as the risk of war, but we propose and strongly advise that expert views on this should be sought at the very earliest opportunity. We also recommend a study of the Suez Canal Authority's capability to react to unpredictable and unforeseeable mishaps and accidents. If we wish to block the waterway for any considerable length of time, those emergency procedures must be taken into account.'

The partners agreed that Ruzicki, as head of security, should seek out and enlist suitable expert saboteurs for the task.

The second document highlighted the crucial elements of potential crises, and areas where syndicate members could profit. It emphasised that the Canal cut the sea-routes between East and West and saved almost half the fuel consumed – a vast amount considering that a large cargo ship might burn 150 tons of oil a day, at almost two hundred dollars a ton: some thirty thousand dollars every twenty-four hours.

Selli's report indicated that the chief advantage to the partners would be their preparedness when the traditionally sensitive, even hysterical, market panicked for at least a week or two. Recent Middle East upheavals revealed that, because there was no oil shortage, prices on the spot market would not be affected immediately, but it would still be very profitable to have oil available at the right spot at the right time. Much more could be made on having tankers in the right position on charter or for sale. A fleet of cargo ships, again in strategic position, could bring in a vast amount without virtually any outlay simply by selling their charter contracts to anxious bidders.

'After all,' said Selli, 'the Canal carries about twenty-three thousand ships a year, something like a million tons of cargo every single solitary day, plus the oil, of course, never forgetting all the oil going through. A third of the cargo arriving in South Asia comes through the Canal. In the Gulf, almost half the essential goods delivered have come that way. If we close the Canal, they'll get nervous and local prices must rise. If we have essential supplies stored on the spot at the right time, the profit potential could be very large and mouth-watering, indeed.

'Then there's the possibility of currency deals. Oil prices may remain steady, at least initially, but we know that, every time the Iranians threaten to close the Hormuz Strait, the dollar shoots up.

'Gold could also profit very considerably – particularly if we could imply and indicate some Israeli mischief and wrongdoing with the risk of hostilities, i.e. war.

'And another essential chance and possibility for our gain, something we could be considered outstanding and foremost experts in – the opportunity to cash in on insurance.

'As you will see from the technical study, if we engineered an explosion, a motorway-type pile-up could occur in the Canal, depending on the position and density of the convoy involved. Ships have no brakes and anything could happen,' he said gleefully. He did not need to explain to this audience that each ship in the convoy could be insured for up to ten times its current market value to cover not the new-for-old price but the mortgage on it, far in excess of the owners' investment. Selli also stressed that those doomed ships could carry over-insured unwanted unsellables, the surplus of the Western world, part of the butter mountain, much of the French and Italian wine lake.

Quincey and Selli were showered with praise for their work, but the partners agreed that further investigations were necessary because, as Ruzicki put it to their delight, 'we certainly won't risk innocent lives while the plan is less than foolproof'.

Hypocrites, thought Savas, but kept it to himself

Early in the evening, Bucken began his drinking seemingly in earnest. The Melkweg was crowded with thirsty strangers: the

Sudanese crew of a German freighter had hit land for the first time in three months. Bucken's men could mingle with them safely, pretending to be docile drunks and buying drinks all round.

As usual, Savas dined with his bodyguard in the corner and made one long-distance call. Bucken waited for them to finish their meal. He knew the bodyguard's routine well. After the last of his wine, the man would go out to urinate from the quay into the water. Savas would be alone for a few minutes. When at last the guard, a Greek of greasy good looks, had left, Bucken gave the signal to his plain-clothes men. The PC stumbled drunkenly, and the sergeant cursed Savas: 'You fuckin' tripped him up, fuck you!'

Savas protested his innocence, but the sergeant would not believe him. Swinging his arms wildly, he pretended to miss the old man's face. The PC also swore at Savas, towering above him menacingly. Their orders were not to damage the target, but push Savas off his chair. That was Bucken's cue. He came out of his corner, fighting mad, fists flailing, like cavalry to the rescue. He would knock one cop down, frighten the other away and, according to the scenario, that would be the end of it. 'Leave the poor old bugger alone!' he yelled with some conviction and hit the sergeant who collapsed groaning like an Argentinian football star. Bucken screened Savas, ready to face any opposition, and it seemed there would be no takers until, unexpectedly, all the Sudanese fell on him willing to fight against such overwhelming odds.

Within a few seconds, everybody had joined in. A bottle hit and stunned Bucken. The returning bodyguard never had a chance to cut his way through the general mêlée to his master. A wiry old Sudanese seaman, with a silver crust atop his five-foot-two, dived from the rail of the bar and caught Bucken's neck from behind in an armlock. His feet were dangling in mid-air, kicking Bucken's calves. His mate broke a bottle – the splash of gin had no cooling effect on anyone – and seemed to contemplate for a second which part of Bucken's anatomy should be his target. Bucken tried in vain to loosen the little man's grip. The other sailor with the fractured bottle seemed to have made his choice. Bucken spun round. The weight of the hanger-on threatened to dislocate his neck, but the body swung in an obedient arc and hit the man with the bottle. And yet the arms held Bucken's neck in a vice.

That was when Bucken noticed that Savas had been reached in his relatively safe corner by two men. They had helped the old man to his feet and were busy forcing him through a broken window to the street. Bucken had no time or inclination to inquire whether they were trying to protect or kidnap Savas in the bodyguard's absence.

Still unable to remove the old sailor's lock, Bucken suddenly moved backwards, smashing his assailant's skull into the wall. As if the crack of bones had failed to tell Bucken he had done enough, the arms peeled away to let him breathe.

He caught up with the two men who were half-helping, half-carrying Savas. The old man looked very pale, his lips quivering, as if he were on the verge of a heart attack. That's all I need, thought Bucken, as he went for one assailant's ankles with a rugby tackle. The four of them ended up in a heap on the ground. One man kicked Bucken in the ribs. Bucken cried out in pain, rolled away and, as the man closed in with a knife in hand, he pulled his bunch of keys at the end of his handkerchief in a vicious sweep out of his pocket. The keys hit the man on the cheekbone and cut a dreadful furrow diagonally downwards. There was blood everywhere.

Savas just sat and stared in horror. Police sirens could be heard. Bucken tried to move but his ribs hurt too much. The injured man staggered about aimlessly, trying to hold his damaged face together. His mate ran into the darkness just as the first policeman arrived. They grabbed Bucken and the injured man. Savas protested but nobody would listen.

The Melkweg had been wrecked. Policemen vied with ambulancemen for access both to crazed fighters and to those already laid up. Bucken would share out his night between the nearest emergency ward and the local cooler.

At the hospital, there was no more animosity. Bucken discovered that one of his London men had escaped with a few cuts and bruises: the other had suffered a dislocated shoulder. The bodyguard was in a bad state: apart from some eye injury treatment, he would have to wait for a set of dentures to be built for him as soon as a broken wristwatch, embedded in his lower gum, could be safely extracted. Six Sudanese and an assortment of fourteen other sailors waited with equanimity to be patched up and transported to the police station.

Bucken himself was X-rayed to reassure him that he had no broken ribs, but he needed four stitches in his forehead to replace some slivers of a *jenever* bottle most of which had to be removed from his hair. It was well after midnight when they released him to the police who then proved themselves most reluctant to accept that he had meant well when, seemingly, he had tried to re-stage Custer's last stand single-handedly. At a quarter past four in the morning, his statement signed, they let him sleep at last, but he was woken barely half an hour later: to his annoyance, he had been bailed out by the barman of what used to be the Melkweg.

'You no friend, you no name only face!' the barman grumbled. 'Tooooook us whole nacht you fined where!'

'Us? Who is us?'

'Old man.' .

'What old man. And why? . . . Okay. Thank you. But why did you get me out?'

The barman signed for him, and he was free to go. Outside the police station, Savas waited for him. Bucken resisted the urge to holler triumphantly.

'He paid you out,' said the barman. He accepted a tip from Savas and left them.

'Thank you, whoever you are,' said Bucken, 'but I have no money to pay you back. Not just now.'

'That's okay,' Savas nodded, 'I reckoned I owed you that much.'

'You did?'

'You may not remember, but you've probably saved, well, if not my life, at least my nose, teeth and wallet.'

Bucken shrugged his shoulders. 'Big deal.'

'Call it what you like. I'm grateful.' Savas pulled a fair wad of banknotes from his pocket and looked at Bucken.

'Don't be stupid, pop, you don't want to insult me, do you?'

'No.'

'Then put it away. I'm no beggar.'

'No, no. Of course not. It's just that . . . '

'Forget it. You could almost be my father.' That's a good line, Bucken thought, a few more words and I'll have him in tears. 'I mean I couldn't let those riff-raff walk all over you. You owe me nothing. And, now that we're quits, I'll say good night. Mind how you go. This is a rough area.'

'I've been here before.'

'Then you ought to know better. That Melkweg is no watering hole for an old pansy looking for sailor boys. Come on. I'll see you to a cab rank.'

Savas smiled. It was flattering to be liked for just what he seemed to be rather than for his position and wealth. 'You're very kind, mister . . . '

'X. Okay? Call me Mr. X.'

'Isn't there anything I could do for you, Mr. X?'

'Well, it depends. If you've got a million or two to spare, buddy . . . no, perhaps it's half your daughter and the hand of your kingdom . . . yes, your highness, you did look distinctly out of place in the Melkweg.'

'So did you. I was doing some business there. What were you doing?'

85

'Ssh.' Bucken looked left and right, then lowered his voice. 'I was on a secret research project comparing the relative efficacy of right upper-cuts and Sudanese beri-beri under the influence of bessenjenever.'

Savas laughed. 'Point taken.' Yes, it was nice to be patronized and perhaps a little cared for by a complete stranger. He felt like a prince incognito – it helped him to distinguish between men of true goodwill and arse-lickers.

Bucken sensed the old man's pleasure – and it shamed him. He was conning Savas. He wondered what sort of sub-human would enjoy the lies and pretence of undercover work as a permanent way of life. He had to vent his anger on someone, and he chose Savas. 'Come on.' His voice roughened. 'I'm too tired to stand here all night. Where do we find a cab?'

Savas led the way. He wondered how to break the suddenly hostile silence and offer to do something for Mr. X without offending his pride. Bucken felt panicky. Had he overplayed his role? Savas's Daimler must be nearby. They would soon say goodbye, and he would have lost his golden opportunity to latch on to the target.

'You're a fool, you know,' Bucken said gruffly. 'You shouldn't have come to the port on your own.'

'I was with a friend.'

'And a fat lot of good it did you, right? Where was that famous friend when you were in trouble?'

'He was injured. He . . . he'll be all right.' Savas did not want to mention that he had already arranged first class medical care for the bodyguard. 'And what's going to happen to you? Where will you go if you have no money?'

'Oh, I'll be all right, too.'

'You've got a job?'

'Why? Can you get me one?' His tone was provocatively mocking.

Savas liked it. 'I . . . I've got a friend or two.'

'Well, what do you know? A prince of industry in disguise. I'd better thank my lucky star, man. Come on, I've got enough to buy you a drink. You look as if you need it badly.'

They turned the corner and Bucken noticed the Daimler. The chauffeur moved to get out as soon as they had come into view, but something stopped him. It must have been a gesture by Savas. They found a bar. Bucken insisted on counting out his last coins for the drinks. He let Savas enjoy the situation. The old man remembered what Bucken had said. You could almost be my father. Well, almost. If only young Savas ever had such guts. He studied Bucken:

the face and the style did not fit the uncouth character he was projecting. 'So how about that job?'

'Yeah. I could do with that. Any suggestions?'

'What's your trade?'

'I'm a greaser. You know what that is?'

Savas nodded. 'You look more the officer kind. Just tell me what ticket you have. First mate? Master? I'll take your word for it.'

'You don't have to. I'm a greaser.'

Savas insisted on buying the next round of drinks. He glanced repeatedly at Bucken's hands, then shook his head. 'No. I've seen a greaser or two in my time . . . '

'Look, I have my card.' Bucken whipped out his seaman's book.

'Bucken?' Savas flicked through the pages. His lips took on a downward curl of open contempt. 'Oh yes. I think I know that consul very well. How much did you pay for this junk? I hope not more than five hundred . . . Mr. Bucken?'

'Now listen, pop, just listen. I didn't ask for a job, did I? And I didn't ask for your birth certificate and pension book before I got that ape off your back!'

'I'm sorry. I didn't mean to be nosey. I'm very sorry.'

'Okay. We'll drink to that.' Reluctantly, he let Savas order one more for him. He needed it, too. Pretending to be drunk might help him in his act.

'You know,' Savas seemed to be talking to himself as much as to Bucken, 'I have a son. And, when I was trying to show you my gratitude, I think I was selfish, too. I thought, who knows? One day my son might get into some sort of trouble. He might try to pose as a greaser. Will anybody help him? I mean help him – no questions. So forget my stupid objections and questions and all that. Let's start again. You say you're a greaser, so you're a greaser.'

'Right,' said Bucken, choking on it. He began to hope that Savas was clean after all, and Spire's hunch would turn out to be groundless. The whole operation could then be cancelled, and he would be free to concentrate on Macao to hunt down whoever had killed the donkeyman and possibly the Malayan girl. But first he would just sleep and sleep . . . Through the window he saw the soft light of dawn with promises of peace, silence and sweet monotony. He battled to prop open his eyelids.

'Okay, I'll get you a ship though I guess you could do a lot better than greasing.'

'I will, mate, I will,' he winked drunkenly, full of fear that, once his eye closed even momentarily, he might not be able to open it again. 'I have *plans*.'

'What plans?'

Bucken tapped his nose with his forefinger.

'Will you tell me something?'

'Depends.'

'What did you do before? I mean before you became a *greaser*.'

'This and that.'

'I don't want to be inquisitive. I'm genuinely interested. Believe me.'

'I don't like to talk about the past. What's gone is gone – that's my philosophy, right?' He was quoting, almost word for word, an ulcerous old safebreaker who had retired into petty thieving from milk floats. Bucken used to lend him the dignity of a conman by pretending to be a sucker for his moronic betting schemes. 'Now I have a new life and that's that.' He let drunkenness loosen his tongue – he had seen it too many times not to know how – and whispered conspiratorially. 'I'll work on a ship, get a little practical experience, and make a reliable friend or two. And then, then I'll get cracking. 'Cause I know a little about that shipping lark and the City. You know what I mean? Ever been to London, pop?'

'Once or twice.'

'Right. Well, let me tell you something. I used to work there. Not in the City itself but . . . never mind. I know the sort of money one can make there with the right ideas, a couple of good mates and a little working capital.' He nodded knowingly, as full of himself as any old safeblower who failed to realise that safes had changed in the decades of his doing bird. 'It's all there for the taking.'

'You want to rob a bank?'

'I'm not stupid. I'll do what the big men do.' He was now letting it all slip freely. About ships. And insurance. Even the Baltic Exchange. Ashenbury and cuddly old Boothy-Graffoe would have been proud of his apparent expertise.

'How come you know all that?'

'I used to watch it all, the craftiness and the fiddles, like honest men do. Now it's time for me to get inside and grab a piece of the action.'

'And become dishonest?'

'No. Just cash in.'

'Isn't that the same thing?'

'Not if you don't get caught.'

Savas liked and pitied him. 'Come on, I'll give you a ride into town and we'll talk tomorrow.'

'You won't get a cab round here.'

'I forgot to tell you – I've got my own transport.'

Bucken looked suitably astonished when the chauffeur opened the door of the Daimler for them. 'You fooled me,' he accused Savas.

'You fooled yourself. Nobody asked you to help me in the first place.'

'I helped a helpless old man, not some rich bugger.'

'You mean the rich can't be helpless?'

'I mean the rich should *buy* help.'

'Okay. How much?'

'Go to hell.'

'Good. Now we're friends again. So listen. You seem a decent enough fellow even if you have crazy ideas about making money in the City. If you still want to be a greaser, so be it. If you want something better, I'll do my best.'

'And no questions?'

'What's gone is gone. Your philosophy is good enough for me.'

Bucken could not afford to react to the mocking. 'What do you suggest?'

'We'll think about it. The 'friend' I had with me in the Melkweg was my bodyguard. How about deputising for him . . . temporarily?'

'Oh, I don't know . . . '

'You seemed to be lively enough with your fists.'

The ride was smooth, the Daimler purred its monotonous lullaby, exhaustion made it easy for Bucken to stay silent and play the reluctant bride.

You've done something you're not proud of, greaser Bucken, thought Savas. But who cares? As long as you're not wanted by the police and willing to toe the line, I'll give you a chance. He decided to use his trump card. 'And I can tell you, Bucken, my man earns a lot more than any greaser.'

'How much?'

'We'll make it a round five hundred bucks a week. Plus all expenses. I mean life won't cost you a cent while you're with me . . . '

'Who says crime doesn't pay?' Bucken smiled.

'But you'll have to look smarter than that,' Savas gestured vaguely. 'I don't know what clothes you have, so you'll get a thousand now to get kitted out. Do we have a deal?'

Bucken nodded. His head failed to rise. He slept all the way to Savas's hotel. The car came softly to a halt yet Savas had to stop him falling off the seat. 'We'll get you a room.'

'Thanks. I'm whacked.'

'Mm.' Savas was studying the seaman's book. 'Bucken? You could have chosen a more interesting name, but it'll do, I suppose.'

'It'll have to. It's my own.'

'Oh, sure.'

'Now listen . . . '

'I'm not arguing.'

'Good.'

'And you're single, I take it.'

'That's right.'

'Anything to prevent you from leaving with me for Piraeus the day after tomorrow?'

Bucken shook his head. At least he meant to.

It was a fine day for contemplating suicide. Prickly cold drizzle sprinkled Athens, dampness penetrated the hotel windows that were unaccustomed to such sneaky, unseasonal onslaughts, and a sequence of minor calamities was triggered off by a whiff of draught that sent a spasm through Don Quincey's chest.

'Can't we keep that goddam' weather out?' he demanded irritably.

The day nurse turned to draw the curtains: Papeete went round the breakfast table to pull his dressing gown tighter. At that point, he sneezed. The two women were too far away to help him with a Kleenex. His only good hand, balancing a cup, moved involuntarily to prevent spittle and snot flooding the table, and splashed hot coffee all over him. Mucus seemed to drip and settle on fresh toast, eggs and all. Quincey blushed and swore. Papeete moved even faster than the nurse.

'It's all right, darling, it's all right.'

'Leave it alone,' he shouted, and reached out to remove the particularly offending sight of fouled marmalade, but burnt his hand on the teapot, and knocked over a jug of juice into the sugar bowl. Other people might have laughed, he did not.

'It's all right, darling.'

'Stop mothering me! I may be a fucking cripple but I can still afford servants to wipe my arse!' His voice tripped.

The nurse took away the cups and began to clear up the mess, but Papeete stopped her. She gathered the four corners of the tablecloth and handed the bundle to her. 'Thank you, nurse,' she said in a thin voice. 'We've finished with breakfast.'

When the nurse had left, she sat down, facing the wheelchair, across the wet, empty expanse of the table.

'I'm sorry,' he said.

'What for?' Now they both had tears in their eyes.

'That's right,darling, it's not me who should be sorry.' His speech was beginning to gain strength and momentum. 'It's them. And by God we'll make *them* sorry. Every one who was party to doing this to me. And once I'm back on my feet . . . '

Papeete turned away. It was one of the increasingly frequent moments when she doubted even the most cautiously optimistic prognoses with which the best specialists in the world had fed them.

'You aren't listening, are you?'

'I am, of course I am. You said once you're back on your feet . . . '

'Then let me *see* you listen.' He launched into one of his long diatribes, regurgitating all the injustice the City had done to him.

Papeete needed no reminders. She knew it all by heart. His youthful drive and enthusiasm had once caught the City with a rabbit punch. His almost naive idealism was magnetic. It certainly drew Papeete irresistibly. His cut-price insurance scheme grew, snowballed and hit many a venerable institution where it hurt most, but it was impossible to denounce him, at least publicly, because his claim – 'I'm backing the punters not The Club' – was substantiated by his taking no more than a very decent salary and a modest bonus from the profits. But the bouncy baby he had created began to grow into an insatiable monster. He needed more and more astronomical finance, and he was drawn into widely practised though unethical and even unlawful schemes.

Having secured regular work for two large freighters, he bought them at market value and sold them at a great loss to a Bahamas-registered *foreign* company he himself owned secretly. Beyond the substantial 'tax loss', he was to make huge profits on the operation of the ships which he leased back at an inflated rate so that most of the real earnings would go to the Bahamas and enjoy all the off-shore tax advantages. The scheme also ensured that the ships could be 'managed' from Korea, supplied with a Korean 'blue certificate' for crewing, and so operated with cut-price labour even when visiting American and other highly unionised ports. The *foreign* company's profits were then loaned to his British company to help his original cut-price insurance venture flourish and let his honourable intentions justify the means.

He also speculated with the steady flow of insurance premiums, though sometimes this left him barely covered against a sudden avalanche of claims, and totally dependent on oft-guaranteed goodwill. It was, in fact, at one such moment that his enemies ganged up on him. The City caught him with a classically simple sucker punch. The financial carpet was pulled, the safety net of goodwill was lowered, and his dubious practices were mercilessly exposed by those who had taught, guided and sometimes partnered him. He was ruined and became a non-person overnight.

His thirst for revenge was always shared by Papeete. His stroke which followed his bankruptcy only strengthened her resolve. His ingenuity had never had a greater admirer than his wife, but lately his brilliantly unorthodox but fraudulent revenge schemes were more and more tainted by elements of common, violent crime. These new tendencies and some new associates worried and upset her, but she knew there was no turning back, not without abandoning revenge and throwing in the towel. And that was not on.

' . . . and if anybody stands in our way,' he thundered, pounding his useless right hand with his left fist, 'they'd better start drawing up their wills.'

'You don't really mean that, do you?'

'I don't need you or anybody else telling me what I *really* mean, thank you.' He stopped as the door opened and the nurse returned.

'Your bath is ready, sir, if you want it now. You said you have an appointment at eleven.'

'Yes. Let's go.'

Papeete stood up. 'That's all right. I'll do it, nurse.'

'No thanks,' said Quincey. 'I'll ask for your help when I want it.'

She stared out at the drizzle and hated it. That was why she decided to defy it and go for a stroll. It would also help her to avoid meeting Ruzicki at eleven. If anything, it was that man and his private deals with Quincey that could have persuaded her to forget revenge and leave the syndicate.

Quincey watched her from the window as she walked out of the hotel without an umbrella. 'Sorry,' he muttered to himself, 'about everything.'

Apart from new plans, Ruzicki wanted to discuss Macao and his concern about that mysterious European with the scarred face his Chinese henchman had mentioned.

'Perhaps they lied to you,' said Quincey, dismissing his worries. 'They invented him because they needed some excuse.'

'Maybe. But that's not good enough. We're vulnerable from several angles. The *Alida* disaster itself. The donkeyman's death. Then the donkeyman's cousin whom we can't trace. If an outsider knows about all this, let alone witnessed some of the events, we're doomed.' He tried to face out Quincey's silence, but his determination did not last. 'Don't you think?'

'Don't fret. Report the facts and leave the thinking to me.'

'Okay. Savas suspects that I had a partner in the *Alida* affair.'

'So what? Aren't you entitled to have any partner you want? What matters is that we should get a frontman urgently for the follow up. The man must be reasonably trustworthy. '

'*Reasonably* trustworthy?'

'Yes, that'll do. He won't know much anyway, will he? And he must be expendable.'

'I'll find a fall-guy, don't worry, Don, but for locating a suitable wreck we must depend on Savas.'

'Just tell him to get his skates on. We must complete that deal well ahead of "Tsunami". I need capital.'

'You know how the old man is. We can't push him too hard. We don't want him to be sore with me.'

'Bullshit. He's a businessman. He'll get his cut, and as long as he finds a wreck he can be as sore as his wife's overworked cunt.'

'If only he knew that we were in this together . . '

'No. There's no need for him to know. Not just now.' Quincey looked away to close the subject, but continued the argument in his mind: just as there's no need for you to know everything, buddy. There was no need for Ruzicki to know *how* the *Alida* deal had been set up – or why Quincey could not object when the phantom 'scarf-ace' decided to go to Macao, take charge if necessary and protect 'our mutual interests'. Quincey remembered the sharpness of the man's voice, and sighed. It was not easy to deal simultaneously with criminals and political thugs from a wheelchair.

Now I know what auctioned slaves must have felt like, thought Bucken, as he stood in what he hoped to be the dignified silence that allowed Mrs. Savas to complete the viewing before making her bid.

'Welcome to Athens . . . and you may call me Greta,' she said at last, watching her husband to detect any nuance of his reaction. But Savas had sculpted his face from stone for the occasion. He felt certain that Greta had slept with his regular bodyguard, now in dry-dock, just to spite him. There was no reason to believe that she would not tempt the replacement, too. So he was more interested in Bucken's response to her instant come-on.

When Bucken said nothing, she asked him after a long pause: 'And what do I call you?'

'Everybody calls me Bucken. So perhaps that's what you ought to call me . . . Greta.' His voice attained a simulated edge to disguise how much he liked what he saw. She was a tall sensuous blonde with slowly roving eyes. Her taut lips suggested inner tension in search of relaxation. He guessed she must be over forty although, forgetting her grown-up children, she looked no more than thirty in the muted, flattering light of the hotel lobby. She had style to flavour her oozing sexuality, and she was a woman rather than a laugh-a-minute good-time bird – qualities he had missed badly since losing his wife and rejecting, foolishly, the drunken and magnetic Papeete in Cairo.

'As you wish . . . Bucken.' She sounded irritated.

I'll give you a rise, Bucken, thought Savas, and double your wages if you also kick her in the teeth. 'I have a meeting in my room, so feel free until three p.m.,' he told Bucken.

'I haven't had a chance to check your room for bugs and security, Mr. Savas,' said Bucken, hoping to have an early opportunity to identify some of Savas's business associates.

'Not to worry. I'm at home here.'

'So you may go,' she said, sensing that Bucken would not adapt easily to playing the servant.

'Thank you . . . Greta.'

To cool his head, Bucken stormed out of the hotel. The drizzle had fattened into juicy rain, but Bucken hardly noticed it. Across the road, with her soaked hair hanging straight, Papeete came running towards the canopy of an umbrella held out by the uniformed doorman. Bucken hesitated. He had a perfect chance simply to step aside and avoid her. But what would that achieve? If she had something to do with Savas, they would soon meet. She, too, would then realise that Bucken's presence might not be any more of a coincidence than hers. In which case, the game would be up. She would tell them about Cairo. Tell them something. And he would have to con them. But could he? There was only one way to tell – and no point in delaying the inevitable.

He moved forward to let the rain and Papeete come to him. 'It was nicer in Cairo,' he said softly.

It stopped her just short of the haven of the large, striped umbrella. She stared at him in disbelief. He knew she would ask him what the hell he was doing there. But he was wrong.

'What happened to you?' She gestured towards the bandage that covered the stitches.

'I was willing but the flesh was weak.'

'And you think the rain will toughen it?'

'No, but it may make me grow enough to go over brick walls instead of through them.'

A slow smile wiped away her screwed-up features. It was such a relief to have a break from reality. 'Do you think we could continue this somewhere dry?'

'I know just the place. In Cairo. Alternatively . . . '

He opened the hotel door for her, but she shook her head almost imperceptibly. It made him feel guilty that he could guess why: she must be staying at the same hotel, and he would have to find out under what name.

They crossed the square, through the maze of white tables and chairs awaiting sunnier days. Rain or no rain, neither of them seemed to be in any particular hurry. The doorman watched them: he always knew that the rich were crazy.

The bar was small with no one else to share its cosiness, and the barman gave them a towel to dry themselves. They huddled near the fire, at the top end of the bar. Bucken meant to say, 'I thought I'd never see you again,' but changed his mind: since his last day in London he had half-expected to see her again and he did not want to lie unnecessarily.

'I never expected to see you again,' she said. 'You disappeared from Cairo without as much as a goodbye.'

'I m sorry.'

She searched his face for clues: did he really believe that I was so paralytically sloshed that night? Had it really been a grand gesture, almost a confession of love, to reject me in the state I seemed to be in? And, if yes, why would he disappear without trace?

Bucken's face told her nothing. 'I'm sorry,' he repeated, 'circumstances beyond my control . . '

Yes, from his behaviour at the time she guessed he might be on the run. She did not care. Cairo belonged to dead yesterdays. Athens was the unborn tomorrow.

'So why fret?' he completed her thought.

The barman stepped closer to take their orders. She nodded towards Bucken: 'Yours is rum, right? White, cold and virginal.'

'Correct. And no, I have no strong principles about who buys whose drink if that's the price of your staying and having one with me.'

'Okay. I'll join you.'

'Two Bacardis,' he told the barman without taking his eyes from her.

She looked away. Then she turned back. She enjoyed this moment of the unreal, of being wanted so fully and openly. And he would never discover how utterly sober she was when she half invited him into her room.

With an effort, he pulled himself together and stopped at least his eyes wanting her. She was probably on the side of the enemy and, if so, he ought to seduce rather than love her. Besides, she might already know about him. She might be play-acting, trying to trap him. He might have no time to waste. 'Are you here on holiday?'

95

She sensed the conversational tone and answered in kind. 'Sort of. I could say yes and no.' Then, quite involuntarily, she lowered her voice and moved a little closer to him. 'Are you . . . are you all right now?'

'What do you mean?'

'You looked as if you were on the run. In Cairo, I mean.'

He shrugged. It was a good moment for lies. 'Yeah. How did you guess?' She just waited, so he turned away thinking: the critics are here, my acting ability is to be tested. 'I . . I had trouble at the time. With the police.'

'Anything . . . anything serious?'

He was pleased that she looked concerned. 'It's over now. Let's forget it.'

'If you say so.'

'Don't worry,' he smiled, 'I'm not Bucken the Ripper.'

'No. You're not. Not even a rapist.'

'How can you tell?'

'You're not the type, that's all.'

'Is there such a thing as type? I mean it could make life,' he almost said a cop's life, 'so much simpler.'

'It does for me. I trust my sixth sense.'

'It can be dangerous.'

She sipped her Bacardi. Her face betrayed her dislike for the sharp taste.

'Would you like something else?'

'No.'

'You don't like it.'

'It takes some getting used to.' She drank up defiantly. 'Most things do.' Like the temptation of adultery, she thought.

During the long pause, both of them were occupied with their private thoughts. He toyed with the idea of telling her everything. Throughout his working life, Bucken considered himself lucky because, somehow, all his villains seemed to fall into three categories: he would hate them, feel indifferent towards them or pity them. It would be much harder to chase them if he liked, let alone loved them. I must be getting on or going soft, he thought. He knew what his mistake was – he had taken a much too close and personal look at his current suspects. No, Bucken concluded, it wouldn't be much fun to put Papeete's wrists in steel bracelets. And, if it had to be done, it would feel better if I knew I had played it straight all along. But how can I? 'Are you married?' he asked her, and even his question was a hateful lie because he knew the answer.

'Yes, yes, I am,' she said defiantly, and let him order another round. 'Are you?'

'Not any more.'

She watched him wistfully. She wanted to ask a few dozen questions – the 'not any more' had told her some long, sad tales – but resisted the urge. Her questions and the depth of her interest were only a short step away from actual adultery – something that would take a lot more getting used to. That moment of weakness in Cairo was different because then she was convinced she would never see the man again. It gave her quite a jolt that he had not taken easy advantage of her. That refusal was both a compliment and a challenge. She still felt like picking up the gauntlet. Was it hurt pride or the makings of love? Perhaps a bit of both with more than a dash of un-diluted sex drive – don't bother too much with the niceties, old girl, just get yourself laid by this bandaged pirate with the warm smile, cold rum, and the whiff of menace.

Papeete was not liable to long periods of kidding herself. For a few months now she had lived with the dreams and physical symptoms of wanting a man. She was eager to touch and longed to be touched, and knew perfectly well that none of it would happen because she was not prepared to cheat. Yes, Cairo and Bucken were something different. Bucken gave substance to the dreams and Cairo offered the opportunity. Don would never have known what happened, and no man, not even this stranger, would ever be able to humiliate her husband, even secretly, by looking at Don and thinking, 'I've enjoyed your wife'. Now if Bucken would promise to disappear . . . She dismissed the thought and pulled herself together.

Don Quincey used to be everything Papeete and her large circle of girl friends had ever dreamt of. His self-assurance, drive, good looks and lifestyle, combined with his open and overwhelming devotion to the woman he courted, had made him the hottest property in Papeete's London. That it was she whom he wanted so much was a triumph. And it needed a triumphant sensation like that rather than just love to help her break off an affair that had held her captive yet poisoned her life from the day of losing her virginity. So when, thanks to Don, that affair was over . . . well, was it over? She used to think it was. Because she used to think she was in love with her husband. Except that there were moments, even at the beginning, when she would admit her doubts at least to herself. Give Don time, let things develop, she would urge herself. But time could not improve things that were not there in the first place. Quincey's inter-ests were limited to business coups, sex and an incessant public demonstration of having a good time with a beautiful woman – more or less in that order. And even in those areas there appeared to be flaws. Papeete tired of his style of good life, his killings in the City failed to stimulate her, and sex, well, she explained to herself, or at least tried to explain, that her sex life had been poisoned and, given time, the poison would work itself out of her system.

There was no time to deal with her doubts: they had been obliterated by the swiftness and thoroughness of Quincey's crash. He was left with nothing, not even a body to make love with. He tried to be fair and did everything in his power to drive her away or into the arms of casual lovers. She was too loyal not to defy him and herself. He would have to be healed, revenge would have to be taken, and then, perhaps then, other parts of their life could be re-examined. Except that, lately, his obsessions and understandable bitterness had made it more and more difficult for her to share his life without any respite.

She looked at Bucken. The sadness in his face intrigued her. She remembered his voice wanting and rejecting her. She noticed that his eyes were looking at something that was not there for her to see. She touched his arm. 'Are you still with me?'

His eyes warmed to her. The sadness was gone.

'Worried?'

'No.'

'What have you done?'

His eyebrows questioned her.

'Why was it that you had to run?'

'I didn't have to. Only that I was accused of something I hadn't done. So I went to Cairo to clear my name.'

'Did you succeed?'

He shrugged his shoulders once again. Acting did not come easy for him. 'Not quite.' The sadness was back in his smile as he raised his glass. 'But here's to a new life. I'm here . . . with you . . . '. He paused, then forced himself to add the words that would bring their relationship to a crunch: ' . . . and I've got a temporary job to keep my head above water.'

'What's that?'

'Would you believe it? I'm a bodyguard.' He could see the fright in her eyes. Savas must have told his friends about the nasty episode in Rotterdam. So now she would make the connection. No point in trying to delay it. 'I'm working for some rich bloke, called Savas.'

He knew what must be going through her mind. It could not be helped and the consequences would have to be faced now or later – so why not now? He pretended to be preoccupied with his drink. He held it to the light and took endless pleasure in its glitter. He thought the notional director putting his act together would approve. She looked confused. Then she excused herself. The sign for the lavatories was twinned with the arrow for the public telephone downstairs. Which one did she want? Would she call Quincey, Ruzicki or Savas? What would she say? That she suspected their meetings in Cairo and Athens were no coincidence? He could do nothing but wait.

When she returned a few minutes later, there was determination in her gait. Would she walk past him? She took her stool at the bar. 'Will you do something for me?'

'Anything.'

'Thank you. Will you please leave Athens – now?'

'Why?'

'As I said, I'm married. My husband knows Savas. It wouldn't be fair. I mean I must tell them that we've met before . . . '

'But that . . . '

'No buts. Please. Just go.'

So she was loyal. To everyone concerned? He felt certain that she suspected him. Of something undefinable. She must also know that they, whoever they were, would suspect him even more. And, if Ruzicki was involved with that death in Macao, another murder might not be too much of a burden on his conscience. That, however, she would not want to happen, Bucken guessed. He knew this recognition ought to delight him. It did not because her fears had confirmed not only her care for him but also her awareness of the ruthless acts her husband or his associates might be capable of.

'Don't ask any questions, please don't. Just do it for me. Go away. Now.' She touched his arm in support of her insistence. 'We might meet again. Somewhere else, some other time.'

'Good. Where and when?'

'I know I have no right to ask . . . '

'Look, it's not a matter of rights. It's just that I don't understand. Ten minutes ago you seemed quite pleased to see me.'

'I was.'

'But not any more.'

'That's right.' Her voice grew croaky. The carefree moment of living in an unreal world was gone. Reality was back and it looked bleaker than ever before. She looked at her hand on his arm then, almost with an effort, she lifted her fingers and drew them away. 'There're things I can't explain.' She watched out for tell-tale signs that might give away how much he understood the unsaid. She saw none. And that made it even harder for her to repeat her pleas driven by concern for him.

It dawned on Bucken that hers was almost as grand a gesture as his that night in Cairo. 'I really fail to understand you,' he said, downed his drink and ordered two more by holding up his thumb and index finger to the barman. Papeete's little finger reached for his thumb and bent it down in slow motion. She smiled, he did not, and the barman looked sad: he could tell that the one-act play for three fingers augured a tragic ending.

'I think you're silly,' Bucken said.

'Am I?'

'Yes. Which is odd because you were rather clever when you spotted instantly that I was in trouble when we'd just met. That's over now. I've finished one life and started afresh. I was on the brink of slipping all the way down when out of the blue I got this job. It's not the most glamorous I can think of, but it's a start. It matters to me. Besides, what have I . . . what have we to hide? Nothing. Unfortunately. There's never been anything, anything factual, between us. So go ahead. Tell Savas what you like. Tell anyone.'

She studied his craggy face and the dark eyes, full of pain, then nodded and drank up. It made her cough. 'I believe you,' she said and walked out into the rain.

Applause, ladies and gentlemen, applaud generously, thought Bucken, there's no dividing line between false pretences and the artistic delivery of someone else's lies. Critics' night has been a success. And now for the real thing . . .

'Tell me about the fight,' said Greta. Her voice had a chesty, intimate resonance. 'How were you hurt? Have you lost a lot of blood?'

Savas found it fascinating to watch her 'in action'. She was wearing ordinary jeans (to avoid too many flights to Sicily for fittings, she always ordered a dozen at a time from The Only man in the world who knew how to cut jeans) and an ordinary T-shirt (designed in Paris to emphasise rather than cover) with a stylised monkey motif (the work of a Chinese finger painter in Singapore). Being a part of the permanent Savas suite, the hotel room was furnished with Greta's French antiques, but she was squatting hunched on the floor, not far from Bucken's feet. She waited patiently for the answers, focusing completely on Bucken, and Savas knew that her eyes would move with his lips when he spoke.

'It was just a fight. I can't even remember what hit me.'

'A bottle was broken on your head,' said Savas.

'Maybe.'

'Did it hurt a lot?'

Bucken raised and dropped his shoulders.

'How about that terrible weapon? Do you always carry it?' She insisted on seeing the keys tied to his handkerchief. 'You must have washed off the blood. They look so innocent and ordinary.'

'They can cause awful injuries.'

'How awful?'

Savas recognised Bucken's reluctance to talk about fights and wounds, but he knew that, sooner or later, men would not only answer but long to answer Greta's questions. She would seduce them to the point where they would start trying to seduce her. That was what she called her inverted fishing, her favourite pastime: instead of playing the fish in order to catch it, she would play her catch when already hooked. And Savas noted the first signs of the man's eagerness to talk to her. Bucken stuffed the keys and the handkerchief in his breast pocket.

'Somebody once threatened me with a sawn-off shotgun.' His eyes detected the slight movement of her arms as they pressed in on her bosom from both sides. 'I pretended to suffer from hayfever. I. . .' he had almost said chummy, the word cops used for villains, 'I mean the man found it funny. That relaxed him. I pretended that I was going to sneeze . . . ha . . . ha . . . ', he gasped for air and twisted his nose. Greta laughed. 'He nodded his permission for me to reach for the hanky . . . ha . . . ha . . . ' He grabbed the corner of the white cloth and brought the keys out with a swish. It throttled Greta's laughter. Bucken dangled the tinkling keys. 'They slashed half his face and jaw away.'

She watched the bunch as if hypnotised. The phone rang and startled her. Savas picked up the receiver. 'Yes . . . Oh yes, by all means.' He rang off. 'It's Papeete. She's coming over for a drink. Would you like another one, Bucken? Feel free. Help yourself.'

'No,' said Greta. 'You give him one. I want to hear more about him. Tell me about yourself.'

'What would you like to know?'

'Anything and everything.'

'There isn't much to tell. I lead a dull and simple life.'

'Be fair, sweetheart,' Savas came to Bucken's rescue, 'only because he's working for me temporarily, we're not entitled to break his privacy.'

'Is that so, darling?' she smiled at her husband. 'Would Mr. Bucken be the first among your friends, partners and employees whose privacy you broke?'

Without knocking, Papeete entered. Bucken already knew that her suite was on the same floor. Clearly, she was shocked to see him there. A single glance at Greta told her much about the mood in the

101

room. Savas began to make the introductions but Papeete cut him short: 'We've met.'

Savas was surprised but said nothing

'Oh, you have,' said Greta. 'Then perhaps you could tell me something about Mr. Bucken. He seems a little reticent . . . or is he so only with me?'

'What will you have, my beautiful?' Savas stepped between the two women. Bucken's eyes caught Papeete's in just a flash. They both knew she ought to ask for a rum. White and virginal. She chose a Martini, then complimented her hosts on a newly-acquired eighteenth-century corner cabinet with fine floral marquetry panels.

'You've answered my husband, but not me, *beautiful*,' Greta mimicked Savas. 'Is *our* Mr. Bucken always so taciturn – or even shy?'

'I wouldn't know.'

'I mean he says his life is dull and simple, but to me he seems a man with delicious secrets. What do you think, beautiful?'

'You'll have to ask him. I'm sure he'll reveal everything to you.' She sounded light and natural, making it quite indisputable that, to her, the subject had been closed. 'May I have a word with you?' she asked Savas.

'By all means. But if it's business . . . ' he gestured towards the door leading to his study.

'It is, in a way, and I'd hate to bore everybody else with it.'

'That's very considerate of you, Papeete,' Greta turned to Bucken, adding: 'She knows I can't stand those excruciatingly dull pow-wows about ships and money.'

'Then you'll excuse us, sweetheart,' said Savas and opened the door for Papeete.

'But of course, Dyonisios.' She noted Bucken's surprise and explained: 'Yes, that's Mr. Savas's actual name even though he prefers to be known as Danny or, more aptly, Oldman Savas.' And without looking at her husband: 'Just don't be too long with it, darling. You know that the Arbouzis are expecting us for some Mexican fiesta on the boat.'

'I . . . I thought we'd agreed not to go.'

'You agreed, darling, I didn't. And they're sending the chopper to take us. They're anchored somewhere near Poros.'

'Then you go, sweetheart. I've got to see some people.'

'Okay. May I borrow Bucken for the evening?' She leaned back and the stylised monkeys jumped to prominence. 'It's only that I'd like to wear some decent jewellery, and you always say "safety first".' She smiled at Bucken: 'Except that I never know whether it's safety first for me – or the rocks.'

'Enjoy yourselves,' said Savas, leading Papeete into the study.

As the door was closing behind her, Papeete heard Greta returning to her questions about Bucken.

'How come you know him?' Savas asked.

'That's what I wanted to tell you.' She described their meeting in Cairo with heavy emphasis on her impression that he had seemed to be in trouble at the time. She told Savas everything, the visit to the Pyramids and the dinner, but only up to the point of her saying goodnight in the bar.

'Was he inquisitive?'

'No.'

'Did he meet Ruzicki?'

'I don't think so. Ruzicki arrived later that night and I only met him for breakfast the following morning. By that time, Bucken had left, I believe. If he had any interest in our affairs, Ruzicki's arrival would have been an incentive for him to stay on. He says he had some trouble with the police.'

'Not an unlikely story judging from his behaviour in Rotterdam where he bought false papers.' He told her what happened, and they agreed that there had been some odd coincidences.

'The point is,' she said, 'that today, when I discovered over a drink that he's now working for you, I asked him to leave. I told him that Don and I knew you. The implication must have been clear. If he was up to something, he'd have fled right away.'

'That makes sense.'

'So I really don't see anything sinister in all this.'

'Then why are you telling me?'

'I thought you ought to know. And he ought to go.'

'What does Don think of it?'

'Haven't yet had a chance to tell him.' It seemed pointless to mention that she had walked for hours in the rain, trying to decide what to do and choosing Savas, a potential ally, to consult first. 'By the time I returned, Don had been taken for physio, and I wanted to know what you think, right away.'

'I think we'll have to tell both Don and Ruzicki before we do anything.'

'Why?'

'Security is Ruzicki's job. He may think we . . . we may have to do something else about Bucken.'

'Are you suggesting . . . ?'

'I'm not suggesting anything. But there's too much at stake.' He smacked his lips and shook his head with disappointment. 'Pity.

103

Bucken seems a good man to have around. And I was hoping to help him.'

'Then do. Send him away – now.'

'Have you . . . ' he avoided her eyes, 'have you slept with him?' It was obvious that the question had hurt him.

'No. Besides, wouldn't I want him to stick around if I have?'

'Not if you felt guilty about it.'

'I wouldn't have done it in the first place if I felt guilty about it.'

'I take your word for it.' He knew he looked more subdued than she had ever seen him, and there was no way to explain to her that his jealousy by proxy was more painful than his own. In fact, in some masochistic fashion, he willed Greta to sleep with Bucken. It would prove at least that nobody in his right mind could resist her. Some day, in anger, she would tell him all about it, with lots of erotic details, some of them real, others pure invention to torment him. And it would be like making love to her for the first time all over again. 'I hope that Don will also believe you.'

'There's no reason why he shouldn't.'

'Okay. Then we'll play it like this. We'll let them go to the party. He must know that you've told me everything. If he's guilty of something, he'll run for it. Ruzicki could still track him down if necessary. If he returns, we'll take it, well, not as proof of innocence, but something in his favour.'

Bucken felt awkwardly self-conscious in the tightness of his borrowed dinner jacket, but luckily in Greta's company nobody had much time to think about him. Before they set off to meet the helicopter Arbouzi, the frozen food magnate with last year's smile, would send for them, Bucken had discovered the Quinceys' alias. They were registered as Mr. and Mrs. Carter. Could Papeete be persuaded to abandon the murky world of Savas and Ruzicki? She would not listen to him, but Lord Ashenbury might have some powerful leverage. Bucken left the hotel in search of a public phone. He caught Ashenbury still in his office, and told him about the *Carters*.

'I m very grateful, Bucken. I thought you might have forgotten my private request to find the Quinceys.'

'What do you intend to do?'

'I'm not sure. The question is what they are up to. Do you know?'

'No. I mean I know no more about Quincey than the rest of them as yet.'

'Well, whatever it is, I think they deserve a better deal than what they've got in the City. I'll try to contact him. Or her.'

'Just make sure that my name won't be mentioned.'

'Goes without saying. Everything okay with you?'

'Mm . . . I guess so. . . . I mean I should know quite soon if I've failed at the second hurdle.'

Normally, he would discuss his doubts and strategy with colleagues, superiors or specialists. He had spent all his life working with teams and plenty of back-up – now, for the first time, he was completely on his own. It gave him the heady feeling of real freedom. The freedom of choice and the freedom of failure. With nothing to fall back on, nobody else to blame for mistakes, and no four-minute warning of impending disaster. For he realised that Papeete might already be talking about him to some people. And they might consider him an intolerable risk. By the time he found out, it might be too late to do anything about it or to get away. Yet he was determined to stay on and try to brazen it out. If it was to be his last, at least it would be a night in the grand style at Greta's side aboard the legendary Arbouzi yacht.

Ruzicki volunteered to deal with the problem: 'Let's not take chances. We can't afford to. So leave it to me.'

Papeete was stunned.

Savas accepted that the coincidences looked suspicious, but argued that 'if Bucken stayed on, it would go a long way towards clearing him. He'd be a fool not to run for it in the light of what he must know that we know'.

'Sure,' said Ruzicki, 'but is that good enough? Let me get on with it and he'll never pass on whatever he's found out.'

Savas resented the crude menace in his tone, but he had run out of argument. Papeete knew she could not repeat her views without calling even more attention to her possible involvement with Bucken. She made just one more faint attempt, as if only thinking aloud: 'If he's found out anything or even if he or anyone else had no more than the vaguest suspicion, the insurance pay-out on the *Alida II* would already be blocked.'

'And it isn't,' Savas supported her. 'The holding company has already been notified that everything is proceeding smoothly.'

'You mean you're against taking immediate action?' Ruzicki asked.

'I haven't said anything like that. I'm only trying to establish the relevant facts.'

'Do you think then that we need to put it to a full vote?'

'May not be a bad idea.'

'What if by then it's too late? Will you take the responsibility?'

Savas was caught. He had only one way out of it: 'Security is your responsibility.'

'But you're opposed to decisive action.'

'I was stating facts, not views.'

Papeete stared at her toes. She knew that deep down she had already made a decision but it was hard to admit it even to herself that she would warn Bucken. And then she would warn Don that she had tipped him off. She refused to contemplate what the consequences of all that might be.

She felt her husband's eyes on her. Throughout the discussion he had been silent but now he asked her: 'Not that you have a vote, Papeete, but do you have any objections to what has been called "decisive action"?'

'No. Why should I? I mean I don't think that any of you would do something . . . something outright criminal.'

'We *are* doing things like that.'

'We've never killed anyone.' The silence that greeted her statement shook her self-assurance. 'Have we? Has any of you?'

'No,' said Savas. 'Obviously not. And we're not discussing anything like that. I think we should all be grateful to you for calling attention to the problem, and now we should just leave it to security to deal with it.'

'And I disagree,' Quincey declared quite categorically. It was a voice Papeete had never heard before. It left no room for argument. 'And I'll tell you why. If, and I emphasise if, this man Bucken knows something, and if he's a snoop for the police or insurance, whatever, and if he disappears, we'll look even more suspicious to whoever they are. If he's gone they'll send someone else whom even Papeete may fail to spot. Therefore, first we must check him out. If he's really bad news, Ruzicki will deal with it as he sees fit.'

'Checking out will take time,' objected Savas.

'Ruzicki will make sure that he stays here as long as we need, and that he won't be able to do us any harm while he's here.'

Ruzicki nodded. 'Good idea. I'll arrange something.'

'What if he checks out okay?' Papeete asked, seeing some hope for everybody concerned.

Quincey smiled at her: 'That would suit us all, I presume. I mean we could use him in all sorts of ways. We need new front men for current operations as well as "Tsunami", and if I understood you and Oldman Savas correctly, Bucken would be quite a tough and plausible one. If he got involved, he'd have to keep his mouth shut. And if

106

we, I mean any of us, tired of him, there would still be plenty of time to hand him over to security.'

All the way to the party Greta sat so close to Bucken that he could feel her body heat through their clothes, and she kept up an incessant patter of sexual innuendoes: but, from time to time, there was a genuine interest in her questions about him. She must be puzzled, he thought, she's probably never seen anyone as ordinary as me. Once or twice when, accidentally, some of his answers about himself happened to be more meaningful than he would have liked, she sensed his sincerity and rewarded it by touching his hand or resting her gaze on his lips for a few seconds. He was sorry when the journey came to an end. They landed on the island of Poros, and a roaring speedboat took them out to the yacht.

There could be no doubt about Greta's popularity. She was swept away – everybody seemed to have something to say to her. It would not have surprised Bucken if men queued up to make her laugh, and he felt like a bumpkin because his conversation with her was dulled by design to give away the minimum.

She danced and drank and flirted with the tireless bounce of a pinball machine. Like players of such a machine devised to give high scores and low pay-outs, her partners had better chances to show off and improve their skill than ever to win. Bucken watched her mostly from a distance. He talked to several people, danced when it was absolutely inevitable, but found his greatest pleasure in allowing his ears to fill with music, laughter and snippets of conversation that might have called normally for thorough investigation – hints of fraud, drug abuse, tax evasion, incest and corruption were just a few items he chose not to pounce on.

He submitted willingly to the lure of mingling with true wealth at close quarters for the first time ever. He was not exactly an honoured guest, but neither was he the intruding cop whose presence would be resented even when welcomed. Power and the joys of hedonism money could buy oozed from every sumptuous corner of that floating gin palace where the host's pleasure seemed to be paramount. Deals and sex added a unique fragrance to the cool air, the island glittered its fairy lights flirtatiously, and a fleet of small boats kept up a ceaseless pilgrimage to bring more and more revellers to the party. Some of those speedboats might cost as much as I make in a year including the modest fiddle on my expenses, Bucken estimated. He thought of the flat in Bayswater and the uncarpeted hallway, and he felt no shame that for once he knew what envying real money meant.

He leaned back against the railing of the spacious poop deck. A steward warned him not to go 'over the wall'. A see-through girl, already high on chasing the heroin dragon through a fine ivory tube, looked up from her silver foil, urged him to take the plunge and promised to join him in the water. She did not realise that she had just messed up his counting of the pairs, threesomes and mixed or unisex groups that had disappeared into the insatiable belly of the yacht. Bucken felt angry with himself. It had been his choice not to participate more actively in the universal fun, and found it unforgivable that he should now experience self-pity as well as envy.

'You seem to be lonely and dry,' Greta offered him a sip of her champagne.

'I'm having a great time even though you're a full-time job.'

'What job? You've done nothing to guard my body all night.'

'People of my most venerable profession are usually discouraged from guarding against the self-inflicted risks you seem to be courting.'

'You're getting very deep,' she laughed.

'I'm sorry. I didn't mean to.'

'Pity. I thought you were beginning to take an interest in me.'

'I was. And it made me wonder how you could have so much fun without ever enjoying yourself.' He paused for the duly light riposte, but she remained silent. 'Tell me something. What is it you're trying to hide or suppress?' He had not meant to go that far, but it was too late to take it back.

For a few seconds, she looked startled and bare. Then, as if frightened by seeing a ghost in her mirror, she laughed with wholly rejuvenating effect, and took refuge in frivolity. 'Ah. A psychologist, are you?'

Bucken bowed with a theatrical gesture: 'Please, please don't tell anyone, kind lady, it's my best party piece.'

'Mine is court jester. I may let you court me if you prove to be a jester of quality, my good man.'

'Oh please, don't be misled. I think it was St. Clement who said that jests and laughter were a prelude to fornication. Little did he know about the superiority of psychology in opening doors.'

'Are you trying to get me on the couch?'

'When was there any doubt about that?'

'Then watch out: it may seem easier than it is.'

'And what makes you think, Greta, that I didn't know?'

They both looked serious – and then they laughed. 'Do you dance?' she asked.

'It could ruin my carefully nurtured image.' It did not, well, not completely.

On the way home it became obvious that their moment of meaningful exchange had erected a barrier between them. She emphasised it by long silences and the absence of her usual provocative banter. During the flight, she chose to leave an empty seat between them. When the helicopter landed and they prepared to alight, she suddenly hugged him, pressing her forehead to his cheek: 'Thank you. I'll borrow you again.' He was not sure whether she had tried to hurt him or herself.

His preoccupation with thoughts about Greta, added to his lack of sleep, prevented him from noticing that their arrival at the hotel had been witnessed. Two men followed him all the way to his room. He opened the door, stepped inside and switched on the light only to find himself peering down the silencer end of a heavy service revolver. Behind him, two men squeezed in and closed the door.

'Sit down please.' The man with the gun gestured. It would have been pointless to argue. The room was in an utter mess, and three pint-sized heavyweights were still busy ransacking it. 'Have you no questions?' It was a Greek accent. 'Don't you want to know what's going on, who we are?'

'No. But I'm sure you're dying to tell me.'

'Oh, I see you're a joker. I hope your sense of humour won't let you down too suddenly, Mis-ter . . . '

'My passport and seaman's book are sticking out of your pocket, so you should know my name, and yes, you may call me Bucken, Mr. Bucken, that is. Now shall I also start calling you names?'

The sarcasm in the words escaped the man but he was a good judge of intonation. Effortlessly, he swiped at Bucken with the gun, and the silencer drew blood from his nose. 'I'm sorry, Mr. Bucken. An accident. It's been witnessed that it was an accident.' The men watching them nodded solemnly. 'It could have been nothing but an accident, Mr. Bucken, because we're not gangsters or something, but officials of the state.'

'Police? You? Then God help all Greek cons.'

'State security.' He flashed a card with no intention of letting Bucken read it. 'And, now that we've been introduced, let's talk a little, shall we?'

'Very little because I'm sleepy.' He stood up and stretched lazily.

'Good. Then we can do this quickly and we can all sleep. Why are you in Greece?'

'I'm working for Mr. Savas. You heard of him?'

'Naturally. But why are you in Greece?'

'I've told you.'

'You've told us nothing. Only jokes.' He nodded, and a heavy shoe landed on Bucken's kidney. 'Quiet, please, other people are asleep. Now tell me, what's your interest in Greek politics?'

'Nothing whatsoever.'

'Are you a Communist?'

'No.'

'Are you an anti-Communist?'

'No.'

'Then you're just a . . . what's the word . . . courier? Is that what you are?'

'You're talking a load of rubbish.'

The second kick in his kidney was harder and hurt much more. Bucken felt like retaliating whatever the odds, but he found it too painful to move. The man behind him must have been a twenty-two carat specialist. 'I hope you have witnesses to this accident, too, because I can't believe that the Greek state would rubber-stamp such barbaric methods.'

'I'm glad we share an interest in safeguarding Greek democracy. So tell us what all these mean?' He held up a much-creased sheet of paper, full of typed rows of numbers. The one of seven digits at the top looked like a telephone number. The rest made no sense at all. The sheet smelled of toothpaste.

'I'd love to tell you but I can't.'

'Then why did you bring it to Greece?'

'I didn't.'

'Oh, perhaps you didn't even know that you had it! Perhaps you always wash your teeth with sheets of paper.' His men laughed as he produced a tube of toothpaste with its top half unscrewed.

I've been set up, thought Bucken, the question is: how deep have they dropped me in the shit? They? Who? It was becoming much harder to pretend the surprise and bewilderment of the bystander: if you have enemies you can't be completely innocent. It was pointless to say anything. Whoever had planted the tube with the creased sheet under the screw-top must be a professional.

'I'm glad that you've stopped arguing, Mr. Bucken. You seem to be a sensible man. So I'll help you. And try to believe you. Perhaps you're just an innocent courier. Perhaps you didn't know what you were carrying. But you must have known whom to contact.' The man pointed at the top of the sheet. 'Perhaps it will refresh your memory if I tell you that this is the last known phone number of a very unpopular man. He's a terrorist, in fact, and we know him extremely well, even if we don't know where he's hiding out. Won't

110

you tell us? . . . Well, perhaps it'll be more convenient to continue our conversation in my office. It's nice and cosy with no neighbours to wake up.' His men laughed heartily.

'I want to see a lawyer.'

'What for? You've just volunteered to come with us and help our inquiries. I have witnesses. You can't go back on your kind offer.'

At the British embassy reception Greta surprised Papeete with questions about Bucken: 'You wouldn't know, darling, where he was, would you?'

'I thought he was away, working for you . . . or rather your husband.'

'And Danny says he's on some errand for somebody else. I thought it might be you. A night errand maybe?'

A silver trayful of champagne came between them. They studied each other over the rims of their glasses. 'When did you see him last?' Papeete asked.

'Two days ago. Just after the Arbouzi party. And you?'

'Just before the Arbouzi party, remember?'

'Oh yes. You came in and wanted to talk to Danny. In private.'

'About business.'

'What business?'

Papeete left the party as soon as she could to question her husband about Ruzicki's ways of making sure that Bucken had not left Athens, but she was told that Quincey was out, taking hydrotherapy.

He was, in fact, strapped in a special harness, suspended in warm water, trying in vain to exercise those limbs he had come to hate so much. At the edge of the water stood a stocky, scarfaced man with hay for hair. His watery eyes were on Quincey, his right hand only an arm's length away from the red switch that operated the pulleys to raise or lower the harness and its helpless load. From time to time, Quincey had the uncomfortable feeling that a flick of that switch could send him sinking to the bottom of the pool. He could do nothing about it, would have no time even to cry out, and nobody would ever know what happened, for his visitor had entered, as arranged,through a manhole and a labyrinth of plumbing below. The nurse had left Quincey alone because he wished 'to meditate, floating in silence'. If he was killed, it would be seen as an accident. At the inquest the nurse would swear that the pool had only one entrance, that she had sat at the door all the time, and that nobody could have entered without passing her.

111

'I thought we'd agreed you'd never initiate a meeting,' said Quincey.

'I'm, sorry, but it seemed urgent and important that we should talk.'

'That's for me to decide. That was the deal.'

'True.'

'You don't want me to complain about you to your chief, do you?'

'No,' he gestured vaguely and his hand strayed towards the red switch, 'but on the other hand . . . '

'What?'

'Forget it, sir. All I meant to say was that Moscow is concerned about the current level of CIA activities.'

'CIA? What has that got to do with me?'

'On this occasion, a great deal, I'm afraid. I know that you're completely non-political and ours is a strictly business arrangement. We respect that. But, just now, the CIA seems to be taking a close interest in every aspect of the *Alida* tragedy.'

'Can you blame them?'

'No, not at all, but it's strange, to say the least, how close they are at every step. As if they had some inside information.'

'Impossible. And if it's anybody's, it's your fault. Your presence in Macao was an unnecessary risk. Ruzicki has heard about you from his Chinese. I talked him out of it, of course, saying that probably that "scarfaced man" didn't exist, but he remained uneasy about it.'

'Do you trust him?'

'Do I trust you? Can I trust anybody? Ruzicki is probably more trustworthy than most.'

'I'm glad you say that, sir,' the man rested his hand on the control console of the pulleys. 'Because, if there're any problems, Moscow may hold you responsible.'

'Now hang on. You seem to forget that I'm working *with* you, not *for* you.'

'Once you work with us, some people may assume, quite wrongly but nevertheless, that you work for us. And, at the moment, some people are very unhappy with the high level of CIA attention.'

'Then go and tell them that I wasn't happy with your doings in Macao either.'

'I'm sorry. It was an emergency. I had to make snap decisions. Unfortunately, the donkeyman sailor died prematurely from shock.'

'How about his cousin? You got no answers from him?'

'It would have been a mistake to exert extreme pressure too soon. And then the police were coming to his hotel. We were warned and had to leave.'

112

'And you still haven't traced him.'

'We're still trying to. The trouble is that we have very little to go on. There seems to be no record of his visit at the Macao police. Inspector Poon who handled him doesn't know his address – or he's distinctly uncooperative. And the worst is that the description we have is very incomplete.'

'How come? Didn't you see him?'

'Only from a distance. My orders were to make it my number one priority that the target wouldn't see me.'

'You were there, in the hotel, when he was questioned by the Chinks.'

'But I never came out of the bathroom. If he caught as much as a glimpse of me, I'd have had to kill him, and that would have looked most suspicious. I mean two deaths in the same family in Macao . . . Anyway, those were my orders from Moscow.'

Quincey wondered where the man had learned his English. His accent was trans-Atlantic with no trace of Slavonic origin. He might have lived all his life as a sleeper in America or he might even be apple-pie American, an actual full-time traitor, Quincey concluded without a thought for his own status. He knew he was no traitor. He was involved with them, making a deal. A profitable deal. He let his bad hand drop into the water and concentrated on exercising his legs. In the last couple of days he had felt some improvement in them. 'How about Bucken?' He sprang the question and noted with pleasure that the man was a little slow to conceal his embarrassment.

'All I can tell you is that our London bureau has activated some inside contacts and it has also commissioned a private detective through a cut-out . . . I mean an intermediary.'

'Are you telling me that you haven't found out anything?'

'No. We've already established that this Bucken has or had some police connections. He was involved in some drunken brawl in a City bar, which was reported briefly in the press. We're still waiting for confirmation from the top.'

'You mean Scotland Yard?'

'I'm too small a cog to know, sir. But we have our sources everywhere.' The scar deepened as the man smiled, and suddenly it looked so freshly red that it made Quincey's stomach turn. 'Can you give us any further lead?'

'Nothing beyond what you already know. From what I've heard from *my* confidential sources, he'll probably turn out to be clean.' Quincey tried to match the man's conceit. His self-assurance was now fuelled by that red scar: the man was obviously a poor choice on Moscow's part. 'Considering that our next deal is progressing quite smoothly, and a suitable wreck has been located, I'd be most grateful if you could pull out all stops and get on with your inquiries. Ruzicki can't force our friends to hold Bucken indefinitely and we must be sure that he's clean before he's let loose. Meanwhile, I'll keep an eye on potential leaks to the CIA. Okay?'

'It's most desirable, sir, because in the light of our information the CIA seem to be rather doubtful about the Tsunami theory. They accept that the *Alida* sank with all the stuff on board, but they can find no evidence that there was an actual Tsunami in the area. And I'm not surprised. Are you?'

The cellar was very cold and completely dark. Whenever the door was opened, the guard used only a small, faint torchlight that gave Bucken no help to familiarise himself with his surroundings.

The cell itself was cleverly constructed to puzzle the prisoner, promote his disorientation and induce an obsession that would help to unhinge his sense of reality. It certainly worked on Bucken. After the painful discovery that he must move slowly because the stone floor was very uneven, at some points shaky, threatening to trip him up unexpectedly, he tried to build up a mental picture of the shape of the cell. Feeling his way along the wall, he found that the cell was three steps by three and a half steps, but the opposite length was four steps, and the opposite width only two and three quarters. So he started again, but the results were different. He suspected that his steps had varied in the darkness. He now measured everything in hands, and then in feet, heel to toe, again and again, and he would still bump into walls whenever he tried to pace up and down.

The only furniture in the cell was a wooden bench. It was shoulder-wide and shorter than him, with its top of a rough slats-and-gaps construction that would inflict pain if he tried to sit or lie on it for more than a few minutes. The whole contraption shook and creaked, ready to collapse – a disgusting prospect considering the state of the stone floor that had a hole in the middle, presumably to gulp down urine, excrement or blood, but mostly to give the rats below access to the cell.

Food came in irregular intervals and in quantities to tease rather than fill the stomach. Stale bread, mouldy cheese, and cold potatoes made up the diet with hardly any liquid. Bucken's shivering became a permanent feature of life, increasing in intensity with his hunger and thirst. No matter how hard he tried not to, he had already lost count of the days. He was now convinced that he had been in there for the better part of a fortnight. It would have meant that the outside

114

world had totally forgotten him, so he tried to reason that he must be wrong: with the lack of liquids he ought to be much weaker by now if his imprisonment had lasted that long.

Once or twice he had been hit and kicked, but the interrogations were not unduly brutal or – and that seemed odd – particularly determined or purposeful. Were they just playing for time? Or waiting for something?

Sleeplessness was the worst. It fogged his thinking. They kept waking him up, depriving him of his only refuge from hardship. Every time it happened, whether it was mere routine or for the purpose of another interrogation session, the temptation grew to tell them everything about himself, everything they did not even ask. In his clearer moments, he realised that the limitations of the questions were significant: his inquisitors were just fishing. He also recognised that they had been careful not to cause obvious injuries that doctors could identify eventually as proof of torture, recently outlawed.

He knew that most of the damage to his sanity and clear reasoning had been self-inflicted, but in the circumstances he could do nothing about it. His most persistent idea was that it might help him if he suggested that, like he himself, his captors were victims of some deliberate set-up. Perhaps they suspected the same themselves. Perhaps that's why they were not yet trying to break him. Yes, that must be it. The temptation to come to terms with them surged once again. For, if they were obliged to maintain at least a semblance of legality, it would not be all that hard to convince them with some half-truths about his innocence. A few cautious words about his real mission . . . a phone call to Scotland Yard . . . no, only Dodd knew the facts, they would have to call Dodd on the emergency number . . . Dodd? He would deny any knowledge of him! He would be obliged to deny everything. 'The Yard would certainly not authorise any investigation in Greece. Surely not, gentlemen, Bucken's a bad apple, to say the least. He's a liar.'

Despair descended upon him once again. He thought about his own interrogation techniques. Yes, he had the reputation of being rough with certain types of hated suspects like child molesters, but he could not imagine himself applying this kind of pressure. And, even if he could, what would it achieve? It would be worthless if the eventual confession mirrored no more than the interrogator's wishful thinking. Except that in his predicament, it would bring at least temporary relief. And he began to feel that he might soon do or say almost anything – even for temporary relief.

Not quite halfway between Abu Dhabi and Sharjah at the foot of the
Persian Gulf, the wreck was seated firmly in shallow water though it
seemed to lean precariously. From a hundred yards it would have
been impossible to recognise it: dust had settled in heavy layers on
every feature of the ship as if trying to turn her into an extension of
the sand dunes. The ancient fishing boat, driven by a gleaming outboard motor, bumped and bounced despite the calmness of the sea as
it approached the wreck. Ruzicki suffered the ride in silence, swallowing a fine assortment of swearwords in his native tongue. His
companions – a fat, ever-sniffing Indian and a lean Arab, of London
chain-store elegance – seemed to be oblivious of his ordeal. They
chatted in flowery pidgin English, trying to estimate the deadweight
of tankers in the distance to the left, and the age of the bullock that
stared out unseeingly from the shore.

Thanks to Savas, Ruzicki already knew as much about the wreck
as he needed to. The *Rose of Stambul*, 6,200 tons dwt, had sailed into
Abu Dhabi under emergency conditions, claiming engine trouble,
fifty-one months ago, and remained there, causing untold headaches,
for almost two years. She was under the Panamanian flag, based in
Turkey, operated by Thai managing agents on behalf of a Sudanese
company that had her on charter. The engine turned out to be the
least of her troubles. She had no food on board, no water, bunkers or
cargo (sold illegally en route in the Lebanon), and her owner had
vanished. Her motley crew's wages had not been paid for eight
months when she berthed, and the men in despair sought hope in
belated unionism. (A copy of their letter to ITF was found eventually
among the ship's papers: ' . . . ve men of above name Stambul in
black touble. Little rice rotten, no oil to vork de generator . . . no
vater, no bear, no vages . . . sertain oder irregulars . . . Please help
. . . Owner gone, no pay port charges, ve in prionment in port
. . . Sank you in anticipation . . . ')

When it seemed that the International Transport Workers Federation could not trace the owner, and all the crew could hope for was
charity repatriation, the men tried to steal the ship. They sailed at
night, chased by a patrol boat (the port authorities could recover
their berthing dues only by arresting the ship), and the wild dash
ended on a sandbank east of Abu Dhabi. The *Rose of Stambul* was
abandoned, and the port authority never got round to selling her for
scrap because the profit would not justify the effort: the scrap value
would hardly cover the cost of refloating and towing the *Rose* to some
breaker's yard.

Yet it was just the wreck Quincey and Ruzicki wanted. When it
transpired that all her documents were available and that the *Rose*

could be bought for no more than fat baksheesh to some port officials, they were most grateful to Savas who had found her.

The small boat ran up the sandbank and stopped with an impact that threatened to disgorge its passengers. The Indian waded through the water and sniffed around the wreck like a young dog off the leash. Ruzicki sat enjoying *terra firma* and running sand through his fingers. The Arab took off his jacket, folded it carefully inside out, and rested it on his knees as he squatted, protecting the seat of his pants. Ruzicki noted that the label had been cut from the jacket: it must have come from some Jewish-owned store, fine for a bargain but a shame to remember. The Indian joined them at last. Ruzicki's raised eyebrows questioned him.

'Yessir. Can be done, can . . . be . . . done,' the Indian scrap merchant clapped his hands. 'But it will cost you, yessir, ve-ry, ve-ry expensive.'

'We'll make a deal.'

'But you . . . '

Ruzicki waved to cut him short. He had no intention to discuss details in front of the Arab who might get some grand ideas about the money to be made when in fact, Ruzicki would actually lose on buying and selling the wreck.

Back in his hotel in Abu Dhabi, Ruzicki spread out the contents of several bulging manila envelopes. This was to be his profit if everything he needed was there. Photographs of the *Rose* in her heyday; full tonnage and other classification certificates; Panama loadline registration; crew rolls going back several years; tonnage tax receipts from Honolulu, New York, Charleston and Baltimore where, apparently, the *Rose* had traded over a long period; inflatable life-raft and other safety equipment re-inspection documents; Japanese reports in English of Survey for Cargo Ship Safety Radiotelegraphy, and the same in Spanish from Panama; health administration and quarantine clearance papers in Chinese; customs declarations from all over the world; Suez and Panama Canal tonnage certificates; oil pollution controls; crew health books; all the documents issued by the builders of the ship; years of cargo and trading evidence; bills of sales and purchases showing previous owners and stating what might have been true once that the ship had been delivered 'free from any encumbrances, maritime lines or mortgages whatsoever' – all in all, the life story of a real ship and evidence of her existence.

When Ruzicki bought the *Rose*, ready to lose some forty thousand dollars on the re-sale to the Indian scrap merchant, it was that heap of papers he was really paying for. Had he tried to buy only the documents without the wreck, suspicions would have been aroused. As it worked out, everybody was happy: Abu Dhabi would get rid of a wreck, the Arab officials would collect some baksheesh, the Indian would buy nondescript scrap metal at some twenty dollars, less than a quarter of the market price per ton, and Quincey would own a ghost ship. Should the non-existent *Rose of Stambul* 'sink' one day, nobody could find a non-existent wreck.

Ruzicki was pleased with himself. He had handled the whole affair with speed, and every partner in the deal had good reasons to keep his mouth shut. Officially, the *Rose of Stambul* had been sold by 'public auction' to an Australian-registered company (Quincey's). The Bill of Sale was completed in English and Arabic with a whole range of impressive duty stamps all over it, signed, initialled and rubber stamped. Although the British Consulate, acting for the Australian government, had no valid reason to play any part in the sale or its legalisation, the vice-consul agreed to initial and stamp the document certifying that the signatories, whoever they were, had signed the deal in his presence on the said date. That made it all look perfectly above board even though the vice-consul had applied another small stamp, tucked away in a corner, saying that: 'No responsibility is accepted by this Consulate for the contents of this document.'

All that remained to be done was to convey the good news with some relevant and urgently needed details to Quincey. Ruzicki composed a note – 'Rose is yours . . . ' – to be telexed to Athens in code. He got out his rarely used but always available fake British passport, and opened it on the last page of NOTES:
'1 Validity A passport is valid for ten years, unless otherwise stated. If issued to a child under sixteen years of age it is normally . . .'

All the letters of the alphabet, except Z, appeared several times on the page, and he could identify any of them by two numbers denoting his random choice of word and the position of letter in that word. Thus, in the first line alone, he had any of four letter R-s to pick for the beginning of his message: 3-7, 6-3, 8-4 or 10-5. It was a system not only to baffle but defeat even the best counter-intelligence computers – anybody not privy to the key itself.

Once that cable was on its way, a replica of the *Alida II* operation had begun in earnest.

Ada Tansley knew beyond any doubt that one day she would become Mrs. Freemantle. What she could not and would not even try to foretell was *when* that day would come. It would be no good guessing, because it would only be pushing her luck. And such things could not be pushed even if one was more than just a pretty face with the longest pair of legs in Fleet Street. She had had an intermittently permanent affair with John Freemantle for most of the last eighteen years, and so it was no news to her that he was not a man to tolerate pressure and impatience. Besides, she felt she had nothing to complain about: she got as much as she gave in loyalty, fidelity, companionship and care – and that was a great deal more than her married, divorced, remarried, widowed and deserted girl friends' lot.

Today, Freemantle was late in from his news round as he dashed across the reception area towards the bank of lifts, though not without grunting something of a greeting to Ada, and dropping a box of Belgian bonbons, her favourites, on her desk almost accidentally. Instead of saying thank-you for the present – 'totally superfluous, I know what you mean anyway,' he would grumble – she only cried, 'Wait!'

'What?'

'Couple of hours ago some bloke was asking questions about your diary piece on Bucken.'

'The fight in the City?'

'What else?'

'Who was it?'

'Some private eye. Library knows more.'

'How do you know?'

Ada glanced at her small switchboard and shrugged her shoulders.

'Ta.' He took off.

The librarian had the name, Joe Mellish, and the number of the detective agency.

Mellish himself answered the call. Freemantle suspected there was no staff. 'Can't say much, old boy,' Mellish apologised in a way that would boost his own ego, 'sorry but, between ourselves you understand, we've been retained to round up what we can about Chief Super – or shall we say *ex* Chief Super Bucken?'

'Oh.'

'Any help would be much appreciated.'

'Really?'

'There could be a shiny farthing or two in it for you if your contacts were better than mine at the Big House.'

'What would you need?'

'The works, old boy, the works.'

'Why?'

'Can't tell, old boy. I'm a pro. Can't divulge client's motives, can I?'

'Of course not.'

'No hassle about your charges, I guarantee that, if you bring me

119

something I don't yet know. But I must warn you, old boy, that I do know quite a bit.'

'Such as?'

'Such as that our Bucken is in the shit. At the deep end. You think you could enlarge on that?'

'I'll see what I can do.' Freemantle rang off and mumbled the invitation to Mellish, old boy, to go and fuck himself. He had no intention of telling him even yesterday's weather forecast, but he was keen to discover what was going on. Perhaps he could warn Bucken if some shitface was on the warpath.

He typed furiously, dropped his five-hundred-word masterpiece in four parts of unsurpassable brilliance on the subs' desk to be pro-cessed for immortality, and half an hour later was sipping his pint of usual – he was a survivor of the mild-and-bitter generation. He ordered a large Irish with no ice, and let it stand, ready and waiting, for Sergeant Connell. With his disguise of rosy cheeks and country bumpkin's awkwardness, Connell was one of the tireless gumshoes of the Yard, checking on erring coppers and merely maligned col-leagues. If anyone, he would know what was going on. The pair of them were old friends with a proven trust record, and there was no need for preliminaries.

'Down the hatch.'

'Up yours, too. What's the rush?'

'Bucken. What's going on?'

'Why do you want to know?'

'He's a friend. And the best.'

'Yet you dropped him in the shit a few weeks ago.'

'Tough.' He could not tell even Connell that Bucken had virtually asked him for the smear. 'You know how it goes. All the news fit to print.'

'Bullshit.'

Freemantle smiled. 'But I still want to know.'

'Off the record?'

'Understood.'

'And I tell you only because something really stinks. Bucken is a good man but, right now, he's bad news. And nobody quite knows why. Which makes it even worse.'

'There must be something on record.'

'Maybe there is. Probably there is. But what? It could be one of two things. He might have gone astray in some stupid way and they're trying to get rid of him without too much embarrassment to him or to us. He could make things awkward, you see. He knows too much.'

'What's the other possibility?'

'Just a guess. He might have pissed into the best vintage port of someone really important, and Dodd could do nothing but drop him in the shit to protect himself.'

'Oh.'

'That's exactly what I think. But, whatever the truth is, I'd be utterly amazed if he ever came back to claim his pension or whatever.'

'It's that bad, is it?'

'It's worse.' Connell drank up and ordered another round to demonstrate that Freemantle had not bought his confidence. 'Pussy is out of the bag.'

'What do you mean?'

'You're not the first to ask about Bucken.'

'Who else?' The long pause meant more bad news to Freemantle. 'Can't you tell?'

'Don't know for sure. But one of them could be uncle.'

'FBI? CIA?'

'You tell me. And you tell me if you hear something.'

'Mellish. Private eye. Also keen to know.'

'Thanks.'

Freemantle telephoned Bucken's home number. There was no answer. He went to the flat in Bayswater and made so much noise with the brass frigate knocker that the porter came up to investigate. He said Bucken was away, it was no good breaking the door down. The milkman and the newsagent next door told Freemantle that deliveries to the flat had been cancelled indefinitely. He phoned Sarah. No, she had not seen Bucken since that scene at the door.

Freemantle regretted that he had ever befriended leggy Ada Tansley. She was too good and too independent ever to marry him. Had she not told him about Mellish and all that, he could sleep in peaceful ignorance tonight, without a care in the world about that bloody cop.

Bucken was woken up at 4.36 a.m. He answered two questions, his name and age, fell asleep, and was woken up, for the ninth time that night, at 4.39. The minute stretches of sleep felt more devastating than being kept awake continuously. He had enough. He decided to answer frankly any question they cared to ask.

'Why are you in Greece, Mr. Bucken?'

He heard victorious irony in the voice, and he disliked it. Yes, he would hold out just one more time. So he repeated his stock answer.

From the intensity of the night session he had already guessed that they were going for broke this time, and he knew he would not be able to resist them any longer. He had no reserves of strength left. But his interrogator's irritation was just one step ahead of his collapse. The incessant pressure worked both ways to some extent. The man stormed out of the cell. Bucken, already half asleep, tried to make himself remember the lesson it had taught him.

At 4.55, two guards strapped him face down on the wooden bench. A nervous and frail civilian was then summoned by the interrogator. They exchanged a few words in Greek. The little man put a leather case on the stone floor, opened it, dropped and smoothed out a piece of white cloth next to it, and began to lay out a fine selection of silvery pins. He worked in silence, fastidiously. After a moment's contemplation, he chose a two-inch needle and approached the bench from the foot.

Bucken felt a single, tiny pinprick at his top vertebra – then such pain shot through him that he lost consciousness.

'I don't like to make people suffer unnecessarily,' said the interrogator when Bucken had come to, 'but my acupuncturist colleague may find it an interesting experiment. After all, the dividing line between causing and – how do you say it? oh yes, between causing and alleviating pain is very, very thin.'

Bucken's lips tightened. His mouth was full of the bitter taste of fury. He suddenly recognised a little of the incredible reserves political prisoners under torture had managed to dredge up from somewhere, sometimes. Yes, he, too, had a speck of it if no more. He would fight them. He would fight them with silence and screams. It would be easier and less exhausting than the composition and utterance of lies. They would not risk killing him. Or would they?

Quincey received a telex from London at 7.45. It was in code. He called for Ruzicki who, using the Notes in his passport, quickly decoded the text.

Bucken is a disgraced detective. He has not been fired or dealt with internally. Prosecution is most unlikely, probably to avoid scandal involving a minister's underage daughter. She was suspected of drug trafficking. Allegedly, Bucken got infatuated with girl and tried to blackmail her for sex in London. Evidence inconclusive but condemning. He pursued girl across Europe and Egypt with alleged intention of trying to make her retract accusations and clear his name, but he propositioned her again in Cairo. On his return, after confrontation with superiors, he hit the bottle in a big way and got into brawling in public. Apparently, Yard just let him run and disappear. They have no record of his whereabouts. Ends.

Quincey smiled. 'A disgraced cop? Could be useful.'

'Or a risk.'

'We need another few plausible and disposable front men. Bucken could be just right for us.'

Ruzicki was full of admiration for Quincey's fighting spirit, clear thinking, ruthlessness and inventiveness, but, this time, he remained unconvinced by his argument. 'Wouldn't anybody who cared to check Bucken's background find out all this?'

'No. Virtually impossible.' Quincey knew that this would suffice for an answer, but the showman in him could not resist the opportunity for flashing his secret powers. 'It took me several contacts, the very best there are, to get the information. Not even Swiss bankers would have access to such sources.'

Watching Ruzicki's amazement, Quincey realised he had almost overstepped the essential mark of secrecy. It worried him. Perhaps it was a sign of frayed nerves. Perhaps the strain was becoming too much for him. He was bursting to reveal it all to someone, not only to show off but also to relieve the burden of his own achievement in manipulating a little the two mightiest secrets merchants for his own gain, insurance and, as in this case, information. He could read the unasked questions in Ruzicki's eyes: how come you have access to such special sources? how come you can deal with them from your wheel-chair? how did you dream up that coding technique with the passports?

Too many questions, Quincey concluded. Ruzicki had no right even to think of them. One of these days, he would have to go – at a price. Police and Western intelligence services would pay handsomely in cash and favours for some incriminating evidence against Ruzicki. It could also prove that Quincey was a businessman, not a traitor. It was a practical rather than ethical consideration for legitimising his future.

'And you think Bucken is ready to play the frontman?' Ruzicki asked, casting aside the more probing questions.

'Wouldn't you be? He needs money. He can have it. He probably wants revenge. We can give him the opportunity. I mean the case against him stinks. The chances are that he's been framed to get him off the minister's back.'

'Or rather his daughter's,' Ruzicki laughed.

'Whichever.' Laughter and jokes, except when the joke was on somebody else, were a waste of time. Quincey re-read the decoded telex. 'Yes, it tallies with what he half admitted to Papeete.'

There was a short pause. Ruzicki was puzzled: was there really no jealousy in Quincey or was he getting his kicks out of the slow, pro- longed destruction of everybody around him? 'Oh well, I have nothing against the guy, and Savas seems to trust him,' he said to break the discomfort of silence. 'He also claims that Bucken is ready to make a fast buck whatever it takes.'

'And we'll let him,' said Quincey, 'for a while.'

Now there was menace and a touch of sadistic pleasure in the voice. It delighted Ruzicki: it's always good to know your friend's weaknesses. 'But no unnecessary risks, okay?'

'Agreed. You yourself will keep an eye on him. We'll use him all out, and burn him out before he knew what hit him.' What Quincey did not say was that, having savoured Papeete's anxiety, he was now keen to see how positive her joy would be on hearing about Bucken's release. 'Tell Savas that he could use him if he wanted to on the Ivory Coast job, and then you could slot him into your *Rose of Stambul* scheme.'

Bucken regained consciousness. He felt no pain. He was numb. Perhaps paralysed. His eyes opened for no more than the span of a flutter, and he would not repeat the exercise. It would only confirm that he had gone mad. For he was imagining that he was tucked between crisp white sheets that smelt of sunshine and sea breezes. He could have sworn that the lights in the spacious room were gentle to the eye, and threw a glowing halo round Papeete who was sitting at the bedside.

'Bucken?'

Oh yes, he was now hallucinating as well. He felt her fingertips on his face. If that was madness, it was better than the sanity of dark- ness. Two nurses came in, the expensive kind in well-cut uniforms, then a white-haired doctor, and Papeete rose to leave.

'Don't go,' Bucken whispered.

'I'll be back.'

'You'll be all right,' the doctor pronounced after a cursory ex- amination. 'What happened to you?' He spoke with a French accent.

'You tell me.' Bucken watched him with suspicion.

'Ooh-la-la,' he made a spiralling upward gesture. His face broke into the smile men use to describe what they would do to the star attraction of the previous night's stag party.

'Explain, please.'

'Exhaustion combined with acute alcohol poisoning. You were

124

found in the company of a dozen empty bottles of Cognac outside a little brothel in Piraeus. And that was two days ago!'

'Thank you.'

Papeete returned and, when they were alone, confirmed the doctor's story. 'You were missing for a week. Savas organised the biggest manhunt Greece had ever seen. He was really concerned.' And after a pause: 'So was I.'

'Don't you find it odd?'

'What?'

'The brandy bottles.'

'You mean . . . ' She stopped. She remembered his usual. Rum. White and virginal. 'Must have been quite a binge if by the end it made no difference what you drank.' She sounded sincere, as if she believed what she said. Perhaps she did.

'Then what?'

'Apparently, the police picked you up, found your driving licence in your pocket, and traced your identity to London.' She gave him a searching look: 'They say you are . . . or were . . . a policeman. Is it true?'

'Sort of.' The double bluff was working.

'When you said you had tried to clear your name, did you mean . . . '

'Yes. You could say, I suppose, that I'm a fallen angel.'

'See if I care.'

She looked relieved. He tried not to look furious. At that moment, he could have killed Greenfingers Dodd for the second time. If it was not only Sarah and Freemantle who could find out something about Bucken's 'corruption' then Dodd must have broken the agreement and planted accessible 'evidence' somewhere. It might have saved Bucken's life on this occasion, but it might cause irreparable damage to his reputation.

Savas sent his own car to collect Bucken from the hospital. Greta found his escapade quite hilarious. 'How on earth could you keep going for a week?' She wanted to know all about it, and insisted that he should dine with them all.

The dinner at Chez Marie, a simple little hole for millionaires, turned out to be a strained affair. Ruzicki wanted to know about Bucken's police work and how he had gone astray. Savas was most forgiving: 'We're men of the world, Bucken, we understand. We all make mistakes, we all have to live with them.'

Halfway through the meal, a cable was delivered by a hotel messenger to the Quinceys. Papeete opened it and held it in front of her husband. They exchanged glances. 'You ought to go.'

125

'I know.' She put the cable in her handbag. 'It would look odd if we didn't respond.'

'Tomorrow?'

'Why not?'

After dinner, Savas asked Bucken if he was too tired to have a quiet drink with him in the hotel room he used as an office. Bucken accepted. Greta declared that she would join them.

'You're, of course, most welcome, honey . . . '

'But?'

'But I must warn you that it's business. We want to talk turkey.'

'After a dinner like this? How disgusting.'

'You'll be bored.'

'How would you know? You've never tried.'

Bucken asked for a brandy as if to confirm the alleged circumstances of his 'escapade'. He wondered how much Savas knew about the real events of his week.

'What do you want to do with your life, Bucken?' Savas's question was so straight and paternal that Bucken once again felt ashamed of his double dealing. No, Savas wouldn't be a party to his arrest. Ruzicki perhaps? Or others. Not him.

'I'll answer you as soon as I have the money to make such decisions.'

'Any idea how you intend to go about it?'

Bucken shrugged his shoulders.

'You mentioned something about your possible interest in shipping.'

'Did I?'

'In Rotterdam. Remember?'

Bucken did not know how to look suitably embarrassed – in Rotterdam he had mentioned some less than ethical ideas – so he drank up.

Greta immediately filled his glass. Her eyes were on him incessantly, as if riveted by some pure, clinical interest in the beginning of yet another possible escapade.

'I may have a better proposition than what you had in mind, Bucken. You could set up a trading company for me to pull off a fair-size deal with an African country. Interested?'

'You think I could do it?'

'Yes. Because I'll be right behind you with advice and any support you need.'

'Then why do you need me or anyone else?'

'Because I'm too busy to deal with the day-to-day details. And it's got to be someone who won't be elbow-deep into the till even before the deal is set up.'

126

'You mean you trust me?'

Savas laughed: 'No, I don't. I don't know you well enough. But I trust my hunches.'

'Thank you,' Bucken muttered. He felt Greta's blue eyes boring into him.

'It's very simple,' said Savas. 'A friend of mine . . . I mean someone at the Greek police has told me what they found out about you in London. And it doesn't sound right. You're not the man to chase children or beg for sex. I'd wager on that.' He turned to his wife: 'Wouldn't you?'

She walked all the way round Bucken, her head tilted, assessing him with the bemused expertise of an art dealer who has recognised a snip at a car boot sale. 'I reserve my right to answer this some other day.'

'Which means she agrees with me for once,' Savas winked at Bucken.

'Well, what can I say?'

'Say thank you,' she urged him. 'Isn't that an easy choice?'

'Thank you. Thank you both.' This time he did not need to pretend: his embarrassment was genuine. 'We'll drink to that.'

Savas raised his glass – and almost dropped it. He went pale and he held his stomach in obvious pain. 'Hope it's not the oysters,' he uttered with great effort as he retreated through the door.

Bucken started towards him, but Greta stopped him with an impatient gesture. 'Shouldn't you go and see what's happening?' he asked.

'No. I'm his wife, not his nurse.' Seeing his open astonishment, she smiled. 'No, don't worry, I'm not that hard.'

'You could have fooled me.'

'Because you don't understand. He's an old man. And age has inflated his natural vanity and Mediterranean macho. He'd rather die than be seen sick and weak by someone he hopes to bed again one day. Is that a satisfactory explanation?'

'Yes.'

'Then show your appreciation. Say thank you. Go on, it's good practice.'

'What do you mean?'

She stepped quite close to him. She was almost as tall as Bucken. Her breath warmed his chin as she spoke. 'What I mean is that I know exactly how you must feel.'

'Tell me.'

'You feel grateful. Indebted. He's offered you something for nothing. Because he's a good man. So you'll hate him for it.'

127

'Nonsense.'

'Please yourself. But, one day, you'll remember every word I said. His genuine, open-hearted helpfulness will make you feel dirty and cheap – and a cheat. So you'll repay him with spite. Oh yes, you'll hurt him one day. And the kinder he is to you, the more you'll hurt him to restore the balance and your self-respect.'

'You must be drunk.'

'If I was, this subject would sober me up right away. Because this is the subject on which I'm the greatest authority alive.' They stood now toe to toe, her lips and breasts only a thin air cushion away. 'Remember,' she whispered, 'we love the helpless and always hate those who are good to us.'

He felt the urge to shout for Savas to take her away before it's too late. He wanted her – and he hated to hurt him. The man is a crook, he reminded himself, don't let his kindness corrupt you. 'Then I must remember,' his voice was low and dry, 'not to be good to you if I don't want you to hate me.'

'Not even if I'm helpless? In need of love?'

'That's another catch twenty-two.'

'Good. Then you're caught.'

They heard the door open. She was in no hurry to move away from him. Bitch, he thought, and stepped back.

She made no effort to disguise her amusement when asking Savas if he was all right now.

'Yes, thank you, I hope I didn't cause undue anxiety.'

'Of course not, darling, you're man enough to deal with your troubles.'

'At least my absence gave you a chance, Bucken, to think about my proposition.'

'No, it didn't, darling,' she answered quickly. 'We were talking about other things. But now I'll leave you to it. Plot, scheme and deal to your heart's delight. Just don't keep him long. Mr. Bucken's had quite a harrowing week, I believe.'

'Sure. There's plenty of time to discuss the details if you say yes, Bucken.'

'I do.' He looked at her. 'And thank you both.'

'Welcome aboard,' said Savas and raised his glass but did not drink. 'We'll leave for Zurich tomorrow.'

In the morning, Bucken went to say goodbye to the Quinceys. Don was already away, taking hydrotherapy. There were packed suitcases everywhere. Papeete seemed very subdued.

'I didn't realise you were also leaving.'

'I'm off to London and Don is . . . ' she paused as she placed some

128

papers in a red leather briefcase with a combination lock and a hand-cuff safety chain, 'he's to see a specialist.'

The phone rang and she walked across the room to answer it. Bucken glanced at the papers in and next to the red case. He had a fairly accurate photographic memory, so he tried to fix the sight in his mind without any effort to take it all in. There was a file on chemical tankers. A great deal about the Suez Canal. A few names – two vaguely familiar – on a list headed 'possibles'. A document with colourful stamps was sticking out of a green folder. The words 'Abu Dhabi' were visible. On the folder somebody had scribbled 'Rose of Stambul'. Bucken walked away so as not to get caught staring at the papers. On a small wine table, next to Papeete's handbag, he spotted her passport and, face down, the cable she had received the previous night.

Papeete rang off and returned to him. 'Are you well?' And without waiting for an answer: 'I hope you weren't kept up too late last night.'

'I wasn't.' He ignored the innuendo. 'How long will you stay in London?'

'Not long. I hear you'll be in Zurich. We may meet there.'

'Would be nice. I mean it.'

She looked at him in search of answers to unasked questions. The phone rang again. He stepped back to let her pass, but this time he moved with purposeful carelessness and kicked the small table to send everything on it flying. 'Oh, I'm sorry,' he mumbled and, clumsily, he began to gather up her papers and handbag from the floor. It gave him a chance to read at least the signature on the cable: Charles Ashenbury.

Midmorning bustle was at its peak in the Filonos, the insomniac street that runs behind and parallel to the port of Piraeus, where the sex bars, gay dives and strip clubs had already closed to give way to indefatigable chandlers, agents, brokers, owners and charterers. Everybody there seemed to be in the shipping game, yielding more operators to the square metre than one-arm bandits in Vegas. It occurred to Bucken that everybody knew, welcomed or at least recognised Savas as the Oldman led him down the Filonos and, through a narrow passage, out into the Aktimiaouli, a street of bazaars, tied-up white liners, dark bulk carriers, sleek or bleak or cumbersome freighters, and all the world's tramps, both human and maritime. 'Would you believe it?' the Oldman sighed. 'This used to be a street where Greeks would promenade their wives on Sundays or even on fine nights not all that long ago.' He turned into a squalid little street with a sleazy taverna where he had a table reserved in the corner, near the telephone. Like the *Melkweg* in Rotterdam, thought Bucken, who was asked to run a few errands, keep strangers away, and deliver a letter.

Over a plate of kebab, salad and feta cheese, Savas held court. He talked business in Greek, negotiated deals on the phone, and received a fourth-generation baker from his grandfather's village to sort out a problem concerning accommodation to entice a new doctor to the village. Savas promised to contribute seven thousand dollars to the good cause. 'I didn't know you were such a charitable man,' said Bucken after the baker had left, but Savas explained that it was not all charity: 'He's not only a baker but also the manning agent for my ships. He recruits locally, knows every man and his family personally, so I can be sure that there's never any trouble with unions, drunkenness and the like.'

At twelve o'clock precisely, an impeccably dressed black businessman arrived. He looked startled that Savas was not alone. The Oldman did not bother to introduce Bucken this time. 'My new bodyguard,' he explained to the man. 'I wanted you to see him because he may be my representative in our deal.' The black man nodded. Savas told Bucken that he could take the afternoon off: 'You might have some shopping to do before the evening flight.'

Bucken swallowed the rude dismissal, trying to look suitably servile, but used his time to wander about, watch the taverna, see the black businessman leave, follow him to his hotel in Athens, and identify him as Amadou Oyouru, some diplomat from the Ivory Coast.

The ante-room was large enough to make two small family flats. The walls were covered by a unique collection of oil paintings, all with naval themes. Ashenbury's personal assistant, whose domain the room was, seemed to match the oils: her classic beauty also needed an increasing amount of daily restoration. She disliked Papeete, always had, but that would not prevent her from apologising profusely on her master's behalf. Lord Ashenbury was exceedingly sorry to keep her waiting. An unexpected visitor and a vital conference of a most urgent nature. As if driven by a timer, she asked Papeete every ninety seconds if she was sitting comfortably, wished to have some reading material or refreshment.

After five minutes, the door opened. Papeete looked up – and flew out of her chair. 'Daddy! What are *you* doing here?'

'Dodecanese!' He was still the most, most handsome man she had ever known, and his favourite joke had not altered either. 'Isn't she lucky?' he asked the secretary. 'Had we been sailing among the Greek islands when she was conceived, her mother might have named her Dodecanese.' He turned back to his daughter: 'Didn't even know that you were in London.'

'Just arrived. I'd have called you.'

'Lucky you didn't. I love surprises. Come on, my pet, let's have a spot of lunch.' It never occurred to him that people, and least of all his daughter, might have other plans than giving him a pleasant surprise.

'I . . . I've got to see Charles.'

'Later.' He took his daughter's arm and glanced at the secretary over his shoulder: 'Tell Ashenbury, will you, that my daughter will be a little late. Alternatively he could join us at the George and Vulture – a fitting location, wouldn't you say?'

He led her into a maze of narrow passages sunshine would never penetrate, demanded and got the best corner table, ordered champagne, and could hardly wait to tell her all about a two-year-old filly he was planning to buy. He produced a photograph. 'Look at that beauty, Papeete, what do you think? Isn't she a sure-fire winner? Isn't she?'

'I wouldn't know, daddy, but I'm pleased to hear that you can afford her.'

'Afford her? That's not a question of affording or not affording her. If you really want something of course you can afford it. Isn't that right? You tell me, you know me better than any woman ever will.'

No, he had not changed: he was still divorced from all his wives and reality. And she had not changed either: she remembered the joy of hearing about her parents' divorce as a small child, believing that she would have him all to herself. 'Yes, daddy, if anyone, it must be you who can afford anything.'

'That's my girl.'

'What were you doing at Ashenbury's?'

'Oh, it's quite boring, really. He phoned out of the blue. He said he needed some *names* on one of his boards, and wanted to know if I'd serve. I said sure enough, guv, if the money's right, I'd say yes, guv, no guv, three bags full, guv.' His Cockney imitation had faded somewhat but still gave her a laugh. 'I mean cor blimey, it's quite a windfall.'

'That's good. Congratulations, daddy.' She wondered how much this sudden windfall had to do with her arrival. Was it Charles Ashenbury's welcome-home present to her? The timing would suggest

131

just that. It would also say: you see how much I can do for people around you? 'I hope the money is right.'

'We're talking about a couple of directorships, that's all.' He had the knack of remaining completely oblivious to every nuance, undertone or possible implication that did not concern him directly. 'We'll see. We – shall – see.' He concentrated on his trout until he suddenly remembered her presence. 'Mm. Well, how about you?' His smile would make pear trees bloom at Christmas.

'How about me?' It always puzzled her how on earth any of his wives had ever let go of him. A nightmare to live with, perhaps, but what fun to love . . .

'Well, how are you? And how's your Mr. Quincey?'

'I'm fine. As for Don . . . '

'You mean Donald, don't you?'

'If you wish.'

'Please. Only because Don, my pet, is not a husband but a quiet-flowing river along which uncouth Cossacks bleed and fornicate. An off-putting thought, wouldn't you say?' He had never liked her husband. In his opinion, Quincey could not enjoy life – meaning wealth, of course – because he sweated too much for it. Money should just be on tap for people who deserved it. 'Anyway, is he well?'

'Getting better.'

'Good, very good.' He said nodding repeatedly, and she had a feeling that the remark had addressed not her but his trout. 'Is he doing business with Ashenbury?'

A mere flicker in his eyes seemed to add an extra dimension to the question. Was he asking her if she had helped Don to some business through Ashenbury? She did not want to know if he had meant that. And she did not want to answer one way or another. Or discuss Ashenbury. She busied herself with her champagne. Otherwise she might have asked her father if he remembered the weekend when he had taken her to Ashenbury's country house in Sussex.

She was just coming up to fourteen. She had offered several times to leave the expensive boarding school to help him. But, whenever she mentioned to him the rather nasty, tendentious remarks the headmistress had made to her about the hardship unpaid bills could cause to the smooth running of the school, he would dismiss it all lightly and most reassuringly: 'Nonsense, my pet, all she wants is to see me. These things have nothing to do with money. You'll understand one day. It's, you see, the limitation our society has imposed on women. They must not appear to be too obvious if they wish to continue to play hard-to-get.'

At the time, Papeete found it a convincing enough argument. She could not imagine any woman failing to be drawn to him. So she went along, playing his game happily, forgetting about bailiffs and the whole caboodle that was part and parcel of his life style, and ignoring poverty that stared them in the face from the bottom of every champagne glass they had emptied.

But then there was that weekend. He had appeared unannounced at the school. He apologised for taking Papeete away two days before the Easter break, and the harshest of her mistresses seemed to wet themselves with joy to reassure him that his wish was no inconvenience to them or to the child.

He had forgotten about clothes for her, and she arrived in her school uniform, the standard one from Howarth, Howarth & Howarth, purveyors of striped blazers, lousy blouses and baggy skirts. Ashenbury thought she looked charming in her boater and all, and refused to allow female house guests, all grown-ups and very tall, to lend her ill-fitting clothes.

'You look lovely, absolutely delightful,' he kept saying, and it pleased her. Ashenbury was almost as handsome as her daddy who might become jealous, she thought. Then her daddy had to leave – 'on business, my pet, quite unavoidable' – and, suddenly, she was a guest in her own right. A guest who would be asked to return after the summer. And again. And stay on. For years. She sometimes wondered if she had ever left Ashenbury. She had not *seen* him since her marriage to Don, but had she *left* him?

Her father sipped champagne and enthused about the filly. She thought about that Easter weekend after which his 'boring financial affairs' had taken a marked turn for the better. Had Ashenbury helped him? She did not really care one way or another. If anything, it pleased her that she had done more for her father than any of his women ever could or would want to.

Without the filly or the encouragement from the champagne, their conversation would have died in less than twenty minutes. By the time she had finished her hors d'oeuvre, they knew it would be painful to stretch the encounter to last through the main course. They agreed she must not keep Ashenbury waiting any longer.

The ante-room beauty showed her right through. Papeete approached the inner sanctum with trepidation. She was afraid the magic might still be there, ready to engulf and unwrap her, hurt and humiliate her, giving her pleasure, want it or not. And what was worse, revulsion or not, if it was there, she would want it, she knew.

Unhurriedly as always, Ashenbury came to meet her at the door. Sorrow, pain, hope and desire clouded his eyes, yet the dignity of his bearing and voice remained unaffected. He took both her hands. 'I'm glad you're here.' He was close enough to greet her with a kiss if so she wished. She noticed a large parcel, tucked away discreetly in a corner. On it, the printed legend said *Howarth, Howarth & Howarth*. It might have been the elaborate lettering that reminded her of the Omar Khayyam in Shepheards. Unborn tomorrow and dead yesterday. In the last second, she turned her head slightly. The kiss landed on her cheek, and he let go of her hands. 'It's good to see you.'

He let her choose her armchair, and noted that she sat with her back to the parcel. Now pain alone remained in his eyes, and she knew he still blamed her for giving him the opportunity to develop a ruinous taste for youth and fetish. It also told her that, at long last, the spell had been truly broken. She was here simply to respond to Ashenbury's kind offer, and so disguise the fact that Don did not and would not need his help any more. The thought left her wondering how much of her liberation had anything to do with her fetish-free desire for Bucken.

The conversation became creaky and rather formal. They both were too preoccupied with the sentences that would stay unsaid.

'How did you find me? I mean us?' she asked.

'One hears about one's friends all the time. Besides, I was asking questions. I knew what had happened to Don, and I fully realised how shabbily he had been treated.'

'Very shabbily.' Ever since the crash, she had been dying to know how much of Don's misfortunes was attributable to his marriage and Ashenbury's revenge. Because Ashenbury had been involved, behind the scenes, to some extent – there was no doubt about that.

He now offered to help him. Give him a new start.

'Why?' Her question was cruel. 'You've never liked him.'

'For your sake. I would have continued to send cables and seek contact until he responded.'

'You knew he wouldn't come.'

'True. I wanted you to come. It would have been unkind to say so.' He glanced towards the parcel in the corner. 'I want you back. At any price.'

She followed his eyes to the Howarth & Howarth, then slowly shook her head. 'Thank you, but no thanks, Charles. I won't lie to you. It's over.'

'It happened before. We thought it was over – and then, suddenly, it wasn't.'

'Not this time, Charles. Now it's really and truly gone. I'll cherish the memories. But that's all.'

'All right, let's leave it for the moment. Doesn't Don need help?'

'Not at that price.'

'That parcel is not a price tag. It's a completely different matter. Quite independent from Don. I'm ready to help him – to help you.' He smiled. 'And, if you suspect that I have ulterior motives, you can take it from me: yes, I have. I want to keep in touch. And live in hope.' He walked over to the parcel and tapped it twice with the fine birch twig that lay on top. 'No, it's not my price.'

'That's good,' her voice warmed to him. 'It would have been awful to see you as a blackmailer.'

She promised to discuss his offer of help with her husband. She knew he would refuse it, and she would want him to. She only hoped that his refusal would not affect her father's new directorship prospects – and his chance to buy that filly.

III

A CLAY PIGEON IN FLIGHT

Bucken's autumn was dizzying and breathless. The sweat of Singapore's tropical sauna had hardly dried on his back when his plane was already being diverted because of icy fog over Zurich. One day he clutched teacups to warm his numb fingers in London, only to guzzle iced drinks in arid Cairo the day after, with no time to pause, reflect, take stock or remember that he was a cop, not a playboy. He lost track of the season as well as the time of day, and only occasionally did it dawn on him that he had been mesmerised by the process that would make him a rich man.

To onlookers, his dazzling business career might have seemed something straight out of a modern fairy tale. By courtesy of Savas and Ruzicki, it took him almost a full day to become a tycoon, and another three hours to blossom into an international shipping magnate – at least on paper. His new name was Booker, his new passport Australian, his ticket invariably first class.

'Sign here, please,' said the deputy manager of the lakeside branch of the Erste Zürcher Stadt und Handelsbankverein – and Mr. Booker became sole holder of a numbered account. The banker's pizza-pastry face remained expressionless as the green olives he had for eyes raced through the anonymous bearer's bond Booker had presented. It was worth a hundred thousand dollars, its number was not on the internationally circulated *stolen/missing* list – why should anyone quibble about it? 'The amount is to be placed in toto in the new account, I understand.'

Bucken nodded as haughtily as he reckoned a tycoon would: Savas had arranged the introduction and warned him to speak no more than the inevitable minimum.

'You wish to have a codeword for telephone instructions and the like?'

'Please.' After a moment's hesitation, he wrote *Sarahelen* in the appropriate section of the document.

'I'm sure you understand the problems involved, Mr. Booker.'

'That's right.'

'Anybody who quotes the code Sarahelen in person or on the telephone, will have disposal rights over your account. Do you wish to
impose any limits on withdrawals on the strength of the code?'

'No.' Only Savas would be privy to the code, and it was Savas's
money, after all, though the banker was not to know that.

'Sign here, please,' said the snooty Swiss estate agent Savas had
roped in, and, with that, Mr. Booker now had a classy business
address to his name. The agent was unimpressed when Bucken
offered to pay a full year's rent in advance for the two-room suite that
sheltered right behind the patrician splendour of the silversmiths'
medieval guildhouse.

'Sign here, please,' said the implacable blonde and, two hours
later, the suite was fully furnished with neo-antiques, complete with
indoor plants, typewriters, telex, intercom, and sumptuously framed
cheap prints – all on hire, all charges duly paid in advance for a year.

By that time, Bucken-Booker was landing at Heathrow. First class
passengers had first class treatment at passport control; the uniformed chauffeur was waiting to drive him to the Hilton.

'Sign here, please,' said the squinting pedlar of limited companies.
He had the complexion of creatures that populate puddles in a cave.
His seediness matched the squalor of his East End office where five
people and six typewriters shared two rooms with a million dusty
files, and where the names of defunct companies could be bought off
miles of shelves. After a random choice, Bucken was to become
chairman and managing director of Fiskal and Kommercial Co. Ltd.
with a fully paid up capital of three pounds sterling. The 'co-
director', signing the papers with him for authenticity, was the dumb
office cleaner, not a marked success in his regular vocation, but an
experienced signatory in anybody's name – for a consideration. His
fee was a fiver that also covered his instant resignation from the
board. The entire charade was arranged in advance by a hard-up
lawyer in Bethnal Green who had taken his instructions – gladly –
from a voice on the telephone and an anonymous money order in the
post.

Bucken had a couple of hours to kill before catching a flight to
Singapore. That gave him an opportunity to check out his suspicion
that he had been followed ever since leaving the airport. He dismissed his chauffeur and walked from the 'names' bureau. Within a
few minutes he spotted the set-up. It was a reasonably professional
job, he concluded. The tail on foot in a nondescript suit now wore a
cloth cap and seemed completely pre-occupied with a recalcitrant
pipe. His back-up, a battered van, cruised along, stopped, and made

occasional detours to reappear in front. It had the speed to chase – it had been doing it on the way from the airport. That told him he had been expected or tailed all the way from Zurich. By whom? Ruzicki? Some foreign police? He would try to find out the answer, but if he failed he would warn Savas. If nothing else, it could earn him some Brownie points in his employer's eyes.

He passed the first telephone booth, then, as if on impulse, doubled back. His turn was too sudden for the tail to stop without calling attention to himself. He would have to walk on a little further before seeking shelter in the entrance of a shop to renew his battle with matches and pipe. By that time, Bucken would have dialled his emergency number without the risk of being overlooked. He needed some answers from Dodd.

On the seventh floor of Scotland Yard, a red light flashed on the miniature switchboard, and the operator answered at once.

'This is the Gardener from Bayswater. Give me Greenfingers.'

'He's away. If it's urgent. . . '

Bucken rang off. It was urgent. But if the Assistant Commissioner was not in the building, he could do nothing quickly enough. He looked up the number of the newspaper where Freemantle worked.

'John? It's Bucken.'

'Well I'll be damned. Where the hell. . . ?'

Bucken cut him short. 'Are we private on this line?'

Freemantle hesitated. Ada Tansley was off sick. The relief girl on the switchboard might listen in. . . 'No. I'll give you a direct number.'

Bucken called again. 'I need some help. And it's between you and me. Okay?'

'Shoot '

'Get on to Lloyd's Register. Find out everything you can about a ship called *Rose of Stambul*.'

'Right away.'

'There's more. I want to know if Quincey owns or has ever owned a chemical tanker.' It was a long shot, but worth a try. 'And another thing.' He reeled off four names he remembered from Quincey's list of 'possibles'. He asked Freemantle to check if there was anything on file about them.

'One of them rings a bell but I don't know where or why,' said the journalist.

'Snap. That's how I feel about two of them.'

'How long have I got?'

'Whatever it takes as long as it doesn't take more than an hour.'

'You're crazy. I'm not the Yard, you know.'

138

'If you were, I'd give you two hours. Meet me at Simpson's. Downstairs.'

'Hang on. Some people have been making inquiries about you.'

'Tell me when we meet.' Bucken hung up. In Dodd's absence, he was more prepared to take a chance on Freemantle than anyone at the Yard where he might be treated with hostile caution at the moment: once the gossip about his alleged indiscretions had spread, even friends might shy away from him. He noted that his tail had been changed. The van was parked a hundred yards further on. He had an hour to lose them.

He walked, changed cabs, doubled back – the tail was still there. He tried the underground routine, jumping into the last car as the door began to close, but the tail was good: he was already inside, ready to get out if Bucken did not get in. Bucken smiled. He decided to try the merry-go-round.

He took a taxi to the City and asked to be driven into Birchin Lane. The van fell back and its place was taken by a Mini with the long-suffering pipe smoker as its passenger. Bucken stopped the cab on the corner of Bengal Court, the first of several alleyways that were too narrow to spread his arms in. The Mini would not want to be spotted so it would have to pass them to the point where the street twisted. Bucken paid the taxi driver to cruise around for a few minutes, then go round the area that contained the labyrinth, and pick him up on the other side, in Leadenhall Street at the entrance of the passage to the Jamaica Inn.

Bucken walked into the maze slowly to give the tail a chance to run back and follow him. The Mini would have no choice but to wait in Birchin Lane. Bucken walked up Bengal Court, through the tunnel that formed the top end of it, and emerged into George Yard, where he sat, dangling his feet, on the rim of the dry pond of green mosaic. The tail's embarrassment amused him. The hapless man struggled with his pipe, but could not stay on and on indefinitely. He kept peeping from behind the corner. He was quite relieved when Bucken got up, strolled past the Inn and emerged in Leadenhall Street. The shock came when the tail saw the cab waiting.

Bucken got in, the tail stepped back to radio, presumably, the cab's number to the Mini. But, even if his set was powerful enough to cope with all the steel structures of tall buildings, the men would be doomed to a wild goose chase. For the cab stopped only a few yards on, Bucken paid the driver to go all the way to the West End, while he slipped into the next dark passage that led into Ball Court – and the rear entrance of Simpson's Tavern.

Freemantle was already there. 'Are we having some more brawling, Bucken?'

'Not this time. I must dash.'

'Whatever you're up to, you'd better watch your back.' He put his hand protectively on Bucken's arm.

'What the fuck is this? You joined some amateur dramatic society for the benefit of gaga newshounds?'

'It's serious. A private eye did some snooping. And there's worse. I know from a source that some powerful outsiders pressed for info from the Yard. Could be Yanks.'

Bucken knew better than to ask for Freemantle's 'source'. Yanks? They might have been on his tail, too. 'Anything else?'

'Yeah. The worst.' He paused.

'I'll recommend you for Hamlet's daddy. Or Dracula.'

'My source thinks that you might have pissed into someone's vintage port, and Dodd is trying to cut your pisser off.'

'Yes, Dracula. If not Frankenstein. Now give. You got what I wanted?'

'Some of it. Chemical tankers. Impossible to say if Quincey owns one or not. You know how it is.'

Bucken saw that Freemantle was building up to some dramatic climax. He did not have the heart to ruin it for him. 'Sure. Just a long shot.'

'*Rose of Stambul* 6,200 tons.' He gave Bucken a slip of paper. 'Here are the details. Panamanian flag, etcetera. Owner disappeared, crew in the shit, there was some accident, and the ship was laid up in Abu Dhabi for a couple of years.'

'Was?'

'Yepp. It's not yet on record, but my source says she has just been sold to the Caryatides Shipping Company in Greece. She was probably worth refloating.'

Or sinking, thought Bucken. 'Anything about this Caryatides?'

Freemantle shook his head.

'Do they have any other ships?'

'Do they ever?' Freemantle laughed at the detective's naivety. 'These days it's the one company one ship principle. If the ship is in the shit, no other assets can be held to cover bad debts. Right?'

'I wouldn't know. I'm not into shipping.'

'Like hell you ain't. You want to know about Quincey, then all this, then your list of names. '

'What about it?'

'Two of the four are mercenaries of the expensive kind.'

That's why they sounded familiar. Now it clicked. 'And the other two?'

'One is unknown. I mean we have nothing on him. But the other sounds interesting. Remember Hitler's commando expert?'

'Skorzeny? Sure. But he's dead '

'He may well be but his spirit lives on in this guy, the fourth on your list. He grew up in Skorzeny's breast pocket. By trade he's a skipper, but he's tops with gelignite, and he must have been good if Skorzeny put him in charge of ships, boats and explosives on some of the famous commando jobs. No known convictions on our files, but he was deported from more countries than you can name.'

Bucken tried not to show that he was stunned. Why would anyone be interested in an old wreck? Was there a connection between the chemical tankers and the mercenaries? Why would they be kept together among Quincey's personal papers? What had an old commando gelly-man got to do with it all? What was Quincey up to? Sabotage? Holding a tanker to ransom? Was that the big conspiracy poor Spire had suspected?

'Aren't you a bit out of your depth these days?' Freemantle asked softly, as if guessing his friend's predicament.

Out of my depth? I'm a bloody marionette who doesn't even know whether he's upside down or what, thought Bucken, but said nothing because he could not tell the truth and would not want to lie to Freemantle. He was fed up with lies anyway. He had played spy, errand boy, bodyguard, common creep and pseudo-tycoon in quick succession, and was not quite sure about right and wrong any more. It was unnerving to operate in a totally new environment, without a power base, legal or moral support of colleagues and superiors, and resist the lure of the good life he had no right to. For deep down he knew he had been tempted. Tempted to reach out for Papeete, grab all that lovely lolly floating about, and make his pile and take revenge for Spire on Dodd in that way. Trouble is, he thought, I haven't got the moral fibre to become a villain. 'Thanks for your help,' he said at last, 'one day I may repay it, but don't count on it.'

'Would I ever?'

'No, not you, sweetheart, you're a fucking altruist, I know. So here's another chance to demonstrate your unselfish goodwill. Find out who Amadou Oyouru is. He's from the Ivory Coast, travelling on a CD passport.'

'You mean seedy passport or corps diplomatique?'

'That's one of the things I want to know, though I guess he may well be in government down there.'

'Anything else?'

'Yes. I want to know more about that wreck in Abu Dhabi. Keep digging, will you?'

'Where can I reach you?'

'I'll let you know from time to time. Right now, I'm off to Singapore.' It was stupid to say it, but irresistible. Bucken knew his own weakness, the craving for a little admiration from a friend or colleague once in a while.

'I thought the government was cutting expenses left, right and centre. I hope you enjoy all that travelling and the bright lights.'

'What the hell do you know about the life of a business tycoon? Most of the time I don't even know where I am. Oh yes, we remember a bit about Macao and Cairo, and a couple of streets in Greece, but the rest is just a blur – cabs, hotels, conferences. We may recall the cabbie's patter or the speciality on a menu, and all we know about the local weather is what we read off some fancy barometer through the plate glass door of the lobby. But that's our lot, sonny, we're on the go, go, go!'

'Remind me to pity you next time we meet.' Freemantle would have hated to admit that he detected a touch of sincerity in Bucken's voice.

Magdalena van Loewe always liked to knit. Now that gout had got the better of her, knitting was a way of life. She lived in one of the beanpole houses in an old, neglected and therefore picturesque quarter of Amsterdam, only a bridge away from the Rapenburgerplein. She did not subscribe to the national pastime of leaning out of windows – even the fattest of window cushions were hard on the elbows after a few hours – but she liked to know what was going on in the neighbourhood. So she relied on the most profound Dutch invention, two long strips of mirrors that were positioned discreetly at the edges of her window, camouflaged by lace curtains, and angled to give a good view up and down the street. Since they had moved the fleamarket to the Rapenburgerplein, there was always something to see.

On Tuesday morning, soon after she had taken her strategic window seat, she saw a taxi roll slowly into view. Magdalena van Loewe was certain that its engine was not running and she would have sworn that it had no driver. The cab crawled along the kerb and came to a halt against a protruding cobble. Four hours later, the cab was still there. On the passenger side, some dark liquid, presumably oil, kept dripping into a slowly growing puddle on the pavement.

By two o'clock in the afternoon, she could not contain her curiosity any longer. When she saw that no-good kid of the Schaaps from No. 5 passing the cab, she urged him to take a look inside. The kid opened the passenger door – and a man's half-naked body fell out. It was covered in blood. It was clear for all to see that the man had been slashed in a thousand places. His skin looked like the surface of an old cheese board, and his hands were missing. Magdalena van Loewe opened her mouth but, before she could scream, the excitement killed her. Her death would not be discovered for several days, but in the street, the police quickly identified the victim as a Greek who had left a Rotterdam hospital only a few days earlier.

'Shipping magnate's bodyguard slain' the morning papers reported on the Wednesday. Over breakfast in Rotterdam, Savas shoved the news item with the sickening photograph under Ruzicki's nose. 'Do I detect your handwriting?'

Ruzicki shrugged his shoulders.

'What happened?'

'I was told he had some mysterious visitors in hospital. Perhaps police. We've never found out who they were, but they wanted to buy some information.'

'Perhaps he would have told me all about it. He was due to report back on duty here this morning.'

Ruzicki smiled: 'That's what I thought. But when he discharged himself a day early, I had him followed to Amsterdam, where he was questioned.'

'You mean killed.'

'It was an accident.'

'Like the one in Macao?'

Ruzicki pretended he had not even heard the question. 'We found these on him.' He gave Savas a folder full of photocopies of various documents. 'I hope this will convince you that we had to act with utmost urgency.'

Savas glanced through the papers, and the blood rushed to his head. All the documents were from his own confidential files, all contained details about his dealings, and the damage their publication could cause him ranged from the embarrassing to the ruinous. 'I should have been warned,' he mumbled.

'I agree.'

'And I should have been consulted.'

'Agreed, once again. But there was no time. I had to make the decision. That's my burden of being in charge of "Tsunami" security.'

'These have nothing to do with "Tsunami".'

'Any danger to any member of the syndicate must have a bearing on "Tsunami". We can't take risks now.'

'You mean you have me watched?'

'My job is to protect all members. And nobody would deny that Oldman Savas is a key member.'

'Thank you.' Savas kept his eyes away from the newspaper photograph of the mutilated corpse. 'I'll need a new bodyguard.'

'I thought you were satisfied with Bucken.'

'He's too good for the job. He's going to do a lot more for me.'

'I'm glad to hear it. He's a slippery customer.'

Savas did not try to conceal how pleased he was with that information: 'You mean he gave you the slip?'

'Temporarily, yes.'

'So you don't even know where he is, do you?'

'That much I do know. He's in Singapore. But when you get a chance, warn him, Oldman, that it's not very healthy for him to make disappearances a habit. After all, I'd also like to give him some work before he slips up like some bodyguards do.'

'Tell him yourself. He'll be here on Friday.'

An hour later, when the television screens had been activated for another syndicate conference, Savas proposed to compel Ruzicki to consult members before taking any extreme or decisive action. The resolution was passed unanimously with a slight modification. Ruzicki would be compelled to consult others in such cases 'if at all possible'. Savas was asked to remonstrate seriously with two partners who had failed, yet again, to turn up at the meeting and listen to the latest feasibility reports by Quincey and Selli on the 'Tsunami' Suez option.

Singapore was to be yet another blurred memory for Bucken. A couple of visits to the local branch of the Russian Narodny, a relative newcomer to the international banking scene, just one night at Raffles, a drink in the Tiffin Room, a stroll down North Bridge Road to Bugis Street, and a peripatetic meal at the last of the street stalls under gaudy lights, where patrons could marvel at the plastic surgeons' art that was paraded by the last of stunningly alluring transvestites. In the morning, he opened an account with Narodny for Fiskal, his new company, transferring a quarter of a million dollars from his Swiss account, then caught the next flight to Rotterdam, enjoying the extra leg room but feeling bored with the champagne infusion of first class travel. The dizzying effect of jetsetting was only worsened by the fact that he could still not figure out in what way Savas was using him.

In Rotterdam he took a cab to the new Eurovista building, a poor millionaires' exquisitely furnished motel, where each suite had fully equipped offices as well as adjoining staff quarters, and where each room was swept electronically for bugs every day – no less a routine chore than hoovering. The Savas suite of rooms clustered around a central hall with twin locks on its own front door.

Savas was pleased with Bucken's reports from London and Singapore. They were talking in the living-room partly because Savas disliked the office ('too many gadgets and computer terminals make me feel old and inadequate'), and partly because the Oldman liked to cart around his current essential documents in an old leather Gladstone bag of advanced pregnancy. As he filed the set of documents relevant to the new account, Bucken caught a few glimpses of a batch of papers that were, apparently, related to some deal with the Ivory Coast.

'Keep up the good work, Bucken,' said the Oldman, 'and you won't regret it that you haven't become a greaser. For the time being, this is a token of my appreciation.' He handed Bucken an anonymous bearer's bond – the international currency of shady deals and tax evasion – worth twenty thousand dollars. 'Eventually, I'll want you to return to Singapore for me and complete some details. That should be worth at least fifty thou to you.'

As if summoned by the rustle of valuable papers, Greta joined them. She wanted to know if Bucken would accompany them to 'this little soirée by some pennypinchers'. 'She means the International Monetary Fund,' Savas explained. 'Come if you like. I'll get you an invitation.'

Bucken hesitated. It could be a good opportunity to meet more of the Oldman's cronies. On the other hand, it could be an even better opportunity to visit the Savas suite and take a look at the Ivory Coast correspondence. Would it be worth the risk? Bucken excused himself: 'Singapore and back was a bit of a rush. So unless you need me in my guard capacity. . . '

'No, no. Have a nice long rest,' said Savas, and Greta supported him enthusiastically.

A secretary came in as Bucken was about to leave. 'A Mr. Ting-chao is here to see you, sir. If you're busy, he'll leave some papers with me.'

'No, I'll see him in a minute.'

On his way out, Bucken passed Ting-chao. The heavy-set Chinaman's face seemed familiar. Ting-chao. Bucken could almost hear the ding-dong the name made. Macao! It was Inspector Poon who pronounced Ting-chao with that ding-dong. The face slipped into place in the memory jigsaw. The hotel room. The weight of Two-ton. The questions. The threats. The liquid opium. Ting-chao was there. Somewhere in the background. Or was it just the name that rang a bell? Was he there when Spire was tortured? The gory pictures on

Dodd's desk. The neatly laid out index fingers. But of course! Second Mate Ting-chao was the senior surviving officer of the *Alida II*. If he left some papers with Savas, Bucken would want to see them whatever the risk.

It was half past nine when Bucken telephoned the Savas apartment to reassure himself that nobody was at home. He let it ring and ring, but there was no answer. Using Spire's burglar set, he broke into the central hall, put out a Do Not Disturb sign to keep servants away, and locked the door from the inside. The master bedroom was to the right, and he decided to start there. He had a small torch but before he would switch it on, he paused in the open door to let his eyes get accustomed to the darkness.

'Don't switch on the light.' The voice was soft yet almost made him drop his torch. 'I knew you'd come here tonight.'

'Greta.'

'You sound surprised. Did you expect somebody else?'

'What a crazy idea.'

'Why are you here if you didn't expect to find me here?'

'Because I didn't expect it. I was merely hoping for it.'

'Liar. But nice.'

He was still standing in the door. As his eyes adjusted to the hint of light seeping through at the edges of the blinds, he could make out the shape of the bed and the ridge her body formed in the middle.

'How did you get in?' She sounded curious rather than suspicious.

'Sheer willpower. It opens doors, you know.'

'Mine, too?'

'I hope so.'

'Then why are you just standing there?'

'I'd never take you for granted.'

'Thank you.'

He could not tell her that he was busy wrapping his burglar tools in his handkerchief and stuffing them tight in his pockets. When his trousers came off, as he hoped they would, it could be embarrassing to have a professional set of skeleton keys scattered all over the floor. And he needed a little more time. 'How did you manage to stay at home?'

'Ah, that would be telling.'

'So?'

'Sorry. Trade secrets.'

'Migraine?'

'Worse.'

'Sudden depression. Allergy to parties. Something reminded you of your favourite uncle's death in a Chinese brothel. Or you remembered that you'd entered a tantrum-throwing contest. Am I on the right track?'

'A good try.'

He walked over to the bed and stared down at the figure in white. Like a modest ghost, he thought. She was covered right up to her chin.

'Any more guesses?'

'I give up.'

'All right. It was a burn.'

'You burned yourself?'

'No.' There was a smile in her voice. 'It was the dress. I said I had bought it for the party and it was the only suitable one I had. But with a hole in a prominent place. . .' She laughed. He joined in.

'You mean you actually. . . '

'Yes. I needed a good excuse.'

'Thank you.' He leaned over to kiss her. It was a light tentative kiss. He stopped when he had a sudden sensation that she was shiverish. Or trembling. As if she was afraid of something. And much too keen to keep the conversation going.

'It was a fantastic Italian model.'

'Was?'

'It's beyond repair.' Her little laugh turned throaty as he touched her face. 'You think it was worth it?'

'You tell me.'

She moved away a little. Was she making room for him? He found the situation a peculiar experience. As a result of long years of happy philandering, his physical approach to women and some of his sex life were ruled by well-rehearsed habits, guided by the subconscious knowledge of what worked for him and what did not. Virtually all his affairs started with almost ritualistic moves and patterns, and yet, like a ballet of temptation choreographed by two wanting, teasing, doubting, begging and finally storming bodies, the performance would remain fresh, never quite repetitive. Of all the great expectations in his life, he found the disrobing of a woman the most awesome. Anticipation only heightened the joy of the throbbing tide in his veins, the urge to race and stand still, the breathless fumbling, and the tumbling of the last taboos – the whole maddening liturgy of the gradual nakedness of her body and will.

He would never undress first. It would take his partner for granted. But, this time, he had no choice. She had given him none. She was there, between the sheets, waiting.

To disguise his apprehension, he tore off his clothes and threw them on the floor in a heap. He felt her eyes on him though he could not be sure. He lifted the edge of the sheet and slipped underneath, beside her, only to recoil with a shock – she was fully dressed. He rose on his elbow. Was that some practical joke? Were there people watching through infra-red viewers from all corners of the room? How should he react? He prepared to laugh with them. But what if there was nobody watching? Nobody but Greta. And she would know that he had been just what he did not want to be – boorish and presumptious.

'I'm sorry,' she whispered as if understanding it all. 'I couldn't face the humiliation if I was waiting here . . . and you didn't return.'

It would have humiliated her even more if she ever found out why, in fact, he had returned. But he was glad he had. He kissed her, and she wanted it. His hands roamed further and further in search of her body, and she willed them to find her skin. Yet, from time to time, he sensed that she was shying away. He dismissed the thought. A ridiculous idea. Man-eaters like Greta would react eagerly to every touch. Her body did. She helped him to get rid of her clothes that separated them. And, yet, there was something . . . hesitation? fear? what? and why?

His lips climbed her breast, the ripples of her ribs, descended upon the curve of her belly – and she backed a fraction away.

He halted his descent: an unasked question. She said nothing. Then, with sudden force, she held his head to her body. Almost as soon as he had begun kissing her, a violent shock ran through her as if she had been electrocuted. Her thighs gripped his face.

She needed a few moments to relax. The tension seeped away, she guided his head upwards to her face, and his body into hers.

Her lovemaking was full of surprises. He expected her to be aggressive and uninhibited. She was not. Her shyness belied the sex-crazed *femme fatale* she always advertised herself to be. But, whatever else she turned out to be, she was fun. And hungry.

Late that night, he asked her if she wanted him to leave.

'No.'

'The party might soon be over.'

'I know.' She walked to the door and locked it. 'We never sleep in the same room,' she said on her way back. Even in the darkness her hands tried to cover herself.

'I want to see you.'

'Lecher.'

'And a voyeur.'

After a moment's hesitation, she switched on the light. It seemed quite an effort for her to remove and raise her hands. She tried to joke it away: 'Please don't shoot, officer.'

'You're beautiful.'

She switched off the light, kissed him, and curled up in his embrace. 'Did I fool you?'

'In some ways, yes. Why do you want to be seen as a three-men-a-day woman?'

'Perhaps because that's what I am.'

'Or want to be?'

'Good question.' She smiled.

'Bad answer.' He smiled with her.

'Leaves you free to take your pick. What do *you* think I am?'

'Can't yet tell. I see too many conflicts in you.'

'Name some.

'All right You're a shy show-off.'

'Go on.'

'You're a lascivious innocent, a peaceful aggressor, a bawdy prude.'

For the first time, she laughed freely. 'You've laid me bare.'

'In more ways than one?' He laughed with her – but a second later he knew he had been lured into a trap, the false security of boxing clever.

She froze their laughter with icy irony. 'Don't kid yourself, Bucken. You're not the first to discover all my secrets. And, for all I know, you may not be the last either.'

'I haven't discovered anything. Perhaps a few questions, if that.'

His sincerity puzzled her. She lived by laying traps – and also saw them, waiting for her, everywhere.

'I'd like to understand.'

'Why?' She felt disarmed. 'Is it always necessary to understand?'

'To me, yes.'

'You want me to massage your ego?'

'You've already done that by being here. Is it just my luck?'

'No. I'm here because . . . perhaps because you insulted me when we met in Athens. In the hotel lobby. Remember?'

'Insulted?'

'Yes. You paid no attention, I mean real attention to me.'

'How wrong can you get?' He caressed her, and her body welcomed it. 'I was on the defensive. You were teasing me.'

'This time it's for me to ask how wrong you can get. I wasn't teasing. I only made allowances for your Englishness. Because, on that island of yours, you've never learned the art of flirtation. You either go for it or you don't.'

'Wrong again. There's a third option.'

She looked surprised.

149

'We joke about it.'

'And you call that flirtation?'

'Sometimes. Depends on the joke.'

'You weren't joking in that hotel lobby, Bucken. You outright rejected me.'

'And it got me here? It should teach me to reject women more regularly.'

They heard the clicking of the lock outside. The front door of the suite opened and shut. Under the edge of the bedroom door a thin strip of light appeared. Greta laughed. 'Oh yes, that should teach you,' she almost shouted. She laughed again. The sound was unnaturally loud.

'It wasn't such a good joke,' he whispered, and gestured towards the door. Perhaps she did not notice that Savas had arrived back.

She waved away his warning and laughed even louder. 'It was very funny.'

Another door could be heard thudding shut. The light disappeared.

'Why do you want to hurt him?' he asked quietly.

She stared up at the dark ceiling.

'Because he's good to you? Because you feel humiliated by gifts you can't return?'

'It's not that simple.'

'I never thought it was.' He knew it was essential to understand Greta well enough to be able to influence her if and when necessary. It was yet another dirty venture but, one day, his mission, even his life, might depend on it. 'Why did you marry him in the first place?' She said nothing. 'I wouldn't have thought that the two of you were an eminently good match.' He had to keep needling her to provoke an argument – and the truth. 'Was it love at first sight?'

Bucken expected a violent explosion, but she ignored the cutting edge of the question. 'Together we created the right impression.' After a long pause, she appeared to be talking to herself. 'I was brought up to believe that white weddings mattered more than virginity, and that manners came before honesty.'

'And Savas knew which fork to use, so you married him.'

'He didn't. I married him for his money. And all that went with it. Security, status, social standing . . . Yes, I know what you're thinking . . . Shall I say it for you? All right, I was behaving like any cheap whore. But cheap I was not. Does that shock you, Mr. Bucken? Are you a moralist, Mr. Bucken?'

'Sadly, I'm not easily shockable any more. But it amazes me how much you can surprise me.'

150

'Good. Because at first I was amazed myself that I could prove to everybody, including Savas, that he didn't buy the freehold on my body. I could do as I pleased with it.'

'And enjoy every minute of it.'

'Wrong again. I didn't enjoy those first affairs. I could go happily without sex for months on end. But, slowly, affairs were becoming a habit.'

'Hurray!' His unbounded enthusiasm broke the solemnity of the moment, and served as an apology for his hurtful questions a little earlier. She embraced him, and the tip of her nose drew spirals skating down his cheek, along his jaw, up and around his lips. 'I can't imagine you *not* enjoying sex.'

'Can't you?'

'No. You're good. Too good.'

She sat up and shook him by the hand with mock formality. 'Thank you, kind sir. And likewise, if I may add, you're very good to me.'

'You mean we'll soon hate each other?'

'Ssh.' She plummeted to kiss him.

'It's your own theory, isn't it? You told me in Athens. You hate Savas for being good to you.'

'He's a genuinely good man. That kind of goodwill not only makes you but also makes you *feel* more dishonest.'

'Is that why you're trying to hurt him?'

'I don't know. I get high on hurting him. I discovered it quite early on. And, what's more, I found that, in some strange way, he enjoyed being hurt. So I perfected the technique. I told him about sex with other men. And I keep feeding him with dreamt-up and true confessions.'

'Will you tell him about us?'

'What do you think?'

'I have no idea.'

'Would it matter to you?'

'No.' Bucken said it a little more loudly than he had intended because he knew it was a lie. Her confession would matter a lot. It could cost him his job with Savas – the job on which he had staked the success of playing dummy.

Once again, she read at least some of his thoughts. 'Don't worry. He wouldn't fire you even if he knew about us. His pride wouldn't allow him to take such cheap revenge. Besides, he'd rather enjoy my little tale about you and me in bed.'

'But isn't there something wrong with your logic? I mean if you really hate him, shouldn't you do and tell him things he dislikes?'

She glared at him.

151

'You haven't answered.'

'You think I must have an answer to everything?'

'Perhaps not.'

'It's a woman's privilege.' She seemed upset. And she was working up more steam. 'You're too goddamn logical anyway.'

Bucken laughed. First it was just a chuckle. Then it burst out.

'What's so funny?'

'I think I have news for you, Greta.' He kissed her. It was just a peck on the cheek. 'I think you're in love with him.'

'Me? With my husband?'

'Yes, a little. In some odd way.'

'You must be out of your mind.'

'Maybe.'

'It's rubbish. Utter rubbish. You don't understand me at all.'

'I never claimed I did.'

'Then stop accusing me.'

'Love, especially marital love, is not a crime.'

'But it's not true. All right, perhaps I pity him. A little.'

'Why?'

'All sorts of things. He's getting old. His machismo and virility don't match up any more. You want to know something? I used to charge him for making love to me. Don't you think he deserves all the pity he can get?'

'Not from those who really hate him.' Bucken was certain about that. For if Savas was involved with Sergeant Spire's death in any way, he would neither deserve nor enjoy any pity from him.

'You'll understand it better when you also learn to hate him. At the moment, all you can see is that he likes you, that he doesn't care how or why you messed up your life as a cop, and that he's good to you. But one day. . . '

"One day, yes, maybe I'll hate him. But I won't pity him. Because I won't need pity or any other sham emotion to cover up feelings like you. He's. . . '

She sealed his lips with a long-nailed finger. 'I don't want to talk about him.' Abruptly, she turned her back on him. 'And I don't want to talk.' Her voice was sleepy.

Bucken lay still and let her be. He remembered their first meeting in Athens. Their night at the party aboard the yacht. Their talks. Their touches. How warm she could be. How vicious she was. No, likeable she was not. But it would not be too difficult to fall in love with her. Love? Certainly not the sort he still reserved for Sarah. And not even the sort he knew he could feel one day for Papeete.

Greta stirred, but her breathing remained deep and even. She

152

must be asleep, Bucken thought. In a few minutes, he would risk leaving her bed to see if he could find the Oldman's Gladstone bag in the study. But, just as abruptly as she had turned her back on him, she rolled over to face him. She flung one leg across him, half straddling him, and covered his chest with darting tongue and kisses.

'I want you to love me,' she whispered. 'Make me whimper and cry . . . You almost made me scream before. Do it again. I want you to make me scream so loud that the whole of Rotterdam can hear it. . . '

The whole of Rotterdam – and mostly Savas, thought Bucken, before he blanked out everything cerebral, abandoned himself to Greta, closed his eyes, and imagined she was Papeete.

Bucken was dispatched to Zurich with great urgency but little to do apart from surrendering to the lure of the good life and holding the fort at the anaemic Fiskal office. For a man who had built all his life on taking the initiative, it was depressing to play the clay pigeon of no free will, circling the horizon, waiting, waiting for anyone to take a shot at him, hoping that, when it did happen, the shattered fragments left of him would crash on the killer's head.

He had no doubt that he was at risk and the explosion could come at any moment. In his blackest moods, he willed it to come whatever the consequences. He knew that he was being tailed again, but this time it was easy to identify the two-man team and lose the bunglers at will. Bunglers? No, they were meant to be seen. They were a constant warning rather than a threat. The question was: who had assigned them? Suspicious Ruzicki or jealous Savas?

Bucken kept regular hours at the Fiskal office so as not to miss any snippet of information he could glean from letters, queries, phone calls and telexes. Some of them came from household names in shipping and international trade. It was impossible to tell whether they were villains or potential victims. When once Boothy-Graffoe telephoned, the temptation was almost irresistible to tell him that the Mr. Booker in Zurich was none other than Chief Superintendent Bucken alias Warman, and to warn him that Fiskal and the whole Savas outfit were crooked, never to be touched except by the robot arms of the law if criminal contamination was to be avoided.

Savas called in frequently from New York, Singapore, Surabaja and Rotterdam. On his instructions, Bucken transferred large sums of money from his Zurich account to the Narodny in Singapore and back as if Fiskal was a very active organisation indeed, engaged in a major deal with the Ivory Coast. Bucken asked Savas for more work,

153

claiming that his talents and eagerness were under-utilised. 'Enjoy yourself, it won't be long now,' Savas assured him. 'We'll soon meet somewhere, and you'll have plenty to do.' He paused, then added, trying but failing to sound jocular: 'And Bucken . . . take care. Don't disappoint me. I mean don't do anything I wouldn't do.'

Making love to Greta would presumably not come into that category, thought Bucken, when she turned up at the hotel unexpectedly. She appeared to be a woman in love and, although the last thing Bucken wanted was any such complication, she had brought a welcome spot of warmth to rainswept, *nasskalt* Zurich.

She was bubbling with excitement. 'What do you want first? The good news or the bad news?' Before he could answer, she blurted out both in one go. 'The good news is that my beloved husband is still somewhere in the Far East, and the bad news is that you're being followed.'

'By whom? Why? And how do you know?'

'That's not very gallant of you. You should have kissed me first for the good news. We have a few days to ourselves.'

'Not if I'm being watched. Have you . . . have you told your husband about us?'

'Perhaps.' She kissed him. 'But perhaps not. Anyway, they can't watch us in bed.'

'Then why did you warn me? And how do you know about the tail?'

'I can't answer all your questions. But I can tell you to watch out because those two are nasty thugs, and that I know for sure even though I can't tell you how come I know.'

For five glorious days, Bucken's time was shared out, rather unevenly, between Greta's bed and Fiskal's telex machine. She shed most of her provocative flippancy, and wanted to find out as much as he would tell about himself, but the more she asked the less he was willing to give. He could sense she was looking for someone to admire just when he would have liked to relax, lay himself open to injury, indulge in self-mocking self-pity, regurgitate mistakes and lost battles, and confess his tormenting doubt in his own abilities. But Greta was in search of a hero as much as Papeete had searched for someone to share her sadness and laughter in Cairo. The conflict was resolved with ease: Bucken was not ashamed to admit to himself that his massive vanity would make him give what she wanted. He spoke about battles he had won, lives he had saved and the moments when he could laugh his fears and doubts away as if they did not exist.

'You've never said you loved me,' she said during their second dawn.

154

'You've never asked.'

'Do you have to be asked?'

'Are you asking?'

She lit one of her occasional slim cigarillos, inhaled, exhaled, and only then did she say, 'No. We're adults, aren't we?'

Twice each day he told himself, cool it, don't let it go too far. Yet every time, he decided to give it just one more day. He would be a fool to reject Greta, who was willing to enjoy everything he could offer.

On the sixth morning, waiting for Greta at the breakfast table – they always came down separately and he always greeted her with some formality for the benefit of the tails – Bucken heard a familiar voice:

'May I join you?'

He spun round. It was Papeete. 'Of course. Hello. And of course again.'

Before they could sit down, Greta appeared. After a few polite exchanges, Papeete announced that Savas would arrive late that night. 'I need to talk to you during the day,' she told Bucken and turned to Greta: 'It's some boring business, darling.'

'Just don't ask me to join in and listen,' said Greta, 'I never compete with anyone for the duller moments of life.'

Bucken suggested they talk at Fiskal, but Papeete refused to go there. So you know that there's something fishy about Fiskal and you don't want to show your face there, thought Bucken.

'How about my room? You choose the time.' Papeete sounded light and businesslike.

'Surely that's the most convenient,' Greta volunteered. 'Do your business now, and we could meet again for lunch.'

Papeete's room was on the same floor as Bucken's. She unlocked Quincey's briefcase and produced a large sheaf of papers. 'You know that on paper you're going to buy a ship for Ruzicki, don't you?'

'So I'm told but I haven't done anything about it.'

'There's no need to. Everything is arranged and all the documents are here. I'll show you what to sign and where. Then you can go to your bank. You'll find that finance has also been arranged. Completion of the deal in Singapore next week. Any questions?'

'Yes. Are you well?'

'Yes, thank you. Any other questions?'

'Yes. Did you think in Cairo that our unborn tomorrow would bring us together in business?'

There was only the slightest hesitation before she said, 'No, but the beauty of the future is that it can bring anything.'

'And the beauty of the cliché is that it can deal with any unexpected question. Where do I sign, boss?' He almost gave himself away when he saw the name of the ship: the *Rose of Stambul*. 'Mm. What a romantic vessel. Is she pink?'

'I don't know. She had a major refit and certification – perhaps they'll let you specify the colour.'

'I'd enjoy that.' He reached for the papers and, accidentally, touched her fingers. She recoiled and snatched her hand away. 'I'm sorry,' he said softly, 'I'd like to, but I didn't mean to rape you.'

'You want to see what you're signing.'

'May I?'

'But of course. It's *your* ship for *your* money.' Her voice was as cosy as the November draught in a derelict house. Yet she hated her role and the whole procedure. She wished they had never met in Cairo. On second thoughts, she wished they had never met. She also wished she was sure about that.

Yes, all the papers seemed to be in order. Bucken – or, rather, Mr. Booker of Fiskal – was to buy the *Rose*. The vendor was Caryatides Shipping, Freemantle had been right. Would he discover that Fiskal was going to be the new owner? The Memorandum of Agreement was the Norwegian Shipbrokers' standard form 'for sale and purchase of ships. Adopted by the Baltic and International Maritime Conference. . . Revised 1966. . . Layout 1974.'

'It's a snip,' said Bucken. 'A fine ship of 6,200 tons deadweight at $300,000? It's a gift.'

'She needed a great deal of work done.'

'And that's included in the price? Amazing.'

'Look, you can do your bedtime reading later. Shall we get on with it?'

'Sure, sure, I'm just rejoicing. Who do I thank for my good luck?'

He noted that the *Rose* was to be re-registered yet again, this time in Singapore with Panama. Fiskal already had a Panamanian company to its name, and that qualified Mr. Booker for owning a ship under that flag, no questions asked. A temporary Certificate of Classification testified that the *Rose of Stambul* had passed all required inspections in the Somalian port of Mogadishu. The date and signature on it were only a week old. Even if the certificate was a fake or bought from some corrupt inspector, there must be some trace of the ship in Mogadishu. Freemantle could investigate.

'Look, I'm sure you'll find everything in order.' She was growing impatient.

'I have no doubt about that.' His eyes fell on the current Crew Roll Agreement, signed as a contract between the Master of the ship and

156

each member of the crew, in the presence of a Panamanian consul. Bucken noticed that most of the crew were described as YB which stood for 'yellow complexion, black hair'. The name of the first mate was Ting-chao. The man in Macao. The man who must have something to do with Sergeant Spire's death. Shock and fury were too potent a mixture to be kept off his face.

'Anything wrong?'

'No, no.' He knew he sounded too eager. 'It's fine. Really.' And then, as casually as he could, he asked if the purchase of the *Rose* had anything to do with the Ivory Coast deal.

'No, nothing at all. This is. . . ' She stopped, she had already said more than she was supposed to. Why had he asked that question? 'I'm helping Ruzicki. That's all. Nothing to do with Oldman Savas.'

His face was taut now, under control. He had only wanted to find out whether she was a mere messenger or someone familiar with the fraud in hand. And now he knew.

She stood up, walked to the window and stared out, complimenting the fine view of the lake, to gain time and compose herself. She wondered if it was the low price of the ship that had prompted his questions. She knew that Ruzicki had paid $160,000 for the wreck and local 'goodwill' in Abu Dhabi; his Australian company resold it to some Indian scrap dealer for forty thousand less but kept the documents; then 'sold' the already scrapped *Rose* on paper to Caryatides, the Greek company that would finance Bucken to buy its ship. She turned back. 'Look, there's no problem. A hundred thousand has been deposited for this purpose on your Swiss account. On the strength of that, the bank will be only too glad to advance the rest of the price.'

'I know They just love mortgaging ships, don't they? I mean it's real estate afloat.'

Suddenly she understood his apparent delaying tactics. Her face and posture stiffened. 'I see.'

'What?'

'You're right. I'm sorry. I should have told you in the first place that you'll get paid extra for this service. The day the papers are through, and it won't take long, I can assure you, you'll get fifteen.'

'Thousand?'

'Yes.'

'Dollars?'

'Yes, and I'm not authorised to haggle with you. But you'll make quite a bit of extra because a London broker is already trying to fix your ship for you. It may be a voyage or time charter, we'll see. Busi-

157

ness is not too good at the Baltic at the moment, so it shouldn't be much of a problem.'

'I'm not worried. You're so efficient that I'm sure you've already fixed a full cargo of fertilizers for my *Rose*.'

Ready to sign, Bucken pulled the papers closer. Papeete's hand came down and held his. He looked up. Her cold business face had slipped, her eyes were a little misty as they had been in Cairo. Her voice shrank to a whisper: 'You don't *have* to sign, you know. . .'

'I know, I could refuse to. But Booker couldn't. And you know it. Because, at the rate you're offering, I can't afford not to sign.' He reached for her hand to remove it. Her grip tightened. The old scars on his wrist reddened. She stared at them, then her fingers slipped away.

'I'm thirsty,' she said, and gestured towards a bottle in the ice bucket.

Bucken opened the champagne with the ease of his newly-learned skill. I could get used to this, he thought, drinking bubbly as a morning refreshment.

'What's that?' she asked about the scars.

'Plastic surgery.'

'How come?'

Only a few days earlier, Greta had asked about them, and he had lied to her – 'As a young cop, I saved a man from a fire' – giving Greta the hero she longed for. Now he said nothing. Then he changed his mind and told the truth. As a young detective he had tracked a suspected con-man to a seemingly deserted house. Then he saw smoke coming through an upstairs window. The man was busy burning all the incriminating evidence, and in his hurry set fire to the house. He was trapped and overcome by smoke.

'And you went in to save him?'

'That's one way of putting it.'

'What other way is there?'

'If you want to know the truth, I'll have to disappoint you. I couldn't care less about saving his life. I was young and keen and ambitious. I wanted my villain. I wanted my conviction. In open court. With a compliment from the judge.' His laugh sounded bitter.

'Did you get it?'

He shook his head. 'A clever lawyer got him off the hook. There was even a half-suggestion that police harassment might have been responsible for the fire. And my sergeant told me that next time, if I wanted justice, I must let them burn in hell.'

She touched the scars, then drank and held out her glass to be refilled.

158

'Don't get drunk, please.'

'Why?'

'Your drunkenness has already robbed me once of your company. In Cairo.' He poured. 'You may not remember.'

'I do. You robbed yourself. I wasn't drunk in Cairo.'

'You could have fooled me.'

'I did.'

'Why?'

'I don't want to talk about it.' She gulped down her drink and poured herself another.

'Pity.'

'Yes. Perhaps.'

'But why? Why did you pretend?'

'You really want the truth?'

'Please.'

'All right, a truth for a truth. I needed an excuse. Such as being drunk. To explain my weakness to myself.'

'Weakness?'

'Yes. Of wanting you. I wanted you that night more than any man since I was sixteen.' She stepped back as if to increase the safe distance between them. She sadly shook her head to prevent him from saying anything. 'This was silly, I mean to tell you, wasn't it?'

'Far from it.'

'You're wrong. Because I won't sleep with you. Not as long as I'm married. And I'll never divorce a helpless cripple. So let's keep away from each other, shall we?' And after a pause: 'Please.'

Bucken watched her, then nodded and walked back to the table. He signed and stamped 'Fiskal' the purchase documents of the *Rose of Stambul*.

'I believe you'll soon be going to Singapore. You can complete the deal and register the ship under the Panamanian flag over there.'

That afternoon, before Bucken went to meet Savas at the airport, Greta visited him.

'You want to come with me?'

'Only as far as the bed to say goodbye. At least until we meet again. Unless the long *business* session with Papeete has blunted your appetite.'

The phone rang and she picked it up angrily. 'Yes. . . yes. . . Hang on. . . ' She turned to Bucken: 'Do you know a John Free-mantle?'

'Oh, yes, some reporter. What the hell does he want?' Bucken took the phone. 'Listen, I haven't got time now to talk to you, but I'll ring you when I'm free. Are you in your office?. . . Oh. . . Okay, stay put.'

He did not feel like getting rid of Greta so quickly, and it was not easy. But it had to be done. He called Freemantle from a public phone booth.

'Good to hear you, Bucken. Sorry about the telephonus interruptus.'

'Just come to the point, please. I must rush.'

'Can't blame you, guv. Doesn't she sound sexy?'

'Why did you call?'

'Oyouru. He's the Deputy Minister of Trade for the Ivory Coast. I've also identified all the names on your list. Mercenaries. All of them. My informer says they'd run invasions, assassination squads, courses for terrorists, you name it, but nothing in South America where they have their sanctuary. You want the names?' He dictated them slowly, and Bucken made mental notes. 'Can you tell me what it's all about, guv?'

'Not now.'

'A hint?'

'The hint is that, one day, it may give you the story of a lifetime. But I can't promise you'll live long enough.'

'Great. I've always loved working for no pay in the dark without a hope.'

'Then you could also do something else for me. I must find out where the *Rose of Stambul* is. She was in Mogadishu about a week ago. She may still be there.'

'Got it.'

'And do me a favour, next time you call and somebody else answers, call yourself something else.'

'Ten-four. This is Mr. Something Else signing off. Over and out.'

Bucken went to the Fiskal office. There was only one telex message waiting for him, an inquiry from London about the *Rose of Stambul*. He nodded in acknowledgement of such efficiency. 'Can fix Rose of S. for 4000 tons lawful general cargo, f.i.o, single voyage Kiel to Helsinki, provided load ready 30th inst. Adapted Gencon Charter Party. 5% commission required. Charterer would agree freight on lump-sum basis. Confirm date availability, min/max seaspeed, precise dimensions of holds, hatches and deck space.'

Bucken tried to recall the meaning of some terms he had learned from Boothy-Graffoe at the Baltic. 'Lump-sum basis' seemed significant. The would-be charterer must know the tonnage capacity of the *Rose* but, irrespective of the weight of his 'general cargo', he wanted the ship on lump-sum basis – all to himself, paying for the full 6200

160

tons rather than sharing the spare capacity with any other shipper. Why? Is the cargo of special value? Or is it a confidential shipment? Or has somebody got some ulterior motive? No, the charterer would not know that. But there must be a reason, otherwise the normal practice would be to 'cut the size of the ship', at least on paper, in order to pay only for the tonnage used.

f.i.o. – free in and out – would not be significant, but viewed in the light of the 'dead freight' option it could imply that the merchant might want the cargo handled at both ends by his own, specially approved stevedores. More indication of confidentiality?

The interest in the various dimensions pointed at large pieces of cargo. Something like machinery. That and Ting-chao's presence on the *Rose* reminded Bucken of the *Alida II*. That ill-fated ship had carried some bulky items of electronic equipment. The memory boosted the flow of adrenalin. Kiel, 30th inst. We've got a date, mate, he thought, whatever happens, I'll be there.

Only now did he look at the signature: Mayor & Heppelstein. Boothy-Graffoe's chartered shipbroking company at the Baltic. In return for a warning that he was dealing with crooks, he would surely help either Bucken or Warman,the Australian scribe, to identify the shippers and the shipment. Bucken decided to contact him at the first suitable opportunity. He pocketed the telex, and took a cab to welcome Oldman Savas at the airport. He watched the inept minders on his tail all the way.

Savas was in an exuberant mood. Things were going well for him. No, he did not mind in the least that Bucken was also doing some work for Ruzicki. 'In a couple of weeks, you'll be quite rich, greaser,' he laughed, 'and my own contribution will be at least fifty thou.' He was pleased to see how deeply Bucken was impressed.

'Fifty? For what?'

'Your loyalty, above all. Because I knew from Ruzicki that you were doing something for him, and I appreciate it that you weren't trying to do things behind my back.'

Over a lavish dinner in the old-fashioned elegance of the Hotel Eden au Lac, Bucken heard that in a few days he would have to go to Singapore and conduct some transaction at the Narodny. 'It's simple and straightforward, but your security is paramount. You'll get the details in Singapore, and I must warn you: it'll be your final test. Don't mess it up. You could go a long way with me, Bucken, and so far you're doing just fine. You're up to expectations . . . in every respect.'

Was that a reference to Greta, too? Bucken had no time to dwell on the thought. He would need some urgent advice, probably from

161

Ashenbury, before going to Singapore. He could give his tail the slip yet again, but if it was ever discovered where he went. . . Not worth the risk. 'If you don't need me for a day or so, I'd like to hop over to London. Some private matters to attend to,' he said with his man-to-man smile that was as good as a wink, heavy with sexual innuendo every time.

Savas was quick to read the message. He smiled: it would be interesting to see Greta's reaction when he mentioned it to her.

From a public phone at Heathrow airport, Bucken dialled Ashenbury's number. The secretary refused to interrupt a board meeting for him.

'It's very urgent. The name is Bucken.'

'I'm sorry, sir, your name doesn't appear on my list.'

Bucken slammed down the receiver and called his emergency number at the Yard.

'This is the Gardener from Bayswater. Give me Greenfingers.' He was connected promptly.

Obliging as ever, and understanding that Bucken would not want to come to the Big House, Dodd promised to pick him up at the Serpentine Gallery in Hyde Park. 'I'll drive a cab, so it won't matter even if you're followed. But I can't meet you in less than two hours.'

Bucken swallowed a few swear words. 'Can you arrange an urgent meeting for me with Ashenbury?'

Dodd promised to do his best.

Bucken called Boothy-Graffoe. 'This is Andrew Warman from Australia. And I'm in a bit of a hurry.'

'Does he know you, sir?'

'Of course, of course. I'm a journalist. I spent several days with him at the Baltic.'

'Well, I can try to contact him, sir, but he won't be back for a day or two from Rotterdam.'

'Rotterdam? What's he doing over there?'

'Just business, sir.'

Damn. There was nothing to be done but wait for Dodd. It gave Bucken a chance to have a look at his post and the state of his flat in Bayswater. But it turned out to be a sour experience. The brass frigate knocker had been torn off by vandals. Fuming, he opened the door to wade into a few letters and tons of unwanted junk mail. Only the musty smell of an unlived-in dump welcomed him home.

He opened all windows, made himself a cup of coffee – most cups were still dirty from the coffee he and Helen and perhaps Sarah had drunk months ago – began to read his letters, mostly from his bank . . . and hit the roof. Again and again, his manager wrote in a gradually sharpening tone, first to advise and warn him about his unauthorised and mounting overdraft, then to demand an explanation, and finally to inform him that his account would be frozen until full settlement of the debts. The statements revealed that none of his monthly pay cheques had been received during his absence. So, presumably, the bank would not have paid his bills either. He picked up the phone – and slammed it down. The line was dead.

By the time Bucken walked into Hyde Park, he felt reasonably certain that he was tailed by nothing except the rain. He was wearing his old, long trench-coat with the permanently upturned collar but got himself soaked to the bones running for shelter. When at long last Dodd turned up, cruising slowly in the opposite direction, Bucken crossed the road and hailed the elderly cab.

Dodd had, of course, an explanation for everything. No, he did not understand how the damaging rumours had spread about Bucken's alleged disgrace. 'As for the financial upheaval, well, I must apologise. Though it's not my fault. I couldn't have guessed that you wanted the bank to pay your bills. Your pay has not been stopped, of course not, but it's been diverted into a special Home Office Fund, gathering interest for you. And only because I had to protect you. If anybody, you must know how easy it is to gain access to somebody's financial status and bank account. So if they investigated your affairs for Savas, and we do know that they did, we wouldn't want them to find out that you were still on the payroll, would we? No, sir, we would not. Right?'

'Right,' said Bucken reluctantly. He hated the thought that he might have to be grateful to Dodd.

'For the same reason, it's been decided at the highest level that, temporarily, you should be reporting not to me but to Lord Ashenbury and a specially formed security committee.'

'What the hell. . . ?'

'Please, please let me explain. I can assure you that everything we've done is in your interest. Everybody appreciates what you're doing and what risks you're taking. Your investigation is vitally important, far beyond any retribution for Spire's death. So your security is paramount.'

The very words Savas had used, thought Bucken bitterly.

They changed cars in an underground parking lot from where two plain clothes policemen drove on in the cab to mislead anyone who might after all have followed Bucken.

163

'You look disappointed,' said Dodd.

'I am. That committee, any committee, must be an additional risk. There could be leaks.'

'Not in this case. The 128 Committee, yes, that's what it's called because it first met in room 128 in . . . well, somewhere in Whitehall, will not even know your identity. It'll be available to advise Ashenbury if and when necessary, and coordinate any action that might be required from various government departments at the highest, and I mean highest, level.'

'They could also drop me like any other hot potato from the highest level, if I became an embarrassment in any way. As long as they keep me at arm's length, they can disown me.'

'How can they? Maritime fraud is costing the world more than ten billion dollars a year, we reckon. You and Spire have convinced us that now there's even more at stake. Britain's shipping earnings have dropped by five hundred million pounds in the past three years. That's nearly fifty per cent. The UK fleet has shrunk from almost thirty to twenty million tons in the same period. We can't withstand any more losses. If there really is something big in the offing, we've got to stop it. We have no option.'

'But I have. I don't have to remain a volunteer for the gallows for ever.'

'No, that's true, but . . . well . . . you need all the goodwill you can get. I mean concocting your cover story prevented me from leaving anything on record. You know what I mean?'

'No, I don't. And I don't want to know. Because I detect a hint of blackmail in your voice. As if you really had something against me, as if I've really done something wrong or even illegal.'

'No,.no, of course you haven't. I know it and you know it, but nobody else, not even the 128 Committee, would know it. Anyway, I'm sure it would never come to that. You're a real cop. You'll go for your quarry wherever it takes you. And I know that you won't let Spire's killers get away with it.'

Bucken opened his mouth, then closed it without uttering a word. His eyes said it all.

'And talking about security,' Dodd smiled to indicate that the subject had been changed amicably, 'I'd advise you to settle your overdraft with the money you're getting from Savas. Where do you keep it? In some Swiss code account? Yum yum. Just don't tell me. I don't want to be a party to any such irregularity.'

Ashenbury's country house nestled among the Sussex hills, forming a natural part of a Gainsborough landscape. A pair of mountainous RAF-trained guard dogs made sure that the doors of Dodd's

164

car remained firmly closed until Price, Ashenbury's butler, reassured them that the visitors were not for mincing.

Dodd followed Price in awed silence to the library. The abundance of museum pieces and exotic indoor plants overwhelmed him. Even with the acres of space around him as he sat sunk into the belly of a leather armchair, he seemed to be all too conscious of his hands and feet that threatened to knock over the Hepplewhite writing desk, an early eighteenth-century reading chair, and a French snuff box collection. He left without waiting for tea.

Ashenbury listened to Bucken's report, not a word, not a hesitant pause would escape him. His interpretation of the clues confirmed Bucken's own. The Fiskal chain of companies existed only on paper, but the transfers of large sums from one account to another would create the impression of healthy trading, mostly for Narodny's benefit. The Ivory Coast minister's involvement with Savas indicated some massive deal with that country, probably an order worth several million dollars.

'Yes,' Ashenbury nodded, 'everything seems to fit. Savas is going to pull off a major documentary fraud. The papers you say you saw, the telexes and all that, give more than a hint that they're placing a vast order probably for a mixed bag of goods with Fiskal.

'Now the money. The routine procedure is that the buyer instructs his own bank to draw up a letter of credit for the full purchase price. A mutually acceptable bank, in this case the Narodny in Singapore, would receive the letter of credit in favour of the vendor, I mean you and Fiskal, but the actual payment would be subject to various conditions. A list of documents would have to satisfy the bank that you actually owned the goods you were purportedly selling, show where and from whom you've bought them, certify that the goods were of an acceptable quality, and prove, above all, that everything according to contract has been loaded aboard a particular ship which would carry it to a port named by the buyer. But that's no problem. Invoices can be obtained, and Certified Bills of Lading are easy to forge. Standard forms can be purchased for a few pence. The vessel referred to in them may never have been near the alleged port of lading or may not even exist.'

'But isn't this where it *can* go sour and indeed *must* go sour?' Bucken burst out indignantly. 'I remember Boothy-Graffoe saying all this to me at the Baltic without a satisfactory explanation. I mean if the bank did no more than telephone Lloyd's to confirm the existence and whereabouts of the ship. . . ' He was stopped by Ashenbury's smile of indulgence. 'You mean you agree with Boothy-Graffoe?'

'I'm afraid so. Because he must have told you that banks do no such thing. They're not interested in ships and all that. They deal in documents. As long as the Letter of Credit is valid and the required papers are duly presented for an exchange, they pay. That's their job, not forgery detection. And the use of the Narodny shows that Savas is clever. Being a relative newcomer on the international banking scene, the Narodny must be even keener than the rest to please and provide an efficient service at speed. They'll probably sit on your documents for a day or two because formal checking of papers is regarded as good practice, but the chances are that they'll pay.'

'And the chances are that I could be caught, waiting in Singapore, during those two days.'

'That's right. That's what you're paid for. And, as Savas's front man, you have a perfect reason to take the risk. Fifty thousand reasons, to be precise, if I remember the figure correctly.'

Both men fell silent as Price entered with a tray and served them tea. Bucken walked to the French windows and stared out into the rain and black skies, trying to imagine how beautiful it all could look on a summer day, over a bowl of strawberries, with bees buzzing, and the aroma of fresh cream mingling with a distant whiff of hay. Behind him, Ashenbury must have placed something on the tray. The gentle tapping noise exploded into an imaginary gunshot shattering Bucken's summer dream: a clay pigeon in the skies had been mortally wounded.

'You could, of course, find some way to torpedo Savas's plan,' said Ashenbury, 'and for a policeman it would be the right thing to do, but then you'd never get to the bottom of it all. You'd save peanuts for some insurance company and the Ivory Coast, but you'd never find out what they're up to with the *Rose of Stambul* and what their ultimate big plan is.'

And I'd never trap Ting-chao and make him pay for Spire, thought Bucken. 'Incidentally,' he said, 'it's Mrs. Quincey who's doing the legwork for Ruzicki.' It was fun to watch Ashenbury's stunned reaction. His Lordship had lied to Bucken, he had denied contacting the Quinceys by cable in Athens, so now it was only right to let him stew. 'She'll also come to Singapore, I believe.'

'Any idea where she'll be staying?'

'Raffles. Not the best these days, I'm told, but still Savas's favourite. We'll all stay there.'

'Thanks.'

'With due respect, sir, I don't think there's any point in trying to help the Quinceys any more. They must be too deeply involved to turn back.'

166

'I appreciate your views.'

'And it is through them that I'm hoping to get to the other conspirators. I have a feeling that we may get a shock or two in the process. I've called, for instance, Boothy-Graffoe only to be told that he's in Rotterdam at precisely the same time as Savas.'

'I don't see anything in that,' said Ashenbury. 'Knowing a little about his wide business interests I'd expect him to go there regularly. Not that that would rule out anything either way. If you have a suspicious gut reaction, perhaps you ought to leave him alone until you find something truly ominous.'

'Would you regard it as ominous that he wants to charter the *Rose?*'

'No. If I were planning some mischief, I'd try to use the most reputable brokers as unwitting partners. Mayor & Heppelstein would be perfect. Everybody deals with them. It would help to create the right image for insurance, etcetera. The only oddity is that if the *Rose* is a replica of the *Alida II* operation, it's not very clever of them to proceed along the same lines and use the same sort of dupes.'

'On the contrary, sir. Villains remain villains whatever level they operate on. They just love to plagiarise themselves in the hope that, if it worked once, it'll work again.'

'Good, then we'll let them get on with it.'

'You mean we'll condone yet another criminal act?'

'Only if there's no other way to uncover and stop Savas's final plans. More tea, Bucken?'

'No, thanks. The *Rose*. . . '

'Try the cake. It's my cook's speciality and she'll never forgive you for not tasting it.'

'The *Rose* could take us to Spire's killers.'

'Let's hope it will. But we can't risk your life. Not at this stage. So just go to Singapore and stay alive, whatever it takes, whatever mischief it involves you in.'

'Talking about mischief,' Bucken recalled Quincey's files in Athens. 'If you were planning something, what would you do with a chemical tanker?'

'Mm. Hold it to ransom?'

'Is the cargo valuable enough?'

'Could be.' Ashenbury thought for a few seconds. 'But the ship is the real value, I'd say. These are purpose-built, very modern ships with special tanks for all sorts of dangerous, corrosive or even explosive substances.'

'Thank you, sir. You've given me an idea.'

'What's that?'

167

'Just an idea. Something to look for.' It was pointless mentioning the mercenaries at this stage. But, if they were employed, and the cargo of such a ship could cause a vast amount of pollution to a beach or an entire coastline around an enclosed sea area like the Mediterranean, even whole countries could be held to ransom. Would that be a big enough target for Savas? Quincey's tanker file was clipped with data on Suez. Was that a coincidence or could there be a connection?

'If you need some advice or even help, do not hesitate to contact me day or night, Bucken. Use your emergency routine with the Yard, and they'll trace me wherever I am. And I hope that Dodd's made it clear what tremendous backing you're going to enjoy through our new ad hoc committee.'

Outside the French window the ferocious pair of dogs made a brief guest appearance. Bucken wondered if they were members of the 128 committee.

The table had been laid for lunch by the time the Quinceys returned from the conference. All the way back to the Eurovista, Papeete listened patiently to her husband's diatribes: Savas was a selfish old fool who had rushed through the meeting to catch his plane to Singapore; Ruzicki was a mindless murderer and not much good even at that; most of the partners lacked vision and initiative; Boothy-Graffoe could not see beyond his bean of a nose and would sell his mother for a fiver if he could pocket it now rather than wait for a million tomorrow. Papeete opened the door and eased the wheelchair through the gap, scraping the frame.

'And you? What about you? You can sulk all right, you're the queen of sulking, but what else? You're no good even at pushing this goddamn chair.'

Papeete positioned the chair at the table only to provoke yet another outburst.

'Don't you know anything at all? Can't you ever learn that I hate facing the window?'

She shifted the chairs to make room for his.

'All right, let's have it. You've maintained that sullen silence long enough. What's ailing you?'

'Well, if you must know, I'm disappointed.'

'Oh, really?'

'Yes. You've always said that you'd make up for all your losses, that you'd hit back and take your revenge, but you'd do it all by using your brains, not violence. And what do we have now? More and more of the physical stuff.'

168

'You haven't been asked to do anything *physical*, have you? You don't even have to fuck me these days. That should be a relief.'

'You know very well what I'm talking about.'

'And I'm talking about fucking. Come to think of it, you've developed your squeamishness only since your London visit. What happened in London? Have you fucked dear old Ashenbury?'

Papeete took a deep breath and examined the drinks trolley. There was some rum. White, virginal and tempting. As an act of defiance to her thought about Bucken, she poured herself a very large gin and tonic.

'You haven't asked if I wanted a drink.'

'You know it's bad for you.'

'And you care, do you? Well, don't worry. You won't be poor as a widow. Or perhaps you don't want to wait. You could be rich now if you returned to your decrepit ex-lover. But is he an ex-lover? Tell me.'

'You know very well that you'll call it a lie whatever I tell you. So try to believe just one thing. Your revenge is my revenge, too. Ashenbury might well have been one of those who ruined you. So I'll stay, and help you, and wheel you about, and do what I'm told to do, until you succeed. I'll stay at least to that day.'

'And then?'

'Then we'll think about it.'

'All right. But tell me something now. What was his hold over you? He's older than your father. Was he so special in bed? Was it sex that bound you to him for all those years?'

'It was an affair. You know it was. And that's that.'

'Some affair it must have been if it managed to spoil your appetite for sex for life. Or was it only me who could never come up to the high standard set by his Lordship?'

Boothy-Graffoe's arrival silenced him. Papeete offered him a drink, but the impish tycoon wanted only 'Jewish champagne'.

'What kind?' Papeete asked. 'We have some château-bottled Perrier and vintage Alka Seltzer.'

'I'll settle for the nectar of your company,' he beamed up at her, and wondered enviously if the gossip was true that she had once been Ashenbury's mistress.

You pathetic creep, thought Papeete, and said 'thank you' engagingly.

He held the chair for her but Quincey intervened: 'She's not lunching with us.' Noticing Boothy-Graffoe's glance towards the table set for three, he gestured vaguely: 'A mistake. Little girls are not meant to sit through serious business. Hop along, darling, play with your things.'

169

Boothy-Graffoe's entire head blushed. Redness shone through in fine stripes where his white mane was thinning. Quincey's crudity upset him but he had been a bridge player long enough to know better than to come between warring spouses. He kept his potentially scathing remarks to himself and waited for Papeete's reaction. To his astonishment, it was only one word: 'Yipeee.' Her voice was wooden, her face a death mask, revealing none of her feelings.

She had been slapped or worse, and it hurt. Yet she was not entirely displeased. As she turned to leave, she thought hard but knew she might never be sure about herself. Was she experiencing the joy of masochism? Did it make her self-imposed loyalty taste sweeter? As soon as the door had closed behind her, Quincey changed the subject. 'I'm sorry that the vote went against you,' he commiserated with Boothy-Graffoe, but his voice betrayed him.

'How would you know that it was against *me*?'

'I guessed it must be you on Screen Two. It's you who has perhaps the greatest though undisclosed insurance interest among us.'

'And I still believe that a rocket attack on something like a chemical tanker would be the best for all of us. That's what would create the biggest panic. And yes, among other things, panic would have an instant effect on insurance rates. It could mean anything up to an extra fifty million takings in a few weeks.'

'Don't worry. There'll be a big enough panic to serve your purpose and keep the Canal blocked for some time. But from now on, you really mustn't stay away or be late at the meetings of the syndicate.'

'Fair enough.'

They paused while lunch was served, but Boothy-Graffoe pushed his plate away after the first few bites. Quincey's rudeness to his wife had put him off his food – no mean achievement – and he wanted to get through the business and leave as soon as possible. 'Listen, Don, I'm a bit concerned about this *Rose of Stambul* deal.'

'Why?'

'Is it once again. . . I mean is she going to carry some politically sensitive electronic stuff?'

'That shouldn't concern you, not at all. We have a new company in Helsinki and an office in Kiel, Ruzicki has a large order, and Savas's frontman in Zurich owns the ship. All you have to do is to get the ship on a single voyage charter.'

'I've already made the approach to this Fiskal and Kommercial in Zurich.'

'Good. Any problems?' Quincey was fed up with the man's belly-aching.

'No, not really. This man, Booker, seems quite an efficient fellow.'

'I'm glad to hear that. We'll want him to do the fronting for us in Kiel, too, if all goes well.'

'What's the value of the cargo?'

'Thirty, maybe forty million. But if you're thinking about insurance – don't.'

'I understand.'

'Nothing to be underwritten by any syndicate in which you have an interest.' Quincey grinned. 'Who knows? They may have to foot a pretty hefty bill.'

'Sad.' They both grinned this time.

'Was that your problem?'

'No.' Boothy-Graffoe drummed on his left palm. 'It's just that I was wondering. I mean, well. Our get-togethers are a risk. And I'm anxious that we should reach the final stage of "Tsunami" safely and without any delays.'

'What's the hurry?'

'I don't know. Gut reaction, I guess.'

'Gut reaction to what?'

'Just . . . just something in the air in the City. People drop odd remarks, I mean remarks that seem to me odd, about Savas. Some members at the Baltic seem to shun Ruzicki. Perhaps he ought to visit less frequently. Then there's a growing interest in and talk about maritime fraud. It's all very vague, you understand, but it's there. A few months ago I was asked to help and brief some Australian journalist on shipping matters. He seemed keen to hear about fraud.'

'It's good copy, isn't it?'

'It is – if it's ever written. But I haven't seen anything yet. He promised to send me his articles but instead he turned up in London again. My office has just told me that he wanted me urgently. And he sounded surprised that I was in Rotterdam. I've already tried, but I can't trace what paper he works for. I could go back, of course, to the man who gave him the introduction, but I don't want to make a fuss.'

'Okay, what's the guy's name?'

'Andrew Warman. A freelance from Sydney, I believe.'

'We'll check him out.'

'Thanks. I mean just to be on the safe side. We don't want to take risks, do we?'

'No.' Like hell we don't, thought Quincey. How else does one make a fortune from nothing? For Boothy-Graffoe, it was, of course, different. He was a very rich man. He could afford not to take risks. And it was nothing but his naked greed that had brought him into 'Tsunami'.

171

One of Ashenbury's Bentleys took Bucken to the Memories of China where he intended to give Freemantle a no-expense-spared lunch: he knew that the journalist was partial to Chinese food, and it was Savas who would pay for it. Freemantle seemed irritated despite the prospect. He cursed his editor. 'Wish I could chuck it all in, start all over again, join the police, and keep flying to lovely places like some,' he grumbled.

'How's the wife?' asked Bucken to change the subject while ordering their meal.

'I'm not married,' said Freemantle primly.

'You're a fool, John, you're having the worst of both worlds. What's the fun in being unfaithful if you haven't made any vows in the first place?'

'What's the fun in playing the field if you keep marrying the same lass every time?'

'Nice backhand, John, love fifteen.' Bucken tried to blot out the surging memory of Sarah's last visit. He rummaged in his travel bag and pulled out a neat little packet, containing a Thai silk scarf. 'It's for the girl with the longest pair of pins in Fleet Street, whoever she may be.'

'Thanks. She loves you, too.' The wrapper said 'Singapore'. Freemantle was pleased that Bucken had thought about his Ada Tansley. 'Very thoughtful of you.'

Bucken knew he ought to blush but he did not know how: his stock of 'thoughtful' presents were assigned only on the spur of the moment.

'I think I've got something for you,' said Freemantle. 'That *Rose of Stambul* you were interested in had a rather colourful life story. She was bought, sold and bought again and again several times over the years. My contact's guess is that the owner was always the same or the same family under different names and flags. She was used in all sorts of devious ways and eventually, as I've already told you, she was abandoned with an unpaid crew and all that. Abu Dhabi decided to arrest her in lieu of port charges, the crew tried to run for it – and ran her aground.'

'How do you know?'

'She was offered for sale as scrap.' The journalist produced a crumpled sheet. 'Sale and purchase boys tried to handle her but for two years there were no takers. The *Rose* needed costly refloating and wasn't worth it at demolition rates.'

Try trading/demo offers. . . said the computer print-out the sale and purchase agent had circulated in vain round the world. On the margin, Freemantle had scrawled in red: *scrap rate cca $100 at the time. Tankers easier to cut up, better value per ton lightweight, no wonder no takers*. 'But suddenly,' Freemantle announced with professional pride, 'there was an upsurge of interest, according to a chum of mine. An Australian company bought the wreck and resold it promptly to a company called Caryatides. Then the track goes cold, but I wouldn't be surprised if she was sold again.'

Bucken was tempted to say that Freemantle was now enjoying the latest owner's company. He checked the urge, but he knew it would have pleased him enormously to get a little admiration. 'Perhaps somebody's found a way to refloat the *Rose* cheaply.'

'Must be a bright bloke, much brighter than you or me, Bucken, to find any use for her. She was no Rose even by Abu Dhabi standards.'

'Why? She was re-fitted and re-certified in Mogadishu.'

'Like hell she was. As far as my best contacts can ascertain, she's never been to Mogadishu. Certainly not in the last few months and certainly not in her own name.'

So the new temporary Certificate of Classification, the proof of sea-worthiness, issued allegedly in that port, must either be a fake or the work of some corrupt inspector, thought Bucken. He felt grateful to Freemantle, and told the headwaiter to bring them the best wine the house had in stock.

'What's wrong with you?' asked Ruzicki, the connoisseur of fear and worried faces.

'Nothing,' said Savas, it's just that I've got a plane to catch.' It was none of Ruzicki's business that in the last twenty-four hours every-body, just everybody, seemed to want money from Oldman Savas. To help them all as he wished to, he had had to stretch his credit to the limit and beyond. In New York, his companies were under a take-over attack by an asset-stripper. His Greeks up and down the East Coast were being forced to play dodgems with creditors and bailiffs though if only they could survive a few more months until the completion of jobs in hand. . . The usual story. There was trouble in Greece, too. His grandfather's village had been flooded and the fourth-generation baker-cum-ship-manning-agent had telephoned for help. Yes, the house to attract the new doctor had been built, everybody was grateful to Oldman Savas, but that was history. This time the village needed some real cash.

Walking through the sea of colours that formed the park surrounding Rotterdam's Euromast, Ruzicki let Savas stew in his worries for a while. Then he decided to be charitable for once. 'You want some good news, Oldman?'

'Please.'

'Your man Bucken seems okay.'

'What do you mean?'

'We had him checked out.'

'What? Again?'

'Only a bit more thoroughly. You may trust your vibes, but if I want to use him with the *Rose of Stambul* deal, I must be sure. Officially, he hasn't been sacked by the police, but his pay has been stopped. He's in trouble at his bank in London.'

Savas was pleased. He did not ask how Ruzicki had broken through banking secrecy – he knew. Computerisation had made it easy for everyone.

'How's your deal going?'

'It's signed and sealed. It'll provide me with sufficient funds for Suez.'

'I'm glad. Bucken told me that you'll want to use him for something more than just buying the ship.'

'He looks plausible, and he has the hard, honest features we need to front for us, I mean for me, in Kiel. If he comes through the Singapore test, that is.'

'I hope he will.'

'That's not good enough. He must be watched and guarded day and night. The men will even have to share his bedroom until payday.'

'What if he objects to such nursing?'

'Then he'll have to be replaced. I mean permanently. Same goes if he wants to lose them this time.'

'You're crazy. Beyond a certain point, one must take a chance. He can wreck the scheme but he won't have evidence against any of us.'

'No chances. Not this time, Oldman.'

'In the final stage, he'll have to go and see the Narodny manager on his own. He could do anything he wanted behind closed doors.'

'Except that he won't go on his own. A big businessman like him will have his PA with him. To carry his papers and all that. You just warn him that the man will be armed.'

'Don't be ridiculous. You can't start shooting in the bank.'

'No shooting. Scout's honour. If Bucken tries anything, he'll suffer a rather painful and fatal heart attack.' Ruzicki stopped and pulled an old-fashioned fountain pen out of his breast pocket. He viewed it, weighed it affectionately for a few seconds. 'Who'd imagine that a

pen like this could write history? At close range it's lethal. Here. . . '
He held it out to Savas who shook his head and stepped back.
'It's. . . '

'I don't want to know.'

'But you must. It fires miniature darts that dissolve in the flesh.
The chemical they carry is a clever combination of *immobilon forte*
with which vets can even knock out elephants, and *tetraethyl lead*
which leaves no pathologic evidence after a sudden and most regrettable death.' They stood at an idyllic spot, where the lakeside path
widened into a neatly kept miniature garden. Savas was staring at the
pen as if hypnotised. He hardly noticed Ruzicki's open and friendly
smile for a middle-aged woman who was approaching them with a
sleek, young dobermann pinscher on a lead.

'Look,' muttered Ruzicki.

'No,' Savas began to protest, but by that time Ruzicki had stepped
back, gallantly, out of the woman's way.

Ruzicki bowed his head. 'What a magnificent creature!' Holding
the pen like a conductor's baton, he gestured with theatrical flourish.
The woman might or might not have understood the words, but
nodded in acknowledgement – she and her dog were used to such
spontaneous accolades. She did not even slow down.

Ruzicki took Savas's arm and dragged him along. The old man
hoped for a second that nothing had happened. Then he heard a
scream. He looked back. The dog had keeled over and was in convulsions. The woman was on her knees. The dog's large eyes went
opaque. The woman screamed again and talked to the dog. The
dobermann's mouth popped open but there was no barking or
movement. Now the woman, too, was silent and immobilised. Her
eyes followed the dog's saliva as it began to drip.

'Stop turning round,' Ruzicki warned Savas, 'mourning is private.'
He would not loosen his grip on Savas. They walked on, seemingly
unaware of the drama behind them. 'Complete paralysis in about five
seconds, death in another five seconds, autopsy would declare heart
failure in the absence of any trace of poison or any other obvious
cause.' Ruzicki's voice sounded awe-stricken by the infinite might
and beauty of science.

Bucken's second Singapore trip appeared to be as smooth and
uneventful as the first. He was accompanied day and night by two
minders. Savas gave him a large set of documents to read in his presence. From then on, one of the minders carried them for him. For
the mixed consignment he had loaded, purportedly, on a probably

175

non-existent ship, the Ivory Coast's Letter of Credit would pay him seven point three million dollars. He had an appointment at the Narodny at half-past ten in the morning. The two minders went with him. One stayed in the general banking hall, the other accompanied him to the manager's office.

Crossing the hall, Bucken noted the glittering eyes of the continuously filming security cameras. My pictures may be splashed across the front pages of the press within days, thought Bucken. But there was no turning back.

He presented the documents, and he could tell that the manager was more interested in making him aware of the opportunities offered by Soviet banking than in checking, verifying invoices and Bills of Lading. The temptation was enormous to do something, make some mistake, let something slip to arouse the man's suspicion. Bucken felt his assistant's eyes on his neck. So what? In the manager's presence the minder could not start shooting to stop him. Bucken found it biliously frustrating to let logic get the better of him, and do nothing.

The bank made him wait and sweat in the two minders' uninspiring company for just twenty-six hours. Then the payment of more than seven millions was duly authorised. The manager was keen to show that handling such amounts was mere routine to him. Bucken, according to Savas's instructions, had the money transferred from his Narodny account to Zurich where, using the code word, Savas would be free to transfer it to somewhere else without ever revealing his own identity. The long preparations had paid off: the whole business was painfully easy. The worst moment was shaking hands with the minders when it was all over.

Bucken mentioned the cameras to Savas but the Oldman had the answer to everything: 'The ship delivering the order is not due in Africa for several weeks. When she's late, inquiries will be made. Then they'll get on to Fiskal which has ceased to exist as of now. Only then will they become truly suspicious. But, by then, the bank's video recordings will have been wiped off. As a former policeman you ought to know that banks are guarded only against daylight robberies.' Savas laughed heartily, and invited Bucken to a celebratory lunch. 'We'll drink to your success, and talk about your prospects . . . unless you feel like retiring right now!'

Bucken thought about retirement and prospects of cops like Spire who were paid peanuts to stop men like Savas and, yes, himself.

The key turned in the lock. The outer door opened.

'Nurse? Is that you, nurse?' Quincey shouted.

176

The door closed with a soft click. Somebody was in the hall. Quincey's emergency bell would normally summon instant assistance but, for once, the nurse was away. A few minutes earlier he sent her to the manager of the Eurovista complex to complain about the telephones that had been playing up all day. It was an utter nuisance when he had so much to do before flying to Hamburg and Kiel. Suddenly, he now saw a potentially sinister connection between the troublesome line and the uninvited visitor outside. Quincey panicked. Ever since Papeete's departure, he had been having nightmares, and now he recognised what they were. Premonitions. The Americans might have discovered the true destination of their computer parts and the *Rose*. Ruzicki might have discovered that the KGB were Quincey's Moscow business contacts. Moscow might have discovered his duplicity. Scarface or some Chinese slash-artist would burst into the room and demand explanations he could not give. His throat ran dry, his lips seized up, he felt certain that another stroke would finish him off long before his executioner had a chance to do it. He heard crockery clatter on a trolley. The door handle moved downwards.

'It's room service, sir.' Through the door the man's meaty Texan accent sounded familiar.

'I haven't asked for anything,' Quincey forced himself to shout back.

'It must have been a mistake.' The door opened.

Quincey recognised his CIA contact in the waiter's uniform. They interfered with the telephone, waited for the nurse to leave . . . what had they found out? 'We . . . we can't talk now. The nurse will be back in a moment.'

'No, sir, she won't. She's been delayed. We can talk.' The Texan's drawl was soporific, his sleepy eyes radiated boredom, his slow approach with the trolley lent a casual air to the visit, yet Quincey knew that the voice could sharpen and the eyes could flash menace without any warning to trap anyone who had been lulled into false security.

'What do you want? Why haven't you waited for my call as agreed?'

'You're quite right, sir, we ought to have done just that. But then, you see, the beeeeg why' cheeeef in Lang-leee is a petulant tyrant of Italian extraction.' The man smiled at his own jocular tone. 'A liddle ole' Mediterranean temperament, that's what he has.'

'Then let's cut the bullshit.' Quincey felt ashamed of his nervousness. If they wanted to kill him, he would be helpless. His cunning was always his only defence. That and a few secrets to bargain with. 'What does he want? Let's have it.'

'I've been asked to convey the sentiment that your input is not evaluated as entirely satisfactory, sir.'

'Tough. Tell them I'm doing my best.'

'I'm sure you do, sir, I wouldn't quarrel with that. But they say it's not quite good enough. They asked you about Mr. Savas repeatedly.'

'And I've told them he's straight. I've told them repeatedly.'

'But can you be sure?'

'Can anybody be sure about anything?'

'Good point, sir, I'll convey it to Langley. But then, they'd welcome some more positive input, I'm sure.'

'I'm working on it. They'll just have to wait without pestering me. I'm not in their pay, you know. I've asked for nothing. I'm a volunteer.'

Quincey was ready for the flash of the eyes. He would not be intimidated by the man's knowledge that the *voluntary* nature of Quincey's service was somewhat questionable. The CIA connection was not his idea or choice. Soon after his financial crash, in the course of his first fraudulent shipping deal, they had approached him for information and reminded him of his civic duties. In the light of what they seemed to know about him and his last remaining secret nest-egg, theirs was an offer he could not refuse. As a reward for his cooperation, they would turn a blind eye on his affairs. Quincey was quick to identify hidden advantages in the deal: at the expense of strangers he betrayed, he could be safe and give some protection to his partners in the syndicate as long as it suited his plans.

Initially, Quincey found his involvement with the Company good clean fun. The secrecy and conspiracy, no different from his business ventures and manipulations in the City of London, sent happy tingles down his dead limbs. The complications set in only when he began his dealings with the Russians. A 'routine business coincidence' brought them together, but he knew they had sought him out deliberately with a request: could he supply certain electronic goods on a confidential basis? A straight business proposition, they claimed. His projected profit: ten to thirty million dollars – repeatable. It needed no explanation that those 'electronic goods' must be highly sensitive, strategic items on the American embargo list. The deal itself seemed irresistible, and Quincey's patriotic misgivings were put to rest when it was made clear to him that Moscow knew just as much about his secrets as Langley. Quincey responded with his scheme for the *Alida II*, and wallowed in the praise showered upon his ingenuity. Then they introduced the scarfaced man as his contact. From then on, fear squeezed the fun out of the game of secrecy, and yet the excitement made him feel more alive than at any time since his massive strokes.

Quincey's game grew more complicated after the success of the *Alida II* operation. The Texan and the CIA began to pressurise him for specific information. Hadn't he heard anything on the grapevine? Wasn't there any lead he could give? He took a calculated gamble and began to feed tit-bits to the Company. When, for instance, he heard that Donkeyman Hiller's cousin was trying to investigate the death in Macao, he obtained CIA assistance in tracing the man. Unfortunately, they never told him what they had found out. On balance, Quincey would have felt more relaxed if the cousin had also died during questioning by the Chinese thugs and Scarface. It did not matter much, but it would have streamlined everything. Quincey liked simplification in his business. He recognised that, sooner or later, many people who were involved in his affairs would have to disappear one way or another. He now looked at the Texan in the ill-fitting waiter's outfit, and wondered if this was the moment to make the first denunciations. He chose not to. He would want to take that sort of important decision with a cool head in his own good time.

The Texan offered him a drink from the trolley. Quincey declined. He would not be seen struggling with a glass of liquid. He took pride in his ability to walk the tightrope no matter how crippled he was. But he was a realist. He knew that one clever step too many could kill him just as easily as a stupid mistake. Fortunately, the last steps to be taken were now in sight: first the *Rose of Stambul* and, finally, Operation Tsunami. Then you can all kiss my arse, he thought gleefully as his mind drifted off on a swell of daydreams. There would be moments of sadness but the end would be sweet. Papeete might cry. She would be devastated when he told her what she had really been involved with. But he would explain it all. By then the healing power of success would have him on his feet. He would stride across the room to her, lift her chin, wipe away her tears, and have the strength to apologise to her. For everything. He would then pick her up, re-create her, and lay all his wealth and new status at her feet. She would love that. She would laugh as she used to. It would be due reward for her suffering and loyalty. And, from then on, no more hotel rooms, no more doubts and fears, no begging for favours, and no more contacts for her with Lord bloody Ashenbury. . .

The Texan brought him back to reality with a photograph: 'Do you know him?'

'I knew him.' Quincey recognised Savas's bodyguard. 'He's dead.'

'Yes. Most inconvenient. He offered us some information but we never established what exactly he had in mind. He died too suddenly.' He produced a second photograph. A naked, clay-white body drained of all blood, spread out on a stone slab in the morgue. 'Heart attack, I guess,' he paused for Quincey's due astonishment, then added, 'yeah, seizure following severe and repeated exposure to some sharp instrument. You wouldn't have heard any details, would you?'

'No.' Quincey felt more and more uncomfortable.

'Looks like some Chink-style execution.'

'Or a clear statement of jealousy.'

'Savas has some Chink connections, I hear.'

'It wouldn't surprise me. Shipping is international.'

'The *Alida II* had a Chink crew.'

'Yes,' Quincey tried to agree wholeheartedly, 'very much so. But, on the other hand, it could be a coincidence. There are some eight hundred million Chinese around and, as far as you can see, the seas are littered with them.'

'You do realise, sir, that the *Alida* had a very special cargo.'

'More's the pity it couldn't be recovered. Have you found any of the wreckage?' Quincey could not have sounded less interested.

'Just a couple of lifebelts and a few fragments that have risen to the surface but even these might have been floating about ever since the sinking. The most peculiar thing is that we can't trace the survivors of the crew.'

'Oh well,' Quincey sighed, 'that's the Orient for you. Pity I can't help you.'

'A great pity, Mr. Quincey, because you put me in a difficult position. How can I keep the wolves from your door if you don't give me any justification?'

For a second, Quincey toyed with the idea of giving Savas and his Ivory Coast deal as a sop to the Company, but he knew it would be a mistake. Before Suez, Savas would be irreplaceable. 'I do have a suspect who may be involved in all sorts of things, but I'm not yet certain.'

'Give me the name and we'll check him out for you.'

'No thanks, I don't spread half-baked hunches. Play cool, and I'll serve him up on a tray if I'm right.' He had Bucken in mind. After the *Rose of Stambul* coup, the ex-cop would not only be superfluous but also a liability. Besides, it would be educational to watch Papeete's reaction. Perhaps he could be fished out of the sea with incriminating evidence in his pockets. It could even develop into front-page news for Papeete to read over breakfast. The thought of newspapers gave him an amusing idea. 'Meanwhile, you could do something for me. There's a guy who could be very helpful in my little investigation. In fact, he'd be obliged to help me if I did him a favour. He's keen to renew contact with an Australian journalist who seems to have gone to ground.'

'We'll find him. What's his name?'

'Andrew Warman.' Quincey almost burst out laughing. He imagined Boothy-Graffoe's face at the moment when he heard that the CIA would do the investigation for him.

'You got a description of the guy?'

'It's all rather vague. Apparently he's a sort of prototype for a seasoned Aussie reporter. Craggy face, tall outdoor type.' A bit like Bucken, he thought.

Savas was in a jubilant mood. Over a drink to celebrate victory, he handed a bearer bond to Bucken. Greta watched the scene with an ironic smile as Bucken stuffed the bond into his pocket and mumbled his thanks. 'You see? It's easy to be grateful,' she said.

'Won't you even look at the value?' Savas asked.

'Oh, yes.' He looked at the bond. 'Oh.' It was for sixty instead of fifty thousand dollars. More thanks were due.

'A little bonus. You've earned it,' Savas beamed.

'It wasn't me – it was Booker,' Bucken protested. He would have liked to believe it, too.

'Booker is dead. It's time to destroy any trace of him, including his passport.'

'Sure.' Bucken was planning to send it to the Yard. One day it could become an exhibit at somebody's trial. 'I'll do it soon as I leave Singapore.'

But Papeete intervened. 'Don't do it just yet. Don called from Hamburg. Ruzicki would like Bucken to do one more job before he casts off his Booker mantle. If it's okay with you, Oldman.'

'As long as it's done within the week or so. Beyond that, the name is a risk.'

'Then you'd better make sure that this doesn't stay on Booker's account,' said Papeete and she gave Bucken a cheque. It was for fifteen thousand dollars.

'Quite a payday.' Bucken tried to look pleased. He was now a fully paid up criminal.

Papeete assured him that it was just a first instalment. There were some papers to sign in order to finalise the purchase of the *Rose*, and he would have to register the ship with the Panamanian consulate. 'We, I mean Ruzicki, would then want you to go to Kiel for a few days. An office has been set up for you and you'll have to see to it that

181

your ship leaves on time for her maiden voyage . . . if that is the right expression.'

'Okay. Anything else?'

'You don't even negotiate your fee?' Greta asked.

'I trust my friends' generosity.'

'You won't be disappointed. Ruzicki will meet you in Kiel to give you the details.'

'Great. Then it's time to celebrate. Dinner, everybody?'

'Some other time,' said Savas. 'Tonight we're the government's guests at some Chamber of Commerce junket. But perhaps Papeete is free.'

Greta was fuming. 'I'm sure she is, aren't you, darling?'

'Sadly, no,' said Papeete. 'I have a previous engagement.'

After the Savases had left, Papeete took a few documents out of a folder. Bucken viewed them with casual interest. He caught a glimpse of some photographs. 'Oh, is that my ship?'

'I'll get you a picture for framing,' said Papeete and shut the folder.

'Thanks. Where do I sign, boss?'

'Don't you want to think about it? You can now afford to quit if you like.'

'What? In the middle of a winning streak? It would be crazy. I'm becoming a highly experienced front man who could soon command very substantial remuneration.' Their eyes met, and she looked away. 'I hope you're not suggesting that secretly you'd want me to remain poor for ever.'

Still anxious to avoid his eyes, Papeete's gaze fell upon the hand-kerchief that was, as always, carelessly stuffed into the breast pocket of his new tropical suit. 'What an untrendy thing to wear,' she said with a smile, remembering what Savas had told her about Bucken's murderous bunch of keys.

'Perhaps I'm an old-fashioned man. In some ways.'

'Stay that way.' She whispered, then rearranged her face. 'And think about the offer.'

'Okay – over a drink.'

'Some other time. I'm sorry. I've got a date.'

'I hope he's trendier than me.'

'Only safer.'

Later that evening, Bucken watched her leave Raffles. A chauffeur-driven limousine picked her up. Bucken went out shop-ping. He needed a small camera with a good lens and a built-in flash. Fortunately, the Change Alley nearby never slept. Only the traders were a little disappointed: Bucken did not even bother to give them a

182

decent bout of haggling, and their extra profit was only partial compensation for the loss of fun.

'Lovely dinner, Charles. Thank you.' Warmed to a faint glow by alcohol, Papeete smiled with relief that might have been mistaken for contentment. Mission accomplished, it would not be long before she could leave. Amundsen must have felt like this on his way back from the Pole, she thought.

How Ashenbury had found out that she was in Singapore she never asked. When out of the blue he asked her to dinner in his penthouse suite just below the revolving tower of Shangri-La, she telephoned her husband in Hamburg. Quincey thought she ought to accept the invitation. He wanted some information from Ashenbury. She got most of it for him before the remnants of a massive Indonesian *Rijstafel* were cleared away. Over a truffle sherbet she secured a half-promise that Ashenbury would throw his weight of influence behind Quincey's eventual rehabilitation in the City.

'And this sherbet. . . ' she exclaimed, wiping the crystal goblet clean, and licking her finger with childish abandon, 'it's just too good for words.'

'I knew it was your favourite.' He did not mention that he had had it flown in on ice from Alba, the hunting ground of the white truffle.

'Thanks again.'

'It's for me to thank you. It's been an enormous pleasure to have you. I mean – it would have been.'

She ignored the undertone. Throughout the dinner she had avoided carefully any hint of appearing flirtatious. If anything, she would have abhorred the thought of sleeping with him ever again, though deep down she knew it was still gratifying to feel wanted by Ashenbury. He was attractive and impressive enough as a man as well as a tycoon to make adulation by him a unique compliment. It only emphasised his strength and integrity that he could now accept that they were friends, just friends, at last. That was why she felt a little ashamed: she had been using him.

She got up, walked over to him and kissed him on his forehead. It was a mere peck. 'Thanks again, Charles. Can we have some coffee before I go?'

'Of course.' He rang for coffee. 'Over there, please,' he told the waiter and gestured towards a recess filled by a huge leather sofa and two low, Japanese lacquer tables.

A little reluctantly she approached the sofa and noticed that he was turning a knob to soften the lights. She stopped. Next to one of the tables in the corner stood a large parcel with a familiarly elaborate logo in gold: *Howarth, Howarth & Howarth.*

'Still black without sugar?' he asked, always the perfect host.

'I'm not sure that I want that coffee any more.'

He looked at the parcel and smiled reassuringly. 'Don't be silly. It mustn't alarm you.' He poured her some coffee. 'It's just that I love my memories, and that's how I refresh them.' As they sat down, she faced a door in the alcove, turning her back to the parcel. 'Don't you love your memories, Papeete?'

'I do. But I never refresh them. They're private.'

'These were *our* memories.'

'They still are. But just memories, no more.'

'That makes them no less lovable.' He walked to the door and opened it. In a sheaf of light, the adult-sized replica of a school uniform came into view. It was laid out on the bed, like a reclining rag doll. There was the blazer with the stripes, the almost deliberately ill-shaped skirt, the boater, the ribbed grey socks with the obvious coarseness that could still make her skin crinkle – everything was there, as if prepared for the beginning of a new term, complete with sports gear and unfeminine knickers that had embittered long years of her youth.

'It's getting late, Charles. I'd better go.' She stood up. 'Of course,' he said, but suddenly he lost his composure. He caught her arm, forced her to face him, and embraced her so hard he seemed to be trying to make love to her through the layers of clothing between them. She tried to wriggle free. 'I want you, Papeete, I want you badly, I want you now.' His voice was throaty.

'You're drunk. Let me go. Please.'

He caressed her hair and his hold slackened. 'I've been waiting. . . I've been patient . . . but it's been too long . . . much too long.'

She tried to back away but he caught her dress at the neck and tore it. 'Charles, please. . . ' She struggled to free herself. They tripped and fell on the sofa in a heap. He hardly noticed. His eyes were on the uniform in the bedroom.

'Would you like to try them on?'

'No.'

'I bet they're a perfect fit.'

'They don't make them for adults.'

'They do for me.' He laughed loudly. But when he noticed her resentment, he suddenly released his grip and stood up. 'I'm sorry.' The fire in his eyes was extinguished by pain. 'Don't they bring back your memories?'

'They do. And I don't want them.'

'Don't you. . . I mean you used to love it. Dressing up. Taking them off. For me. And for yourself. Because you enjoyed it. I mean it wasn't just me. It wasn't. . . Tell me.'

'No. It wasn't just you.'

'We were addicts. Both of us. And it was . . . wasn't it beautiful?'

She closed her eyes. She felt pity for him, and pity was more humiliating than anger. She hoped that, if she counted slowly to ten, the whole scene and the memories would go away, vanish forever, by the time she opened her eyes. One . . . two. . .

'Those socks. . . ' He was in and out of the bedroom in a flash. He held the grey socks to his face, then touched hers. 'These awful socks, my God.'

Five . . . six. . .

' You hated them. You used to hide them under the bed . . . just anywhere out of sight. . . ' He laughed, this time with warmth. 'Remember when you flung them out of the window? The gardener burnt them the next day because he didn't know how to cope with the embarrassment of finding them under my bedroom.'

She laughed with him to avoid crying. Seven . . . eight. . .

'You see? You remember. You want to remember. Do you still hate those knickers?'

This time, her chuckles were genuine. 'You seriously contemplated roping in some tame MP of yours to propose a law banning knickers throughout the country.'

'And you seconded the motion!' He kissed her gently. 'Remember the first time?'

She lost count. Seven . . . eight. . .

'The first time I thought I'd never get them off you.'

'Rubbish.' Too late she realised it had been a mistake. She should have counted to ten first.

'What's rubbish?'

'The first time you didn't need to get them off. I was in bed, feeling very, very wicked without a stitch on.'

'Were you expecting me? You never told me.'

'There was no need.'

'There is now. Were you?'

'You were so wonderful. The way you looked. The way you treated me, not as a little girl, but a woman. Your style. Your self-assurance. Every schoolgirl's dream.'

'Were you expecting me?'

'No. I didn't think a fourteen-year-old would have a chance among all your ravishing house guests. And that's how I'd like to remember you. Always.'

'Why only remember? Why?' His begging was even more distressing than his aggression. 'Tell me why?'

'Because it's over.'

'Then let's celebrate the memory. Just this once. Put the clothes on. The boater. The blazer. Please.'

'No Charles, I've grown up. And so have you, I hope, for your sake.'

'Look, it wasn't just the sex. It was the game. Our game. The hunt. The anticipation. Admit it that you just loved to seduce this old man.'

'You weren't old.'

'I was your father's age.'

'And you were as wonderful as he was. You were devastating. You could do no wrong. You were my dream even when you spanked me, even if I could have killed you for it every time.'

'All right. No spanking. It's a deal. I promise. No spanking, not even pretending. Just dress up, once more, and come to me.'

'I can't, Charles.'

'I'll do anything for you.'

'I don't want anything from you.' She could not be sure that she was not blushing.

'You used to love me.'

'True. Used to.'

'And your love used to be pure, right? It wasn't just a pretence to get me to do something for your father.'

'Of course not. I didn't even understand the relationship. I didn't know that you *could* help him or that he might need it.'

'But you do understand now, don't you?'

'What?'

'That I could help your father, that I could get him out of debt, help him buy that filly and the rest of it. And you do understand how much I could do for your wretched husband, don't you?'

She felt like dying: she had been blind, she had been a fool, he had known all along why she was there.

He grabbed her and fondled her harshly, kissing her neck. 'Go and get changed, you cheap little whore. Help your father now that he needs it most. Because now you know what his game was.'

'What game?'

'That he brought you to my place in the country in the hope that something might happen between us and he'd benefit. Don't tell me that you've never guessed. He certainly didn't make much of a secret of it when we talked about it.'

'That's a lie.'

186

'You want to ask him? Shall I call him? It was he who told me that you were in Singapore.'

'Liar!' She hit him and stepped back in fright. She suddenly felt Bucken's fist smashing her teeth. He would not let her hit him. He'd . . . he'd . . . Ashenbury smiled with the old cool composure. 'All right. Here's the number. Call your wonderful daddy.'

'No.'

'Go ahead. And, if he needs any prodding, I'll order him to tell you the truth. Or even to *ask* you to be *nice* to me.'

She reached for her richly-embroidered shawl to cover the tear in her dress. 'No, Charles. We'll just forget about all this, about Singapore, the dinner and what followed, and we'll remain friends, distant friends, who share a happy but fading secret for ever.'

Like a drunk in a downpour, he was beginning to sober up, regretfully. His head hung in despair, his eyes were closed, perhaps he was counting to ten, hoping that the whole scene would just evaporate. 'I'm sorry,' he mumbled.

'What for? It was a lovely dinner, Charles. And that sherbet . . . it was just too good for words.' There was nothing in this world that could force her to put on that uniform, take it off, and let him make love to her. But the memories would be wiped out only if one day she could talk about them freely, seeking absolution from someone like Bucken.

Ashenbury kissed her lightly on the cheek, then sat down, on the edge of the sofa, the outsize garments leaving the ridiculously long shadow of a schoolgirl behind him.

She opened the door and he looked up. His eyes and voice belonged now to the chairman of the board. 'Thanks for the evening, my dear. My driver will take you back to Raffles.' He raised his hand to stop her answer. 'And don't say goodbye. You'll be back.'

Soon after eleven that evening, while Papeete was finishing her truffle sherbet, Bucken broke into Papeete's suite as smoothly as if he had borrowed a key. Spire's old lock-picking kit was the best Bucken had ever used.

He knew that she was out, and yet he stopped just inside the door to listen, half-fearing, half-hoping to hear her breathing and some sarcastic remark – don't you ever knock? In the same situation, Greta's first words had been *don't switch on the light.* And she had said she knew he would come in that night. What would Papeete say? He waited, but there was only silence to greet him.

It was tempting to waste a few minutes just rummaging in her cupboard, touching her clothes, catching a whiff of perfume among her underwear, but he searched purposefully, for the *Rose of Stambul* folder. He found it in a locked briefcase, but the lock was no match for Spire's kit. He photographed the papers without reading any of them. There would be plenty of time later on. The fading pictures of the ship were a problem. Some showed the *Rose* in her bloom, others were snapshots of a withered and tatty tramp. Bucken tried to spot key features for eventual identification, but to his untrained eyes she looked just like any other smallish freighter. Her shape was a little pregnant. That might have been the heavy-lift jumbo derrick's doing – it seemed to dwarf everything else in sight. Bucken did not quite trust his camera to capture sufficient details. After a moment's hesitation, he decided to take a chance and nick one of the pictures. If it was ever missed, Papeete would think she had mislaid it.

He packed everything away, checked that half-open drawers were left as he had found them, and relocked the briefcase. He opened the door of the suite slightly, and peeped through the gap. The corridor was deserted. He stepped outside and shut the door with a soft click. In a few seconds, he would turn the second safety lock. That was when Savas appeared in the corridor. His astonishment quickly turned into wolfish admiration. A wink and a nod said it all.

Bucken smiled at him inanely. He could not ask Savas not to jump to conclusions. And now he could not lock the door. That would tell Savas that Papeete was not inside.

Savas put his hands to his eyes, ears and mouth, impersonating the three monkeys of utter discretion. 'But I can't say I don't envy you.'

'I . . . I thought you were still at the party.'

'We returned early. Greta didn't feel well. I'm just going down to the bar for a nightcap. Care to join me?'

'No, thanks. I want to catch the first flight out of here. Ruzicki needs me in Kiel as soon as possible. So I'll have to be up early.'

'I understand,' said Savas with yet another man-to-man wink. He wondered how Greta would react to his little discovery of the night. She would be pleased because she had been right once again: Papeete did have affairs after all. She would also be angry. She did not take it kindly when men in her vicinity wanted anyone but her.

Early next morning, before the farewell breakfast with the Savases and Papeete, Bucken slipped out of the hotel to call London and report briefly to Ashenbury. He was told that his Lordship was out of the country but would be back by the evening. Bucken left a message for him at the emergency switchboard of the Yard that he would call again from Kiel.

188

While he was out, the phone rang in the Savas suite, and Greta answered it.

'Sorry to call you so early,' said Quincey, 'but I'm in Hamburg and I must talk to Bucken urgently.'

'Then why don't you call him? This is not his room, you know.'

'I'm sorry, but he seems to be out, and I thought he might be with Oldman.'

'He isn't. Why don't you try Papeete's room?' By the time she had said it, she knew she might cause more damage than intended with that random swipe. It was, however, too late to take it back – and she only half-regretted it.

Quincey rang off, and stared ahead, right through the Hamburg hotel wall, across continents. He then called Confidential Couriers, Worldwide, a company whose phones would be manned twenty-four hours a day. It was a front organisation to set up meetings with his KGB contact. In an innocuous-sounding conversation he used the code word that meant he would want to meet him at midday in the hydro brothel where clients were guaranteed maximum privacy.

'Moscow has approved the arrangements. . . ' announced the scar-faced, baby-blond man, and let it hang in the air on a high note as if expecting the applause his statement must have earned him. Alas, this was not the carefully orchestrated plenary session of the Cent-Com or even a *Pravda*-appreciation seminar in a kolkhoz, so all he got from Quincey was a terse 'sure', and on second thoughts, 'Why shouldn't they approve? It's a good plan. But have they agreed the price?'

'They think that thirty five million is a bit steep.'

'Tough. Setting up a viable front company in Helsinki is not as cheap as in Cairo. The whole deal is much more expensive. The Americans are jittery about the sale of embargoed goods, particularly from government stocks. We had to find a Finnish buyer of long-established trading reputation – a buyer who could never afford to reveal how he had been *persuaded* to make this purchase. Then we needed a top-drawer London broker to charter the ship, and I haven't even mentioned yet the cost of a first-rate front man to hold the fort in the Kiel office during loading and possible American spot-checks.'

'Yes, Moscow understands but. . . '

'I'm sorry. No buts.' Quincey raised his good hand to stop any further argument. 'I've made the arrangements, you know the price, if they're not acceptable, no deal.'

Both of them knew that, if there was no deal, there would be no Quincey either. Yet in moments like that, Quincey positively enjoyed to be strapped in a wheelchair. It was even more humiliating to the other party, in this case the mighty Bolshevik Party of the Soviet Union, that they could do nothing, nothing but accept the terms set by a clever cripple.

The agent knew when he was beaten, and acknowledged it with a silent nod. While Moscow needed desperately the embargoed American goods, one had to pay the price. And part of the price was to kowtow to the cripple and meet him anywhere, even in a hydro brothel where private pools could be hired by the kinky.

Quincey was in a good mood. This was his second visit to the establishment, and this time, just before the agent's visit, it had worked: suspended in warm water, submitting to the girl who offered underwater oral sex, he became almost the man he used to be. Now that he knew what the answer to his problem was, he might be only one step away from getting Papeete to do the same for him. His voice reflected his sexual triumph, too: 'So this is what we do. The ship will load in Kiel. The goods will include all the computer parts and other electronics you require. They're genuine American products, coming from a NATO store in West Germany, and their sale has been cleared to Helsinki. Adjust that, will you?' He gestured towards a large dial. 'I like the water two degrees warmer. . . Thank you. Er. . . Oh yes. Those American spot checks may involve visits to the Kiel office and the ship. That could cause slight delays.'

'Moscow won't be pleased,' said the agent, fingering his facial scar. After all those years it still throbbed every time he felt agitated. Moscow would hold him responsible even if he had every justification for blaming Quincey for delays and unforeseen complications.

'Can't be helped,' said Quincey without any pity for the man's predicament. 'In a situation like this, the CIA is entitled to initiate checks and double-checks or even a last-minute cancellation of the whole deal. Just think what caution Moscow would apply the other way round.'

'Don't they trust the buyer? Or is there a problem with the *Rose?*'

'Don't worry. They trust everybody involved. Otherwise the deal would already be off. But the various agencies involved must cover themselves. That's why we need a cool front-man. And our Mr. Booker is first class.'

'How about the voyage?' The agent prepared himself for battle. He had news Quincey might not like.

'No problem. The voyage of the *Rose* will terminate some forty miles from the island of Götland, where there's a sort of well in the

Baltic. It's about 8,000 feet deep, so the Americans will understand why they can't find the wreck. I'll give you the precise location in a day or two, and we can finalise all details.'

'That's fine, just fine.' The agent paused. 'There is, however, something Moscow will insist on. I don't like it, you may not like it, none of us likes unnecessary bloodshed, but Moscow is adamant that, this time, there must be no witnesses. I mean we had a lot of trouble with the dispersal of the *Alida* crew, and we can't afford any more skulduggery in port. Helsinki is not Macao, you know.'

Quincey hesitated. There would be several good and useful men aboard the *Rose*. But, he had to admit, all good things must come to an end. 'All right, but for the same reasons of security you'll have to deal with a problem for me.'

'Anything you say.' I'd have never guessed that you're as big a shit as I am, thought the agent, *and* you're a volunteer. 'What's your problem?'

'Booker.'

'I thought he was a major asset.'

'He is right now, and he'll be a tremendous asset in Kiel until the loading is completed. Beyond that, he could be a liability.'

'You mean. . . '

'Yes. And, for reasons of my own, he's to be found floating in the harbour. Make the identification difficult.' Quincey could not suppress a little grin in the corner of his mouth. There would be photographs. Gruesome details. Something for Papeete to think about. 'But you may have to keep him on ice for a day or two. If he's found and identified during the voyage, somebody might have bright ideas about stopping the *Rose* in the Baltic.'

'Where is he now?'

'He'll be in Kiel in a day or two.'

'Okay. We'll start tailing him right away.'

'Don't. It would only alert him. Besides, I can tell you precisely where he will be at all times. I'll let you know when to go ahead.'

Quincey felt pleased with himself. The ingenuity of the double and treble cross appealed to him. If the discovery and identification of Bucken/Booker's corpse coincided with the *Rose of Stambul* disaster, the Americans would look for Russian culprits. If he himself then tipped off his Texan contact and the CIA about Booker's true identity and perhaps even this scarfaced killer, he would strengthen his credentials on both sides, cover his flank for Operation Tsunami, and, simultaneously, get rid of the man Papeete found attractive.

191

IV

MAYDAY IN DECEMBER

The office in Kiel was not as grand as the one in Zurich, but it would be used only by Bucken for no more than a couple of days. Ruzicki met him at the airport with some papers and instructions: 'Man the office until nine in the evening – you never know who might want to contact the owner urgently during the loading of your ship. Take a lunch break because all Germans in the building would be most suspicious if you didn't, but keep it short. Now sign these, please. It's for the insurance. You don't have to read them.'

A quick glance told Bucken that, apparently, some Cayman Island company had lent him six million dollars for the purchase and refit of the *Rose*. The ship was assigned to them as security, and now his signature would name them as beneficiaries of the insurance on the voyage. 'You may get a call from an American government official. Handle him with care,' said Ruzicki, 'but try to see him in the office not aboard ship. Keep me informed of everything that may come up.'

The morning in the office was quiet. Bucken received two telexes from Helsinki, and reported them by telephone to Ruzicki. There was also a brief phone call from Boothy-Graffoe. Bucken resisted the temptation to ask him about Warman or tell him that he was dealing with crooks. It was upsetting to be stuck in the office when he was itching to go down to the port and see his very own ship loading.

At lunchtime, Bucken took a cab to the port. As he was an owner, it would have been easy enough to enter, but the guard on the gate might call the *Rose* and that, let alone a visit aboard, would certainly be reported by the crew to Ruzicki who would demand an explanation he could not give: he had no business at the quayside. So Bucken satisfied himself with locating the berth of the ship and catching a glimpse of her from a fair distance. He spotted a six-storey *Parkhaus* near the harbour, a promising vantage point for initial reconnaissance. Before returning to his office, he went to a department store where he bought himself a pair of shoes and powerful

192

binoculars, in that order, so that he could carry the latter in the shoebox without arousing suspicion if he was tailed.

In the afternoon, the American called from Hamburg and volunteered to visit the office the following day: 'Just routine, sir, it won't take long, I can assure you. We're obliged to examine certain documents relevant to the ownership and the chartering of the *Rose*. If they're available, we'll be through in no time at all.'

That evening, after some arduous anti-surveillance detours, Bucken went up to the top floor of the *Parkhaus*, and scanned the harbour. It was easy to pick out the pregnant, elderly design of the *Rose* with the bulky superstructure amidships. But, somehow, her silhouette did not quite match the photograph he had stolen from Papeete's file. The fo'c'sle seemed taller and longer in reality. In the faint lights of the port, through the drifting mist and the glare of spotlights playing on the water, the shadow pattern of the swinging derricks and deck cranes did not seem to tally either with the outline in the old photo. The equipment must have been renewed since the picture was taken. The most prominent characteristic of the *Rose*, the heavy-lift jumbo derrick at the foremast, was clearly recognisable, so anybody who had known the old ship would readily identify her from memory. It was just the repeated comparisons between picture and ship that left Bucken a little uneasy. He decided to continue his scrutiny at first light the next morning, before going to the office to meet the American inspector.

He returned to his hotel by cab, watching the blurred streets of yet another strange city he might never get a chance to explore. Then came another night enduring the tycoon's lot – the speciality of the chef, a wide range of the world's most expensive booze, and the limited choice of whores recommended by the hall porter. Bucken rejected all of them, longed for a steak and kidney pud and settled for some schnitzel, then went for a walk so that from a café of random choice he could telephone Ashenbury. For all he knew, he might have been on the moon.

At dawn he was back in the *Parkhaus*. The early rays of the reddish sun that seemed to be floating on the waves made Bucken blink: the light was piercing the superstructure. The ship swayed gently, and the hole where the light came through grew into a vertical gap. What seemed a single block in the picture, the actual superstructure was in two sections. Admittedly, the gap would be visible only when viewed from the side, virtually at right angles, whereas the picture had been taken from much further aft.

Yet another detailed study revealed that, although the ship was in excellent condition for her age, not all the paintwork was new. She could not have been badly ravaged by her years grounded near the desert, and her rejuvenation must have been only partial. There was nothing definite either to confirm or to dispel Bucken's unease. He hoped against hope that the American would spot something in the documents to necessitate a visit aboard or to cancel sailing the following day. But Bucken's hopes were short-lived. The American was anxious to return to Hamburg, and conducted a most perfunctory examination of the papers. Obviously, his aim was merely to make a routine entry and put a tick or two on some official document that would cover him and his department. He seemed to be suitably impressed by the history of the ship, the Bills of Sale, and the British vice-consul's meaningless stamp ('no responsibility is accepted . . . for the contents of this document'). He congratulated Mr. Booker on bringing a fine ship back to life, and he was ready to leave.

Bucken was fretting. He had no hard evidence against Ruzicki, the ship or the Helsinki deal. If he made the American suspicious and the *Rose* was prevented from leaving port, not only Savas's big, final plan would become unassailable, but nobody might ever find out the truth about the *Alida II*. And yet, for a policeman, it was hard not to do something: at least pray for some supernatural intervention. He proudly showed the photograph to the American.

'Mm. Cute. Not new, but cute.'

'Would you like to see her?'

'No time. Pressure of work.'

'I understand, but I thought a visit on board...'

'I'm no sailor or engineer, Mr. Booker. I can tell right from wrong only on paper. Thanks all the same.'

Bucken reported the satisfactory outcome of the visit to Ruzicki who was very pleased: 'You've done a good job. Many thanks. And let me tell you this: you won't regret it. Now return to your hotel and stay there until tomorrow afternoon when the *Rose* sails.'

'I thought she wouldn't leave before the weekend. I mean Helsinki doesn't expect her before the middle of next week.'

'Not to worry, the loading is completed, all the papers are in order – why hang about? Right?'

As soon as Ruzicki was off the phone, Bucken called the port for the latest weather forecast for the Baltic. The outlook was not good. A considerable storm was blowing up in the whole area. Bursts of gale force ten and eleven were already reported everywhere north of the 55th parallel. Bucken did not need any more: *Alida II* had also sailed into a potentially devastating storm. He knew now that the night was his last chance to get on board and try to see what was going on.

194

On his way to the hotel, Bucken identified his newly-acquired tail, an agile though pot-bellied man with sleepy eyes and an improbable beard, who wore a noisy donkey jacket of extra large technicolour checks. Bucken recognised the trick: if anybody ever tried to describe him, only the beard and the jacket would be remembered. A short detour, more to verify the fact than to lose the tail, confirmed Bucken's suspicion. Having been followed all the way to the hotel, Bucken took a look at the street from the darkness of his room: the tail was on the far side of the road, perching on the edge of a wind-swept bench, watching Bucken's window. So he knew which room to watch and waited, perhaps, only for the light to come on. Bucken obliged, moved about to make himself visible for a few minutes, then switched off the light and looked out again: the man had disappeared. He would be a fool not to get out of the icy wind. Bucken went down to the bar. As he was crossing the lobby, he saw his man reading a paper, soaking up the heat in a cosy corner.

Bucken dined in his room and made plans for losing his tail. At midnight, he ordered a taxi. Dressed in jeans and a heavy jersey he hurriedly crossed the lobby. The man was still there, the beard looked as phoney as ever, but he would not even get up to follow his quarry. Bucken asked the driver to go round the block and cruise slowly past the hotel. The man in the lobby seemed to be snoozing. He's not interested in me, only in my room, Bucken concluded, and ran a quick mental check on the contents of his room and luggage. Australian passport, ID papers, a couple of telexes, no, there was nothing there to identify him as anything but Mr. Booker. He decided not to return to that particular hotel because the man might already be investigating the Narodny affair. Ruzicki would understand. He would have to be notified in the morning.

Using both hands and pidgin-Deutsch, Bucken indicated to the driver that he was late returning to his ship and needed to get to the berth fast and quietly. The flash of a handful of notes completed his explanation – the driver was not new to these games, the guard on the gate would wave him through. He dropped off his fare near a Dutch tanker, as requested, and refused to sample the bottle of Aschbach Bucken had bought on the way. When the car had disappeared from sight, Bucken rinsed his mouth with the German brandy and splashed half the bottle on his clothes: even armed patrols would have some sympathy for inane drunks. Luckily, the brandy had been wasted: the quayside was completely deserted. It was probably the relentless gale and the occasional freezing spray that forced everyone to seek shelter whatever the regulations: thieves would be crazy to work on a night like that.

195

Aboard the *Rose*, high up behind the bridge, light was oozing from a few adjoining portholes. The rest of the ship was in virtual darkness. In the wheelhouse, a man was busying himself with his nose, taking lucky dips and examining its contents lovingly. He would have the port side in view and, as the gangway was up, Bucken could not risk any acrobatics to get on board. It was a leisurely cluck-cluck, cluck-cluck, near the stem that caught his attention. A small motor boat swung at the end of a Jacob's ladder that was hugging the hull of the *Rose*. Bucken retreated, took two doubles of a gulp from the brandy, and lowered himself into the water. I may not be shot, he thought, but it's not a nice way to go having my arse frozen off. He reached the boat, silently climbed the ladder and hoped that his clattering teeth would not give him away during his brief visit.

The lay-out of the ship seemed familiar from the drawings he had seen. That was what probably saved him when a door opened and two men appeared. One was Ruzicki, the other a Chinese sailor. Bucken would have sworn it was Ting-chao, but he had no time to take a second look. He ducked behind the windlass and dropped rather than descended through an open hatch. Only the faintly exotic smell told him he might be in some ropes locker. The steps above stopped. If anybody came down into the locker, Bucken would have nowhere to hide. He crawled inside a coil of rope, thick as his forearm.

'Oh well, can't be helped. These things happen. You'd better get some sleep.' Bucken recognised Ruzicki's voice and wondered if the man was carrying the stiletto with which he had probably caused that ghastly carnage in Macao. 'And thanks for everything. You're a good man, Ting...' Ting-chao. Was that the final link with the *Alida*? 'So take care of yourself, will you?' It sounded more like a grave *farewell* than a *bon voyage*. A little like Ruzicki's 'many thanks' to Bucken earlier that evening.

'Sank you, sah. Don't wohhy. No p-hoblems. Just tell me, why change plans?'

'Because the forecast is that the storm may not last long.'

The other man chuckled. 'Now I understand, sah. A little tsunami, yes?'

Judging from the noises, somebody was climbing down the ladder. A few seconds later, the engine of the small boat fired. 'Goodbye, Ting.'

The engine roared and the boat left at a fair speed. Bucken tried to figure out why Ruzicki had visited the ship at night and why by boat rather than car. Perhaps he did not want to have his visit logged at the gate of the port. And what was the change of plan? The earlier sailing time? Bucken heard some clattering noise. Ting must be rolling up the ladder. Somebody shouted in Chinese. Ting answered, coughed, spat. The phlegm landed with a clang on metal a couple of feet away from Bucken.

When Ting's departing steps had faded away, Bucken climbed on deck. Keeping to the starboard side, he ran past large covered holds and two towering crates tightly lashed down and protected by thick tarpaulins. Voices could be heard faintly from high above, but otherwise all was quiet and the ship seemed deserted. Perhaps the crew had the night off before sailing. He tried a massive metal door – it opened with hardly more than a hiss. Subconsciously he noted the amazingly good condition of the *Rose*. Not a trace of rust anywhere. She could easily have been half her age. In the silence, he let the distant hum of a generator guide him towards the engine room.

The pot-bellied man worked with a powerful portable microlight, and searched Booker's hotel room thoroughly. He prepared to photograph all papers, passport and whatever else he found indiscriminately. It was not for him to guess why Frankfurt wanted it done. God and goddamn CIA station chiefs moved in mysterious ways. Somebody might be trying to build a career on swinging some deal with Helsinki – someone else might hope to gain something else from stopping or just discovering the full background of the same heist. All I get is a cold day and a sleepless night, he thought, and tore off the beard that made his chin itch.

Steps and a squeaking noise stopped outside the door. The agent switched off the torch. Booker wouldn't be back so soon, surely. Room service? At this hour? A key turned in the lock. He lay down on the bed, pretending to have fallen asleep. From under his arm which lay across his face, he saw a hotel valet pushing a large box of a trolley through the door. Why kill him unless it was inevitable? The agent decided to bluff it out. 'Who's that?' He switched on the bedside light.

'Laundry, sir.'

'What? In the middle of the night?'

'I'm sorry, Mr. Booker, I was told you wanted the shirts right away.' The voice lacked any German accent.

The agent got up slowly. 'I'll complain about this.'

'I'm very sorry, sir, but now that I've woken you up, you might as well have them.' He held out a sheet of paper and a pen. 'Could you please sign for it?'

'Sure.' Better to sign Booker's name than to fight and leave the

197

search incomplete. He made the signature illegible. It was his last act for the almighty station chief of Frankfurt. The valet broke his windpipe with a single chop. He never saw the second man who rushed in and completed the bloodless killing with protracted pressure on his throat. Throughout the strangling, the valet kept checking the victim's pulse. The body was bundled into the trolley. The inevitably bloody disidentification of the face would be carried out elsewhere, later on.

The valet checked the room: he was to leave no trace of his visit. On the way out, the trolley squeaked a little more loudly under the extra weight. Is that the famous German efficiency? the valet asked himself. Can't they oil those bloody wheels? He massaged his face in annoyance. The old scar was throbbing again.

Bucken relied on his ears for security. He was using his pocket camera and Sergeant Spire's kit for wax impressions to record engine numbers and the ship's other identification markings. He knew already he was gathering good, hard evidence. The numbers and coding were nothing like those he remembered from the Bill of Sale and Classification Society documents. If this was the *Rose of Stambul*, she must have been gutted and everything inside, including the engine, replaced. That's as far as Spire got on the *Alida*. But he must also have known the full meaning of his evidence. That's why he was ready to die and withstand even torture. The photographs on Greenfinger Dodd's desk. Spire's clothes on the bed. His hands and index fingers laid out neatly on the bedside table. Did he know what ship he was serving on? Did he know what relationship there must have been between the *Alida II* and the Russian *Lena*? And back to the old question that had bugged Bucken and Poon in Macao: if it was the *Lena* that had sunk in the Tsunami, where was the *Alida*? The search had continued ever since the sinking yet nobody had reported any sighting of the *Alida II*. Did she sink or did she vanish?

A door was slammed hard. Heavy steps approached. Why don't the bastards sleep? Bucken fled noiselessly in his plimsolls along the dimmed lights of the passage. Somewhere ahead of him, a hydraulic door opened and began to close with an endless sigh. Then two breathlessly chattering Chinese voices could be heard. Bucken forgot about the icy water in his clothes. It was the sweat of fear that made his jersey cling to his back. He tried a door on the right. It was open. He slipped into complete darkness. A mixture of strange smells greeted him. He was probably in some store room. Voices and increasing traffic in the corridor outside urged him to seek some hiding place. He had to risk brief flashes with his torch in order to orientate himself. There were cans of oil and grease, a workshop corner, deep packed shelves rising above his head, a variety of tools and spares, coils of ropes, and figure-eight-shaped bundles of indestructible string soaked in tar with a pungent yet pleasantly intriguing odour, probably the last relic of sailing days carried on modern ships perhaps to satisfy nothing better than the bosun's whim.

Bucken clambered to the top shelf. It was much deeper than the lower ones, almost half a false ceiling. He could not even start making plans for getting out and away, when with a groan, murmur and throb the ship's engines came to life. He knew nothing about the working of the ship. Did she need warming up for several hours before sailing? The vibration and clangour increased. The traffic outside became incessant. The door opened and somebody came in. Bucken could not see him. He kept his head down, hoping for the best. And the best did not seem good enough.

The mahogany lining of the lift smelt pleasantly of fresh beeswax polish. The shiny brass of the control panel showed no marks or fingerprints. That was exactly the way Savas liked it. One of these days, soon, the Rotterdam office would be abandoned. The thought left him with a mixture of sadness and elation. He tapped out the combination code, and the lift ascended smoothly to the 'non-existent' ninth floor of the eight-storey building.

Savas was early. He sat with his back to the bank of blind TV screens and stared out, over the roofs of Rotterdam, towards the port and the ceaseless procession of ships. Every one of them, even the rusty, the old and the cumbersome, seemed beautiful to him. For a few seconds, he was tempted once again to pray. He was strong enough not to. It shamed him that in critical moments he could even be tempted. And, just now, calling on God's help could weaken his resolve when he needed it most. He had just received some details about the two German mercenaries recruited by Ruzicki, and hated them. Throughout his long career in shipping, he could not avoid mixing occasionally with thieves, con-men, fraudsters and other villains of varying degrees of crookedness, but he had never associated with professional killers. Not until now. Those two made him feel uncomfortable because he would have to – and he knew he somehow would – come to terms with the nature of their service.

In the distance, a pack of tugs busied themselves like well-trained sheepdogs around a chemical tanker. What a lovely ship! Purpose-built, every inch of her planned ingeniously for maximum utilisation, efficiency and safety . . . yet she could be the one to face a horrible fate. Or another one like that. There were four ships on the short-list: the choice would soon have to be made. Savas did not want to think about it.

In a few minutes, members of the syndicate would arrive. Savas would chair their most crucial conference on the closed-circuit system. Each would have some selfish motives to fight for. If agreement could be reached, preparations for buying and chartering a major fleet and lining up several valuable deals would have to begin. The projected date for Operation Tsunami could be brought forward to as early as the end of January if all went well. Savas closed his eyes. His thoughts raced along the Suez Canal from Port Said to the Red Sea, with whistle-stops at the Ballah by-pass, Ismailia and the Great Bitter Lake. Imaginary flames shot up. The tanker was alight from stem to stern. Screaming sailors were going over her walls in a mad rush, their distorted faces reflecting the certainty that something much worse than an inferno could await them in the water. Savas's guts shook as they did in rare moments of crying. He opened his eyes to chase the vision away. The tugs strained, the tanker began to turn in majestic slow motion, the anaemic November sun glittered on the windscreen of the bridge – all was well in the port of Rotterdam.

A buzzer sounded, and Savas activated the TV camera in the lift. On a small screen he saw Papeete and Quincey ascending to his floor. He opened the door for them.

Quincey glowed with excitement. He had nothing but good news from Kiel: despite last-minute US government double-checking, everything had turned out well, and the *Rose* was on her way. It was hard to keep it all to himself. He was also enthusiastic about the mercenaries.

'Can we trust them?' Savas asked.

'As much as we can trust anyone.' Quincey was relaxed. Papeete seemed absentminded.

'I'd prefer to have someone we know with them. Someone to let them get on with it but remain in ultimate charge in case sudden decisions have to be made.'

'No problem. Do you have anyone particular in mind?'

'Yes. Bucken.' Savas noticed that Papeete looked up with sudden interest in the subject.

Quincey shrugged his shoulders. 'Whatever you say, Oldman, whatever you say.'

'You'll have to ask him. I mean he may not be interested,' said Papeete.

'Why shouldn't he be, darling?' Quincey smiled at his wife. 'And if he wasn't, you could always try to persuade him.'

'He did a good job for you, did'nt he?'

'No complaints, darling, he did everything I had in mind.'

'So where is he now?' Savas asked.

'All I know is that he's left Kiel. I thought you were expecting him back only next week or so.'

'That's right, he'll call me. He...' Savas glanced at Papeete, 'he wanted a holiday to enjoy his new money.'

'There you are then.' Quincey turned towards his wife and winked. 'He's probably enjoying some well-earned female company in Hamburg. There's a lot of talent there, I bet.'

Hunger was easier to bear than thirst and seasickness in the rising heat of the store room. Stale air became trapped on Bucken's shelf and made breathing an unpleasant task. Some twenty hours out of Kiel, relative silence descended upon the store and the world outside: nothing but trumpeting gusts and the drone of the engines filtered through the door. Bucken decided to take a chance and reconnoitre the corridor. He did not hope to find a better hiding place easily, but he might be able to forage for food and water. He opened the door cautiously. There were no voices, no movement. He slipped outside and turned left. He remembered passing the galley on his way in. Now he could not find it. Was it one floor up? A wild movement of the ship thrust him against the wall, then made him stumble blindly to regain his balance. He felt sick.

Unsteady on his feet, Bucken retraced his steps towards and past the store room. The noise of the engines grew louder. Then a hydraulically-operated door blocked his progress. Next to it, the 'opening instructions' were badly glued to the bulkhead. The sheet of print was peeling at the edges. Another note, above the red handle, said

ATTENTION
ALARM
DOOR ABOUT TO SHUT – KEEP CLEAR

That could indicate only one thing: in case of fire or flooding or merely for the sake of good housekeeping, the door could be worked by remote control, probably from the bridge. It meant that some warning light up there would tell anyone who cared to look if any of those doors was open. If they realised that nobody was supposed to be down here just now. . . It was yet another risk Bucken had to take. He was about to pull the handle when it occurred to him that

201

such sophisticated electronics might not be in keeping with the age of the *Rose*. Like her good, rust-free condition. And unlike the peeling sheets of print. Wouldn't such instructions be painted or embossed on the metal itself? With a sudden urge he pinched the corner of the WARNING, and pulled it. It lifted away easily. Underneath, several words in identical layout were embossed in metal. But he could not read them. The writing was Cyrillic.

The thoughts triggered by the discovery came in a single flash. The ship was not the *Rose*. She was Russian. Spire must have made the same discovery aboard the *Alida II* which was probably the *Lena*. And, if this was not the *Rose*, she might not be intended to sink at all. The printed sheets would be removed, the ship would change her identity and sail away with all the embargoed goods. But then where was the real *Rose*? What would be sunk in her place? And finally, the simplicity of it all struck Bucken: the sinking would be publicised freely but, in fact, nothing would sink and so nothing could ever be found on the seabed. The *Rose*? And the *Alida II*? Neither of them would ever be seen in any port in the world. They were ghosts that existed only on paper. The grounded wrecks they once had been must have been cut up for scrap, leaving no trace.

Bucken pulled the handle and the door opened in slow motion with the familiar sigh as if resenting the nocturnal disturbance. There might be people on the other side. They would be shocked to see a stranger on board. Ready to exploit surprise, his only potential advantage, Bucken dived through as soon as the gap was wide enough.

The passage and the small electronic control room beyond were deserted. Facing a wall of row upon row of gauges, switches and red buttons, a well-worn swivel chair was still warm. Its user could be behind the panel. A single leap took Bucken to his target but there was nobody there. His foot hurt: accidentally he had kicked and over-turned a heavy can. He picked it up and touched the liquid, a little of which he had spilled. It smelled foul but at least it was not oily. He drank some lukewarm water. On his wet lips he could detect a faint draught of air. He drank some more, hoped not to be sick, washed his face, and followed the draught. It led him to a metal ladder that was fixed vertically to the wall. At its top, he could make out the shape of an escape hatch in the eerie light. He took a few more gulps, and began to climb the ladder. The rungs were clean. Another sign of good housekeeping. Did it mean that someone on the bridge would soon notice some warning light indicating an open hydraulic door? Bucken knew he ought to rush back and shut it, but could not resist the lure of that hatch above.

202

He climbed to the top. The hatch cover was heavy but it opened smoothly. As soon as he began to raise it, a fierce wind peppered his eyes with icy droplets of seawater. Blinking desperately, he scanned the deck. Nothing was moving up there. Only madmen would venture out on a night like that. The ship heaved and pitched, only to come down corkscrewing. As she ran into a dark pit of waves, Bucken's stomach turned. He looked up to keep his eyes from the sea. High above the bow, a single speck of light danced in the black sky. Bucken threw up violently. His whole body convulsed again and again, weakening his grip on the ladder, increasing the weight of the hatch cover on the back of his head. The ship rolled and began to rise but the convulsions would not stop. The mixed smell of diesel and vomit would continue to make Bucken sick without any help from the sea. Yet the urge to escape was almost irresistible. A few steps could take him across the deck. Anything, even a crazy plunge into the darkness, would be better than staying on board. But he knew that the sea would offer him nothing beyond the choice between freezing and drowning.

Lowering the hatch, he retreated. His knees wobbled as he slid down: seasickness and the bleak prospects ahead had taken their toll. His only chance would come when the ship reached Helsinki and. . . His thoughts collapsed in a heap. The ship would never go to Helsinki. He might have to make his getaway in a hostile port when the crew were taken off. But how? Somehow. He longed to be back in the womb of his top shelf where he could curl up, feel the hard support of the wall, and think in peace, more clearly, hoping that the mess and stink he had left behind would not lead the crew to his perch.

He ran back through the open hydraulic door, pausing only to reach for the operating handle – but he was knocked off balance. The ship reared up and crashed down as if the waves had had enough of playing with this useless toy. Bucken would not let go of his can of water. His flailing arms sought support to keep him upright. He never saw the short metal rod that tore into his temple.

When Bucken came to, he was lying in a pool of blood and water. A Chinaman was slapping his face hard. 'Wake ahup. Wake ahup, foreign devil. Who arle you? I'm sure I know you. Who arle you?'

Seeking his way back to the world, Bucken was uncertain where he was or what had happened. The voice amused him. The r-s were as soft as l-s, and the frequent, unwarranted ha-s in various words lent the man's speech a humorous quality. But there was no joke, only punchlines. The slaps grew harder. 'Wake up.' Bucken felt the repeated prodding of the metal rod. He opened his eyes and closed them again. He tried to take stock. The other man had all the advantage. Bucken needed time to regain his strength. But time he would not be given. His attack would have to be unexpected to be effective. He groaned and began to turn. The man stepped aside and reached for the can to see how much water was left in it. Bucken kicked the man's knee and pushed himself away from the floor, hoping to jump to his feet in the same movement.

The plan failed. The kick had caught the man unawares but failed to hurt him sufficiently. And, instead of leaping, Bucken was barely staggering to his feet. As they both turned so as to keep facing each other, the light fell on the man's face. Bucken recognised him. It was Ting-chao. His unblinking eyes reflected boredom rather than any urgency. More at home on the rolling, uneven rhythm of waves, he feigned his first attack, a thrust with his outstretched fingers towards Bucken's eyes, knowing full well that it would drive his opponent right into the path of the metal rod. Unceremoniously, he clubbed Bucken to the floor once again.

Bucken fell readily to avoid further blows. He was hurt but exaggerated how dazed he was. The last of his strength would have to be used sparingly.

'Who arle you?' Ting-chao closed in and put his foot on Bucken's chest. He was so sure of himself that he dropped the rod on the floor. But then he whipped a bayonet-shaped knife out of a sheath under his shirt. 'You say nothin', Misteh? All rhight. Firhst it will be one fingel . . . then two . . . then three. . . You want that? Everybody talks, Misteh, I tell you. Only one man didn't, but he was cra-hazy. And he is dead. Vely, vely dead.'

And I know who it was, thought Bucken, though the recognition of Ting's crazy victim was no consolation. He found it easier now to avoid Ting's eyes and pretend exhaustion and helplessness. The pressure of Ting's foot increased. 'Talk. Now.' The foot shifted towards Bucken's neck. 'Who arle you?' The knife glittered as it plunged with measured menace. Behind Ting, a croaky klaxon gave the alarm: the hydraulic door was about to close. Someone on the bridge had noticed it was open. The harsh sound would give sufficient time for anybody in the door to get clear.

'My name is Booker. I'm the owner of this ship.' Bucken felt proud of his presence of mind: saying 'ship' was right, mentioning the *Rose* would give him away because Ting must know the truth.

'The owneh?' Ting sounded startled. He knew that a Mr. Booker worked for Ruzicki. Why hadn't Ruzicki told him that the owner would be on board? What was going on? He thought hard to solve the puzzle without clues, and reduced his concentration on his helpless victim. It did not concern him that, behind him, the sound of the klaxon pitched to a shrill. But Bucken heard the sigh of the closing door. He grabbed Ting's foot and yanked it with all he had left in him. As his body flew backwards, Ting dropped the knife so as to grab something for support, and his fingernails spurted blood as he tried to maul a hold out of bare metal. His head hit a large fuse-box on the wall, and bounced, in a half-turn, into the path of the slowly-sliding door that closed on him with unstoppable power. It caught him in a vice, squeezing his neck into his right armpit. There was a sickening crunch. An embryo of a scream did not live long. The rattle of death rose from his broken throat, and the pressure on it remained constant – the machine was neither cruel nor merciful.

Bucken was on his feet, holding Ting's knife, thinking about Sergeant Spire, and telling himself that he must exact his revenge. He could not kill in cold blood, but not pulling the handle to open the door was as good as murder. It would take several minutes for someone to come down from the wheelhouse to investigate why the door would not close properly. By that time Ting would be dead. Bucken felt no remorse, relief or satisfaction.

Fear and exhaustion urging him to run and hide on his shelf, Bucken forced himself to stay and think for a few more moments. The can. He must not lose the can however little was left of the water. And the knife. He saw the scene with his policeman's eyes. If this death was an accident, the knife would not be lying there. Ting's body was still writhing in mute agony when Bucken's searching fingers located the sheath under the shirt. Bucken could see no other tell-tale sign that there had been a fight. He ran.

When, much too late, Ting was found and freed, the bleeding bump on his head testified to an accidental fall. Nobody would investigate any further, nobody cared. If anything, it was anger the captain felt towards his dead first officer. Accidents and suchlike were a nuisance. The corpse could not even be dumped in the sea because the captain had strict orders that, at the time of the hand-over of the ship, every member of the crew must be present or accounted for. A burial at sea might require a great deal of explanation. It was not worth the hassle and the argument with Ruzicki.

The morning after the night of the *Rose*'s departure, a corpse with a severely-disfigured face was washed ashore in Kiel harbour. Cause of death: strangling and-or multiple injuries. Because the police had found a valuable ring and almost two thousand Deutschmarks on him, robbery was ruled out as the probable motive for the murder.

205

The vicious battering of the face could have indicated an attempt at disidentification, but Inspector Kohl, the detective in charge, decided that this must be a case of some vendetta, probably involving a jilted and possibly homosexual lover. Routine checks on hotels revealed that Reg Booker, an Australian shipowner, was missing. Kohl put two and two together. Feeling certain that the killer would be caught within a few days, he was already losing serious professional interest.

At midday, the lab reported an intriguing complication: Booker's passport, found in the hotel, was a first-rate forgery. The detective contemplated it over his lengthy lunch. On his return to his office, he heard that the Kiel police had been alerted to look out for an American who was also missing. The alert was raised by Bonn, and the level of pressure to find the man was ominous. It would have told any policeman of minimal logic that the missing American, although of no official status, must be of considerable importance, i.e. CIA. Inspector Kohl was inclined to put two and two together yet again, but chose to hold off for at least twenty-four hours, try to carry out a more positive identification of the body first, and offer Bonn a neat solution on a plate. This time he would not be passed over when it came to promotion. He reasoned that two missing men plus one corpse must equal one murderer plus one victim.

At about the same time, a Kiel shipping agent was asked to do a most confidential favour to Lord Ashenbury, an old friend and business associate, who was interested in the loading and sailing time of the *Rose of Stambul*. An hour later, Ashenbury was infuriated by the news that the *Rose* had sailed during the night. So where the hell was Bucken? Why wasn't he in touch?

The following morning, the corpse of Kiel harbour merited a bloated headline, a skimpy news item with homosexual undertones, and a gruesome photograph in the *Bild Zeitung*. Ruzicki bought a copy of the paper at Hamburg airport, and took it with him on the early flight to Rotterdam where he would join the Quinceys for breakfast. He showed them the picture and translated the words.

Quincey watched the blood drain from Papeete's face. 'Yes,' he said, 'it's very sad, and most inconvenient for Savas. We must let him know'.

'I'll do it,' Ruzicki volunteered. 'I can try to find out some details if you want me to.'

Quincey turned to his wife. He saw she must be on the verge of fainting. 'Do you think we need any details, honey? I mean they must be quite distasteful. Who would have guessed that Bucken was a pansy?'

206

She stood up and left the room. Quincey watched her closely as she passed him. She was not yet crying. She soon would be, he thought, and it both pleased and irked him.

Bucken woke with a fright. The cessation of noise and the ensuing plunge into silence were as stirring to him as a gunshot to birds in a cherry tree. He did not know how long he had slept – only the cramp in his joints was a clue – or how long before the engine had stopped. The ship was rolling from side to side. Waves were banging on the bulkheads. From above he heard heavy objects being dragged along the deck. He drank the last of his water. Pangs of hunger combined with night-long seasickness to torment his stomach. He had no room to sit up. He shifted and turned uncomfortably. He remembered his nightmare of falling off his top shelf, breaking his arms, and being found helplessly by the crew of the *Rose* who then proceeded to snip off his fingers and toes, one by one. He knew he was awake but the darkness perpetuated the dream. In the torch-light he looked at his watch. Twenty to six. Dawn or day? He wished he had a twenty-four-hour digital. What if they were already in some port, some Russian port? Startled, he sat up only to crash his skull into the deckhead.

Bucken exercised his left arm to remove the pins and needles before he would lower himself to the floor. Once again, the corridor outside was dark and silent. The hydraulic door, Ting's killer, was closed. The corpse was gone. In trepidation, he pulled the red handle. The sigh could have been his own: he had to make a move if he did not want just to wait to be found. He made his way to the ladder with the hatch on top, paused for steps or other sounds of warning from above, and opened the hatch just enough to peer out. He was ready for the breathtaking gusts of icy wind but, this time, the air was merely bracing. He took a huge gulp of it.

At first he saw only dimmed lights – daybreak in the Baltic was still battling with darkness below the horizon. Then, gradually, he could make out some activities on deck. There were several waterproof-clad figures hurrying about, most of them hooded and faceless like monks, a few wore sou'westers that threw off a wet glitter as they passed under the lights. Bucken scanned the horizon as far as he could in a half-circle. He saw nothing but a black seascape in a black sky. The ship must be stationary at open sea.

A stocky figure with a bucket wobbled along the icy deck, his feet wide apart for better balance, and stopped next to the portside life-boat, only a couple of yards away from the slightly-raised hatch.

Bucken could not see what the man was using, but a pungent smell drifted towards him, and soon the words ROSE OF STAMBUL were beginning to melt away from the side of the lifeboat. The man was scrubbing it furiously. After a few minutes, a second man arrived with a tin of paint and a strip of cardboard with some pattern cut out of it. Bucken watched them mesmerised as they began to stencil an R, an 0 and then double SS on the side of the boat.

The captain stood on the bridge and ticked off items on a check-list. The name on the bow had already been repainted, the gondola with two men was just now being lowered behind the stern: soon the *Rose of Stambul* would revert to *Rossiya Nyeva*. The captain ticked two more items and looked towards the lifeboats: the starboard one would remain untouched; on the portside boat, the stencil was in position, the letters, R, 0, S, S and I appeared one by one. He was waiting for the change of funnel cladding. Another five minutes – and the transformation of the ship would be completed. Signs and markings on the bridge, in the engine room and the crew's quarters had already been changed to Russian, below deck there was nothing else to be done. Embossed numbers on the various parts of the engine and power plants had never been altered: there was no need, nobody in port would examine those during routine loading.

On deck, men began to gather around the foremast where the mock-up of the heavy-lift jumbo derrick, perhaps the most prominent feature which could identify the *Rose*, had already been dismantled. It would soon be jettisoned and sunk.

The captain walked over to the radar and scrutinised the bleak and desolate picture. Apart from a fine spray of lights, the circling trace revealed no recognisable bleeps. Nothing moved. Nothing but the clutter of echoes from rain and sea. There were no ships in the sight of the radar. He switched over to the twenty-four-mile range. Still nothing. In disbelief, he picked up his binoculars hoping to prove the radar wrong by spotting a distant light approaching his ship. He found nothing. His disappointment turned into anger. He hated sloppy operations. Until that cursed collision near the Horn and that unfair court hearing, he used to take pride in the discipline of the Royal Dutch Navy, particularly his own minesweeper. All right, this was not the Navy, but if a rendezvous was scheduled for zero six hundred hours, it should not be effected at zero five fifty nine or zero six zero one. Yet now that damned Greek rescue ship which would bring fresh crew and take off his men before the 'sinking' was already ten minutes late. According to his schedule, by now he ought to have transmitted his first Mayday call announcing explosions and fire all over the *Rose*, and requesting immediate assistance from all ships. The Mayday would be picked up on the island of Götland and in the Latvian ports, the nearest land, as well as by any ships in the vicinity, but the 'rescue' would be carried out by the Greeks, as arranged, because they 'happened' to be most conveniently positioned. But where the hell were they? What if the wind got up again? He would not fancy transferring his men to lifeboats, even with the Greek ship standing by, in a full Baltic storm.

The distant whizz, then chuck-chuck, of a helicopter attracted his attention. It was approaching without any navigation lights. What the hell was that? Some Swedish sea patrol? Why? Was something wrong? The men on deck must also have sensed danger. They stopped working.

Soon the chopper was overhead. It began to hover and flashed B-Q-S, the agreed recognition signal for proper authority to take command and for radio communications in an emergency. The captain stepped out on the wing of the bridge, picked up the Aldis lamp and flashed B. Q. B, the correct answer code skywards. The chopper came lower and lower. The door on its side opened, and a man in a green overall was winched down. The captain ordered the crew on board to catch him. While two more men followed, the first down started towards the bridge. The captain decided to wait for him rather than meet him halfway. An officer of the Royal Dutch Navy. . . Shit, he mumbled to himself. There was nothing royal or even naval about himself or this operation. But it would be the last, he promised himself.

The visitor was young, his face full of acne. He came up on the bridge and glanced knowingly at the radar even before saying a word. Not a stranger to ships, thought the captain, and let him say good morning first. They spoke English, the language of the sea.

'Good morning, captain. Sorry about the change of plans.'

'What change?'

'The rescue ship has been delayed but she'll be here in no time.' The man's voice had a military clip. 'Please collect all your men on deck. We must have a roll-call.'

'I know.' The captain issued his orders.

'I take it that everything is prepared.'

'And you'll be right in that.'

Both men moved over to the radar. The revolving sweep showed up a glowing orange dot that was approaching fast from the edge of the dark concentric circles, cutting through the sprinkling of lights on the screen. The captain sighed with relief.

The young lout, who failed to show even the basic courtesy of introducing himself, reviewed the ship from the bridge. He noted the obligatory two red lights that had been hoisted to pretend that the ship was 'not under command', i.e. drifting, the furious activities on deck, and the jettisoning of the mock jumbo derrick. He nodded with satisfaction, and turned to the captain: 'Time for your Mayday.'

The captain started towards the radio cubicle. 'I'll tell Sparks.'

The visitor raised his eyebrows. He seemed puzzled. Let him be, thought the captain, why should I help?

'Oh yes.' The man remembered that most radio officers were nicknamed Sparks. He was proud of his command of English. 'No, captain,' he smiled, 'I tell Sparks.'

'As you wish.'

The sweet smell of hashish permeated the radio room. The Chinese radio officer would not even remove the joint from his mouth when the captain and the visitor entered. Why should he? This was not the Navy. He was a partner, not a 'fooking servant'. 'What?' he asked without looking at them.

'Mayday. Make the distress call brief and garbled. Try to sound excited.'

'I know my fooking yob, misteh – you know yours?' He activated the auto-key device. It began to send out SOS signals followed by the ship's call sign and long, four-second dashes to enable all shipping to take bearings. It would activate auto-alarms aboard all ships on 500 kiloHertz within receiving distance. It would initially keep transmitting for two minutes to allow radio officers to come on duty and get ready to receive the distress message.

After only thirty seconds, the stranger snapped: 'That's enough.'

'I am radio officeh, I know when enough.'

'And I tell you it's now.' He pulled out a gun and pointed it at Sparks.

'There's no need. . . ' the captain began, but the pimply youth cut him short:

'Then tell him to do as I say.'

Sparks reached for the Morse key, but the man ordered him to use RT. Morse would be too clear, easier to read and take bearings on. Radio-Telephony could be a mess, a victim of noise, static and other radio traffic. Sparks shrugged his shoulders, tuned to 2182 kHz, the distress frequency that would be heard on the insomniac Channel 16 on the bridge of every ship and land-based monitoring stations.

'CQD. . . CQD. . . ' he began his message. It would warn everybody that an emergency call was being made, keep the airwaves free of traffic. 'CQD,' he repeated with a smile: the code was generally nicknamed Come Quick, Distress, but the last thing anybody aboard the *Rose* wanted was for some intruder to come quickly to the unwanted rescue. 'CQD. Vessel *Rose of Stambul*. Ten. . . ' he mumbled the tonnage and spoke with admirable incoherence about explosions, fire, heavy weather and the ship's position that could send searchers on a wild goose chase over hundreds of square miles. '. . . immediately need help. Twenty-two crew abandoning ship. Immediate help, all shipping. . . '

At a signal from the visitor, Sparks switched off the transmitter and beamed: 'Okay, misteh?'

'No.' He refused to share his moment of amusement. 'Switch on, please.' He grabbed the microphone and, affecting a heavy Russian accent, began to answer the distress call: '*Rose of Stambul*. Your Mayday not loud not clear. Soviet vessel *Rossiya Nyeva in distress area. No see on radar. We full speed to help. Please give good bearings.*'

Clever, thought the captain. Everybody in the Baltic would be assured that the *Rossiya* was already standing by to pick up survivors. It would also serve as proof that the *Rossiya* was making no secret of her presence in the area at the time of the sinking.

The youth ordered Sparks to transmit a final 'CQD, abandoning ship' message and close down.

'Are all your men on deck, captain?'

'Except one. My first officer is dead. An accident.'

'Where is the body?'

'On ice in a store room. It's being brought up.'

'Good. Let's go. You, too, Sparks.'

Bucken climbed down a couple of rungs to give a rest to his aching neck which had to support the weight of the hatch cover. He had already armed himself with a grappling-hook and now he began to formulate his escape plan. His ideas ranged from the insane to the crazy. He closed his eyes to concentrate – and he was fast asleep. Greta told him to be grateful. Papeete said that the unborn tomorrow was today. He woke up with a start. It was the chirp and rumble above that saved him from falling off the ladder. He recognised the sound. A helicopter was approaching. Then another one. Were they going to take off the crew? He would have to get among them. But how? He could perhaps grab a man, knock him out, pull him down through the hatch, and take his waterproofs in the hope that the darkness and the hood would give him momentary safety. It was madness but he had no choice.

He climbed back to the top and raised the cover a fraction. The crew were standing in a tight group. A man in green overalls was counting them. At their feet lay Ting-chao. His head was at a permanent tilt. The small chopper overhead was moving out of the way. Two large ones took its place above. Guide ropes were dropped and caught on deck. From both machines simultaneously, men began a fast and orderly descent. Each of them carried a long, slim duffle bag that seemed heavy. It looked like a military operation. Marines? Commandos? They were spreading out in a half-circle.

The man in overalls finished the count. 'Please get the starboard lifeboat lowered, captain, ready for embarkation.'

'Sure. As soon as the rescue ship is here. I'm not going to let my men. . . '

The stranger pulled out his gun. 'Now,' he said with quiet authority.

'Now hang on, sonny. . . ' He never finished the sentence. The bullet blew half his head away.

The crew stood stunned for a second, then began to move menacingly. A series of clicking noises concentrated their attention. They were surrounded by the new arrivals who had pulled submachine guns out of the duffle bags.

'Behave yourselves and nobody else will be hurt.'

Bucken did not believe him. He was glad not to be wearing a waterproof and standing among them.

The marines were backing away from the bunched crew of the *Rose*. The man in overalls glanced around, checking the situation. He raised his hand. The guns opened up. It was over in seven seconds. Ting's corpse was not the odd man out any more. On the wildly-rolling deck blood was flowing everywhere. The captain's body was beginning to slide towards the railing. The man in charge trod on the face to stop it. He was counting once again – the roll call had become a body count. The two large helicopters swivelled round and departed.

Brief orders were issued in Russian. The men worked with the efficiency of well-rehearsed extras on a film set. A tarpaulin was removed to uncover a massive metal container. While the corpses were being thrown into it, oxyacetylene equipment was winched down from the small chopper which was then ready to follow its big brothers.

In the distance, Bucken spotted a ship. Judging from its silhouette, it could be a warship. Home for the aircraft, escort for the *Rossiya Nyeva*. Bucken just stared, unable to move, paralysed by the repugnant sight of the massacre and the growing certainty that, if he could escape at all, a few minutes' survival in the freezing waters would be all he could hope for.

The dead filled the container almost to the brim. The metal lid was welded into position. It had holes to let the sea in. A crane lifted the spare anchor of the ship and it was welded to the container by a chain. Meanwhile hoses were run out all over the deck. Two derricks lifted the container and swung it out towards the sea. The chain was too short, and the anchor was torn from the crane. It came down with a crash, cut a furrow in the deck as the roll drove it to the port side, amputated a stretch of railing, and plunged towards the waves. Swearing men swarmed everywhere to save the lifting gear. The container, a potential battering ram, was swinging dangerously, but the teams worked well. They released the load, and the boxed crew of the *Rose* were on their way to their sea grave.

The hoses were turned on. Bucken got a drenching. The blood was washed away. From the bridge, someone issued Russian commands through a hailer. Bucken did not understand a word, but instinct told him that the *Rossiya* would soon be underway. Half the men were disappearing from the deck. The killers must be putting on their sailors' hats – they would soon be down in the engine room. Yet he could not go on to the deck: the last team up there were working only a few feet away from his hatch. Below and behind him, he heard the hiss of the hydraulic door. Then men came running. Bucken climbed further up until he was in a crouching position. His neck ached. Weighed down by the metal cover as he was, it was impossible to tell how long he could perch like that. The engine room crew were passing right below him. He hoped they would be too busy to look up.

The men on deck broke up various wooden objects collected from all over the ship. They tore away bits of a lifeboat, then hurled all the wreckage overboard. The job was completed by the jettisoning of half a dozen lifebelts with the name *Rose of Stambul*, and the launching of the starboard lifeboat, the only one that had not been repainted. In his mind's eye, Bucken could see all the wreckage floating away to provide proof of the sinking. If only the team on deck finished the job. . . How long will they be? Shit! The engine was starting up.

The deck team hosed down the starboard side. Much of the water froze to the deck. The ship began to vibrate in earnest. The men turned to run in the hoses. Bucken knew it was his last chance. He shoved the hatch cover upwards and decided to take his last chance. He could already see himself diving into the sea, but in fact he was not yet through the hatch. His body was too numb to obey. Instead of taking a few leaps, he was dragging himself along, skating, stumbling, forgetting that he was still swinging the grappling-iron, forcing himself not to look back: there would be no advantage in facing the guns.

His luck, if the prospect of the Baltic could be called luck, still held – or the men were too well drilled to look anywhere but at the job in hand. Instead of executing a grand dive, Bucken tumbled over the broken railing, hit the water awkwardly, and began to swim towards a lifebelt. The boat was not far beyond it. If he did not freeze or drown first, he might be sucked under the hull of the ship as she began to move, only to be minced up by the screws astern. And yet he was still holding on to the grappling iron. It might have been a subconscious act of defiance or the shackles of lifelong habits: he would never let go of evidence. The markings on the handle were in Cyrillic. I must be mad to risk my life for it, he thought, as he battled with the waves and the cold and the conviction that a spotlight and a hail of bullets would find him . . . just about now . . . or now. . .

A mighty roller lifted him playfully and dropped him into the jaws of another two. The sea isn't cruel, he thought as he went under, it's just too big to notice me and make allowances for the weak. His lungs were bursting. Let me go! He thought he was shouting. There was nothing else he could do. Swimming and thrashing about would be as effective as spitting into an inferno. That much he had already learned, and now he felt at peace with the sea. It was the peace of helpless despair, the first step into death. His mouth demanded air – and let in the sea. It did not taste salty. Was it that the Baltic was different or did taste make no difference to the dead? Suddenly he was breathing again. And seeing the sky in a whirl. Something crashed into him. He hit back angrily with the grappling iron. He held on – and the next wave failed to suck him under.

Swamped by headlines about mysterious EXPLOSIONS IN THE GULF OF SUEZ and MINES AT BAB EL MANDEB, the world press could spare hardly any space for the *Rose of Stambul* disaster, though papers on the Baltic Coast made the most of it.

ROSE OF STAMBUL SINKS WITHOUT TRACE

Storm or Sabotage? New Baltic Enigma

Baltic Winter Arrives With A Bang

MAYDAY IN DECEMBER: crew missing, presumed dead

There was plenty of room for hot speculation. The *Rose* must have sunk almost immediately after the Mayday call. Why? What went wrong? Instant accusations and counter-accusations answered the questions concerning the delays and inefficiency in the mounting of search and rescue operations.

The role of the *Rossiya Nyeva* puzzled and infuriated the shipping world. She was on record as receiving and answering the Mayday call, and asking for precise location co-ordinates from the foundering *Rose*. But, apparently, the Soviet vessel was late on the scene. She reported finding nothing but a couple of lifebelts and several pieces of floating wreckage. She marked out the spots with a few buoys, then left with inexplicable speed, using the excuses of 'running out of fuel' and having 'food poisoning of epidemic proportions' on board. The news was that she would steam for Pavilosta, the nearest Latvian port, where she would land all she had recovered at the scene of the disaster. The Soviet authorities volunteered to deliver everything, without delay, into the hands of the investigators or other rightful claimants.

The role of bad weather was also debatable. The consensus of opinion was that the storm had subsided to manageable levels by the time of the SOS message: and, even at its peak, a *truly seaworthy* ship would have ridden it comfortably. So was the *Rose* truly seaworthy? Yes, initial inquiries indicated that she had recently undergone a major refit and overhaul prior to the issue of her new Classification Certificate in Mogadishu. That would support the sudden disaster theory also confirmed by a reference to the explosion in the Mayday message and the fact that, apparently, all hands had gone down with the ship.

When all this was published, the day after the sinking, ships and aircraft were still converging to search for survivors, but nobody had any real hope of finding anything better than some wreckage and perhaps a corpse or two.

There was considerable interest in the cargo of the *Rose* because its would-be recipients in Helsinki refused to give any press interviews or statements about the value of the loss. But none of the papers would yet connect the disaster with the 'Mystery Death in Kiel Harbour', merely a news item on the previous day's inside pages.

Oldman Savas liked to joke about the disadvantages of being rich. If you own several homes, castles, *pieds-à-terre*, floating palaces and love-nests in Paris, New York, Athens and Rotterdam, he would sigh in mock despair, you only multiply your chances of the roof falling in on you somewhere or other. This time, it was no joke. All the roofs seemed to be falling in simultaneously in the last few days.

His run of misfortune began with a midnight telephone call from Greece: an earthquake had left most of his villagers homeless. So soon after the flood, it came at one of the worst possible moments. He would have to arrange a massive financial operation to help just when a sudden weakening of the dollar and a potentially devastating run on his business interests in the United States had already rendered him particularly vulnerable. Under such pressures, the multi-million yield from the Ivory Coast fraud was dwindling away at a stunning speed. Operation Tsunami would put an end to all such worries and enable him to deal even with the most monstrous demands on his resources, but the smooth development of the syndicate's Suez plans had suffered an unexpected setback and could be torpedoed by the appearance of mines in the Gulf of Suez. Like everybody else, Savas was desperate to figure out who would and could have planted them. Should Iraq and Iran be his prime suspects? Were the Egyptians up to something? Had the Israeli elections anything to do with it? Why would Israel open a new front? And then there could be something in it for Libya. Wasn't the Colonel always trying to catch something in the muddiest waters of international politics?

None of this helped Savas in his planning. If the Straits of Hormuz and Bab el Mandeb were closed to shipping. . . He was afraid even to contemplate the prospect. And, if all this was not enough to unhinge the imperturbability of old age, there were the two phone calls from his daughter. One had come the previous night, announcing that she was engaged to an Italian count who was probably more of a conman than an aristocrat. The second call came the following morning to say that the engagement was off, but she was four months pregnant, and two gynaecologists had already refused to carry out an abortion.

Savas woke Greta to deal with it. He could not tell which made her more furious – the pregnancy or the interference with her normal hours of sleep. Savas did not care. He ordered coffee for her, but the next knock at the door was not room service. It was Papeete with the *Bild Zeitung* and the news that 'Herr Booker' had been found floating in Kiel harbour. It shook him badly. He liked Bucken. Occasionally, he would even toy with the idea of training the disgraced cop for a major role in the Savas empire. The old man closed his eyes and swore at the gods who denied him a son or heir or at least a friend. He did not even begrudge Bucken the pain his death caused to the two women. Both of them were fighting back their tears, both seemed bereft of speech.

Then a call from New York came through. Savas had to deal with it and concentrate in order to make snap decisions involving millions of dollars. That was why he only half-heard the conversation at the far end of the room.

Greta made the first vicious thrust. 'Couldn't you protect him? Couldn't you do at least that much for him?'

'What on earth are you talking about?'

'He was killed. Was it because he loved you?'

'You're out of your mind.'

'Am I? Or is it you who's crazy?' Pain and anger wiped out Greta's memory of her betrayal. She had never meant to tell Quincey on the phone that Bucken might have spent that night in Singapore in Papeete's room. 'I hope you enjoy ruining men. Is that what you get your kicks from or is it simply a pathological compulsion to betray every man you know and sleep with?'

Papeete would not let Greta see how deeply hurt she was. She kept her voice cool. 'I, for one, don't sleep with every man I know.'

'Oh, good. Then we both go only halfway. Because I don't know every man I sleep with. At least, my way there's no temptation to betray them all.'

Papeete turned away. She hunched her shoulders and tried to calm her breathing. In . . . out. In . . . out. Isn't that what they do during childbirth? In . . . out. She would never have a baby. Not from Quincey, and not from Bucken any more. His tomorrow would remain unborn forever.

Behind her, Greta was whispering more to herself than anybody else: 'If *I* were his lover, I'd have saved him.'

The CIA's Frankfurt station chief knew he could never come much nearer to a stroke or a heart attack or both. He decided to break his lifelong self-imposed rule of not touching bourbon before breakfast, and poured himself the first two fingers of Jack Daniels of the day. He must try to think clearly. There might be only a few minutes left until urgent demands for a whole range of explanations started flooding his desk, telephones and telex lines. Right, then.

Why was the loading of the *Rose of Stambul* authorised?

I wouldn't know. Ask the Pentagon.

Then why did you send a man to see the ship-owner and check out the final arrangements?

Because the whole thing looked odd. Yes, odd, irregular, but not suspicious, nothing to warrant a double check with Langley.

Then why did you detail an agent to tail and check out Booker?

No connection between the two. I mean, at that stage, the lines didn't cross. We didn't even realise that Booker and the ship-owner were one and the same person. We only had a tip-off that Booker might be of interest to us.

Tip-off?

Sure. From an adopted son.

You mean an informer?

Yeah. Don Quincey. Useful guy. If he had already seen the papers, he would think that Booker was dead. He wouldn't know, of course, what the Kiel police told me alone, that the corpse was not Booker but my man.

So what's your theory?

The station chief leaned back in his chair and closed his eyes. So far so good. Now a touch of brilliant reasoning, and he's safe. Right. He awarded himself a second dash of bourbon.

My guess is that Booker is KGB. He spotted the tail, then set up the murder and the disidentification to gain time and disappear. Why? Because his job was finished. He somehow got his ship chartered to carry the computer stuff to Helsinki. My guess is that they never loaded any of it on the *Rose*. It was perhaps flown to Moscow. If we ever recover the *Rose*, we'll find only junk aboard.

The third drink gave him an idea. He got on to Langley, Central Computers, and fed in Booker's description just to see if by any chance he was already wanted or being watched or noted for possible interest under his own or any other name, worldwide. He waited, taking sips that would not count because they came straight from the bottle, and smiled triumphantly when he discovered that he had struck gold: the computer told him that Booker was already wanted for a heist he had pulled in Singapore at the expense of the Ivory Coast, possibly in collusion with the Narodny Bank's local branch. The descriptions matched. The teleprinter supplied Frankfurt with a blurred photograph that had been taken by the security camera in the main hall of the Singapore bank.

'Not good enough to tell a spy from a cow in labour,' mumbled the station chief but that made no difference to his projected self-defence. By the time the demands for urgent explanations began to roll in, he would be on the offensive: with due respect, sir, whoever handled the sale of these embargoed goods must be responsible for a universal cock-up; I mean they kept checking the destination of the computers, they demanded an end-user certificate from the Helsinki buyer who was, presumably, kosher, and they checked out the ship, her seaworthiness and the rest without ever looking at the owner!

By mid-morning, the station chief was in the clear. Using diplomatic channels via Bonn, he strongly requested that the Kiel police should not disclose the true identity of the harbour corpse. The Kiel police chief was not pleased. He interpreted the order from Bonn as a sign of Inspector Kohl's unwarranted dabbling in politics, and quietly placed a black mark on the man's record: the Inspector would

218

never get promotion and would be pensioned off at the first suitable opportunity.

At midday, the Frankfurt chief's recommendation was approved by Langley: a worldwide search would begin henceforth to locate/ detain/eliminate – in that order of preference – the Australian, known as Booker, under whatever alias the man might reappear.

The chief then telephoned Quincey in Rotterdam. 'Hi, Don, this is your buddy from Frankie de Furt.'

'Hi, buddy, what's up?'

'You remember the poker player you mentioned to me the other day? Where can I find him? I need a game but now.'

'Tough shit, buddy. The guy's gone bankrupt. No more card games. He's on cold turkey, so to speak. Know what I mean? He's dropped out of sight. And that's final.' Quincey felt angry. Doesn't the fool read the papers? Doesn't he know that Booker is dead?

'So I hear, Don, old buddy, yeah, so I hear. But I'm real keen, you see? So in case he comes up for air and looks for a real hot game, perhaps under his wife's name or something, I wanna know right away. Right?'

'Right.' Quincey rang off. The guy must be off his rocker. How could a corpse resurface in any shape to be of further interest to the Frankfurt station? He couldn't. Not unless. . . Quincey's eyes began to bulge out. He felt like drowning. Not unless. . .

'Are you all right?'

Papeete's concern was an extra irritation. Her eyes revealed that she had been crying yet again. 'Sure I'm all right. Just leave me alone, will you? Go.'

Not unless the corpse in Kiel was not Booker-Bucken's after all. Not unless fucking scarface and his gangsters made a mistake. Yet another mistake. He picked up the phone and asked for a London number.

'Confidential Couriers, Worldwide. Can I help you?'

'You've gotta be joking.'

'Sorry, sir, it's not funny. You got the right number?'

'Okay, okay, the joke's on me, it's me who'll pay twenty thousand rupees for the call.'

Quincey then asked the operator to check if he had the right number for a London shipping company. He was duly told it was a different number, and he said he would talk to them later. That covered him with the switchboard. Meanwhile, 'Confidential Couriers, Worldwide', the KGB shop-front, would be busy identifying the caller and decoding his message: Quincey requested a top priority meeting with the scarfaced agent, his direct controller.

219

Room one hundred and twenty-eight was a creation of inverted Civil Service snobbery that took pride in ostentatious austerity. Its bareness, basic furniture and cheap prints contrasted favourably with its priceless views of Big Ben and the Thames – in effect it was a most economically composed wordless memo to the Cabinet that the Service was doing its best to cut overheads. It was merely incidental that Room 128 was surplus to requirements, had been for years. It was resurrected for Ashenbury's mob, a motley collection of *éminences grises* apart from one actual Face, known to the public as a junior member of the Cabinet.

Once again, it was Ashenbury who had called the meeting of the ad hoc committee. More than the news from Kiel and the sinking of the *Rose*, it was the developing Suez situation that worried him. And, once again, everybody was punctual except Edwin Wade, the chubby, evergreen representative of MI5, but knowing the fellow's peculiar views about the 'prudent modes of passage' that was only to be expected. He arrived ten minutes late and, with utter disregard for the discussion in progress, blurted out that he had bad news about Bucken.

'I think I may assume I am speaking for all members of this Committee when I say that we're quite capable of reading *The Times* ourselves,' said Ashenbury, 'and as the bad news is about three days old, we may presume that everybody here knows that Bucken is dead.'

'My news is worse.' Wade seemed as unmoved as if Ashenbury had only said good morning. 'Bucken may be alive.'

'But we know that Booker . . .'

'Yes, sir, we know about the corpse in Kiel. But we have no proof that it was Booker alias Bucken.'

'Do you have proof that it wasn't?'

'No, I'm going only on the fact that the Americans want Mr. Booker dead or alive. And I'm not given to dramatics, sir. The CIA has placed Booker on the most wanted list. Why, I do not know. They're keen to catch him but, failing that, they want him dead. And I'm afraid that's all I know.'

'Can you name your source?' the Cabinet minister asked.

'Yes, sir, but only if ordered specifically by the PM.'

'If Bucken was alive, he'd be in touch with me, I'm sure of that,' said Ashenbury.

'Unless he knows he's in danger and must lie low.' The pasty face remained expressionless, the voice retained its plum-in-the-cheek echo, the man did not even bother to sound contemptuous. 'There

220

are, of course, other possibilities. Perhaps he *wanted* to disappear. From them as well as us. Perhaps he arranged his own murder using a substitute for the corpse. Let's not forget the facial mutilation might have served as the means of disidentification. Or the means of suggesting some false motive, something like jealousy, for police consumption. We'd then need a replacement. And finally there is the alternative the Committee must have considered, I'm sure.' He paused. 'I'm talking, of course, about the possibility that your man managed to board the *Rose* and vanished with the rest of the crew. This alternative would leave him dead once again and give us a free hand to put in a new man.'

'How?'

'We'd have to find a way.'

'We have no time.' Ashenbury pushed a sheaf of newspaper cuttings towards him. 'This developing Suez crisis may well be a part of the plan Bucken was investigating. For all we know, it may already be in full swing.'

'Yes, sir, I do follow the news.' While the rest of the Committee watched the duel impassively, Wade covered the headlines with short-nailed sausage fingers.'But perhaps a real professional could infiltrate the set-up more effectively.'

'Are you suggesting that Bucken wasn't, I mean isn't, I mean wouldn't be a good enough policeman?'

'No, no, not at all, sir. He's done extremely well. Without his achievements, we couldn't even begin to contemplate our next move. But with due respect, sir, you may not be fully versed in the humdrum details of *my* trade. Where Bucken may tip-toe and box clever, my man would use speedier and, let's say more direct methods. On the other hand, there could be situations where cops would tend to run because they're trained to chase, spies would walk to avoid calling attention to themselves, while counter-intelligence would choose to crawl, yes, gentlemen, in more ways than one, no need to remind me, but crawling is good because in that way you're least likely to miss anything in sight.' Noting Ashenbury's smile he knew as soon as he said it that he had made a mistake.

'Thank you, Mr. Wade, a most enlightening if somewhat self-defeating exposé. You see, we can't really advocate high speed and crawling in the same breath.'

After a brief debate, the Committee decided to watch closely the development of the possible crisis in the Gulf, but take no steps until there were reasonable assurances that the move could not be counter-productive. 'After all, in the light of what we know and suspect,' Ashenbury concluded, 'we may be able to avert serious damage even without Bucken's help if we can spot in good time which way the cat is about to jump.'

Bullshit, thought Wade, and permitted himself a polite smile for the first time.

There remained only one question to be answered: should the Committee inform the CIA about Booker's true identity and mission? The decision against it was unanimous, even though it meant that, if Bucken was alive, the CIA might kill him. Revelations, however, would make the CIA suspicious that not even half the truth was being revealed. To explain Bucken's role, they would have to disclose the facts about Spire, too. In view of all that, the CIA might suspect that the British investigation was never a purely police matter. It might even question the motives behind the unexpected gift of shared intelligence. Why now? Why at all? What if some bright light in Washington accused Britain of actually helping the Russians to obtain those embargoed goods?

'Our decision may entail sacrificing a good man, but I'm sure Bucken would understand. So mum's the word, gentlemen . . . at least for the time being,' said the Cabinet minister who had built a spectacular career on always having the last word – a word of agreement with everybody else. 'Our duty is to our country above all, I mean without doing anything detrimental to our allies.'

Not in his dream of dreams would cub reporter Lars Björkman have scooped the world press twice in one day. Yet it was true, it had happened to him, he had to keep reminding himself as he was yapping away in Swedish and English, choking with excitement, first on the telephone to Radio Götland in Visby, the capital city of the island, and then directly to Stockholm itself where, he knew, the lines were open to the world, and he could be heard live on radio in London, Sydney, Milan and Karachi. Well, he knew that not absolutely everybody and every station would be interested, but the possibility was there, and that was good enough for him. And yet it had all begun with such a routine little assignment, suitable for a beginner: a day after the sinking of the *Rose of Stambul*, his editor had sent him to Herrvik, the thriving fishing port on the east coast of the island, to snoop around and pick up some comments. It would be good if someone ventured to say that 'the captain of the *Rose* must have been a fool, nobody should be at sea in such weather' or something like that. No such luck. The fishermen kept shrugging their shoulders and turned away from his microphone. 'It's bad. But these things happen. It's the risk you take every time you're out there,' was the most promising comment he could cajole out of an old sea-dog.

Ready to return to Visby, he spotted a fishing boat on her way to the harbour. She had a lifeboat in tow, too large for a vessel like that. So Björkman waited, and his patience paid off. He borrowed a pair of binoculars and read the name on the lifeboat: *Rose of Stambul*. They had found something! Were there survivors, too? He ran down to the quay. A shout came from the fishing boat: 'Get an ambulance!' There must be a survivor! Björkman telephoned Visby, collected some brief interviews for the midnight news, and half an hour later he was on the air.

He tried to calm himself but could not. He was reporting a miracle. The survivor had been unconscious in the lifeboat when the fisherman found him. He had suffered from exposure, but old hands at the survival game gave him a fifty-fifty chance. On the way to the port, warmed up by blankets, coffee and akvavit, the man kept passing out and coming to, shivering, looking grateful, but saying nothing as yet about his ordeal or the ship. It seemed he could not or would not release his frozen grip on an iron hook. 'A miracle, a miracle, however it came about!' Björkman panted down the line.

The village hospital felt quite capable of dealing with the case. They kept the survivor there, and the doctor in charge promised Björkman that he would be the first to interview him.

'We've scooped the world,' the editor in Visby said on the phone, claiming a share in the glory. 'Now listen Lars, old son, local stringers and even bigshot reporters from Stockholm and abroad may soon begin flying in. But don't you budge. The story is ours. We have first shot. As soon as the bloke is awake, you talk to him and call me. We'll try to sign him up for an exclusive. I'll make arrangements with the network. Got it?'

The midnight news from Sweden was monitored in Moscow. Because the *Rossiya Nyeva* was also mentioned, it was routine to pass the news item to the KGB shipping section. Two hours later, the helicopter boarding party and the entire crew of the *Rossiya*, still in Pavilosta harbour, were rounded up and driven twenty miles south, to the nearest large KGB centre at Liepaja. At 4.30 a.m., after a brief interrogation and a makeshift trial, the young marine officer in charge of the boarding party was found guilty of negligence. His pro-testations of innocence and excuses that he had counted the crew of the *Rose* before the execution and the bodies afterwards, twice, were not acceptable. At 4.40, he was shot through the temple by a KGB colonel who later boasted about his unique way of curing young men's acne for good. A brief report was signed and sent with all the arrested men under guard to Riga HQ.

At five in the morning, Björkman breakfasted with some fishermen and picked up a potential bombshell: the lifeboat of the *Rose* had been found a long way from the buoys dropped by the *Rossiya*. It would be wide open to speculation how that had come about. Some theories were kicked around, winds and currents were debated, and the young reporter stayed on to listen. He returned to the hospital at 6.15 to hugely disappointing news: some time around dawn, the survivor had bolted. Yet, on second thoughts, that could be another world scoop! An immediate search was organised because it was feared that the survivor might not be in full control of his senses, might do something irrational, commit suicide or get exposed to another cold night in the open with fatal effects. Björkman himself rushed around with the search parties. He would wonder forever how it was possible that the survivor was never seen again. He could just about foresee the birth of another ghost story from the Baltic: fishermen and islanders in the neighbourhood would report sightings from time to time for hundreds of years. Sometimes the ghost would save lives from the clutches of a storm, sometimes he would avenge mercilessly the lost lives of the *Rose*.

Yet the explanation of the disappearance was relatively simple. When Bucken came to, having regained some of his strength, the last thing he wanted to do was to talk to anyone about his ordeal and the sinking of the *Rose*. So he dressed, picked up the grappling iron, climbed through his ground floor window – nobody had foreseen any need to guard him – and went to the local police station from where he telephoned Ashenbury, reversing the charge.

Ashenbury lived up to his reputation of efficiency. Within twenty-five minutes, through Edwin Wade of the 128 Committee, he had enlisted the help of Swedish intelligence. Explanations would be offered later. First, any news about the survivor must be blacked out. As it was too late for that, at least Bucken must be kept under wraps and flown out in complete secrecy. That could be done. The local police chief at Herrvik never understood why he personally had to take the stranger to his own home, why he then had to continue the 'search' for the survivor who was sleeping with a grappling iron in his bed, and why he was burdened with keeping such a good yarn a secret forever – but he accepted that it would not be for him to know the answers.

The tall man wore his peaked cap and black uniform with too much relaxed elegance for a messenger. The gold emblem on his chest had a new shine. Encircling a Hermes figure in winged boots, the logo said Confidential Couriers, Worldwide. Papeete wanted to accept and sign for the delivery, but the man insisted that the message was verbal and person to person for her husband. His eyes were watery, and it was disconcerting that they never seemed to focus. Papeete was not prepared to argue with him or with Don who wanted to receive the message in private.

'And who the hell are you?' Quincey asked angrily when they were alone.

'I'm your contact, sir.'

'Like hell you are.'

'You wanted urgent contact – and here I am.'

'Where's the man with the scar?'

'He's not available. Please do not concern yourself with such details.'

'Why not? It's my fucking neck not yours.'

'I can assure you that you'll get more dependable and trouble-free service from me.'

'You mean fewer mistakes? High time, too.'

'We're very sorry about the mistake my predecessor and his men made in Kiel. I'm to apologise to you.'

'Then apologise for the second mistake, too. The arrangement was "no survivors" and yet . . . '

'That wasn't our fault. It's a different department. But I can assure you that the culprit has already been found and punished.'

'Not good enough. The survivor is a witness.'

'I know, sir. But we're looking for him. And we do have the resources to stop him.' For the first time, the man looked straight at Quincey to reassure him.

'Who is he?'

The man's gaze dissipated yet again.

'Is he one of the Chinese?'

'I'm not involved with him. I don't know.'

'But you're involved with me. So tell me, why haven't I been paid?'

'Fifteen million dollars have been deposited with the Cayman Island company named by you, sir.'

'That's not the agreed price. Don't tell me you've made yet another mistake.'

'No, sir, the full amount will be paid as soon as the survivor is found and dealt with.'

'That's none of my business. I did what I promised, you've got what you wanted, don't tell me your government is not as good as its word.'

'I can assure you. . . '

'Assure me with the cash. At once. Otherwise no more deals.'

'I'll convey the message to Moscow. Now let's discuss the next step, shall we?'

'No. Not until payment is made in full.'

'As you wish, sir. But I must remind you that nobody, absolutely nobody is irreplaceable.'

'And that goes for you, too. Your job is to keep me sweet. Now piss off.'

Quincey sounded more certain of himself than he actually was. The Russians now knew the technique he used. They would have problems with securing further sales of embargoed goods to whatever new company they created – it took Quincey and Ruzicki several months to find the man who could be bribed even with five million in cash every time – but they might seek out another corrupt official in the Pentagon, offer him ten millions, and cut out the most expensive part of the deal, the middleman. Yes, Quincey was ready to face facts and accept his own weakness. It was high time to cash in his chips, make one more, the biggest, financial killing, and get out. As soon as the messenger had left, he telephoned Savas to arrange an urgent meeting, and asked Papeete to accompany him. He wanted to watch her face.

The old man was in a foul mood. 'Everything is going sour. This Suez crisis is about the last thing we wanted. And what about this *Rose of Stambul* tragedy? How come there was only one survivor?'

'It's not as black as it looks. Just a technique to let the crew disappear. We don't want them to hang around and answer questions by the press as happened in Macao. That's all.'

'Then why haven't the whole crew gone to ground the same way? Now everybody suspects everything because there's only one survivor – and he simply disappears.'

'Please don't worry about minor details.'

'Minor details? Trying to be funny, Don? The whole affair stinks. Can you really assure me that the crew got away safely?'

'You're not suggesting that I'd get involved with mass murder, are you?'

'I'm not suggesting anything. But can you vouch for your partners?'

'I can vouch for one thing. And that should please you. Both of you.' He paused. His eyes were on Papeete. 'I have confidential information that Bucken must be alive.'

'How come?' Savas asked, but Quincey continued to address Papeete: 'All I know is that the corpse at Kiel wasn't Booker's.'

She paled, then blushed, then paled again. She was holding on to the edge of the table with both hands. Her fingertips went chalky from the effort. Quincey thought she would faint. And that was good enough for him. His hunch about the need to get rid of Bucken for good had been correct, and now it ceased to be just a hunch.

'That's the best news for weeks!' Savas exclaimed. 'Are you quite sure about it?'

'Trust me, Oldman, trust me. And I'm specially glad about it because I know you wanted him to be in on the action at Suez.'

'You had certain reservations about it.'

'Not any more.' Quincey smiled submissively. It made Papeete feel uneasy. She could not explain to herself why, but it took all the joy out of the news about Bucken. Quincey had plans. Private plans. There was menace in that smile. Yet she refused to believe that Don would do anything more criminal than double-crossing his partners. Except that Bucken was not a partner.

Savas was too preoccupied with Suez to notice whatever was going on between the Quinceys. 'But the problem is,' he said, continuing his dark thoughts aloud, 'that the hostilities in the Gulf and the mines near the Canal could reduce the impact of our plan.'

'On the contrary, Oldman, it's not at all like you to miss the point. The war and the mines and the current crisis would only enhance the panic we intend to cause. Everybody will think that there's a war about to erupt. Papeete's done some research into this for us, haven't you, honey?'

'Research? . . . ' She was still far away. Where would Bucken be now? Should he be warned that something was wrong? Warned about what? That Don didn't like him?

'A mink coat for your thoughts, honey.'

Savas came to her rescue: 'About Suez. What have you found out?'

She nodded to him gratefully. 'Oh yes. I asked around. I was just trying to summarise it in my mind. All it comes to is that most of the oil people are jittery but not particularly worried, as yet. But the shipping market is panicky and ready to clutch at straws. And so is international trade. The current trend of economic recovery looks much too fragile to them. One good push and they'll go over the brink.'

'And if we're ready for it. . . ' Savas did not need to finish the sentence.

'We are,' said Quincey. 'The mercenaries have already come up with some plans.'

Savas grabbed his shoulder. 'Don. Are you crazy? Has Ruzicki told them what exactly we want?'

'He's not that crazy, don't worry, they don't even know who their employers are. And, if you like, it could be one of your own trusties, perhaps Bucken – why not? – who'd give them the target ship and their duties at the last moment. But now we'd better move fast.'

They began to discuss the final scenario. Savas had already rented a suitable Spanish hide-away, a villa compound near Marbella, and a part of that would now be speedily converted into the operational headquarters of 'Tsunami'. Aldo Selli, one of the American partners who had prepared the original Suez assessment, was to submit daily reports on the shipping scene from now on. Boothy-Graffoe would have to prepare a list of ships and chartering agents who would be used as dupes and dummy fronts. Finance would have to be arranged for putting down deposits on several ro-ro ships, long range refrigerated and other vessels. Was there any need to book port and bunkering facilities round the Cape? Savas would report on that. A final 'summit' for all syndicate members would be held on 'D-day minus seven' – Ruzicki loved terms like that. Quincey insisted that, on that occasion, Boothy-Graffoe must also make himself available for personal consultation: 'No excuses, this time, for not turning up or being late as usual. This is the point where even he may have to take a bit of a risk.'

Papeete heard none of it. She felt like screaming a word of warning to Bucken so loud that he would hear her, wherever he was. Don't come back! Don't ever come back. At that moment, if Bucken had been there, she might have broken free of the chains of her self-imposed morality and crippling loyalty to Don Quincey.

A minion in Swedish intelligence was quick to leak it to the CIA that somebody had spirited the *Rose* survivor out of Götland. Ashenbury did everything in his power to ensure Bucken's security. Until the next step was decided by the 128 Committee, even Washington's potential demands for information would be stonewalled by London and Stockholm out of necessity and guilt respectively.

It was an Andover with RAF markings that flew Bucken home. 'It's like one of the Queen's Flight,' Bucken said. A knowing smile was all the otherwise chatty pilot gave as an answer, and Bucken chose not to press the point. He would have liked to believe that he was that important to someone.

They landed in rain, at Northolt, a bleak military airfield. Bucken was ushered to a midnight-blue Bentley. Ashenbury was waiting for him on the back seat.

'Welcome home, Bucken. Well done.' He touched Bucken's shoulder, and for a couple of seconds both men seemed to be overwhelmed by the sheer force of this emotional outburst. He listened impassively to Bucken's brief and strictly factual account of events in Kiel and the Baltic, poured some Chivas Regal into cut-glass tumblers, and said, 'Mm. Pretty terrifying.'

'A bad scene, you could say. Cheers.' And fuck you, too, thought Bucken.

'The Baltic is no fun in December. Cheers. You did well.'

'I was lucky. There was nothing I could actually do for myself.'

'Presumably, you haven't heard that you're dead.'

'Am I?'

'The Krauts fished a mutilated corpse out of Kiel harbour. It's reported to be Herr Booker. Any idea who it could be?'

'A bloke was tailing me right up until I left the hotel to visit the *Rose*. He was still in the lobby as I was going out. All my papers were left in my room because I didn't want to carry any identification and I didn't expect to be away for long. So somebody could have ransacked my room and pinched my passport. My tail must know who it was . . . unless the corpse they fished out was his own. Can't the German police identify him?'

'They believe that the body was yours. I mean Booker's At least that's what they say. And that's what all the press said.'

'Oh.' Bucken wondered how Papeete and the Savases would have taken the news.

'The difficulty is that, apparently, the face of the victim was badly mutilated or battered or something.'

'So they wanted to prevent or at least slow down the identification process. Which means murder with more careful planning than it seemed at first. The question is: who was the intended victim? If it was me, there must have been a mix-up. Which poses the next question: who would want me dead?'

'Just about everybody,' said Ashenbury with a faint smile that was apologetic and only emphasised the gravity of the glib answer. 'I'll tell you about it.' Ashenbury looked out. The car was turning to leave Hyde Park, cross Park Lane, and squeeze itself into the narrow streets behind the Dorchester. 'We'll drop you at a service entrance. You'll be met there by a chubby man with the youthful features of an old midget. He's Edwin Wade of the one-two-eight committee. He'll take you to the suite permanently reserved for my company. I'll meet

229

you there.' The Bentley slowed down. 'Sorry, Bucken, this charade was Wade's idea. He thinks you'll be safe here.'

Ed Wade glanced at the grappling iron Bucken was carrying wrapped in a plastic bag, but asked no questions. Bucken liked him.

'Make yourself comfortable, Bucken,' said Ashenbury as he joined them in the suite exquisitely furnished with several of his own antiques. 'You may have to stay here for a few days, but room service will get you absolutely everything you may need. And I do mean everything, including company for light relief.'

The two men listened to Bucken's tale, and Wade made no secret of how astounded he was: 'Do I get this clear, Bucken? You claim that the *Rose of Stambul* doesn't exist, that it's been the *Rossiya* all along, masquerading as the *Rose* with a few alterations to increase the resemblance between the two, and that it was the *Rossiya* that loaded all the American high-tech stuff in the first place?'

'That's right. It's embargo-busting without a trace. The Americans can throw in the best deep-sea hardware they've got but they'll never find their computers, which didn't sink, or the *Rose* that didn't even exist. The Baltic storm and the Mayday messages were a smokescreen. Same as the Tsunami that swallowed, supposedly, the *Alida II*. In that case, it was the *Lena*, another Soviet vessel, all along, and we identified it from the engine numbers Sergeant Spire had wax-printed, except that at the time we couldn't make head or tail of it all. Now we know. And we know why Spire was ready to die for the info he had.'

'How about the print you took in the engine room?' Ashenbury asked.

'It's here, intact. The film in the camera must be damaged, but perhaps the lab can do something with it, whatever it's worth.'

'Quite a lot,' said Ashenbury.

'Is it?' Bucken asked with a tired smile, and suddenly there was an understanding, the bond of the professionals, between Bucken and Wade. 'It only proves that some time or other I was on board the *Rossiya* and managed to identify her engine. But that's no connection with the *Rose*. Strictly speaking, my word is the only evidence we've got at this stage.'

'Good enough for me,' said Ashenbury.

'But is it good enough for the prosecution?'

'Who's talking about prosecution?' Ashenbury looked away. 'No, stirring up some international scandal is not the next step for us, as far as I'm concerned. What do you say, Wade?'

The man from counter-intelligence was busy feeling the weight of the grappling iron Bucken had brought back with him. 'Quite a

230

weapon,' he said at last. It seemed to please him irritating Ashenbury. 'The best you could have picked in the circumstances, I reckon.'

'It saved my life. Without it I couldn't have caught and climbed into that lifeboat. The sea was not exactly calm and I wasn't feeling particularly fit just then.'

Wade studied the inscription on the metal. 'It's Russian all right, but is it evidence?'

'Not really.'

'I thought we'd already discussed that,' snapped Ashenbury. 'It helped you to hang on, and again that's good enough for me.'

'Oddly enough, it wasn't the greatest thing it did for me. My fingers were freezing to it in that boat. I could do nothing for myself, I knew, but that piece of metal gave me a lot of strength when I needed it most. It helped me to fool myself. It gave me hope against hope. It made me believe that I did have something vital to bring back. So I had to come back. I had to survive until some miracle saved me: such as blankets and emergency rations in the boat.'

After a moment's heavy silence, Wade told Ashenbury: 'We must inform the Yanks. Proof or no proof, it's essential for them to know what happened.'

'What's done is done. We can't undo it.'

'We must warn them.'

'We? It's up to the Committee.'

'Aren't they supposed to be our special allies?' Bucken butted in.

'Of course they are. They're friends. But not family. Do they restrain the dollar to protect the pound? Do they stop the guns for the IRA at the insignificant cost of the Irish vote in New York? No, gentlemen, they don't. But all right. Don't say that I'm trying to be a dictator. I'll put it to the one-two-eight though, I warn you, I'll argue that you ought to concentrate on Suez and the implications of the chemical tanker and the mercenaries, whatever the connection may be. Then the Committee's decision will be final. Fair enough?'

'Yes, it may be fair, but it's wrong.'

'My dear Bucken, right and wrong are not absolute terms. They do attain different meanings in the light of the national interest. And Savas's plan seems to threaten nothing if not that.' Ashenbury turned to Wade: 'What's your opinion?'

'I disagree about withholding information from the Yanks, but I accept that it's up to the Committee. What I don't understand at all, sir, is that you seem to suggest that Bucken should continue his investigation. He's no good to us, I'm afraid, and he's at risk. We know that the CIA wants Booker dead or alive. We also know that the Narodny has submitted evidence complete with photo and description to Interpol. And we must assume, well, we can take it for granted, that the whole of Europe must be swarming with KGB agents hunting for the unknown sole survivor of the *Rose*. If the killing in Kiel was their doing, and if they know they made a mistake, they must be desperate to eliminate the real Booker, too. It's obvious that they didn't want to have any witnesses left. So it wouldn't surprise me if they also wiped out Ruzicki and Quincey.'

'Unless they still hope to do more business with them,' said Bucken.

'In which case Ruzicki would try to protect Bucken in turn. After all, he's proved himself to be a perfect front man both in Singapore and Kiel. And my guess is, they can't even admit to the Russians what Bucken's real background is,' Ashenbury concluded triumphantly, and the others had to admit that he might have a valid point.

After a moment's hesitation, Wade returned to the attack: 'That may reduce but certainly not eliminate the danger. Because we haven't even mentioned yet that the CIA is also looking for Mr. Warman. And I think it's quite lucky for you that they haven't connected the two inquiries as yet. Their computers could match Booker with Warman in no time. All it needs is some little clerk to put the right question to the machine.'

'How do you know about this?' Bucken asked.

'It was me who picked it up first,' said Ashenbury. 'According to a friend of mine, an American was making inquiries in the City. He was such an obviously clean-living, all-American college boy, that he just had to be a CIA junior. He was bandying about a cock-and-bull story about having some real big scoop for Warman. All my friend could say to him was that he didn't know where to find Warman just now. But here comes the twist. It was this same friend I used as an intermediary to introduce you as Warman to Boothy-Graffoe and two others. And why would they want to contact Warman?'

'They may be wondering what happened to me. Why I haven't been in touch since then. Why I haven't sent them the articles I promised to write . . . ' Bucken paused, trying to put himself in their shoes. 'Yes, if they suspect that I used or even misused some information they gave me, they'd be worried that something has already been published, perhaps misquoting them or plain detrimental to them. But, if then they wanted to find Warman, they'd go back straight to the man who gave the introduction. Why would they turn to a CIA contact?'

'And which of them would have such a contact?' Ashenbury was quite amused by the question.

232

Wade was more interested in the people who had briefed Bucken in the first place. 'You don't think that any of them could be connected with Quincey, do you?'

'Yes, Boothy-Graffoe,' answered Bucken without any hesitation, 'but he's associating with Savas and the rest of them quite openly. It's a matter of interpretation and I have no evidence.'

'And you're convinced that Quincey was the brain behind the *Rose of Stambul*.'

Bucken nodded and watched Ashenbury's face.

'Incredible. Such a good man. Such a tragic story.'

'I know you were keen to help him, sir, but he's been a prime suspect all along.'

'And you think his wife is also involved?'

'I don't know,' Bucken lied. 'I can't be sure one way or another.' He was. It was Papeete who had told him to buy the *Rose*. She had played a part throughout. She had to know the truth, but he was reluctant to admit it even to himself.

'Such a charming woman,' said Ashenbury. 'Not much of a life for her, is it?'

Nobody answered him.

'Do you know anything about the casualties on the *Alida II*?' Wade asked, to break the silence. 'The captain and eight men were said to have gone down with the ship. You think they were killed?'

'Perhaps they refused to cooperate for some reason, and that's why they had to die.'

'You don't sound convinced, Bucken.'

'Perhaps because I'm not. I have a different theory. Perhaps the captain and the eight sailors were Russians with false papers. Like the *Alida*, they existed only on paper. Then they could disappear with the ship while the news of "heavy casualties" would help to convince everybody about the horrors of the Tsunami disaster.'

'Right or wrong, one thing is certain, old boy,' Wade's pasty face beamed a smile of boredom, 'if I were you, I'd look for a new identity in a hurry.'

'That's for the Committee to decide,' said Ashenbury. 'We have a meeting tonight. So have a good rest, Bucken, tomorrow you may be back in action or on the run.'

'Action? He's finished.' Wade saw Bucken as a spent force. 'As dead as the Spires.' He noticed how startled Bucken looked. 'Oh yes, I'm sorry, we haven't yet had a chance to tell you that Spire's widow killed herself. Well, some combination of alcohol and an overdose. The child is in an orphanage.' Wade pulled a buff envelope out of his pocket. 'There was a makeshift will on the mantelpiece. You've been named as executor and the child's guardian.'

'Shit,' was the only word Bucken could utter. At that moment, he could have beaten Sugar into a pulp.

The two men promised to be back late that night, and suggested Bucken should stay in the relative safety of the hotel. As soon as they had left, Bucken ordered a cab, went to his flat for a change of clothes, and called Sarah from the café round the corner because his own phone was still disconnected.

'Is that my wife twice removed?' he asked and heard the smile in her voice as she remembered the way he had once introduced her in his kitchen to a naked Helen. Reluctantly, Sarah agreed to meet him a couple of hours later.

It had begun to snow lightly, but only a few flakes survived contact with London's pavements. The sight added, Bucken thought, to the Christmassy mood the stores were so keen to project. He paid his cab driver to cruise around and wait for him in Regent Street while he went shopping for toys. He bought indiscriminately – he had never regarded the Singapore pay-off as his own or even real money – and spent almost six hundred pounds. Bloody nouveau riche, that's what you are, he chided himself, a real shipping magnate would spend more prudently. He also bought a card for Spire's little girl, but threw it away when he realised with embarrassment that he could not even remember her name.

Christmas decorations were making vague promises of merriment in the orphanage, too, and the presents were most welcome. The Matron offered to bring 'lucky Miss Spire' to her own office to meet the generous benefactor of the establishment, but Bucken felt it would be kinder or more appropriate or both if he went to meet the child in the crowded playroom. As soon as he entered, he knew it had been a mistake. The orphanage seemed to have everything that made a home. Everything public expenditure could buy, that is. The clatter of toys and babble of voices churned about in Bucken's stomach. He knew that nobody could be blamed for the fact that all the inmates of all ages seemed to present themselves as so many little whores vying for attention, making eyes and funny faces, withdrawing shyly in the forlorn hope of surviving yet another rejection when every visitor was a potential customer for love. They swarmed around him as, led by the Matron, he made his way through the crowd.

He would not have been able to pick out Spire's daughter, and she did not show any sign of recognising Bucken. She could not perceive what an executor of a will or a guardian was, and would not even care. She would not understand that mummy used to be an alcoholic

234

or what the difference between mummy's absence and death could be. She did not even look at the stranger who had brought her the presents. She just held his hand and would not let go. Bucken fought to suppress surging shame, guilt and helplessness. He had no idea what to do with or say to a small child. He felt responsible for her, but he could not even begin to contemplate an application for adoption. All he could offer was money, any or all his ill-gotten gains, and that, he was told, was not her most immediate need.

He turned down an invitation to 'our happy little Christmas show presented by our children for our honoured guests'. And no, he would not take tea with 'lucky Miss Spire' either – she had already lost her parents, why cause her the pain of befriending and losing someone yet again when he might never be able to return and see her even once more?

He met Sarah in one of their old haunts, a shoe-box of a pub on the river near the foot of Blackfriars Bridge. 'It was a summer night when we last came here,' said Bucken as he bought her a tomato juice and a very large Bacardi for himself. 'It was very hot and we sat out on the bank.' The colour of her drink reminded him of Cairo: Papeete had drunk Campari soda. 'Don't you remember?'

'I do.' She looked at her watch with emphasis: she had already told him she did not have much time.

'It's good to see you.'

'Likewise,' she said wryly. She tried to keep a stern face, but failed. A burst of laughter loosened her tight mouth. 'I mean it.' It was the old warmth of her voice.

'Are you happy?'

'How do you define happiness?' She concentrated on her drink.

'I'm sorry. I only asked because I care.'

'I know. Thank you.' She was about to say something else but held it back. She looked at her watch. It was a cheap and cumbersome contraption – it was all young PC Bucken could afford on their first wedding anniversary. She still wore it with pride. 'You have twelve minutes left, Bucken, no more, because I have to pick up my husband at Victoria.' She paused. She used to pick up Bucken, too, when returning from a trip. 'So if there really was something urgent you had to tell me . . .'

'There was. Remember Sergeant Spire?'

'Sure, I've heard, I'm sorry. I know how much you liked him.'

'His wife's committed suicide.'

Sarah looked stunned. 'Wasn't there a baby?'

'There is one. In an orphanage. That's why I wanted to see you. I'm her guardian or something.'

235

'And a fat lot of good that would be to anyone.'

'I can make sure that she'll never have any financial problems. No, please, don't ask questions. The money is there, and that's that.'

Sarah turned away. She was ashamed of him and for him. She suspected the source of his sudden wealth. So were the rumours true? She did not want to know.

It was maddening that he could say nothing. So he raised his voice almost to a shout. 'Don't be so bloody squeamish! Don't you trust me?'

'It's just . . . '

'It's just you're passing sentence before the hearing. You have no right to judge me on sight, and it's none of your bloody business anyway *what* money and *how much* I'm talking about.'

'Then why am I here?'

'Because it's a lot of money. Because . . . ' he noticed the shocked faces of a couple of old-timers at the corner table, near the fire, reserved for regulars, 'because the kid needs someone,' his voice softened, 'and because I'm going away . . . well, you know . . . these things may take time.'

Suddenly she heard Captain Oates leaving Scott's tent saying that he 'may be some time' out there in the Antarctic night. Questions of concern threatened to burst but Sarah respected the rules of the game, and knew what not to ask. 'What am I to do?'

'Try to keep an eye on the kid. Make decisions about the money if necessary.'

'I may not be any good with either of them. We've never had money. Or kids.'

'No.'

'And I can't adopt her. I mean my husband . . . '

'I know, love. I know. Just do what you can. It can't be any less than I could do.'

The CIA's urgent request for information about Booker was circulated confidentially, worldwide. In Macao, Inspector Poon matched the description with his own memories, and all but identified Booker as Donkeyman Hiller's cousin, who had visited him after the *Alida* disaster, proving himself a good colleague and an astute investigator. The CIA interest indicated that Booker might be political, probably someone on the Russian side. Poon was fond of the man but hated politics. Still, through a convenient cut-out he leaked the information to a contact who, he knew, would convey it to Peking right away. If it was Booker/Hiller's fate to be caught or killed, it should at

236

least benefit the Chinese, even red Chinese, rather than any of the foreign devils.

By the time Ashenbury and Wade returned to the Dorchester, Bucken had managed to snatch a couple of hours' sleep. The chubby man from MI5 seemed to have aged a decade or two, but Ashenbury was still as alert, freshly shaven and impeccably dressed as he had been more than six hours earlier. Bucken wondered if he had a barber and a wardrobe complete with a valet tucked away in that low-flying Jumbo he used for a car.

'Sorry, Bucken, it's been a long session. The Committee was most concerned about your well-being.' Ashenbury rummaged in an early Victorian corner cabinet, and came up with a bottle of thirty-year-old Macallan. 'It's the best I can offer, in fact the best I've ever had.' He half-filled a crystal tumbler for Bucken. 'What do you think of it?'

Bucken gulped down the whisky without any of the reverence the Macallan's exclusivity and price tag commanded, and held out his glass for another shot to demonstrate how unimpressed he was. Which was not true. Except that being fêted by Ashenbury felt no less ominous than the offer of a last cigarette from a compassionate hangman.

Wade was completely preoccupied with his drink. He seemed to avoid Bucken's eyes.

'Your good health, Bucken,' said Ashenbury. 'Happy days.'

'In other words, you need a volunteer.' Bucken drank up and helped himself to more of the same.

'Don't ever think that people in very high places have taken their recommendation lightly. You're certainly not being ordered to volunteer.'

'Or even asked to do anything at all if in *my* professional judgment the risk is unacceptable – whatever the country's need,' added Wade in a firm tone that verged on rudeness. 'Not because your country would never ask people to die for a cause, but because if we lose you, we lose the game, too.'

'So any amount of backing will be yours for the asking,' said Ashenbury.

Asking? Bucken just stared at him. I may never get the chance even to cry for help, he thought, and you're whistling in the dark on my behalf.

Wade at least proved himself sharp and inventive when it came to concocting a cover story for Bucken's missing days. He listened in on the line when eventually Bucken called Savas in Rotterdam, and felt satisfied that 'the old bastard swallowed it hook, line and sinker'. He would have felt a great deal less confident if he had had a chance to assess the mood of the meeting at which Savas reported Bucken's call to the Quinceys and Ruzicki.

'Just as you expected, Don, he's spent a few days away from it all in some godforsaken Cornish cottage with no papers, no telephone, no radio or television.'

'You mean nothing but a bird or two.'

Ruzicki's interruption was ignored, and Savas concluded that Bucken sounded genuinely shocked to hear not so much that the *Rose* had sunk but that there had been no survivors. 'He's living it up in the Dorchester now and will wait for my call telling him what to do next.'

'Nothing until I've checked out his tale,' said Ruzicki.

'It may help you that he asked if he could bring his girl friend with him.' Savas saw that Papeete had winced. He looked forward to mentioning it all to Greta, too. 'I said, of course, that at the moment, that would not be a good idea.'

Quincey agreed, but argued with Ruzicki: 'There's no reason to keep him away while you're checking. The nearer he is the better we can control him and see what needs to be done. Besides, even if we decided to use him in the Suez operation, he wouldn't know what was going on until the last moment – and then it would be too late. So yes, let's have him over here. We'll fly him to Marbella for a little extra holiday.'

When Savas called back, asking Bucken to be in Rotterdam the following day, he cracked a few jokes about Bucken's escapade, enquired if it had been exhausting, and hinted that he himself might like to borrow that cottage some day for a leisurely weekend with a friend. He was reassured when Bucken was most forthcoming about the place, giving him the address, at the bottom of some unmapped country lane up Bodmin Moor, and the telephone number of the nearest village shop and post office where he would only have to mention Bucken's name to get all he needed. Wade had already made the arrangements with the shopkeeper who was on his occasional payroll to look after the safe house on the moor.

'There's an element of risk, of course, and we must prepare for eventualities.' Ashenbury's tone of objectivity slipped off key, revealing his concern for Bucken. He looked embarrassed. 'What I mean is that your job will be like dismantling a new type of unex-ploded bomb. I must know at all times how far you've got. So if any-thing happens to you . . . '

'Okay, okay,' Bucken cut him short impatiently: the tone of concern had begun to embarrass him, too. 'I'll submit regular reports as we go along. The question is: how? Savas has half-mentioned that eventually I'll have to spend some time near Marbella, where he's renting some villa. If anything, it sounds like an operations HQ. If I have to stay with him, the use of telex and phones from there would be out.'

'We could make arrangements . . . ' Wade began.

'What? Carrier pigeons?'

'How about the Marbella post office?' Ashenbury suggested.

'Sure. If I was bent on suicide, I'd go there twice a day.'

The use of a go-between with an airtight cover seemed the only solution. By a process of elimination, policemen were ruled out: high-powered tracers could identify them. 'What about a reporter? His presence on the celebrity-infested Costa would be quite plaus-ible. He could interview British ex-pats and fugitives.'

Bucken shrugged his shoulders. He knew that Wade was right, but he also knew the next logical question and did not like it.

'You could meet him openly and regularly. There would be nothing suspicious about friendship between a reporter and an ex-policeman. Right?'

Bucken helped himself to another drink.

'Somebody you actually knew would be ideal.'

'Somebody I actually trusted would be even better.' Everything began to focus on Freemantle.

'Who was the chap you tipped off in advance about your drunken brawl in the City?'

'Freemantle. But his job ties him to London.' Bucken was clutching at straws. He did not want his friend to be brought into this.

'You could whet his appetite with an eventual scoop, and I could have a word with his editor. All Freemantle needs to know is that he's going to pass coded messages for you.'

'I won't fool him. I must warn him about the risks.'

'That in itself could be a risk.'

'But it would be his choice. If he refuses to play, we must find some other solution,' said Bucken more in hope than expectation: Freemantle would be much too gullible, and certainly not the first reporter to be seduced by an opportunity to dip actively into the secret world of cops and spies.

'All right, but tell him what's at stake. Tell him what we're fighting for.'

Bucken shook his head. He would not use moral blackmail against a friend.

'Thanks, Bucken, count me in,' said Freemantle, salivating copiously over the prospect of a hyper-scoop, but it was obvious that he had been lured more by Bucken's secretive and reluctant request than by the thought of an exclusive. The national interest was never mentioned. Freemantle would have pooh-poohed it with all the irony he could muster. He had his bread-and-butter image of the cynic to safeguard. At his age, he could not afford to lose it. Among his younger colleagues, old-fashioned patriotism was as shameful an affliction as consumption used to be among the poor. He only wished those famous whizz-kids could see him now, talking to Bucken in a deserted car park at dead of night.

'There's just one other thing. Something I must tell you.'

'I didn't ask questions, did I?'

'No. But I must tell you that you may be in danger. You may get hurt.'

'Do I draw up my will or is it enough to wear a false beard?'

'I wasn't joking.'

'And I wasn't laughing.' But the boyish glitter in his eyes belied the reporter's words.

V

SHANGHAIED IN PORT SAID

The young officer of the Guardia Civil extracted his index finger from his nostril, and waved to the pilot – welcome to Malaga. The private jet taxied to a halt behind the maintenance sheds. Formalities for VIPs were restricted to the barest minimum. Quincey's chair was wheeled straight from the aircraft into the waiting helicopter.

'You want Bucken out of the way . . . ?' Ruzicki himself was not quite sure if he meant it as a question or a statement. He was watching the topless sights of a Spanish December as the chopper flew above beaches and private pools, hugging the southern coastline. 'I mean do you?'

'No. Not just yet.' Quincey turned his eyes away only to catch a glimpse of the short golden hairs on his nurse's neck as she sat, in animated conversation, up front with the pilot. The bile in his mouth told him how much he hated Bucken and all men who would want such women, and Ruzicki who would not. 'I don't know why, but Oldman Savas is suspicious about that killing in Kiel. As if I had anything to do with that botched-up job.'

'Didn't you?'

'You'd be the first to know if I did.'

I wonder, thought Ruzicki, but said nothing. He did not like the fact that certain of Quincey's contacts were strictly private. If Quincey was in the habit of double-crossing his other partners, he would do it to him too without compunction. 'Okay, give the word when the time comes.'

'I will. But I don't want to antagonise Savas just now when he seems to have a grand design. I think he wants to train Bucken to run his show one day.'

'Sure. Why else would the Oldman lay on this welcome-home-from-the-dead champagne breakfast for him?' Ruzicki speculated if there would be a special dish for Bucken, and if so, who would it be? Greta or Papeete? 'Mind you, he's done well for us. Our sources were right when they checked him out. He's capable and reliable.'

241

'And we'll use him to the full, don't worry.'

Just beyond Marbella, Pueblo Yasmin, the villa compound with its sumptuous mansion and guest houses within walled grounds, came into view. It had a roll-out pier to receive small craft direct from the sea, a helicopter landing pad and a first-rate security system – everything a sheik would want and oil could buy, everything Savas might need for the final planning and execution of Operation Tsunami. The Arab owner had used it only once for three days in as many years, but now even the private mosque and part of the adjoining harem building were utilised: they had been converted into a sophisticated communications centre with high-powered transmitters, telex, a telephone exchange and computer facilities. Using one of his Greek cronies as a front man, Savas had rented the compound for three hundred thousand dollars for six months knowing full well that it would be used for no more than six weeks. The surplus time would eliminate the possibility of some snooper noticing the coincidence between the rental period and 'Tsunami'.

'Fine choice,' said Quincey as the helicopter settled down on the pad with hardly a tap. 'Any number of people could visit by road, sea and air without any of the neighbours getting suspicious about the commotion.'

'There are no neighbours.' Ruzicki's voice was sour, he envied the Oldman's style and easy way with money. Yet he knew that, if he played his cards right, he might come out on top. None of the partners seemed to realise what he saw so clearly, that a secret shared could one day become a secret used against all of them.

Savas was in high spirits. His guests were seated round a large circular table sculpted out of a single slab of Carrara marble. He was pleased with himself that his protégé, on his right, was making a good impression on everybody, including two more of the partners.

Bucken sensed his mood and felt like Judas. He would fight rather than con Savas whom he had grown to like despite everything, crimes and all, yet his job was to lie low, observe, stay alive, spy and betray. He found it loathsome. Having spent a week wheeler-dealing on Oldman's behalf up and down Europe, he had come to the conclusion that his trustworthiness rating among the crooks was up, and he was now the joker rather than the Number One fall guy in the pack. The obvious front companies were now in the names of two new dummies while he had the responsibility for some legitimate negotiations, representing people who, he suspected, might be partners in the syndicate. He was posing as himself once again. and Savas had hinted that he must conduct himself with dignity because better things and major assignments were in store for him. After two days in

Gibraltar where a small warehouse had to be rented for Ruzicki, he had arrived at the villa compound by speedboat only to be told that he would soon have to go to Casablanca and buy a new ship.

Unlike Savas, Greta greeted him rather coldly and made no secret of the fact that she felt hurt. 'So where's your favourite girl friend?' she asked. 'Will you survive without her for a few days?'

So Savas must have told her about his cover story, the Cornwall escapade. It would help Bucken to cool the affair and avoid antagonising Savas too much, but at the same time it was important to keep her sweet. Bucken was not proud of the manoeuvre. 'It was a big joke, of course. I wouldn't dream of bringing anyone here while there was half a chance that somebody like you might be around.'

'Liar. But it's nice to hear it.'

'Am I forgiven then?'

Conscious of Papeete's gaze upon the two of them, Greta answered him loudly enough for her to hear it: 'We'll see. I may tell you tonight.'

Papeete smiled at both of them, and Bucken wondered if he had just made yet another enemy. Then he returned to his main task, that of memorising new names and faces round the table. Lazily he touched the third button of his shirt with the built-in microphone. What would they do if they found out? When he reached for the champagne bottle, he had almost forgotten how cautiously he must move: he was wired up from top to toe with the latest bugging devices. Baby-faced Ed Wade had offered to get some of the circuits printed on his skin, but Bucken turned the idea down. An electronic tattoo? What if he had to join the party for a midnight swim or Greta in her room on the spur of the moment?

His thoughts were so far away that he almost missed what Savas was telling him. 'Invest a hundred thou of your own money with me, and you'll come out of this a millionaire.'

Bucken hesitated. He was fumbling in his pocket to activate the bug. The new turn of the conversation might be worth recording.

'I'd like to, but . . . '

'But what?'

'It's just that I'm not a gambler.' Too late Bucken realised the mistake.

'Oh.' Savas looked disappointed.

'I mean I don't gamble without having a chance to influence the odds.'

People laughed and Savas brightened up. 'Don't worry, you'll have a chance to do just that. Because we may have an important job for you. Interested?'

243

'As long as I don't have to work.' He got the laughs but not from Papeete.

'It's a sort of commando operation. You could go along as my representative, and you'd have two jobs. One to make sure that nobody gets hurt, and two, to press the button on my say so.'

'What? Where? I don't understand a word.'

'You're not supposed to. You do your job, others do theirs. Some will know what to do, one will tell them where to do it, and you'll say when.'

'What? No button to press?' Fingering the switch that had been sewn into the lining of his pocket, he hoped the damned thing was working. He abhorred bugs, of whatever kind.

'Well, as a matter of fact . . . '

Quincey interrupted him: 'It's too early for serious discussions, Oldman. Let's just celebrate our Mr. Booker's safe return. I mean Booker, Bucken . . . what's in a name?'

'A would-be millionaire is entitled to the choice,' said Savas. 'So tell me, do I or don't I have your hundred thou?'

Bucken thought that Papeete had moved her head imperceptibly from left to right and back. Or was he just imagining it? 'Any time, any place!' he exclaimed with all the enthusiasm he could muster.

When the party broke up, Bucken set out to explore the compound. He would also engineer some informal chats with the people he had never met before, and tape something useful for Ashenbury. As he left the breakfast enclosure in the perfect circle of orange trees, and entered the main building, he heard a clicking sound. He looked back and saw a sign light up: THANK YOU FOR PASSING THROUGH OUR DEGAUSSING FRAME. He would soon discover that there was one like that above every main door. He hoped that was more the sheik's private joke than a serious security device. He was wrong. There was no sound left on his tape.

Throughout the day, there were conferences and ceaseless activities in and around the mosque, now the communications centre, but Bucken was not invited to participate. Savas urged him to rest and enjoy himself. Greta was away, shopping in Marbella. Papeete seemed to be seeking Bucken's company at the poolside and in the cool of the library where every single book was leatherbound and not one had ever been opened, but could not find one opportunity to talk to him alone.

Shortly before ten in the evening, Ruzicki invited him to go to Puerto Banus, the yachtsmen's and their groupies' playground, a few miles down the road. He suggested they could dine together and perhaps gamble a little. 'What's your game, Bucken?'

'As I said at breakfast, I gamble only when I can influence the odds.'

'Okay, let's buy the Casino.'

Bucken found it irksome that it was no joke. 'Perhaps tomorrow. I feel a hundred thou was a big enough stake for me for a Thursday.'

Bucken planned to have a night-cap with Greta. He already knew that she occupied the harem wing of the main house because, as she had said, 'the thought of having me in his harem gave darling Dyonisios a kick'. Bucken's mini-suite was in one of the guest houses that had the convenient lay-out of a motel, offering each occupant his own front door behind a clump of olive trees for privacy. He had just put his matchbox-sized camera, courtesy of Ed Wade, in his pocket (you never know what papers there might be lying about), when there was a hesitant knock at the door.

'Papeete . . .' For a second, he tried desperately to believe that her loyalty to Quincey had snapped, and she was ready to reopen the wound of Cairo, the memory she had once cauterized so painfully. Was this the unborn tomorrow?

'May I come in?' She sounded harassed and out of breath as if she had been running away from someone. 'May I?'

'Of course. Please.' He peered into the darkness beyond the olive trees but nothing seemed to move. He shut the door. 'How about a drink?'

'There's no time. I don't want to be found here. So listen, and do something for me without asking questions. Go away. Now. Don't even bother to say goodbye to anyone. Just go.'

'It's the second time you've tried to get rid of me.'

'I wish you'd listened to me in Athens. I wish you'd never got involved with all this.' She kept her eyes on his shoes.

He lifted her chin. There was no resistance. 'You're a better liar than your eyes.'

'Perhaps I'm drunk.'

'Oh yes, a drunk of convenience.'

'You could be in danger. Some people around here don't like you.'

'Nonsense. We're all friends. Win or loose, we cheat together.' He reached for the switch in the lining of his pocket. He was glad now he had not kissed her. 'We have strong bonds, haven't we? Singapore, Kiel, the Narodny and the *Rose of Stambul* . . . we're doing well, aren't we?'

'Haven't you made enough money?' She sounded angry. 'Do you really have to go through with "Tsunami"?'

'Tsunami?'

245

'Oh, just a name, forget it. Forget I've come to see you tonight. You're just too greedy to understand. Pity.' She started towards the door.

'We'll talk more about it, shall we?' The tape would have to be dropped through the window to be safe. 'Tomorrow?'

She shook her head. 'I'm going away. And I hope I'll never see you again.'

'It sounds as if you meant it.'

'I did. Because, by the time I'm back, you'll have become a crook or a corpse or both.' Her body seemed to grow more rigid, her eyes lost their glow as if they had just been bathed in some emotional disinfectant. 'It was bad enough to read about your death in Kiel. I don't want to be asked to identify the body in a morgue some day.' She managed a smile. 'Goodbye, Bucken.'

He said nothing. The bugging device, to him, oozed the stench of betrayal.

She stepped outside and moved back a couple of steps as if to put a safe distance between them. 'You know something? If you cared less about getting rich quick, and if the circumstances were different, I could have gone for you in a really big way.'

Behind her, a shadow peeled away from the trees and melted into the darkness of an arched doorway. Bucken could have sworn it was Greta. If she was hurt before, she might be mortally wounded by now. She might fight back or, probably, just ignore Bucken from now on. Yes, that's what she would do, he hoped.

On Friday morning, the villa compound seemed to be dead and deserted by everyone except the security guards. Bucken knew that Savas and Quincey had been in a huddle in the mosque since dawn. He would have liked to 'drop in' on them in the course of his seemingly aimless wanderings, but a guard turned him away even from the approach corridor. He planned to go into Marbella for his first meeting with Freemantle but, sensing the air of expectation all over the place, he delayed his departure. He breakfasted with Ruzicki who kept looking at his watch. Then a telephone was brought to the large marble table, and Ruzicki took the call. 'Yes, fine, I'll be coming over right away,' was all Bucken heard from the conversation. While Ruzicki rushed to the mosque, Bucken decided to tail Ruzicki if he left the compound, but his idea was stillborn: Ruzicki was picked up by the helicopter, and Bucken could only wave goodbye to him. He would therefore keep the meeting with Freemantle after all.

Surrounded by clattering telex machines and desk-top VDUs, Quincey watched Savas, who seemed to be doing ten different jobs simultaneously, and surprised him with a question: 'You don't like Ruzicki, do you?'

'Does it show?'

'No, let me correct the question. You don't even trust him, do you?' And without waiting for an answer: 'Any particular reason why?'

'Er . . . just a hunch.' He squinted at the glitter of large Arabic letters on the eastern wall. It would have been pointless to spell out what worried him. Less than twenty-four hours ago he had found out some of the causes of his old troubles which had driven him originally to the brink of bankruptcy. According to his fresh information, it was probably Ruzicki who had played a decisive role in the unexpected and inexplicable misfortunes of the Savas empire and the Greek community in the States. In the light of this, everything else could make sense. It was Ruzicki who had volunteered, just in time, to help him out with some shady deals. It was Ruzicki who was gaining control over some Savas interests. It was Ruzicki who knew a great deal about Greta and the rest of the Savas family, and used everything to manipulate the Oldman. By the time Papeete had reactivated Quincey's ideas for revenge through fraud, Savas had virtually no other choice left but to go along, form the syndicate – and accept Ruzicki as a founding partner.

In the last few hours, Savas had been wondering if Quincey had entered into some secret pact in advance so as to ensnare him, but the thought made him angry with himself. He tried to stamp out his suspicions. If you can't trust your friends, he scolded himself, what is left for you in this life? Yes, he was ashamed to tell Quincey how strongly he felt tempted to hit back, lay a few traps for Ruzicki, and make sure that the bastard would come out of 'Tsunami' a loser. No, there was no point in saying so. He could never go through with it.

Quincey was aware of the long pause, and watched Savas intently without a word. 'Yes, just a hunch,' Savas repeated the lie, 'and no, I can't say I like him.'

'Snap,' said Quincey, and smiled.

A couple of hours later, Ruzicki returned. Savas switched the telephones to answering machines, and gave instructions to the guard outside that they were not to be disturbed.

'It's all go,' Ruzicki beamed. 'Go, go, go! We could be in business soon after Christmas.' In Malaga, he had just had his final meeting with the two mercenaries whom he called 'the two gentlemen of Vill-arica', and who, in turn, kept treating him as Mr. Intermediary Ple-nipotentiary because, he explained, 'it probably gave them some hope that their dirty work would be done for a government, any government I represented.'

'I thought they were pros,' Savas interjected.

'They are, but they prefer to work for governments or big business as long as they are anti-terrorist and anti-Jewish – otherwise they'd probably charge double. Anyway, they know they're lucky to get work at all these days, and they like the idea of blocking the Canal because they hope that their endeavours could start a Middle East war and kill a few more Jews and niggers – their words, not mine.'

The older of the two, codenamed Hans, had once been a preco-cious wizard with explosives in the service of the commando supremo Skorzeny, and was handpicked by Ruzicki straight from the boring pastures of the Nazi reservation in the Paraguay jungles. He, like his partner, stood to receive a hundred thousand dollars plus bonus plus generous expenses. He thought that the recent hostilities in the Gulf and the mines in the Canal had prepared the ground work for the venture. He proposed to heighten international tension, Ruzicki recounted, by spreading rumours of a growing terrorist threat to the Panama Canal, too, and eventually by setting off a small bomb at the Pedro Miguel Lock or the Gaillard Cut. The damage would be minimal but it would look like the botched attempt at a major attack. Simultaneously, Hans would also cause two minor explosions, to cut the Saudi pipeline and the new Egyptian one along the Suez Canal. These would interrupt the flow of oil only momentarily, but the psychological effect would be considerable, coinciding with the main part of the operation. 'It was Hans who came up with these ideas, and I must say, I like his way of thinking,' said Ruzicki.

'So do I,' Quincey enthused, 'and I guess he's going all out for his bonus.'

'It's also a matter of professional pride with him. For the same reason he was not very pleased with the idea that I'd be there with him. He'd prefer to work without supervision, but he accepted that he would not know his actual main target until the last minute.'

'And we're still assuming,' Savas was thinking aloud, 'that your target ship will be riding at anchor somewhere off Port Said, waiting to join a convoy for the transit. Correct?'

'We can't assume anything,' Quincey snapped. 'We've got to be sure that she's there.'

'No problem,' said Ruzicki, 'it's a matter of timing. Hans wants to raid the ship just before sailing, keep her under control with the use of minimum force, lock up most of the crew, and place explosives at critical points all over the ship. He'll want instructions about whether he should use American, Israeli, Libyan or Czech explosives, whichever implication we wish to create. His preference is, of course, for some Israeli stuff. Partly because it's good, partly because he doesn't like the makers. But that's immaterial to us, I guess. What matters is to choose the right spot for the detonation. He wants to do it by some radio signal after his men and I are safely away.'

'Hey, wait a minute!' Savas was on his feet. 'What the fuck is he planning to do with the crew? He can't just let them perish with the ship!'

'You mean you want Hans to free the crew?' Ruzicki found the thought amusing.

'I want more than that. I want the crew *ordered* to abandon ship before Hansie boy shifts his own fat arse.'

'Fair enough,' said Quincey, 'we're not murderers.'

'Surely not, but we're interfering with the operation,' Ruzicki argued. 'Hans and his men would want to protect themselves.'

'Tell them to wear face masks.'

'Okay.' Ruzicki shrugged his shoulders.

Savas knew Ruzicki better than to believe that he could be convinced as easily as that. What was he planning? To kill off all witnesses? 'Not good enough. I want to be sure about the crew. And as we'll have Bucken on board . . . '

Both men interrupted him with questions.

'What?'

'Is that definite?'

'Let's make it definite now. Your men supply the know-how and the muscle. You alone will know the target until the last moment. And Bucken will be there to receive the final signal to blow the ship after, and he's to make sure that it is after, complete evacuation.'

Quincey acceded to the Oldman's demand right away. Ruzicki just shrugged his shoulders once again. He had his private plans anyway. Although he had given Hans full details of his escape arrangements for the raiding party, and although he had made them sound as if the facilities were to be laid on and backed at a very high political level, his secret intention was that none of the saboteurs would leave Sinai alive. After all, he was the only syndicate member they knew personally, so that Savas and the rest of them could remain nameless and faceless shadows, and he would certainly not want to spend the rest of his life wondering who might try to blackmail him one day. 'Okay, anything you say, Oldman,' he forced himself to say, and quickly changed the subject: 'Hans wants to organise a raid on the nerve centre of the Canal at Ismailia during our transit, and force the staff to transmit special orders for the entire convoy to maximise speed. That would certainly help the pile-up.'

'No,' Quincey objected quite categorically. 'It's an unncessary risk. It can go wrong, the men can be caught and made to confess, Ismailia must be better guarded than Fort Knox.'

'Don't you believe it, Don.'

'If we need to sow confusion at Ismailia, why don't we settle for some mechanical sabotage without any risk of bloodshed?' Savas asked.

'Yes, tell Hans to look into it.'

'Okay,' Ruzicki nodded, 'that will, in fact, keep the cost below the projected one million dollar mark. As for the pile-up to maximise the duration of the closure . . . '

Savas was only half-listening. He could not suppress a little smile of vanity. What none of the others could predict, though he knew for certain, was that the pile-up would be very substantial indeed. He would have two tankers, about 300,000 tons each, sailing in ballast, in that convoy. Both ships were owned by his front companies, registered under Flags of Convenience, and manned by trusted Greeks who would ensure that those monsters, unstoppable at the best of times, would just plough into ships and shore alike. Purchased at knock-down scrap prices but insured at current nominal market value, their wrecking would bring Savas some quick extra profits in the region of ten million dollars net.

Ruzicki was still summarising the assessment the younger of the two mercenaries, a second-generation Nazi codenamed Franz, had submitted. The estimate was that 'a reasonable pile-up' would take from three months upwards, probably more like six months, to clear up.

'Couldn't we be more certain?' Quincey wanted to know.

'I don't think so. Franz, in fact, quoted to me someone who works for Smit itself in Rotterdam. I think the exact words were that ship salvage is a science of vague assumptions, based on debatable figures, from inconclusive instruments, performed with equipment of problematical accuracy, by persons of doubtful reliability and questionable mentality.' He paused for effect, then concluded Franz's thesis: 'jokes apart, he says that sometimes, salvors can perform miracles. The Canal is not very deep, and that's also against us. Salvage equipment could be flown in and taken to the spot by road. The use of floating cranes would also be possible at least as far as the two ends of the pile-up. But delays are likely. First salvage engineers would have to be flown in to assess the risks. If there were tankers with no inert

250

gas system fitted, there could be gas explosions. There might be undeclared dangerous cargo in the wrecks. Some ships could be refloated, others would have to be cut up by divers or controlled explosions or if possible by chain cutters worked by two huge cranes in a sawing action.

'And that's not all. Many owners would fight cannibalism and demand refloating. That's more time wasted with plenty of room for international legal arguments. So it's not unreasonable to think in terms of even twelve months.'

'And even that's not all,' said Quincey. 'Because Hans and Franz do not know our chosen target. A chemical tanker is a floating bomb in herself, and with all that corrosive, poisonous and inflammable stuff loose in the Canal . . . well, gentlemen, I think we really are in business.'

As they drank to the success of 'Tsunami', Quincey tried to assess his two main partners. Savas would play it straight, maximise his own profit, but that was only fair. Ruzicki might have some secrets to protect himself: might even double-cross people if he saw any advantage in it. Yet Quincey did not feel troubled. He had his own scheme that was progressing smoothly in tandem with 'Tsunami' itself.

In the Marbella yacht harbour, Bucken's fortuitous meeting with Freemantle was meticulously planned and staged. Bucken knew that he might be watched by somebody in Ruzicki's pay, but Freemantle was playing his part well, unwanted witnesses would see nothing but the joy of a chance encounter, and at least the pleasure of the shirt-sleeve December day needed no faking. Bucken told himself again and again that, as long as they adhered to their carefully devised routine, his friend would be in no danger, but he could not be sure. They walked down the long pier where they could be seen but not overheard. Along their route, gleaming, deserted yachts stood shoulder to shoulder, forming a guard of honour on both sides. Most of those floating palaces would hardly ever put to sea or receive visitors even in the high season, and their nickname – the Holes, through which rich men poured fortunes into the water – seemed well deserved.

'Thanks for the arrangements,' Freemantle beamed. 'I've never been on such generous expenses.'

'Not my money,' said Bucken curtly.

'That won't make me or Ada any less grateful.'

Bucken reacted as if stung. 'What has she got to do with it?'

'Oh, come now, paid leave and a holiday with me?'

251

'You mean she's here?'

'Waiting for us in the hotel. She wants to say thanks personally.'

'That had nothing to do with me. It never occurred to me that she should come.'

'I thought so. You bloody cops wouldn't have the heart, would you?' But Freemantle knew that Bucken must be lying. His editor was not in the habit of encouraging reporters to take their time on plum assignments. Bucken must have used a lot of muscle to make the editor grit his teeth and offer an extended holiday, as a reward for hard work and years of loyalty, to Ada Tansley, Freemantle's intermittently permanent lover who had never tried to rush him into marriage in eighteen years.

Bucken was fuming. Ada's holiday must have been Ashenbury's idea for a perfect cover story. In sullen silence he turned back towards the shore.

'Don't worry,' said Freemantle, 'she hasn't got a clue what we're up to.'

'I'm not worried.'

'You could have fooled me.'

Bucken forced himself to smile. 'I did. Now listen. I want you to send your first telex to Ashenbury. Use the code I gave you. The message is simple. Chummy is on course to pull off the big 'un. The enterprise is codenamed Tsunami. You know the word?'

'Sure thing. I was brought up on magazines where every cub reporter had to make up stories of white slavery and the Krakatoa disaster with homicidal tidal waves.'

'Good. Just mention in the telex that the name may imply a connection with the *Alida II* sinking.' Bucken did not elaborate, and Freemantle had the good sense not to ask questions. Finally, Bucken gave him the names of his new acquaintances. 'Ask Ashenbury to identify them and let me know.'

'I think I can help you a little. Mahoudi is a Lebanese super-fixer of tankers. He's a specialist in twisting arms and recruiting cut-price crews, and corrupt to the tip of his fourteen-carat fountain pen, but that's part of his charm, and inevitable, I suppose, if you want to thrive on recession.'

'Anything on the others?'

'Aldo Selli rings a bell. My guess is that he's an American big-shot in insurance.'

'Okay. Make sure you get the spelling right when you encode the telex.'

'All very hush-hush,' Freemantle mocked Bucken as much as himself, because he would never admit how strongly all this secrecy appealed to the Walter Mitty in him. It stirred him even more when Bucken outlined the daily routine to be followed for keeping in touch: 'If at any time I fail to call you as agreed, you wait for six hours in case I've just been delayed, then take the first available flight wherever it goes. Just get out of here.'

'Very dramatic.' Freemantle had no special respect for premonitions – he had concocted real life dramas galore of that kind for a demanding editor in his youth – but now something tightened in his throat. He had to fight off the urge to embrace Bucken and plead with him to take care, whatever he might be up to. The thought embarrassed him, so he laughed: 'Draw, man, draw! Bang, bang! You're dead.'

'I'm serious, you bloody scribe.'

'Serious?' Bucken's momentary weakness and the tone of genuine concern threw the reporter even more. 'You're just a fastidious fusspot.'

'Piss off.'

'You know something? I find you a lot more bearable when you're plain nasty like any other fucking cop.'

Passers-by would have been hard put to guess that they just loved each other.

They had a drink in the port, another in Millionaires' Row, and a third as they started up the hilly streets of the old town where Freemantle's modest hotel nestled behind luxury boutiques and the kitchen doors of chic watering holes. That was where they ran into Greta who had just come out of a shop specialising in kid-glove leather slacks. Her new bodyguard was three feet behind her. Bucken hesitated for a second but decided there was no reason to play hide and seek or to lie and introduce his friend under some assumed name.

Freemantle? It sounded familiar to her. Wasn't that the man who had once called Bucken in Athens? Or was it Zurich? All she remembered for certain was that the call made Bucken rush out and break the spell of a sexy afternoon. 'Wasn't there a London telephone exchange called Freemantle in the old days?'

'Fremantle, with one e, ma'am, but long before your time,' answered Freemantle gallantly. They all smiled but Bucken knew he had made a mistake.

Ed Wade was pleased with himself. The agent he had dispatched to 'watch the boats go by in Götland' noted the arrival of strangers at Herrvik. He heard them talk in bars about the *Rose of Stambul* disaster and the lone sailor's miraculous survival. Their interest was understandable: everybody up and down the island seemed to be puzzled by the survivor's mysterious disappearance from the hospital. And yet there was something peculiar about the newcomers, a certain eagerness without the voyeur's morbid pleasure in their questions. So it was instinct rather than anything tangible that alerted Wade's man, and made him speculate, though not for long, about the strangers. They might be from the KGB, he thought. Or the CIA. Or both. Under the terms of his assignment, it made no difference. If those men wanted to find out more about the survivor and his fate, they would have to approach the sergeant who played police chief in the fishing village. Under some pressure, he might or might not reveal the little he knew that could be too much. *Could go comme ci, comme ça*, he concluded with some pride: he always saw himself as a bit of a linguist of humorous disposition.

Just to be on the safe side, the agent promptly shot the policeman with a poison dart gun of Soviet manufacture, a known darling of the KGB. He stayed for the funeral to pay his respects and photograph the mourners, then left them to sort out the implications of the death for themselves, whoever they might be.

Yes, Ed Wade was reasonably pleased with himself, though less so with his agent's rashness in trying to claim expenses for five lavish dinners in four days on Götland.

Christmas on the beach in sunshine was a revelation to Bucken. He decided to make it a regular feature of his life if he ever got rich or retired young enough to enjoy the sun – two likely impossibilities. On Boxing Day, however, he was asked to run another 'little errand' for Savas: he was to fly to Casablanca for 'just a whistle stop to complete the purchase of a nippy little tramp ship going for a song for two hundred and ten thou U.S.' As he would be away for only a few days, it seemed best that Freemantle should stay put in Marbella. That required some gentle pressure on his irascible editor, but after a few words, whispered by Ashenbury's friend of a friend, the great man was *delighted* to extend the time allocated to Freemantle's Spanish assignment and Ada Tansley's supportive presence.

Two days later, Bucken took possession of the *Aloha*, the 2,400-ton tramp, and dismissed the Maltese captain and his crew. He then appointed a reputable local agent to get a few minor repairs done on the *Aloha*, kit her out for a long voyage, and hire a Moroccan crew who would sail her only as far as Gibraltar. Bucken had no idea where she would go from there, but he knew that Savas would supply the crew. Before leaving Casablanca, he telephoned Ashenbury: 'I think it's well worth keeping an eye on the *Aloha*. Can you arrange it? She'll be in Gib by the beginning of January.'

'What do you know of the history of the ship?'

'Not much. But, as I'm the owner, I can send you photostats of the documentation.'

'Who holds the mortgage on her?'

'No mortgage. I always pay cash. A snip at two hundred and ten thou.'

Savas had mortgaged himself as well as all his protégés to the hilt and beyond. He knew that the stress would soon begin to take its toll. Yet there was no way to stop and rest now, not even over Christmas. Ships did not take holidays and neither would recession-struck owners, brokers, insurers and pedlars of other shipping services who were only too keen to pick up crumbs of business at any hour of any day of anybody's festive season. Savas's Nordic physician in Marbella, one of the gold-diggers of the Costa who would treat emergencies outside banking hours only if his secretaries had already diagnosed a large wad of cash in hard currency, warned the old man that his blood pressure was much too high. He urged Savas to take it easy, and the good patient promised to do just that in a month or two.

In the mosque of the Pueblo Yasmin, Savas worked twenty-hour days peppered with catnaps. The telephones and telex machines seemed never to stop, and visitors were unwelcome. Big killings come at a premium and if you're keen, you've got to pay, Savas kept telling himself in moments of flagging energy, stomach pains, dizziness and despair. When he repeated this to Greta, she deemed it 'the most boring remark of the decade. Please don't use it tonight even if anybody cares to ask how you spend your day.'

'Tonight?'

'Have you forgotten The Party of The Season at The Club?'

'Er . . . I'm sorry. We'll go next year.'

'I'll go tonight.'

'Okay, Bucken will take you.'

'He may not want to.'

'He'll have to if I tell him.'

'No thanks. You don't have to pay anyone to screw me. Men still want me, you know? It's only you who's dead between your knees and your nose.'

She had said worse things to him on many occasions over the years, but now he was infuriated beyond endurance. He took a wild swipe

255

at her with the back of his hand. It caused as much pain to him as to her, even physically. And it left her speechless. It did not make sense. Such things happened only to other women. Things like beatings or the humiliation of finding your lover with somebody else just when he was supposed to be in your bed. She waited. She was not sure if she was waiting for a second blow or an apology. Then the phone rang.

'Excuse me,' said Savas, squeezing past her to reach the set. It was not clear what he was apologising for.

Greta slammed the door as she left. She blamed Bucken for the unpleasant scene, for her need to ask her husband of all people to escort her to the party, for everything. You'll pay for that, she swore, both of you.

It was Savas's main American banker on the line. Out of sheer goodwill, the man was trying to warn Savas that he might be over-extending himself: 'Listen, Danny, I know you've borrowed left, right and centre on everything you've got, homes, ships, offices, real estate, the goddam' lot, and now you're mortgaging your reputation, too. Is that wise?'

Savas had no time for him or his caution. 'Help me or say "no" and I promise to turn to someone else with no hard feelings.' But his mind was fixed on making up mental excuses for hitting Greta. He decided to say his apologies with diamonds, the 'erring husband's Esperanto', in his experience.

Another phone rang, and even Greta was forgotten. One of his lawyers was calling from Bermuda to report that 'a two-bucket deal' – tankers, this time – was through.

While the other syndicate members dreamt up exotic schemes (Ruzicki was buying unsellable and perishable goods at give-away prices to rot for him, well insured, in the blocked waterway), Savas concentrated on taking advantage of the main forecast of the effects of the Canal closure and momentary war hysteria. His calculations were based on simple home truths: the Canal saved some twenty per cent in distance and, depending on cargo and speed, up to half the fuel consumption for the east-west trade; every day, up to seventy ships used Suez for transit; the Canal carried half the oil coming out of the Gulf; a tanker trip round the Cape could double the time and cost; a closure and fear of worse to come would hit oil prices, industry and stock markets everywhere; even if the effects were ephemeral, those who were prepared for them would get rich.

Savas opened a file and took out a sheaf of notes he had scribbled and typed (badly) himself. With his 'Tsunami' thoughts, plans, and all the interlocking interests in three dozen nameplate companies set up specifically for the exercise, he could hardly trust himself (what if I talked in my sleep?), let alone anybody else. It was time for him to finalise his moves and close the deals.

The top sheet was headed *OIL PRICES*, and began with a list of objections: *Miracles in the seventies . . . 5% cut in Mid-East production then raised prices 150%. No more miracles to be expected. Oil glut: producers desperate to sell and maintain falling prices at same time; West has big reserves; Japan, still dependent on imports and therefore vulnerable, holds buffer stock enough for four months . . .* Savas smiled: yes, all that was still true, but he knew that oil- and money-men had lived on their nerves for too long. They lived or died by their gut reactions. To be on the safe side, they would panic first – think later. *So spot rates could still jump six or seven dollars a barrel . . .* For Savas's pre-emptive strike at the markets, even a few days' panic would be sufficient.

He fed the sheet to the shredder. He knew the calculations that followed by heart. 'Gambling' on future oil prices, he would make about two million dollars on every ten promised (not invested!). He would skim his profits quickly, soon after 'Tsunami', still at the height of the panic.

The next sheet for the shredder referred to *STERLING*. *Buy. Specify all payments for services to be received during Tsunami in sterling, oil-rich Britain's petro-currency. North Sea oil independent of Suez: sterling must rise at least for a short while . . .*

Savas's bankers were already buying forward currency. Short-term sterling and oil gains would then be poured into Japanese stock:

TOKYO. Stock market will tumble. Always does when oil threatened. Buy heavily with minimum delay . . . Recovery could occur within weeks . . .

All prepared. No more reminders needed.

INSURANCE. Bonanza for B-G . . . Insurance cost would at least treble from one to three per cent of insured value of cargo and hull . . . To insure just one tanker for one Mid-East voyage will be up to about a mill and a half . . .

That, however, was Boothy-Graffoe's pigeon. He would make yet another fortune insuring ships readily at inflated war risk rates, knowing full well that there was no special risk. Savas could have claimed a piece of that action, too, but chose not to. He only accepted an assurance of preferential terms. It was not because he did not want the extra profit, it was merely a matter of his own brand of machismo. He prided himself on being 'a ships man' who would rather work than pray insurer-style for his luck.

Savas took out a pink folder, marked *TANKERS*. The thoughts

257

accumulated therein gave him an almost sensual pleasure. The well-thumbed pages attested to a great deal of slave labour, sleepless nights and foresight. He, like most ship-owners, had visions of grandeur on the Onassis scale.

One sheet dealt with ULCCs. The 400,000-ton Ultra Large Crude Carriers, queens of the seas in the seventies, had deteriorated to the point of extinction, doomed dinosaurs rusting away in ship cemeteries, pitiful eyesores dotting the bays of shelter. They had been killed by the sudden glut of tanker tonnage following the days when a single voyage would earn back the price of a ship, and received the coup de grâce from the Coast Guard decision to exclude everything but double-skinned hulls from US ports.

But, Savas thought, with his chest bursting, there was a big, big BUT. Following the Suez closure, the law could be revoked temporarily. The price of a fit-to-float ULCC could overnight soar to a thousand per cent or more of her mortgage value. If such ships were on hand when the war hysteria began, the Saudis and other Arab producers would fight to rent them for off-shore oil storage. The charter rate for just riding at anchor outside the war zone could easily be thirty thousand dollars a day – more than ten million for the year. Beyond that, she could be scrapped. 'Who cares?' Savas had scrawled in the margin even though he knew the answer: he did. He just loved big things afloat.

Savas's ULCCs, each owned by a different front company, were to be near the Gulf in good time to enjoy a head-start against competitors who might try to climb on the bandwagon and would need seven or eight weeks to find ships, get them out of mothballs, resurrect and position them.

Other, handier-sized tankers also figured heavily in the calculations Savas had prepared for the syndicate. Currently, tankers were queueing in the Gulf, under-cutting each other to get fixed for the odd voyage, willing to work at rates below the breadline to stay alive until a new dawn. Only the shrewdest and occasionally ruthless managed to squeeze a small profit out of tankers in the eighties. To an owner, sailing under the Japanese or American flag, the running cost of a 150,000-ton tanker was about ten thousand dollars a day. A Greek, under the less demanding Liberian flag of convenience, would find cheap labour and run the ship at half the cost. The vast bunker bills, almost half a million dollars' Canal fee, and port charges would be the same for everyone but the *fixture* would probably go to the cheapest ship and the owner who knew whom to bribe. Even so, the sporadic sixty-six-day round-trip would net no more than a quarter of a million profit that would hardly cover losses caused by the long periods of idling.

The Suez closure would change all that for a while. The queues would melt away, worldscale rates would shoot up from 27 to 50 or more, every available ship would be fixed, possibly for several voyages, and a single round-trip would bring in more than two million profit. Savas planned to have a small fleet on hand to pick up the long-term contracts of affreightment and to work in rotation to keep the oil flowing the long way round the Cape. Once the papers had been signed, it would make no difference if the Canal was reopened and the work ran out: idling would be well paid.

Papeete wheeled in Quincey just as a telex began to chatter. One of the most reputable brokers who had been dealing with the Savas family's shipping division was reporting from London that the owners of the *Chittagong Star* and *Marques of Ponta Grossa* had accepted Savas's offer to charter the ships at three thousand dollars a day, 'delivery January 16 and 18, Port Sudan and Haifa respectively, 3 option 3 option 3'.

'Perfect,' said Quincey, and hurriedly explained to Papeete with undisguised glee that Ashenbury had a well-concealed interest in both ships. 'Your old darling will be stung in more ways than one. Do you mind?'

Papeete shrugged her shoulders and turned away to marvel at some inscription on the wall in Arabic.

Quincey was already talking to Savas: 'Shouldn't we make it six option six?'

'If you wish. But I think it's good enough as it is.'

The chartering of the two ships for three months with options to extend it for a second and third similar period at fixed rates was only a small part of the syndicate's most ambitious and delicate operation. The principle behind it was simple enough. Speculative ship-building and the world recession in trade and industry had created a tremendous surplus in available tonnage. Owners of general cargo ships, bulk carriers, roll-on roll-off RoRo vessels, refrigerated cargo and container ships went begging for work. Charter rates were rock-bottom, throat-cutting competition was expected and accepted on all fronts. Savas and other experts deemed a Suez closure and threat of war 'the best thing to happen for shipping in a decade of misery'. Freight rates would jump by some thirty per cent overnight because everybody would at least assume that it was inevitable. Apart from the increased risk, there would be pressure on shipping to cope with the longer routes and keep delivery dates for traders and manufac-turers who were threatened by massive penalty clauses for delays.

The syndicate planned to profit in two ways. Members who owned cargo-starved, loss-making fleets would keep their ships free and available in crucial ports from January onwards. But the sweetest profits would derive from ordinary charter deals. The *Chittagong Star*, for instance, was now available to Savas at three thousand dollars a day. No money would be handed over before delivery date. From then on, ninety thousand dollars would be payable to cover a month, always a month in advance. The moment the Canal was closed, the going rate for the *Chittagong* could become one or two thousand dollars a day more. Savas would simply sub-let the ship and pocket the difference.

As it had to be done on a large scale all over the world, secrecy was the cornerstone of the whole plan. The Baltic and other exchanges were extremely sensitive to any whiff of gossip. Yet operations like that were not without precedent: the Russians organised it expertly to ensure cheap transport when they did their vast shopping and shipping of grain each year. Savas therefore used front companies, and dealt with owners directly whenever possible. He also knew the discreet and 'keen' clerks in major brokers' offices who would be willing *not* to put the deal through the books: that would help to preserve the secret – and line their own pockets with the brokerage fee. At times of recession, everybody was keen to please in any way the would-be charterer of good standing and, all too frequently, even the one who had just walked in from the street.

For the syndicate it was crucial to deal with reputable owners and brokers who knew that shipping had to live up to its 'my word is my bond' motto to survive, and who would not renege and do a bunk when it mattered most. Savas recognised that he was about to exploit hard-up owners, and felt sorry for them. Pity did not prevent him from going ahead – nobody had helped him in his gravest moment of need – but at least he did not gloat over their misfortunes. Quincey had no feeling for the would-be victims, least of all for Ashenbury.

The red phone rang and Papeete answered it. She listened, covered the mouthpiece, and whispered to her husband: 'It's that creepy dwarf from London.'

Quincey nodded and she switched the line to the speaker, thus allowing him to talk to Boothy-Graffoe without holding the receiver. Boothy-Graffoe was full of good news for everybody. Thinly veiled, he reported that the insurance claims on the *Rose* were soon to go through, and that he had chartered, clandestinely, several more ships for the syndicate, as requested. 'How are things going at your end?'

'Smoothly. We're about to move, so we'll have to discuss final, yes, *final* details eyeball to eyeball. The Oldman wants everybody here by Friday, Saturday at the latest. Can you make it?'

'But of course.'

'Good. Anything else?'

'Yes. There's something that bugs me. Remember the Australian journalist I've been trying to contact?'

'Sure. Any luck?'

'No. Even though your American friend seemed to do whatever he could. Has he given up now?'

'I'll find out. Don't worry. We'll get there.'

'It's easy for you to say not to worry.'

Quincey sighed. His grimace told Savas: I wish the fucking dwarf dropped dead. What did this idiot expect? An international manhunt and a full discussion on an open line? Quincey had used his CIA contact only to keep Boothy-Graffoe sweet and happy because the little man's expertise and contacts in the City were vital to the whole syndicate. So, more reassurance was needed before Boothy-Graffoe, wealthy enough not to take any risks, got frightened by his own shadow, and backed out of 'Tsunami' even at the last minute. 'I'll tell my friend to make some more urgent inquiries.'

'Thanks, Don, I appreciate it, and please don't think that I'm seeing ghosts or something, because just the other day I bumped into that broker friend of mine who introduced Warman in the first place. So I asked him if they were still in touch. When our American friend asked him the same question, he could afford to fob him off. Not me, he couldn't do it to me. He couldn't say he knew absolutely nothing about that reporter because then why did he introduce him, right? So he was forced to think back and recall that Warman got to him via Ashenbury and that was good enough for him.' He paused to let it sink in. He knew that Ashenbury was the Quinceys' friend and helped Papeete's father now and then.

'Well, that's something else we could look into.'

'I've already done just that, and I didn't like what I saw. His lordship and I met at some reception last night, and I asked him casually about Warman. First he didn't seem to remember him at all, then he said "oh, yes, some scribbler from down under, isn't he?" He told me he hardly knew him. Now that's not like Ashenbury at all. He's real City. Normally, if you wanted to buy an *Evening Standard*, he'd check and double-check your school, family, character, motives and financial status before he'd tell you where the nearest news-stand was.'

'I tell you what,' said Quincey. 'I'll ask my friend to contact you right away. He might even enlist some help from the police, and you could then construct Warman's identikit picture or whatever they call it. That would give us something to go on, wouldn't it? And we could talk more about it on Friday when you get here.'

261

Bucken was at a low ebb, and the January sunshine failed to cheer him up. He felt used, abused and exploited all round, making no headway since his return from Casablanca. He knew that patience was the name of his game, but he had had enough of his odyssey in a one-way system of dead ends. He wanted to wind up his mission one way or another, but thought with apprehension about the vacuum beyond. He would have a hard time disentangling the mess about his job, and coming to terms with the fact that he had been cheated and manipulated, sometimes ruthlessly.

Then, suddenly, all his dark thoughts were forgotten. The adrenalin began to flow. Long before he would see or hear anything concrete, he sensed that things were coming to the crunch.

On Wednesday, Ruzicki arrived back from some confidential mission and went straight into a breakfast huddle with Savas. That gave Bucken a chance to look at the name-tag on Ruzicki's luggage. It said: H. Wetzel. The name under which he ran his front company in Cairo. Suez, Tsunami, Cairo. Had Ruzicki gone there to make some final arrangements?

Bucken would have liked to search the suitcase, but could not afford the risk. He wandered towards the mosque, and stopped to chat to the duty officer in the security centre of the Pueblo. Over the man's shoulder he could see the bank of closed-circuit TV sets: security cameras were scanning all approaches to the gates, key areas inside the compound, and the walls that were also protected by electronic sensors. One of the screens sprang to life: a cab with a Malaga registration drove up to the main entrance. The passenger, obviously familiar with the procedure, leaned out of the window and spoke towards the keyhole in the unmanned, eight-foot-tall gate that looked just a sheet of metal but would have withstood the impact of a speeding lorry.

'My name is Pullen. I'm expected '

'Just a second, sir.' The guard checked a list, studied the face on the screen. and compared it with a photograph attached to the list. 'Okay, Mr. Pullen. Please dismiss the cab. Transport is waiting for you inside the gate.'

The man on the screen nodded and paid the driver.

Your name is not Pullen, thought Bucken, I know who you are, 'Rabbit' Schwarzberg, owner of a pair of ears big enough to sail a Chinese junk, a wayward genius with explosives and electronics. Bucken himself had interrogated him several times, and like other detectives failed ever to convict him. Yet he knew, everybody knew, that the Rabbit supplied all the high-tech gear to rich villains whose bank robberies could pay for his exclusive services. Bucken considered himself lucky to have caught an early glimpse of the Rabbit. Not that his police background was a secret to Savas and the rest of them, but it was better to safeguard his composure at all times.

He decided to wait for developments at the poolside. As he was crossing the large patio of the harem area, Papeete stopped him. 'I thought you'd never speak to me again. Have I done something wrong?'

She stared at him in silence for a second, her face reflected that she was about to answer but then changed her mind. 'I'm off for a few days.'

'Oh.' He did not know how to react. She was not in the habit of informing him about her movements. If she did, it must have some significance.

'I didn't want to leave without saying goodbye and wishing you luck.'

'Luck?'

'Well, you never know when you may need it, do you?'

'I'll tell you when you return.'

'By then you may not be here.' Suddenly she grabbed both his hands, and lowered her voice: 'Take care.'

'Hey, what's this?' His smile always rearranged his craggy features into what Sarah used to call 'semi-cuddly'. 'An undeserved demo of care and concern?' He wanted to kiss her and knew that she would not reject it even though both of them were conscious of the vast expanse of tinted glass wall behind which Quincey had his own private electronic sanctuary. She let go of his hands but would not move out of his reach. The intensity of her gaze carried the message: it's up to you, Bucken, this time it's up to you.

He stepped back. 'Well, bon voyage.'

Her sad smile said *thank you for making the right decision for both of us*, but she longed to know if he could ever make an unselfish decision about anything or anyone.

'I hope I'll see you soon in . . . let's say some other place.'

'Don't. Don't hope. Things will change. For all of us.' She turned to go, but stopped. 'Incidentally, I couldn't find Greta and you're bound to see her. Give her my love, will you?'

'Love?' Has she ever known the true meaning of the word?

'I'll let you choose the word, okay?' She began to feel shivery despite the heat. It was like the real scorcher of a day in Biarritz when she had last seen her mother, emotionally neglected and sick, with cold sweaty hands conjuring up visions of death. I'm crazy, Bucken's hands were warm, she thought, as she left.

A couple of hours later, Bucken was summoned to the mosque. The Rabbit looked up from a heap of gadgetry – and gasped. 'It's a set up. It's a bloody trap!' He lunged towards Savas who stepped back in horror. 'What on earth . . . ?'

'It's all right, sir, the memories we share with Mr. Schwarzberg are not mutually happy ones.'

It took a great deal of convincing to reassure the Rabbit that he had not been set up by the police, but then he began to enjoy himself, teasing, taunting Bucken, calling him a born-again ex-cop. 'I'm glad, guv, that you've seen the light.' His accent retained a Viennese tang that grew even more prominent when trying to imitate some Cockney villain. 'You were so righteous, guv, when we last met at the Met. How's Old Bill taking it that you've strayed?'

'Let's not waste time, gentlemen.' Savas turned to Bucken. 'Mr. Schwarzberg is here to deliver some equipment and teach you how to use that,' he gestured towards a small bright yellow box that looked like a cross between a cheap transistor and a calculator. 'When the two of you have finished, he's to go to see Don, and you wait for me. I won't be long.'

Gleefully, Schwarzberg explained to Bucken that the yellow set had two functions. 'Firstly it can bring you your master's voice.' He pressed a button on a similar but red set, and the yellow one sounded a croaky klaxon. 'With that your boss, whoever he is, can give you the signal that the game is to begin and you are to do whatever you're meant to do.' He smirked and asked in a silky voice: 'What's your game, Superintendent Bucken? Or was it *Chief* Superintendent? I'm sorry, I didn't mean to offend. And I didn't mean to ask in what way you superintended to debase your fine and shiny character. I'm not even curious, to tell you the truth. I'm just an honest trader. I sell customised electronic equipment to men of means and sophisticated needs.'

'When you've stopped enjoying yourself, *chummy*,' the word stung the Rabbit, 'perhaps we could get on with it.'

'You're not working for Old Bill any more, you know,' Schwarzberg snapped indignantly.

'But I could still kick your balls for a hundred-yard birdie, and this time it's me who'd deal with your complaints, too.'

'Oh well, once a guv, always a guv, it seems.'

'Look, let's be serious, Rabbit. If you have any grand ideas of telling tales about me in London, I suggest you forget it. My new friends have longer arms than the law, and they don't bother to sue for slander. Just remember that.'

Schwarzberg stiffened and reverted to his favourite professorial voice. 'The red set is a rather powerful little transmitter. If your boss programmes it with the correct code, it will transmit to you and set off the klaxon in your yellow set from anywhere within five miles, from the ground, a moving car or even an aircraft. I've already given the code to Mr. Savas. Now if you care to look at the set, please. not that, the yellow one, thank you, you'll note that you can tap out numbers in any combination on it. It will not tell you sine, cosine or tangent, I'm afraid, but it will transmit a signal to these little darlings,' he pointed at a neat pile of match-sized boxes, 'and activate them.'

'To do what?'

'Oh well, it's up to you. They may start machinery, switch on and off a conveyor belt, an automated bakery, anything you like, and may even detonate bombs.' He paused to watch Bucken's reaction but was not surprised to see none. 'For simplicity, and in order to avoid mishaps or unauthorised usage in case this yellow devil falls into the wrong hands, the detonators respond only to a specific code. So attention, please. It's three, seven, double two, eight tapped out twice in quick succession. That helps to avoid accidents. Now will you please memorise it?'

'Will anybody else know the code?'

'Your set, your code. Three-seven, double-two, eight – twice. Got it? Good. So if you hear the klaxon, you tap in your code, and whoosh, it all begins to happen. What will it be? Fireworks for the kids?'

'You mean it happens at once?'

'Good question, guv. You can use it as a direct transmitter activator or you can press button T and you've got a timer for up to twenty hours – so. Press button T and, say, fourteen, then T again and your code. Now you can dump the set, you have fourteen minutes to get away without carrying any incriminating evidence.'

'Clever.' Bucken began to see the meaning of a couple of unguarded remarks over the breakfast that had honoured his safe arrival. He was to go somewhere as Savas's representative. When Savas gave the word, he would have to press the button. Suez? What was the role of *Aloha*, the tramp he had just bought in Casablanca?

A security guard came to collect the Rabbit and take him to Quincey. Bucken had to wait for Savas. It was a good opportunity to look around, but apart from the communication machines there was not much to see. The red and yellow sets revealed nothing about their intended functions. Would the black matchboxes be used as radio detonators? The large metal filing cabinets did not seem to be locked

– one drawer was slightly open – but to look inside could be risky. Bucken did not know the security arrangements. He slowly scanned the walls, air vents, light fittings: no sign of concealed TV cameras.

He still had his miniature tape recorder. Although it could not be moved about because of the degaussing frames of the doors, it could still be used as a bug, left *in situ* to record every sound in the mosque. As it was voice-activated with auto-shut-off after fifteen seconds of silence, it could record four hours of continuous or intermittent conversation. It had both magnetic and super-glue fixing facilities, and the only problem was to find a safe nook for it. It had to be something permanent – desks, telexes, filing cabinets would be removed when Savas cleared out of the Pueblo.

Unfortunately, the mosque itself was too bare. Bucken wandered about aimlessly, admiring the rich carvings of the marble walls. On the main, eastern, wall, shiny yellow metal formed an intricate pattern at a kneeling man's eye level. Bucken recognised it as ALLAH AKHBAR. In its deep crevices, the magnet would hold. He walked on, found the recorder in his pocket, palmed it, returned and rested his back aqainst the Arabic lettering, hoping that Allah was not only great but also kind to policemen. Damn. Whatever it was made of, probably pure gold, the inscription was non-magnetic. Removing the glue-protector strip behind his back, he managed to slip the device in the belly of a letter A – and it held. Praise be to Ed Wade, he thought. One day the device will be recovered, by me if I'm still alive, Bucken pondered without self-pity, to provide condemning evidence – or a recording of the muezzin's high-pitched calls for prayers to the faithful.

Savas returned full of beans, and Bucken stepped aside to take a quick look at the inscription. Among all the glitter, there was no obvious sign of the recorder. He sighed with relief when Savas declared: 'It's all GO! You'll soon be rich, very rich, if you invest with me, I mean if you trust me . . . Well, do you want to be a millionaire overnight?'

'Sure.' Bucken tried to look suitably enthusiastic.

'Good. Then give me a hundred grand.'

Bucken hoped his hand would not shake writing out a cheque of funny-money magnitude.

'Now listen. You'll be leaving shortly for Gibraltar to join the *Aloha*. You'll take a trip aboard your new ship. No,' he raised his hand, 'don't ask questions, you'll be told all you need to know in good time. What you must remember is that, from this moment, you carry that yellow set on your body at all times and everywhere, in the shithouse and, well, even in your lover's bed. But don't worry,' Savas laughed, 'even if you lose it somehow, there'll be people to retrieve it for you. From now on, you're a VIP as far as I'm concerned. Like the rest of us, you'll have your own bodyguards.'

'Great.' Bucken's heart sank. He did not cherish the memory of his minders in Singapore. Under their watchful eyes it could be suicidal to pass the information to Freemantle however careful contingency plans he had devised, but he knew he had no choice but to risk it. It gave him no satisfaction that hindsight might vindicate his precautions and prove to the reporter that he was not 'just a fastidious fusspot' with games of secrecy and fall-back arrangements.

'I must emphasise that I'm counting on you, Bucken. You'll be guarded because you'll be the man acting on my behalf alone. Now listen. If all is well and I want things to go ahead, you'll hear the klaxon in your yellow box for several seconds. If I see a last-minute hitch in my plans, I'll just call them off. In that case, you'll hear five short bursts of the klaxon, and you'll tell Ruzicki to stop everything. He'll tell you what to do next. But, if you do get the one long wail of the klaxon, I want you to make absolutely certain that you and everybody else can get away safely before you activate the second function of the yellow box. Is that clear?'

'As far as it goes, yes.'

'Good.' Savas began to explain how Bucken's money would be made. He was talking about a share in tankers and some chartering business, but Bucken concentrated only on trying to steer him towards self-incriminating admissions. It did not feel good playing the worm.

Savas remained admirably cautious throughout. He would not spell out anything precisely, but Bucken understood clearly that in some way, probably with the aid of *Aloha* the tramp, the Suez Canal would soon be closed, and a monumental fraud was to be perpetrated – just as he had suspected all along. Because of the security arrangements, Savas and the rest of them could be caught only in the act of conspiring to cause an explosion resulting in the closure – a criminal act he himself was now assigned to commit. Charming, he thought in despair. Get him at least to admit it, he urged himself.

'In other words,' Bucken said breezily, 'you're preparing deals with enormous profits that depend on something . . . something disastrous to disrupt shipping.'

'Life is a gamble.' Savas gestured benignly, 'but foresight may turn the odds in your favour.'

'Foresight and something like a war or the closure of a major waterway,' Bucken probed.

'I've never said that . . . but feel free to make your own deductions. But, Bucken,' he lowered his voice to suggest avuncular concern, 'it doesn't pay to be too clever. Stay ignorant. That's your key to success. And, if I were you, I wouldn't mention my private deductions to Ruzicki or anyone else.'

'How come *you* don't mind what I think or may deduce?'

'It's because I've come to trust you. You virtually saved my life in Rotterdam. You asked for nothing in return. Just a job.' He laughed. 'As a greaser. Did you really want to be a greaser?'

'I had no choice.'

'You called me a prince of industry in disguise and thought I'd fall for your fake seaman's book.'

'In a way you did. I'm here, greasing palms. You were taken in, Oldman.' Bucken was playing with fire but could not resist the dare.

'No. I followed my instinct about you, and you proved me right. After all, even Greta seemed to like and trust you, right?'

'I hope it is.'

'I'm sure it is. In one's old age one must rely on instinct, foresight, people's loyalty and friends, while recognising the laws of youth and nature, and make allowances for them.'

'What allowances?' Bucken asked angrily, remembering Greta's warning: he'd be good to you, and you'd learn to hate him for it.

Savas ignored the question. 'And you've done everything I asked and expected you to do. You were loyal in Singapore, and you did well for Ruzicki in Kiel.'

'You mean the *Rose of Stambul* and . . . '

'Whatever it was. And I'm grateful for . . . for everything. That's why you have a future with me. We'll make, er, more straightforward deals together. One day I'll need someone in my business, someone I can trust with everything, even with . . . well, never mind. Go now. Ruzicki wants to see you.'

Bucken was already at the door when Savas called after him. 'And, Bucken . . . I'm glad you're not the nosey type. Most people I know would never miss a chance to look at my files.' He pulled a drawer open. It was full of pink and buff dossiers.

'Perhaps I did. How would you know?' He glanced around: had he missed something?

'No. No hidden cameras.' Savas crossed the mosque to the wall facing the filing cabinet. 'The Arabs have always been keen to know what went on behind their backs. This compound, even the mosque, is full of spy-holes. Look. Simpler and more infallible than television.'

'But with no scanning facility', Bucken tried to joke and praise

Allah at the same time. For had the spy-hole been among the gold letters . . . the thought made him choke, but Savas was still smiling.

Ruzicki was already waiting for Bucken. 'On about Sunday, we'll go together to Gibraltar. I'll introduce you to a friend with whom you'll sail, but we'll meet again a few days later.'

'Anything you say.' Bucken was more concerned about that night than the future. As it was a Wednesday, Freemantle would be in the Casino where they had already had two meetings. If Bucken failed to turn up or send a message, he would get out of Spain in the morning. Bucken pretended to have a brainwave: 'Hey, how about a spot of gambling? I haven't forgotten your idea that some day, perhaps, you and I could make a bid for that Casino!'

'It's still a good idea. Shall we dine there?'

'Why not?' As Bucken was leaving Ruzicki's chalet, he saw the Rabbit scurrying from Quincey's glass-walled office. He would have given a finger for a chance to discover what those two might be up to. What he could not even guess was that the information might be worth a hand or even both arms to him.

Bucken spent the rest of the afternoon writing out a summary of what he had gleaned from Savas and the Rabbit. Using a pin-pointed pen from an art shop, his tiny lettering looked like lace on a small card that he taped, eventually, to his wrist under his shirt.

In the evening, Ruzicki drove and two goons took the back seat. As the foursome entered the Casino, Bucken noted that Freemantle was perching in the piano bar on the left, as usual. Bucken stopped at the door and made as much as possible out of his 'frantic search' for his membership card until the manager assured him that he was a known and valued customer and no proof would be required. That would have alerted the reporter to follow a planned routine, make himself scarce, but keep an eye on the seat Bucken would occupy in the restaurant or at one of the roulette tables.

On his way to the restaurant, Bucken waved a breezy hello to Freemantle and Ada Tansley who waved back enthusiastically.

'Don't you understand?' Freemantle grumbled. 'He doesn't want to meet us tonight. Why don't you just go and throw your arms around him?'

'Oh? Jealous again?'

'Me? Of you? Don't be so stupid. Who'd want you apart from me?'

'Wanna give it a try, Mister?' She crossed her shapely legs with a flourish. On top of the tall bar stool it was an eye-catching sight, most appreciated by Freemantle himself. Neither of them felt hurt or amused: the whole exchange was just one of the stock jokes of a long

269

relationship in which nobody remembered the original punch line that used to make them laugh. Freemantle ordered more drinks, and Ada made no secret of her displeasure. The more refined the food and the later it was consumed, the more bloated she would get because of it. She hated midnight dinners, But she would eat herself silly, again and again, and then toss and turn all night.

At long last, Bucken and his companions rose from their dinner. Freemantle rushed in and grabbed the table even before it could be cleared. While Ada studied the menu, Freemantle found the little card taped to the underside of the table-top. He removed it, excused himself, and locked himself in a cubicle in the marble-clad *Caball-eros*. His eyes were not very good, the writing hardly legible. Much of it seemed speculation about the *Aloha* in Gibraltar, the Rabbit, tanker deals and charter operations. He hoped that it would make more sense to Ashenbury who must know the background and nature of Bucken's suspicions. The last line said it all: 'Hopefully, details by tomorrow: meet according to schedule for Thursdays.' In that case, it would be wise to delay the telex to Ashenbury. Wasn't that what Bucken always advocated? 'If we can transmit full information, we get full attention. It's the strange mathematics of bureaucracy. One bit today plus one bit tomorrow never equals two bits in one go.' So be it.

By the time Freemantle pocketed the card, Bucken had already lost the equivalent of his three weeks' salary at the Yard. Ruzicki, winning steadily, thought he understood Bucken's anger, but he was wrong. The policeman was swearing at himself only for having forgotten to mention in his note the tape recorder and its location in the mosque. Now it would just have to wait until tomorrow.

Thursday for Ruzicki began at the uncivilised hour of four a.m. After the long, boozy session at the Casino, he had slept for less than forty minutes but the telex woke and sobered him up. He fished his fake British passport out of the lining of a suitcase, and began to decode the all-numeral text.

The message was a shocker: his hand-picked German chemical tanker *Chemi-Lippstadt* had completed loading two days early, and slipped out of Bordeaux harbour on Wednesday evening. Depending on weather conditions (currently stormy, gale force 10 in the Bay of Biscay, gusting to 12 around Cap Finisterre), the following Wednesday, eighteen hundred hours, was her Estimated Time of Arrival at Port Said. If she maintained her normal 17 knots average speed, she would cover the approximately three thousand nautical miles in just about seven days, keep to her ETA Port Said, and join the Suez convoy before daybreak on Thursday. That would impose an unexpectedly tight schedule on the syndicate's plan.

Ruzicki telephoned Savas and Quincey. A few minutes later, three sleepy figures gathered in Quincey's bedroom. 'We're cutting it a bit too fine,' said Savas.

The tone of reproach was not lost on Ruzicki. He apologised. It would have been pointless to offer his excuses however justifiable.

Savas knew that his oil tankers could reach Port Said in time. His captains were well versed in the art of dropping baksheesh to key officials who would make doubly sure that the tankers were not delayed and could be in the same convoy as the *Lippstadt*. 'The question is: when can the *Aloha* sail? She must make Port Said by the time the *Lippstadt* drops anchor, and definitely not later than Wednesday midnight.'

'I believe she's ready to leave Gibraltar at short notice,' said Ruzicki. 'Both her declared general cargo and the crates Hans needs are on board. Hans is there, waiting for final instructions and Bucken. If we flew there right away, she could sail by about noon. Franz is in Benghazi, and I could telex him to bring the rendezvous forward two days.' He looked at Savas. 'You think the *Aloha* can be there to pick us up?'

Savas made some calculations. The little tramp had the speed and, although rust was spreading on her like livery blotches of old age, mechanically she was in sound condition. He was pleased with his foresight when choosing her. With her two S.A. Sulzer engines developing 5,000 BHP, she could do twelve. probably even fourteen knots despite the current storm in the Mediterranean if the utter discomfort of crew and passengers was disregarded. And it would be disregarded. But I'll be damned, he thought, if I make it easy for Ruzicki. 'Well, you've certainly created a totally unnecessary problem. But somehow we'll have to cope with it.' He turned to Quincey. 'We've come a long way, Don. And now we have a seven-day count-down. Let's move, gentlemen without waiting for the partners.'

Ruzicki alerted the helicopter pilot and Bucken. 'We leave for Gib at five-fifteen.'

Savas instructed the staff to begin dismantling equipment in the mosque and prepare the evacuation of Pueblo Yasmin by Sunday evening. There was no need to disturb Greta with the news. What did she care where the money came from? She could spend the next fortnight in Switzerland.

Quincey telephoned New York but missed Papeete by a few

271

minutes. He left a message for her to take the first available flight back to the Pueblo.

Throughout the short hop by helicopter, Bucken tried not to look perturbed. Legitimately, he had no unfinished business, no reason for any delays. He knew that Freemantle would keep their evening rendezvous, as arranged, in the cramped *tapas* bar, off the Plaza de los Naranjos in Marbella. Ada would grumble, as usual, but the reporter would wait, leave, return, leave, return hourly until midnight. He would then go to his hotel nearby and, if there was no news from Bucken, prepare to take the first flight to London. He would go to meet Ashenbury straight from the airport on Friday morning. By lunchtime at the latest. Even if Freemantle did not telex Bucken's last message on Thursday, Ashenbury would have plenty of time to deduce that the *Aloha* must be playing a crucial role and, whatever it was, she must be apprehended. Apprehended, my foot, Bucken smiled inwardly, don't I ever stop playing policeman? He was looking forward to the moment when some military or armed police patrol craft of whatever nationality ordered the *Aloha* to heave to. It might happen en route or at Port Said. Ashenbury knew that whatever was to happen would happen near or in the Canal.

Bucken hoped that the intervention would come only in the last moment when all other parts of the plan were in full swing and the syndicate was committed irrevocably. For, even if the notoriously tortuous process of international law failed to catch up with the criminals, they would suffer crippling losses and could never resurrect their grand design. Yes, it would be quite obvious to Ashenbury that the *Aloha* must be prevented from entering the Suez Canal. And, even if all else failed, Bucken would still have the yellow box, the key to whatever it was designed to trigger off.

The Rock grew taller and taller as the chopper descended. The door opened, the in-rush of air drew Bucken's attention: he would have sworn he could smell the welcome of fish and chips.

Savas supervised the final preparations for the *Aloha* from a safe distance. Ruzicki introduced Bucken to Hans and a morose, muscular punk – all three of them would appear as supernumeraries on the crew list to overcome union and other seafaring regulations.

'See you Sunday evening,' said Ruzicki. Hans nodded knowlingly. Bucken could not afford to ask questions. The *Aloha* sailed at eleven zero seven, declared destination Karachi, calling at Port Said, Jiddah, Aden and Mukalla.

'Thanks for the offer,' said Greta, 'but I'm staying with you.'

'I'll be very busy, honey,' Savas warned her. 'And I'll be leaving in a few days.'

'Then we'll leave together.'

'You'll be bored.'

'So what's new?'

Savas did not know what to make of it. It could not be for his sake. Surely not. And yet for once there was no bodyguard, no Bucken, no young male in sight for whom Greta would swap a holiday in the Alps. Did she sense that he might need some moral support as he turned an ominous corner in his life? 'I . . . er . . . '

'Don't bore me with facts, Danny. Just let me know if I can be of any use.' And she was gone.

Savas had no time to ponder. Events threatened to overtake him. In the evening, Boothy-Graffoe arrived earlier than expected. He was bubbling with qood news: things were going well. Over dinner, he thanked Quincey for the help 'your American friend gave me. Rum fellow, but it was quite good fun: I've never seen it done before.'

'Sounds very mysterious,' said Greta.

'It isn't really, I'm looking for an Aussie chappie, that's all. The name is Warman. Don's friend helped me to compile an identikit picture. Great fun.' He pulled a copy of the segmented portrait out of his pocket and showed it to her. She gave a choking sound as she struggled to get her mouthful of food down.

Savas leaned across to take a look. He could not pretend that he was any less shocked than Greta. The picture went round the table. Ruzicki clenched his fists and swore mutely at the ceiling. None of them doubted that Warman and Bucken looked astonishingly alike. Quincey seemed amused when he broke the silence: 'A remarkable similarity. I wonder what Papeete would think of it.'

'Think of what?' Boothy-Graffoe looked bewildered.

'It's Bucken. You'd know him as Booker.'

It was Boothy-Graffoe's turn to pale. 'You mean the fellow on the phone in Kiel and Zurich?'

'We can't be sure.' Savas's hand was shaking as he raised his glass. 'It's just . . . just a likeness.'

'If we're uncertain, we've got to assume that the man is Bucken. We can't take chances.' Ruzicki brought his fist down on the table and the glasses danced. Greta's sharp glance forced him to apologise.

Let them stew, thought Quincey. He had taken out some 'insurance' against unforeseen mishaps like that. No need to tell them – yet. Might teach Savas a lesson or two.

'If, and I mean if, he's some sort of a spy . . . ' Savas began.

'You mean a cop working undercover.' Quincey made an effort to

273

sound objective and helpful as if merely suggesting a more precise definition, but the words rolled off his tongue with too much relish. 'It's unlikely, but our checking on him might have slipped up. Perhaps he's never left the police service.'

'Impossible,' Savas argued. 'If this picture, this Warman *is* Bucken, perhaps he tried journalism after getting the sack. If Bucken is working for the police, he'd have found a way to stop me in Singapore – and you in Kiel.'

'Perhaps he couldn't.'

Greta looked away. She never wanted to know exactly what was going on. About Bucken, her feelings were confused. She would never admit that she was jealous of him, least of all on Papeete's account. She thought she had been slighted, even insulted and hurt by him, but perhaps she was wrong. She studied the picture. 'We may all be jumping the gun, whatever you're talking about,' she said at last. 'This certainly resembles Bucken, but would you put me in a film only because some people think I look like Catherine Deneuve?' She noticed that Savas kept nodding gratefully, and that was too much for her. 'On the other hand, Don may be right. Bucken certainly has the crudeness to fit a cop – in some circumstances.'

Her outburst was followed by yet another portentous silence. Everybody round the table sat contemplating the implications. Quincey reached for his glass but knocked it over. It made him wince. Everybody else pretended it had not happened. His eyes narrowed as he viewed Greta: 'You certainly looked shocked by the possibility that Bucken might be a cop. Imagine how shocked Papeete would be. You may not know it, but she rather likes the guy.'

Boothy-Graffoe was on his feet. 'For Pete's sake! Does it matter who likes the guy and who doesn't? We need facts. But, at the moment, I'm inclined to agree with Savas. The man had any number of opportunities to expose Singapore long before Kiel. He could have stopped payment at the Narodny. He could have prevented the insurance pay-out on the *Rose*.'

'And what's more,' Savas was regaining his authority, 'he could have made things rather uncomfortable for us right here. He'd have made phone calls. But he didn't. He'd have sent messages. He did not. He'd have tried to spy on me in the mosque. He did not. He'd have used contacts or couriers . . '

'He has.' Greta's two words were spoken in a whisper.

Pandemonium broke out. Savas reached across and grabbed her arm. 'Say that again?'

'I said he has a contact. In Marbella.'

'You mean he has acquaintances. Like you or any of us. But that's nothing. He's been watched. He never visited anyone.'

'Yesterday, in the Casino, he nodded to someone,' said Ruzicki, 'but I thought it was a woman.'

'You mean a woman can't be a police contact?' Greta asked contemptuously.

'I didn't mean that.'

'Makes no difference what you meant. The contact happens to be a man. I met them by chance as they were strolling in Marbella a day or two after his arrival.' She lit a cigarette. Let them drag the details out of her. She forgot about her quest for reasons to harm Bucken and, through him, Papeete.

'What makes you think that it's a contact, I mean of some sinister kind?'

'Only that the same man once telephoned Bucken in Athens . . . no, Zurich. I'm not sure. Just let me think.' She was enjoying herself now. It certainly made a change to be the centre of attention in this anxious little gathering of crooked merchants.

'How do you know about that phone call?' Savas sensed that a shock was in store for him. He knew his wife. And he was not to be disappointed.

'Oh, I happened to be in Bucken's room when the call came through, and I picked up the phone. The caller's name was both ridiculous and memorable.'

'What was it?'

'Freemantle. Like one of the old London telephone exchanges with an extra e in it. Anyway, Bucken spoke to him, got rather agitated, excused himself in the middle of . . . our conversation, and left. To meet him, I guess.'

'How do you know it was the same man in Marbella?'

'We were introduced. That's how.'

'Right.' Ruzicki stood up. 'Let's get him.'

'There's no need to rush.' Quincey was calm and collected. 'We know where Bucken is, and he's not going anywhere from the *Aloha*. So take it easy. And let me offer a vote of thanks to Greta who may have done an invaluable service to all of us.'

They raised their glasses, but it was Ruzicki's face that held her attention. It conveyed a menace she had not bargained for. 'I'm glad to help,' she paused, frightened, 'you as well as Bucken. After all, he may be . . . I mean the whole thing may be just an innocent coincidence.'

'Quite. We'll have to ask this Freemantle about the relationship,' said Quincey reassuringly. 'But how do we find him? And will you recognise him?'

'I think so. In fact, I saw him once again in the old town. He was with a woman. And, when Bucken introduced us, he said something that he was staying in some small hotel up there, near that Orange square.'

'There're dozens of them.' Ruzicki despaired of the prospect.

'Then why don't you get on with it? The night is long.'

'If that's what you call a holiday, thank God that it's over.' Ada Tansley could not throw her clothes into the suitcase fast enough. 'Was tonight meant to crown it all? Come and see the old town, luv, sure, luv, what else? Sample the delights of wind and drizzle and sea-rubbish they dish out in spicy washing-up liquid.'

'Come on now, I quite like their *tapas* and *cerveza*,' Freemantle tried to pacify her.

'Then why do you throw up every other night?'

He had no answer to that. He was no jet-set reporter. He was out of his depth here. He preferred to operate in the murky waters of the London he knew so well. Railway sandwiches and egg-and-chips in cheap caffs were his regular sustenance except when living on pub-grub through long days of muck-raking in the City. He listened to Ada's cascade of complaints, and could not find it in himself to stop her. Yes, as far as she was concerned, the holiday had been a shambles. On Wednesday, she never got a decent meal in the Casino. On Thursday, her fare was 'savoury appetizers'. By midnight, both of them had stuffed themselves full of *tapas*. They returned to the hotel, and Freemantle began to track down Ashenbury. He caught him in his club and told him that 'my friend failed to show or leave any messages'. They agreed that Freemantle should return to London by the first available flight Friday morning.

Ada's voice was still droning on and on.

'The main thing is that it's over,' said Freemantle cheerfully.

'Oh, yeah? Then what about me 'oliday!'

He could never work out why she slipped into an ill-fitting, whining Cockney everytime she wanted to reveal the full might of her fury. He was still preoccupied with that enigma when he began to answer without thinking. 'Holiday? I tell you what. I'll take you on a real holiday at Skegness if you marry me.'

Her mouth popped open but no sound escaped, the long legs felt like jelly as she swayed, and she began to sob quietly. 'Marry you?' It was the light at the end of an eighteen-year long tunnel: it had paid off not to be pushy too soon. 'Marry you?'

'Sure.' There was no chance to back-pedal.

'And Skegness?'

'Blackpool if you like.' Bloody Bucken. Freemantle blamed him for all that, and decided to make the cop pay for it. Pay for the honeymoon, yes, and make him pay the way it would hurt most. Freemantle would make it a formal wedding with Bucken as best man in grey topper. What a laugh that would be!

She sidled up to him, still sobbing. 'You mean a real honeymoon?'

'Hey. Have you no feminist pride, woman? Pull yourself together. We haven't got much time to sleep, and it's only a wedding.' Now that he had said it the second time, the prospect seemed less daunting.

A joy ride it is not, thought Bucken, as his stomach struggled to disgorge everything that was not there any more. Like a schizophrenic carousel that saw itself as a big dipper and could not make up its mind which way to go, the *Aloha* danced, shuddered and groaned but kept up her speed. Enveloped in sickening diesel fumes even on deck, Bucken had visions of the *Aloha* turning into a fireball. His only cheerful sight was Hans who had put on his death mask and, spouting water incessantly, began to look more and more like a gargoyle on York Minster. Bucken contemplated pushing him over the taffrail, but Hans was constantly shadowed by the beefy punk who found the storm quite amusing. Crests towered, troughs yawned, the *Aloha* corkscrewed sluggishly, but her crew went about their jobs vomiting freely into the wind.

Bucken stumbled and staggered drunkenly up some ladders and into the wheelhouse the ancient White Russian captain insisted on calling his bridge, perhaps because of some pronunciation problems with that treacherous WH device.

'Forrtinn notts!' the captain announced proudly. 'You sink good? Very good.' He kept stabbing the air with his index finger. 'Vee make good time,' stab, 'very good time.' The final stab might have been his leaning tower of Pisa imitation because just then the sea rose to peep through the windscreen, mocking the wipers and rolling the ship to starboard. It seemed to take an eternity for the *Aloha* to right herself. She might be too tired to fight any more, thought Bucken, and not without justification. For the *Aloha* would not have been a reassuring sight even in a sunny bay in Hawaii. She was covered with scars some people might have called welding; she sported a great variety of pockmarks and bullet-holes from the glorious days of running refugees and contraband according to the changing fortunes of some African revolutions; and her eight-man motley crew liked to amuse themselves taking bets on how many layers of paint could be found on her two decks, open shelter, and wildly-coloured, exposed pipes everywhere. But, undoubtedly, she was doing *forrtinn notts*.

Before they sailed, Bucken had toyed with some grand idea of taking over the ship single-handed or conning the radio officer into sending coded messages to Ashenbury. Now he knew there was no radio officer on board, and he was too weak to take control of a push-cart even if he lived to see Friday dawn, still two long hours away.

The barman at the Marbella Club, a giant among international authorities on rich people's infidelity, introduced Señor Zaragoza, a private detective, to Greta. She commissioned him and his associates to go gum-shoeing all over Marbella old town and all through the night in search of Freemantle. At five past eight, Friday morning, Zaragoza himself won the bonus Greta had offered, but his news was bad: 'the gentleman in question and his travelling companion of a different name' had already checked out of the ingeniously-named Mar Bella guest house and, according to the 'financially induced receptionist', booked two first-class seats on the Iberia flight leaving Malaga for London at half-past eight.

Ruzicki knew that passengers must have checked in by now, and at short notice nothing could be arranged to prevent Freemantle from boarding the aircraft. Ruzicki called London and talked to a trusted friend who, despite his wealth, lived 'above the shop', a dingy Chinese restaurant in Soho. They exchanged a few words of compulsory courtesy, and then Ruzicki asked the venerable restaurateur if certain happy moments of their mutual past would still be remembered. They were, he was assured. 'I'd be eternally obliged if you could help out a friend in need,' Ruzicki pleaded, knowing full well that the I.O.U. he was about to call in would be honoured.

Less than three hours later, at ten o'clock local time, a Chinese and an English thug, plausibly dressed, planned to put through a public announcement in Terminal No. 2 at Heathrow, requesting Mr. Freemantle to call at the airport information desk. They were to use persuasion and minimum force to take Freemantle to Chinatown and hold him till Ruzicki's arrival. With commendable prudence, they did a little recce before making their move, and discovered that a uniformed chauffeur was waiting with a large board for Mr. Freemantle at Arrivals. So they changed their plan. Soon after the Iberia flight had touched down, they asked for a public announcement: 'Will the driver meeting Mr. Freemantle please go to Terminal No. 1, as his passenger is arriving by British Airways via Madrid.'

They watched the angry driver disappear in the maze of corridors, then calmly took his place among waiting relatives and drivers with a makeshift Mr. FREEMANTLE board.

On Friday afternoon, it seemed a miracle to Bucken that he was still alive to witness the *Aloha* maintaining *forrtinn notts*. The horizon had grown longer, and there was only a slight sea running with hardly any swell. Occasionally, the waves got up and the bow dug into them, shipping green, foaming water over the deck, only to climb away, pause and dive again with a shuddering blow: but Bucken was cheered by his first pangs of hunger in the past thirty hours. He borrowed the captain's binoculars and scanned the seascape. There was no sign of warships or fast patrol boats closing in on the *Aloha*. Too early, he reassured himself, Ashenbury would hardly have had time to digest Freemantle's report.

Too early for dinner, too late for lunch, Ruzicki knew he was expected to take Dim Sum with the restaurateur and the males among his numerous children and grandchildren. They sat behind a curtain of plastic beads, with the man's womenfolk playing mah-jong in the background whenever not serving tea and more tea or Daan Tart, Cheen Chung Go and other sickly sweet delicacies. In lieu of conversation there were smiles all round, and in lieu of saying thank you, Ruzicki dutifully tapped twice on the table every time his cup was refilled. Having demonstrated hospitality and good manners, the host declared that Mr. Freemantle and companion had been a little restless, so Ruzicki expected to find them tied and gagged, which suited him fine.

They were trussed up, lying on a bed on the fourth floor of the narrow building, and Ruzicki was disinclined to waste any more time on niceties. With the gag removed, Freemantle started to shout and demand explanations. Ruzicki slapped him across the mouth, drawing a trickle of blood.

'I ask the questions,' he said and noted with quiet satisfaction that it was understood at once. So it was reasonable to assume that with some patient pressure he would get all the answers he needed – if only he had the time. 'Who is Bucken?' There was no answer. 'Why were you in Marbella? Come on, man, I don't like unnecessary violence, do you?'

279

'I'm a journalist, I was holidaying in Marbella with my fiancée, and Bucken is a guy I used to know.'

'A policeman?'

'Ex-policeman. He was booted out.'

'Was he?'

'Ask anyone.'

'When did you see him last?'

'Before Marbella? Oh, many months ago. He was drunk, started a fight in a City pub, and I did a story on him.'

'Didn't he mind?'

'He promised to kill me.'

'He didn't try to in Marbella.'

'Perhaps he forgot about it.'

'Didn't you meet him in Athens? Or was it Zurich?'

'I can't recall meeting him.'

This time Ruzicki hit him on the nose. Blood spurted, and Freemantle wriggled to turn his head to avoid choking. 'Try again, Mr. Freemantle.'

'Perhaps I did. I can't remember.'

'You telephoned him in his hotel. He must have told you where he was staying. What did he want from you?'

'He enjoyed fresh gossip from London.'

Gagged and frightened, Ada Tansley glowed with admiration.

Ruzicki sighed and brought a stiletto out of his pocket. It opened with the soft click of a fine instrument. 'I don't make idle threats, Mr. Freemantle. I want honest answers to my honest questions. Are you going to tell me what the relationship is between you and Mr. Bucken?'

'Piss off and drop dead on the way.'

'As you wish.' Ruzicki turned and, with the flowing gesture of a Karajan, slit Ada Tansley's skirt and thigh. She passed out with a muted scream as a slice of her flesh was folded back. Freemantle's eyes bulged with the vain effort to free himself and yell loud enough to bring the walls down. Ruzicki replaced his gag. 'Mr. Freemantle. You must relax. You'll note that her blood is flowing freely. She could bleed to death. She'll need help. But that's not what she's going to get if you make me lose my temper again.' He wiped the stiletto on the journalist's jacket. 'So let's be friends and start again, shall we?' He paused to review the prospects of the whole scene: if Freemantle did not break after the removal of one, possibly two more slices of her flesh, it would be a certainty that Bucken was innocent and the journalist had no secrets to reveal. Ruzicki contemplated the shine of the stiletto. 'Well? What do you say? Shall we make a fresh start?'

Freemantle nodded.

'And you'll cooperate.' He followed his victim's eyes to Ada. 'Oh yes, of course. I'll get her bandaged right away. And of course pain-killers. She'll need those when she comes to.'

Waiting for the gag to come off, Freemantle had a few seconds to think. There was no guarantee that he or Ada would be allowed to survive even if he told the truth and the whole truth. But he had no alternative but to take that last gamble. He could not witness her gradual mutilation to death. *Sorry, Bucken, I'm sorry.* He hoped he had not said it aloud but could not be sure. He tried to pray, as much for Bucken as for himself, but could not remember how. He then answered all the questions as curtly as he was allowed to. Which was not much of an achievement. Then Ruzicki found Bucken's card with the report in his pocket.

Twenty minutes later, Ruzicki took one more cup of tea down-stairs with his host. They both smiled: the debt had been paid. 'But I have a request,' said Ruzicki as if continuing a silent conversation. 'Those two upstairs could be an embarrassment to me.' The Chin-aman answered with a quizzical look. Ruzicki nodded – it was as good as signing a new I.O.U., this time the other way round.

Weary and jet-lagged from her dash by Concorde and connecting flights, Papeete was getting punch drunk as she listened to Quincey's juicy account of the identikit picture and Greta's revelation about Bucken's contact. Her incredulity mingled with anger and self-accusation. Every feature of her face began to droop, her mind demanded its rightful escape into sleep, and she was too stunned to speak, but she held out with her senses registering independently of each other the words that were spoken, the open irony in Quincey's tone, Savas's stoop and bloodshot eyes, Greta's emphatic absence (she had gone to the grand opening of a new watering hole for oil-sheiks and super-whores), and the faint smell of passing sardine boats. She stood up and paced the heated patio to keep awake. Again and again she stopped to re-read Ruzicki's laconic telex that had come in code – 'suspicion confirmed beyond doubt' – and look at the crude picture that resembled Bucken but lacked the warmth, humour and magnetism of the man with the unborn tomorrow. Were all criminals degraded and dehumanised the moment they got on the Wanted list?

'We could still call it off,' Savas suggested without conviction.

'What for?' Quincey seemed admirably unperturbed. 'Now that we know the facts, we can deal with them.'

281

'How?'

'Bucken must be counting on outside help as well as his own opportunity to sabotage the operation with that yellow box – thanks to your gullibility.'

'Okay, okay, you don't have to rub it in.'

'I'm merely trying to face the facts. And I think I have the answer to them.'

The others could only sense what sort of an answer it might be, and it horrified them.

'We ought to discuss it with the partners,' Savas proposed half-heartedly. All members of the syndicate were due to arrive within twenty-four hours although the evacuation plan for the Pueblo was already in progress.

'No. It would be pointless, don't you think, honey?'

'I don't know.'

'No, of course not. You weren't here when we identified Bucken as a spy. You didn't see how badly Boothy-Graffoe took it. We don't know how the others might react. They'd be upset and confused, and one of them might run to the police to make a deal and save his own neck.' The self-assurance of his argument seemed all the more menacing. He obviously had something appalling up his sleeve. 'Let's try to get some sleep.'

Ruzicki arrived back at two in the morning. He had had to bribe his way on to one of the late charter flights. His report was devoid of emotion and other irrelevancies. The only vague suggestion of some gory details was contained in his choice of one word when he said that he had *extracted* all the information from Bucken's associate. He then put Bucken's card on the table, and waited patiently while the others were reading it.

'It's obvious that Bucken is still only guessing,' said Savas with a glimmer of hope.

'That's bad enough,' Quincey slammed him down. 'What puzzles me is why this Freemantle was to report to Ashenbury rather than the police. Did you ask him about it?'

Ruzicki nodded: 'Repeatedly. And I'm sure he doesn't know. In return for the promise of a big scoop, he supplied Bucken with bits and pieces of background information as if the police couldn't or wouldn't give it to him, and his main role was to play the courier from Marbella. He forwarded telexes to Ashenbury, but Bucken's vague suspicions and guesses made no sense to him.'

'Are you sure that Freemantle didn't hold back crucial details?'

'I'm sure.' At least Ruzicki had been sure at the time. He was contemptuous of the journalist who had broken so easily for the sake of a woman. But, now that the question had been posed, he was not so certain any more. 'Of course I'm sure.'

'What could Ashenbury's role be in all this? Any idea, honey?' Quincey asked his wife mainly to embarrass her. 'It's you who knows him best.'

'I have no idea. He may be the link between police and shipping or government.'

'The real question is,' Savas viewed the little card gravely, 'how much had Bucken told Ashenbury or others before this card was written? The chances are that he could not offer them any proof. Otherwise there would be warrants out for our arrests.' When they all agreed, he continued. 'Now, "Tsunami". If they can't prevent it, we're okay. There won't be any proof to connect us with the closure itself.'

'No?' Quincey sounded amused.

'No. The mercenaries know only Ruzicki, and who the hell would accept their word against his?'

Ruzicki had his private views about that, but it would be pointless to argue with Oldman.

'So what's your conclusion?' asked Quincey.

'Only that, if there's no proof concerning the explosion and the closure, we're in the clear. All our gains will be in a variety of names, all will come from highly speculative but legitimate deals.'

'And I agree,' Quincey enthused, 'I suggest we go ahead as planned.'

'How about Bucken?' Ruzicki asked, and noted fear in Papeete's eyes. 'The bastard must have staged that brawl in the City and the report by Freemantle. His dismissal from the police must have been a smokescreen.'

'I think it's simple,' Quincey volunteered. 'You keep the rendez-vous with the *Aloha* as planned. Say nothing to Bucken. He'll be waiting for outside help that won't come. His note makes it obvious that his superiors don't know enough about the *Aloha* to make them stop her at sea.'

'It would be better to deal with him as soon as I get on board.' He saw that Savas was twitching.

'And I disagree,' Quincey declared quite categorically. 'Anything unexpected would only worry Hans and his men. I don't want them to smell a rat and pull out prematurely. You just get on with it, but stick to Bucken like gum all the way down the Canal, and neutralise him when he fails to obey the klaxon. You'll then take the yellow box from him, and that's that. It should be quite easy to . . . to lose him. One more corpse in the Great Bitter Lake won't make too much difference. The locals have been killing each other for centuries all round there.'

'So we turn into murderers.' Papeete's harsh objectivity surprised Savas, but he said nothing.

'That's not murder,' Quincey corrected her. 'That's self-preservation. A preventive measure, if you like, the elimination of a hostile witness and proof against us.'

There may remain no proof against you, man, thought Ruzicki, but there'll be plenty against me. I'll be open to blackmail forever. Was there any point in telling his queasy partners that he had already made his plans for losing the mercenaries, too, during the get-away? No. Such things were best left unsaid.

Saturday's first light illuminated a strip of horizon. The sea breeze attained a more distinct smell of fish. Somewhere out there, the *Aloha* must already be calling Port Said, giving her ETA, and booking a place in the Thursday dawn convoy. There remained only a few details to be discussed. Ruzicki was persuaded to snatch a couple of hours' sleep: he would have to catch an early flight to Benghazi via Madrid and Tripoli.

Over a sunrise breakfast, Quincey proved himself to be the only one with a hearty appetite. 'You know, of course, the flaw in the plan,' he said casually.

'Yes,' Savas nodded gravely.

'What flaw?' Papeete asked. Her ignorance was suspect at least.

'Whatever it is, we can leave it to Don to deal with.' Savas did not want to know Quincey's answer to the problem.

'But you can't,' Quincey protested. 'This is no one-man-show. You must know that the tanker crew as well as Ruzicki and the mercenaries are a risk.' He paused and savoured the moment, then softened his voice. 'Look, Oldman, the three of us started all this to take revenge for various grievances. We have a just cause. We've worked for it ceaselessly. Success is now in sight. We can't let it just slip away. We owe it to ourselves, and to our partners, to exercise self-protection, right?'

'I guess so.'

Papeete's premonitions of worse to come made her turn away and stare out to sea. She, too, knew that, somewhere out there, the *Aloha* was carrying Bucken and others to their doom.

'I'm glad you see it my way, Oldman.' Quincey sighed. 'When you wanted Bucken in with that yellow box, I didn't argue. I trusted your judgment of character. Despite my doubts, I thought you must be right. But it was my duty to myself and all of you to take out insurance.'

'What insurance?'

'Just that . . . ' he almost answered, but then he changed his mind. He had made private arrangements with Rabbit Schwarzberg who was now on his way to Egypt. Would it serve any useful purpose to spell out what Schwarzberg's role was to be? He started again: 'Just that we're talking about scum. A spy, a Ruzicki and his shitty band of flotsam and jetsam. After "Tsunami", they all become a liability. Let's just say that my insurance applies to all of them.'

The last of the blood drained from Savas's cheeks. 'So we're not talking about self-protection but slaughter of the innocent.'

'Nobody is innocent in this game.'

'Not even the tanker crew?' Papeete challenged him meekly.

'I'll see what we can do for them.'

Savas knew that it was a lie. It had to be. And he knew that Quincey was right. One day, those men out there could undo everything they were about to accomplish. Ruzicki and Bucken deserved no mercy. At some point, the final step must be taken. He had always known that, it had always troubled him from the beginning, but every time he managed to look the other way. Now there was nowhere else to look.

Quincey knew precisely how the Oldman must feel. He remembered the time when he himself used to feel like that. If he had to cope with the true implications, why should others be spared? He looked at Papeete. No hysterics, no frothing at the mouth, no hypocrisy. He appreciated that. She was sitting with her arms and head dangling loosely like a rag doll's. It seemed she had finally crumbled. Not a bad point from where to start afresh some day soon.

It was snowing gently all over Sussex. With his hands in a numbing clasp behind his back, Ashenbury was gazing blindly at the rolling hills. Through the leaded panes of the massive French windows he thought he could hear the flakes settle on the ground. Too taut nerves, he warned himself, relax. Easier said than done. Where the hell could that journalist be? According to the police, the man and his woman friend were on yesterday's first flight from Malaga, and collected their luggage at Heathrow. After the driver had been diverted by the false call, both passengers had disappeared without trace. Twenty-four sleepless hours later, with no news from Bucken or Freemantle, Ashenbury had asked for an urgent inquiry to be carried out in Marbella. By Saturday evening, it produced another blow: the Pueblo Yasmin seemed quite deserted. And now, all this . . .

285

Ashenbury spun round. His eyes firmly fixed on his shoes, he walked the length of the library only to return with equal speed and determination. Crackles from the open fire broke the silence. It was a comforting sound: logs must be snuggling up to one another. His eyes bore into the dusk outside. As he began to speak, his breath clouded the window pane: 'Why have you told me?'

'Isn't it obvious?'

'Make it obvious.' This time he turned slowly. In the dark room, lit only by the fire, his eyes took in the familiar shapes and shadows, then came to rest on Papeete's seated figure in the far corner. Her white blouse seemed to be the stage for dancing flames.

'I thought it would be obvious that I wanted to avert a disaster. Whatever else I might have been willing to do or close my eyes to, that was my bottom line. I just had to prevent slaughter. Isn't that a good and obvious enough reason?'

It was the first time that she could put it into words even for herself. She had had no time to think before Quincey asked her to return to America right away. He wanted everything to continue according to plan, and her station was to be New York. She had left the Pueblo before Saturday noon but broken her journey secretly in London to visit Ashenbury. If Bucken was reporting to him, he must be able to save his man. Now she felt disappointed.

'Yes, that's a very good reason, Papeete. But it's got to be substantiated with many more details.'

'What details?'

'Who's planning the *disaster* you're talking about?'

'I don't know.'

'Or you don't want to say.'

She shrugged her shoulders. Even betrayal must have its limits.

'What's the role of the *Aloha*?'

'As I said, if it's stopped by the coastguard or whatever, you'll find all the answers.'

'Who's on board?'

'A bunch of men.'

'Including Bucken?'

'Yes.'

'Are you trying to save Bucken?'

'I'm trying to prevent murders. And worse.'

'What do you know about Bucken?'

'That he's going to die. I mean with the others.'

'Things like that must be planned in someone's interest. Whose is it? Don's? Savas's? Look, it's no good shrugging your shoulders. You've dropped a bombshell. You can't just leave it at that and walk away.'

'You can't stop me.'

'Can't I?'

She remembered the pair of bullock-sized ex-RAF guard dogs that roamed the grounds of the house. A sign on the gate advised visitors not to alight from their vehicles in the absence of staff. 'I must call Don,' she said.

'Why?'

'To tell him that I missed the connecting flight to New York.'

'You mean he'll be calling you there?'

'Probably.'

'What would he suspect if you weren't there?'

'I don't know. But he might . . . I don't know.'

'He might what? Warn the *Aloha*? Do something to the ship or the people on board?'

'I don't know.'

'Is he in control of the ship?'

'He knows the captain. That's all. And, if you don't do something about it soon, all the risk I've taken might be wasted.'

'Do you love him?'

'He's my husband.'

'I meant Bucken, not Don. And I asked – do you love him?'

Their eyes locked. There was a long pause. 'I don't know,' she said quietly.

'Thank you for trying to be honest.' He felt worn out and irritated now, too.

The phone rang. Price, the butler, reported that a Mr. Wade had arrived. 'Show him into the estate office.' On Saturday evening it would be deserted, and it had telephones and telex. 'I'll join him shortly.' He rang off. 'I've got to see someone, Papeete. Feel free to order what you like and call Don. But think about the situation. I can't just mobilise a destroyer or something to arrest the *Aloha* without giving reasons. Good reasons beyond a beautiful woman's gushing altruism.'

Wade was the first of the 128 Committee to arrive in answer to Ashenbury's alert. He had heard it briefly on the telephone, now he listened impatiently to a most unsatisfactory summary of information received. He volunteered to take over the interrogation without any further delay. Ashenbury refused to let him.

'With due respect, sir, I have more experience in these things.'

'And with equally due respect, Mr. Wade, I have more experience in handling this particular informer.'

'I know, sir.'

'And what is that supposed to mean?'

287

'In my profession, one hears about things, sir. I'm sorry.'

'Forget it.'

'Do you think that it's because of this, this personal relationship, that she came to you?'

'Possibly.'

'It could be some trap. Or a diversion.'

'Unlikely.'

'As far as we know, whatever Quincey is up to, she must be a party to it. Why would she betray him?'

'Split loyalties?'

'I see.'

Ashenbury meant to say *you see nothing*, but chose to defend Papeete instead. 'She has a playboy of a father who might sell his own daughter if it suited him. She has a rather insecure life story. Her husband's bankruptcy and tragic illness might have driven her to do things she otherwise wouldn't even contemplate. And she wouldn't be the first fraudster who drew the line somewhere.'

'Such as murder?'

'Such as. So why antagonise her unless we must?'

'Do we have a choice?'

'Perhaps. After all, we know that they were planning some monumental fraud. Bucken conveyed his various suspicions, and Mrs. Quincey's information is in line with those. If the *Aloha* is to cause a disaster, it's likely to block Suez. It's again in line with Bucken's thinking. What their plans are, how they would benefit, these are secondary questions.' Ashenbury paused to smile: 'Anyway. If you were familiar with shipping problems, you'd guess what they might be up to.'

'But we still ought to ascertain that Suez is the ultimate target.'

'Quite. And I'll try to "ascertain" that as well as her motives.'

'But do we have time to proceed as gently as you propose, sir?'

'She says we have until Wednesday night. That's four long days.'

'For Allah and the Ayatollah,' whispered Naji al Sabah as he slipped three pounds of gelignite behind the wall panel. He would have prayed, too, but quickly checked himself because he had been warned: 'Even if you know there's nobody around, you never know.' There was no reason to doubt his paternal uncle's wisdom, and had he not been proven right yet again? Although he was still in jail for his part in President Sadat's assassination, nothing could prevent him from sending a word to his nephew. His message only said 'be my sword and strike a blow for the Jihad', but the messenger

288

explained that Naji would have nothing to fear: 'Allah will be with you. And the job is easy. Aren't you the most trusted cleaning officer at the Ismailia control centre of the Suez Canal?'

'I am,' Naji agreed readily because *cleaning officer* sounded far more impressive than *general cleaner*. 'And on Saturdays I'm cleaning supervisor, too, in charge of another cleaner!'

'You see? It'll be easy.'

And so it was. In the evening, when the communications centre was deserted, he smuggled in the gelignite hidden in his bucket, unscrewed a wall panel, and slotted the bomb. When would it go off? He was assured not before Wednesday night. 'But don't mess about with it,' the messenger said, 'because it's booby-trapped and it might kill you. You see, it's a clever bomb. Working for the Ayatollah it's got to be. It has something inside that knows when it's Wednesday night and knows what to do.'

Overawed, Naji had no more questions. He was proud that his uncle had chosen him to be the sword that would make a thousand cuts. He quickly restored the wall panel, and listened. He still half-expected to hear a little ticking at least, but there was no sound. It was a clever bomb. He began to clean the ashtrays and viewed the banks of sleeping TV screens and radios lovingly. They were so beautiful and mysterious. And everybody was so proud of them even if they served the imperialists and a government of imperfect faith. Ardently he hoped that the damage would be bad enough without devastating all that beauty. For that reason he decided to offer the poor half, well, perhaps a quarter of the money he had received as a gift of goodwill from his uncle's messenger.

Under growing pressure, Papeete admitted that the *Aloha* would cause a disaster in the Suez Canal.

'How?'

'I don't exactly know. Something to do with some chemical tanker.'

In the light of the flickering fire, Ashenbury could see the crippling strain on her face. She sounded drained but, to his surprise, not for a moment did she weaken. He had ordered sandwiches and drinks but everything remained untouched. 'And you think,' he began with slow deliberation, 'that Don would benefit from the disaster. Is that right?'

'Your guess is as good as mine.'

'But he wouldn't kill people, would he?'

'Of course not.'

289

'Then who would?'

'I don't know.'

'Do you realise that, if Don's plans fail because of what you've told me, he might be ruined for good?'

'Yes.'

'Don't you mind?'

She was poking at the logs, squatting so close to the fire that the heat made her eyes water, but she hardly noticed it. The questions forced her to admit to herself something she had suppressed in her mind all along, that no matter what she did or said from now on, she would be doomed. Secretly, she had hoped right from the start that if 'Tsunami' succeeded, she might be able to leave her husband. If it failed, if he was ruined again, it would be her lifelong, self-imposed penance to support him.

She felt Ashenbury's eyes on her back. Oh yes, she understood his concern. Her news must have been a tremendous jolt. He was bound to ask for details and evidence. And, now that she had betrayed the *Aloha*, she might as well go the whole hog. Yet something made her hold back. She had to retain *some* integrity, she had to hold on to *some* secrets, if she wanted to find a way to live with herself. She would put up with any amount of pressure, ridicule or humiliation: she would say anything, do anything to convince Ashenbury – anything short of telling all about 'Tsunami'. Crazy? Yes. But, if it was madness that had driven her all the way here, madness must have its own logic.

He waited patiently, then repeated the question almost apologetically. 'Don't you mind that Don might now be ruined for good because of you?'

'I do.'

'Don't you love him at all?'

'It's not a question of love.'

'What then? Loyalty?'

'Sort of.'

'A rather twisted sort, don't you think?'

'Maybe.'

'What if he goes to jail for a long, long time?'

'He won't.'

'His illness won't keep him out.'

'But lack of evidence against him will,' she said with conviction. 'You have no evidence, and I can't give you any.'

'You mean you don't want to.'

'Whatever you say.'

'And that's exactly my problem, Papeete. Be sensible. You come to me with this cock and bull story about some massacre and a disaster. You ask me to save lives, Bucken's life, but you don't want to see that I'd have to call in some international police force or one of Her Majesty's warships, arrange an arrest on the high seas, create a huge political upheaval, and all this on the strength of your word alone. Give me proof of your sincerity, and I'll do my best. For you. I promise.' He walked away from her and pressed his forehead against the cold glass of the French window. Again he had the weird sensation of hearing the drop of the snowflakes.

When he turned back, she was standing in front of the fire, where they used to make love in happier days. The shadows reduced her figure to the girlish silhouette he had once been addicted to. She was standing on the very spot where he had first seen her naked, on her first visit as a house guest. Then, she was a statue, petrified but waiting. Now she moved. She began to unbutton her blouse.

'What the hell are you doing?' He shouted at her with venomous indignation. Or was it self-defence?

'I'm offering you proof of sincerity.'

She slipped out of her blouse.

'That's not proof. That's prostitution.'

'Not if I ask for no reward.'

'You've asked for a lot more than money.'

'And I'm offering you a lot more than a fuck.'

He was suddenly hit by the truth: she might have been honest, she might not know it herself, but she was in love with Bucken. Ashenbury wished she loved him, that anybody would ever love him that much. And that made him hate Bucken. 'Get dressed,' he commanded. His voice was so hoarse that he would not have recognised it himself. 'Please.' He stepped closer to her and picked up her blouse from the floor. 'Please.'

'You believe me?'

'I'm trying to. But I need proof, not just a fuck, as you put it.'

'I understand.' She nodded, backed away, and walked to the corner where she tapped the last volume of a set of old encyclopaedias. The shelf, although laden, turned smoothly on its pivot. She reached inside – and snatched her hand away as if it had been burnt. She forced herself to persevere, and found what she was looking for. He watched her, mesmerised, unable to speak or intervene, as she pulled out a large parcel from *Howarth, Howarth & Howarth*. The gold logo glittered brightly, just as it had in Singapore where he had predicted 'you'll be back'. Was she? She was gasping for air under the flood of memories. They frightened her. What if I'm going to enjoy this? The thought made her shudder. Then revulsion took over. But she would not stop. Not now. She opened the bag.

291

Everything was there. The boater came out first. She let it float to the floor.

He could hear his own prediction, screaming at him all the way from Singapore: 'You'll be back.' Was she? Was that the moment he had been waiting for? He had slept with no one ever since Papeete left him. Was it worth waiting for her?

Her clothes dropped, one by one, to her feet. A few seconds later, after a flash of nakedness, she was an overgrown schoolgirl. She thought she was. Or perhaps a dummy in the shop window. Mr. Howarth himself or the fussy headmistress could not have faulted her uniform. She topped it with the boater, and waited. 'You wanted proof. Take it.'

Ashenbury moved like a robot. He stepped closer, and slowly, as if performing a ritual, fondled her from almost an arm's length away. She stood motionless as at the first time. Except that then it had been a child-woman's curiosity and excitement that paralysed her. Now it was humiliation. She only hoped she would not cry.

Without any warning, Ashenbury lost control. He was tearing wildly at her clothes with both hands, kissing every spot of skin he had bared. There was no trace of the sophisticated, superb lover he used to be. In his rush, they stumbled and fell. It was going to be rape, yes, rape! The thought excited him. Why was she not resisting?

Her skirt was ripped off. And still no reaction from her. She was neither willing nor, even worse, unwilling to make love. She was there, and he could do as he pleased. Suddenly he realised that his blood had stopped racing. He froze. She was not a child any more, and he blamed her for it. He blamed her for being a woman who might be thinking about another man. She was there, he was free to do anything with her. But he could not. His hands grew shaky, his limbs went numb, he felt spent as he lay on top of her in a heap, terrified by the vision of witnessing the last of his desire oozing away. And he blamed her for that, too.

Blindly, in a frenzied fury, he hit her. His fists broke free from his will and pounded flesh and bones indiscriminately. A trickle of blood appeared on her face but that would not stop him.

Her lips began to swell, her nose began to bleed, but she would still not scream, fight back or even try to wriggle free. 'Damn you! You . . . you fake! Damn you!' He heard the voice faintly without identifying the source of all the abuse and swearing.

There were three hard knocks at the door. 'Yes, your lordship? . . . Did your lordship call?' The heavy oak thinned the butler's voice, but sobered Ashenbury. The man must have heard the shouting but not the words because discretion would not allow him to overhear anything specific. It was most embarrassing. 'It's all right, Price. Just go and check if my visitors have arrived.'

Ashenbury struggled to his feet. His eyes avoided Papeete. She was lying on the floor, prostrate, but somehow with all the humiliation gone.

The 128 Committee had already been briefed by Ed Wade when Ashenbury entered the estate manager's office. He summarised Papeete's information and concluded: 'I now understand her motivation, and in the light of everything we've heard from Bucken, I've no reason whatsoever to doubt her goodwill any more. The scheme, codenamed Tsunami, is based on forcing the closure of the Suez Canal. Now where do we go from here?'

Wade volunteered the first two suggestions. 'Mrs. Quincey ought to spend the night in a London hotel in case her husband tries to call her. We don't want him to get suspicious. She then ought to take an early flight to New York tomorrow morning. I'll arrange for her to be watched both for her security and our convenience in case we need her. As for the *Aloha*, well, she must be close to Sicily. She ought to be stopped and searched, let's say for drugs, probably by the Italians who could be tipped off through Interpol.'

Members of the committee gave various sounds of approval, but Ashenbury had reservations. 'Yes, you're right about Mrs. Quincey. But I've made some calculations about the *Aloha*. She definitely can't reach Port Said before Wednesday evening. Being forewarned, perhaps we could gain more than just a few random arrests.'

'But Bucken . . . ' Wade began, only to be cut short by Ashenbury:

'Oh yes, Bucken. We'll bear his fate in mind, but first I think we ought to have some consulations at the highest level.' He paused for emphasis. 'After all, the national interest deserves to override all other considerations.'

The weather had cleared and the horizon grew longer. There was only a slight sea running with hardly any swell, giving Bucken's stomach some well-earned respite. Yet he felt forlorn and restless. When Malta was visible in the distance, he expected something to happen, something like the silhouettes of fast, armed vessels detaching themselves from the shore, vessels of hope and charity to close in on the *Aloha*, order her to heave to, take over from him, let him go home and let him sleep in his own bed – a desire that was as much a stranger to him as it would be a source of amusement to Sarah. There was, of course, no good reason to have such expectations or feel disappointed when Sunday came and passed with no gunboats in sight. Ashenbury had plenty of time to act, and the *Aloha* would be, in fact, a much better catch with Ruzicki on board.

Sunday was expiring under midnight stars when the *Aloha* rendez-voused with a sleek motor launch. Bucken noticed that her markings were in Arabic. He had to admire the precision of the operation: everything went without a hitch, within hailing distance of Benghazi, a paltry ten minutes later than planned. Ruzicki and a man, intro-duced only as Franz, climbed the gently-swaying Jacob's ladder. The long arm of a three-ton derrick swung out to haul three crates aboard the *Aloha*. Its bigger brother lifted the launch out of the water. When the boat was secured, two Arabs emerged and climbed on board. Ruzicki did not bother to introduce them.

The crew of the *Aloha*, convinced that their passengers were poli-tical or criminal fugitives, seemed a little surprised by the new-comers, but asked no questions. Ruzicki was more talkative than usual. He was impressed by Bucken's enthusiasm over the meticu-lously planned and executed rendezvous. He even toyed with the idea that Bucken might not be a traitor after all. Yes, perhaps he used to be a cop but, once within grasp of easy wealth, he had changed sides and would never return to the humdrum ways of salaried exist-ence. Ruzicki would find that plain common sense. He decided to watch Bucken closely through the next three days of finalising plans for the raid.

Quincey called New York yet again, the third time that Sunday. He just had to know that Papeete was there. This time he woke her up with the flimsy excuse of asking some questions. She sounded perfec-tly relaxed, so all must be well, but her whimsical overnight stay and shopping in London bothered him. He disliked the unexpected, par-ticularly if it meant any diversion from the plans. Yet he knew that the root of his worries lay elsewhere. As soon as he had arrived at Rotterdam, he arranged two meetings. He had to continue his tightrope-walking, playing out his CIA and KGB contacts against each other, because he sensed suspicion against him from both sides. Now he hinted to each contact in turn that the other side might be planning to kill him. Both sides promised him protection in the hope of further services. What he banked on was that the watchers would spot the watchers from the other side and mistake them for would-be assassins. Barring accidents, that could only raise his credit on both sides.

He then spent the night awake, irritated at failing to find a feasible excuse to call any of the partners in London or Rome or Tokyo or Savas in Piraeus where the silly old man was attending a local baker's all-day all-night wedding.

Ashenbury was arguably the least popular man in London that Sunday, but achieved what he wanted. After two preliminary meetings, he was invited to Chequers. The Tudor mansion was swarming with Japanese dignitaries and would-be investors, being wooed and entertained in style. Ashenbury was received in a small office, well away from Cromwellian relics and frontline hospitality, by one of the PM's personal aides and a faceless backroom eminence who held undue sway over the economy.

Ashenbury tabled his facts free of frills and irrelevant details such as Papeete's role and Bucken's presence aboard the *Aloha*. He outlined the likely aims of a major fraudulent conspiracy. He said if it succeeded, the damage could be incalculable. He added somewhat pointedly: 'Due to the recession, the oil and shipping glut, and to a great extent misguided governmental policy, Britain has not only ceased to be a major maritime power, but her merchant fleet has shrunk from half the world's total to eighteen million tonnes compared with Liberia's hundred and twenty million and Greece's sixty-two million tonnes. As Don Quincey, the discredited speculator, seems to be one of the conspirators, it is fair to assume that he hopes to cash in as well as take revenge on the City by driving the last nail into the coffin of our shipping and insurance industries.'

'I don't see what your problem is,' the economic adviser retorted. 'We'll arrange the arrest of the *Aloha*, thereby preventing the Canal closure, and that's that.'

'On top of that, of course, justice will be done,' said the aide.

'Justice?' Ashenbury contemplated the word. 'What justice? I mean, yes, a few mercenaries will be locked up and we or some other government can throw away the key. But how about those real criminals who have planned this outrage? They'll lose some money, but they'll remain free to plan something else another day. Even if we obtain evidence against some, we'll get nowhere. It's hardly ever clear-cut who can and what country will prosecute. For most of their crimes, extradition treaties are not applicable. Then there's all the plea bargaining that can enable them to keep their millions after a short spell behind bars.'

'So what are you proposing?'

'I'd like to keep the national interest as our number one consideration. I'd like to see our shipping and finances receive the kiss of life, a major infusion of plasma, instead of the coup de grâce.'

'Do I understand . . . ' the aide began hesitantly.

'Yes, sir,' Ashenbury cut in to make it easier for him. 'I'm proposing *not* to stop the *Aloha* and *not* to prevent this horrendous event. I'm proposing to let it happen and take advantage of it by preempting the conspiracy. They must be planning to gain from massive charter deals, oil and currency speculation. We could muscle in on their deals and we ourselves could do everything they hope to achieve – except that we could do it on an even bigger scale. Think of the boost to North Sea oil and British shipping, gentlemen.'

'Expediency is no substitute for the law.' The aide was on the retreat, hiding behind sententious pronouncements.

'You're advocating a crime, Ashenbury,' the economic adviser sneered.

'Not a crime, certainly not. Maybe an oversight. It wouldn't be without precedent. And, of course, we'd back an international outcry against terrorism, and support the clearing of the Canal with specialists, salvage teams, hard cash and aid to grief-stricken Egypt.'

What he did not mention was that the unexpected bonus would seep into the national coffer just at the time of approaching elections, and silence all critics of governmental shipping policies. He knew that everybody present would recognise that without prodding.

The two men said nothing. Ashenbury was asked to wait. An hour later, the aide informed him that the PM could not be disturbed, but it would appear, nevertheless, that there was nothing Her Majesty's Government could or should do in the circumstances. If anything, Ashenbury's information was no more than hearsay about some purely criminal matter concerning a foreign trampship on the high seas and non-British nationals' underhand schemes.

That was as good as a nod. 'Thank you,' said Ashenbury. Nothing would be official, no record would be kept, nobody could trace his visit to Chequers. 'As for our economic allies, and particularly the American cousins . . . '

It was the aide's turn to interrupt him: 'Let's not be concerned with political considerations. If anything actually happened, our friends would be informed with the utmost urgency, needless to say, and it would be *most* regrettable if the information reached them only when it was too late for them to act upon.'

Ashenbury left in a hurry. He had three days to prepare his moves, charter a fleet at low rates in great secrecy, place his bets and let a few personal friends take advantage of being forewarned. It was not much time, but it would be enough. Ships and shipping never slept, so he could also utilise the precious little that was left of Sunday and the night. As a prelude to what he saw as a master stroke, he called New York to wake Papeete, allay all her fears, and assure her that everything was in hand: the *Aloha* would be tailed and arrested at Port Said.

'Fortinn notts. All ze vay!' the White Russian captain declared proudly. 'Vee make good time? Very good time!' On Wednesday evening, when the lights of Port Said appeared like a horizontal Christmas tree, he knew that his bonus for being punctual had been earned. All that remained to be done was to get rid of his unsavoury passengers.

Ashenbury is cutting it a bit too fine, thought Bucken, as the annoyingly uneventful voyage was coming to an end. Perhaps London had made some different plans. Perhaps Ruzicki and his gang were to be caught in action. In that case, marine commandos might be watching the *Aloha* right now. Oh yes, she was entering the Port Said roads, an area that was under full control like an airport from the Port Fuad radar station at the northern entrance of the Canal by-pass.

From the wheelhouse and deck of the *Aloha*, six pairs of binoculars were scanning the sea for the *Chemi-Lippstadt*. Throughout their *fortinn notts* approach, the trampship's specially powerful radio equipment had been monitoring all Port Said radio traffic on VHF and the interference-free UHF, used by the Canal pilots, so Ruzicki knew that the chemical tanker was already anchored in the roads.

To search for the *Lippstadt*, the *Aloha* would have to find an excuse for not going straight into the harbour but sail up and down in the open sea that served as a parking lot only for the big ships.

'Call Traffic Office as agreed,' Ruzicki told the captain who then radioed the port:

'Zis is *Aloha*. Entering roads, slowing down because little engine troubly.'

'Do you need any assistance?'

'No, sir, sank you, sir. Vee can repair engine, but perhaps stop a little. Vill call soon. Any possibility to join second convoy?'

'You mean instead of the first?'

'Yes, please.'

'We'll let you know.'

As the *Aloha* moved slowly along the line of tankers and other big ships, the monitoring of all communications with Traffic Office began to reveal the plans for the two Thursday convoys. The first

297

southbound convoy would comprise thirty-nine ships in two groups. Group A would be made up of the smaller vessels that were already made fast in Port Said harbour. It would follow the shorter route along the old Canal and wait, if necessary, for Group B at Ras El Ish.

Group B, according to normal pattern, would be led by the chemical tanker, except that in this case a cumbersome car-carrier would take precedence. *Chemi-Lippstadt* would be in the Number Two position, followed by a 'third generation' container ship, three VLCC-s sailing in ballast, and other vessels of over thirty-eight feet draught. That group would take the long, new Port Said by-pass, join the main Canal at Ras El Ish, and combine with Group A to form a single convoy for the rest of the way to the Great Bitter Lake and Suez.

'*Lippstadt* . . . *Chemi-Lippstadt* . . . Please prepare to leave anchorage at oh-one hundred,' Ruzicki heard Traffic Control advising the tanker, and almost at the same time Franz cried from the deck:

'There she is!'

The *Aloha* sailed on, passing the *Lippstadt* on her starboard, towards the by-pass entrance. The magnificent, purpose-built 23,000-tonner looked like a ghost ship. Her appearance would have been no different if she were sailing at full speed through the night: under the guidance of satellite navigation and autopilot, her crew would be in bed, the engine room working unattended, the bridge manned by a solitary officer with one seaman to take the wheel in emergencies.

Hans and Ruzicki had to make a quick decision. They could raid the ship now and have her fully under control by the time the pilot and a steady stream of other officials came on board. The risk would be that someone might spot some irregularity and report to Port Said on leaving the ship. They decided against it. Close to the entrance of the by-pass, the *Aloha* dropped anchor and reported to Traffic Office that the engine problem was being sorted out, the ship would return to Port Said in time for the second convoy.

Sea and wind turned the *Aloha* as she rode at anchor. Once she had settled, the motor boat with the Arabic markings was launched on her port side where it would be invisible to the harbour radar. Franz climbed down into the launch and prepared a very fast, inflatable rubber dinghy, ready for a flying start. Then the crates were lowered into the launch. From one of them, Franz took out four submachine guns, heavy revolvers with silencers, boxes of flares, and what looked to Bucken like stun grenades. Ruzicki asked

Bucken to check the yellow box: yes, in its waterproof wrapping it was taped securely to Bucken's side under his shirt.

Captain Neuburg loved the *Lippstadt*, even though lately she had sailed under the Panamanian flag with a Korean crew and half the UN represented among her officers. He loved the ship perhaps more than any other vessel he had ever commanded, and certainly more than Beatrix, his wife, with whom he was yet to find something in common – something beyond a taste for prolonged absences from each other. Neuburg had given the crew a few hours' rest before the long day ahead, and now he was up early, pacing up and down the bridge in the eerie green light, listening to the constant and reassuring high-pitched whine of the radar.

It was Third Officer Schneider, the man on bridge duty, who broke the silence. 'Did you know, sir, that animal life began on earth some three hundred and fifty million years ago?'

'No, I wouldn't have guessed that it happened a day over three hundred and forty million years ago.'

The little joke, completely free of irony, escaped Schneider, a professional bore of genuine goodwill. 'It's just that I was reading this magazine, and I suddenly thought of my granny. She always told me, "Erich, watch out: you learn something new, every day in your life." And she was right, sir, you do.'

'Quite,' said Neuburg, and studied the computerised wall-chart that set out the nature and location of his entire cargo. Although the designers of the ship had catered for every foreseeable operational hazard with due separation between chemicals, and double-bottomed, double-skinned construction, this time Neuburg felt a little uneasy about the voyage ahead. He had just heard on the radio that a pipeline had been blown up somewhere along the Canal, that there was renewed tension in the Middle East, and that confrontation in the Gulf threatened to spill over.

He listened to the latest report from the Alexandria pipeline control centre claiming that the damage was limited. It might be a lie, he thought, but even if it was the truth, it was the intention that mattered most. Was it the prelude to more terrorist action or another war with Israel? Neuburg's eyes ran down the cargo list. The *Lippstadt* was a floating bomb, fully laden with a particularly potent mixture of deadly chemicals – hazards his crew of twenty officers and men were well trained to deal with in normal circumstances, yet hazards the world was still unprepared for on a major scale despite the incessant 'alarmist wailing' by the environmentalists.

In the huge stainless steel and specially lined tanks, many of the chemicals on board were highly toxic, ready to react with water, sunlight and each other, producing a variety of lethal gases and other agents to set the sea ablaze, cripple people by inhalation or skin absorption, cause cancer, insanity and painful death. There were six reinforced drums of radio-active material; a deck tank of three hundred cubic metres full of some isocyanate compound, a key component of plastics, that would react with water, burn readily and produce both carbon and nitrogen dioxide; the second of the four deck tanks contained ACN, short for Acrylonitrile, a suspected carcinogen and a major source of cyanide gas; there were a few drums of mercury, enough to poison the Gulf and half the Mediterranean, and lead-based anti-knock additive to petrol that would kill divers and salvors or at least induce incurable insanity. And then he had not yet even contemplated the thousand tons of yellow and white phosphorus, shipped under a water blanket to keep the air away from it.

'Morning, Captain. Morning all.' The Swedish First Officer arrived to take over from the bore on the bridge.

'Erich!' Neuburg stopped Schneider at the door.

'Sir?'

'Use the satellite to phone your wife. It's on the company. Who knows? You may already be a father.'

People winked, as always when a sailor was 'expecting', and Schneider mumbled something about his granny who, no doubt, would have some specific wisdom for the occasion.

Neuburg looked out towards the bow, surveying the rust-reddish expanse of the deck, the maze of pipes and ladders, the deck tanks, catwalks with foam-cannons. From the bridge, atop the four-storey tall aft accommodation block, it was a magnificent sight of ingenious engineering. The deck was coming to life. A single gangway was lowered almost to sea level to receive a procession of motor launches. A derrick swung out, ready to hoist a mooring boat out of the water and carry it all the way to Suez so that, at a moment's notice, its Arab crew could if need be take mooring ropes to bollards along the shore of the Canal.

The harbour pilot, seen as a nuisance, one of the jumped-up boat people, was the first to arrive. 'Please, Captain, heave up now,' he requested officiously and handed over his little plastic carrier bag to be filled with goodies. When the Canal was nationalised by Nasser, everybody thought that operations would end in chaos. They were wrong. The service became more efficient – only the number of official visitors with plastic bags grew. They would all receive cartons of cigarettes and whisky, according to their status, but it was a small price to pay in baksheesh for smooth procedures when the Canal crossing cost up to a hundred thousand dollars.

The *Lippstadt* began to move towards the by-pass entrance. Fast launches would soon form a queue behind the gangway. One by one they would draw level and adjust their speed to keep up with the tanker and allow the visitors to come on board. First the ship agent, then the Health Authority – no problem? good, thank you – Canal Authority Inspector, and other inspectors – what? only one carton this time? – all with plastic bags, all with paraphernalia to stamp crew lists, health forms, Double Bottom form, Declaration E for hazardous cargo, dozens of documents and everything in sight, only to hurry on and visit the next ship, refill the bag, and be off before the arrival of the Canal pilot.

'There it comes,' said Ruzicki, pointing at the mooring boat from Port Said.

Franz and an Arab, both sporting colourful headdresses, jumped into the dinghy. The engine roared, and they were off, skimming the bumpy water at high speed. They caught up with the mooring boat and hailed it down. The Arab caught and held the boat with a hook, while Franz stepped on board, smiled at the two-man crew, and shot them dead with the equanimity of counting sheep.

The bodies were then placed in the dinghy, and tied to the heavy outboard motor that would pull them to the bottom of the sea when Franz opened the valves to let the air out of the inflatable.

The Arab then took the wheel of their prize. Franz observed the death throes of the dinghy. When the corpses had sunk, and the last of the air bubbles had risen to the surface, he gestured let's go. After a short chase, they manoeuvred the mooring boat alongside the *Lippstadt*, behind the gangway. Steel wire ropes ran down from the derrick, two massive hooks were fastened, and the boat was hoisted to deck level, just abaft the bridge. Franz and his man knew they were expected to stay in their boat. They were given sandwiches and coffee, and they handed over their plastic bags secure in their conviction that, at Suez, every day was Christmas. Their boat, hanging like a window-cleaner's gondola, gave them a commanding position with the gangway, the wing-bridge and much of the deck in sight. Had they craned their necks, they could have seen the receding starboard side of the *Aloha*, but they did not bother.

Ruzicki watched the approach of the *Lippstadt* and her flock of motor

301

boats. Through binoculars he could see the activities on the bridge. The chemical tanker began to turn slowly to starboard, preparing to swing round a marker and enter the route between two rows of light-buoys that would guide her into the by-pass. Ruzicki climbed down into the launch, and signalled to the Russian captain: time to part company. The trampship headed back towards Port Said, the launch followed and joined the dwindling queue behind the *Lippstadt* gangway.

Hans was at the wheel, the Arab mercenary was strap-hanging on the side, the punkish muscleman squatted idly on the roof of the wheel-house. Ruzicki and Bucken were hiding two steps down, in the cramped engine enclosure. Ruzicki slipped a handgun into his belt, and hung a short-muzzled Uzzi round his neck. Bucken reached for the remaining heavy revolver.

'You know how to handle it?' Ruzicki asked with open sarcasm.

'I can always learn on the job.'

'Don't. Your job is to look after and operate the yellow box.'

It seemed pointless to argue. Commandos must be waiting aboard the *Lippstadt*. Bucken did not want to get shot in the confusion. He would make sure he was the last on board.

On the bridge wing of the *Lippstadt*, the Arab electrician whose presence was compulsory emplaced a split-beamed projector that would light up a channel of cat's eyes along the Canal. That the cat's eyes had long been replaced by buoys made no difference. Pilots still loved the projector, and it gave a job to the electrician who otherwise would have nothing to do but eat, sleep and scrounge all the way to Suez.

The bosun, in charge of the gangway, helped the Canal pilot, a true professional, aboard. They had known each other for years. The pilot carried his own UHF as well as the LORAN transmitter that would enable the computers at Ismailia to calculate the precise location of every ship throughout transit. The harbour pilot picked up his plastic bag, descended the gangway, and stepped across to the Canal pilot's launch moving side by side with the ship.

That's it, sighed the bosun with relief. He was about to give the signal to raise the gangway when, to his surprise, yet another launch speeded into place. 'I thought we had everybody,' his mate shouted from above.

The Arab on the side of the launch caught the railing of the gangway and leapt across. 'Spare equipment for Mister Pilot!' He held a large bag aloft. The bosun began to swear at him, but the muscleman drew his gun and shot him between the eyes.

The silenced shot could not be heard on deck, but the bosun's mate saw the flash. Just in front of the tank of firefighting foam, he leaned over the taffrail. 'Hey. what's going on?' He never found out. Franz, seated comfortably in his gondola, shot him twice to be sure, and once more for luck.

Bucken had witnessed the killings and waited in vain for the return of fire. There was only ominous silence. It was obvious now: Freemantle had had an accident; Ashenbury had never received his message; there would be no commandos, no arrests. Bucken scrambled aboard with the others while the muscleman began to scuttle the launch as planned.

On deck, they were joined by Franz and his Arab to help with the crates from the launch. 'You,' said Hans quietly, pointing at the Arab, 'you come with me to the bridge. The rest of you, let me just repeat, spread out and round up everybody in the block. The engine room can wait. Anybody inclined to resist you or waste your time must be shot. Is that clear?'

'You stick to me like glue,' Ruzicki told Bucken who was by now on the look-out for some weapon, any weapon. 'After all, your box of tricks is our most valuable asset, and I'm responsible for you.'

'Don't you think you've had enough?' Greta asked, knowing full well that the Oldman would only shake his head, drink up, and let his glass be refilled yet again. She had spent the night with him, in his favourite taverna in Piraeus, perhaps the first time ever. He appreciated her gesture but nothing in this world would induce him to show it.

She hated the taverna, the uncomfortable chairs, the sour air of cheap wine, sweat and black tobacco, her husband's incessant drinking and his determination to be one of the lads dancing and throwing plates, but she held out. She was not quite sure why. She did not know what was going on, but she sensed its importance, whatever it was. She would not even start asking questions. He was not in the mood to answer them. And his apparent lack of caring about past, present and future impressed her more than anything throughout their stormy marriage. For the first time, she saw him as a stern, taciturn man in command, a shark, a killer. And she found it exciting.

Savas was past caring about anything, that much was true. It was all in the lap of the gods. After sporadic phone calls, in came the one he was waiting for from Gibraltar: message had been received from the *Aloha* in code – everything was going according to plan. Savas called Rotterdam to tell Quincey, then turned to Greta: 'We'll go home now.' She noted that he did not say *darling*, did not ask if she wanted to go, just stood up and walked out into the misty dawn, expecting to be followed or not giving a damn. He looked at his watch: it was three o'clock, the same as in Egypt. Barring disasters, he was one breath away from becoming a multi-multi-millionaire.

Papeete's flight was climbing out of Kennedy. She had to deliver some papers to Boothy-Graffoe in London on Thursday morning. All day Wednesday she had been calling Ashenbury, but according to his vitriolic secretary, 'His Lordship could not be contacted anywhere.' That seemed reasonable. Arresting the *Aloha* and the follow-up might well take up all his time. Papeete calculated the time differences. Seven p.m. in New York, one a.m. Thursday in London, three a.m. almost first light over the Canal. If not before, by now it must be all over. Don and the others might already be under arrest. She wondered what she herself would be charged with, and what it would be like to face Bucken, the key witness for the prosecution, across the court room.

'Steer one, nine, seven,' said the pilot.
   'One, nine, seven,' echoed the Korean sailor at the wheel of the *Lippstadt*, and made the necessary slight adjustment to the compass course.
   Nobody else spoke. An Arab with a submachinegun stood at the pilot's elbow. Hans with another submachinegun controlled the length of the bridge. When the *Lippstadt* had been stormed, the Swedish First Officer was foolish enough to hit Hans with a heavy torch. He was shot dead. Neuburg had been shot through the arm as a precaution, but he stayed on the bridge to do what he could for his ship and to find out at least who the attackers were and what they were after. Ginger, the radio officer, watched the scene intently: he had been ordered to leave his cubicle and stay in sight. Ever since then, only essential commands broke the eerie silence. Everybody understood that a single false move would bring instant death rather than any outside help.
   'Increase the speed, please, and tell the tanker pilot behind us to come closer and reduce the gap.' Hans spoke very quietly.
   'But . . . ' the pilot began indignantly, then stopped and shrugged his shoulders. What else could he do? It was crazy! They were already moving at eleven knots, too fast for the Canal, and the statutory separation between ships had already been halved. If there was

an accident, a ship was grounded or went out of control, none of the convoy behind could stop in time or take evasive action to avoid a disastrous pile-up. Didn't these terrorists care? Were they suicidal maniacs?

The pilot glanced at the Arab at his elbow – why in Allah's name was he carrying an Israeli weapon? 'Faster! Haven't you heard your orders?' the gunman asked in Arabic.

'Twelve knots, please,' the pilot sighed.

'Twelve knots,' came the echo.

Neuburg and the pilot exchanged glances: the extra speed and the closing gaps in the convoy would at least alert Ismailia. But then there was a sudden burst of cacophony on UHF.

Hans listened, then asked the pilot: 'What's the routine?'

'I must call S.U.Q . . . I mean Canal Authority on four-two-five, four-five-four or four-six-eight kilohertz.'

'Do it. Just watch what you say. You understand?'

The pilot understood it only too well. He tried but could not raise Ismailia. Eventually, excited messages began to seep through. Something had happened at Ismailia. A break-down at the Centre. Will the pilots please ensure the safe transit of the convoy? No shore control would be available for a while.

Hans permitted himself a smile of self-satisfaction: the bomb planted at the Centre must have gone off at the right time. The news and the words terrified Neuburg: 'a while' could mean anything up to a few months in Egypt. Were his worst premonitions beginning to materialise? Perhaps Ismailia was under attack. He looked up at the sky. Was an air raid on the Canal imminent? No, perhaps they would not bomb their own men, whoever they were. He only wished he could be sure. He knew that most of his crew had been locked up in small groups in workshops, tool stores, even in decontamination cubicles. If something went wrong . . . no, it was pointless to contemplate it, because he was helpless. Most of them would die before they could be freed. And, if fire broke out, who would fight it? The men who were essential to sailing the ship were all guarded by the terrorists. If only he could establish some contact with his chief engineer.

Neuburg turned to Hans and pointed at an instrument panel on the central console: 'I must talk to the Chief. We're having some problem with the number two engine.'

'What's that?'

'Overheating.'

'Bullshit. Do you want a second bullet, this time perhaps in your mouth?'

The chief engineer, a stubborn, sarcastic Scotsman in the guise of an amiable giant, had, in fact, got into Ruzicki's bad books very early on, and was now lying, clubbed semi-conscious, in the enclosure housing the stand-by generator. Bucken gave him some water once, but could not do anything for him since then. Right now he was busy sharing a hip-flask and making friends with a cheerfully tipsy Welsh electrician right under Ruzicki's nose. The man's unsteady gait, glazed and hopeful eyes, and sparse, gingery beard lent him an air of innocence. Ruzicki judged him harmless and used him as a messenger boy. But Bucken had more experience with drunks in his youth on his beat in London's dockland. He recognised that the man's drunkenness was a state of mind rather than a weakness. Like all drinking men, the electrician loved company. So Bucken drank with him. When Ruzicki was busy beating the Chief, Bucken whispered: 'I need a small screwdriver.' The electrician gave him one searching, sober glance, but asked no questions.

With the screwdriver, Bucken began to dismantle the yellow box under his shirt. It was a desperately slow process.

'Itchy?' Ruzicki asked.

'Sure. I've got the bug, haven't I?'

'Very clever.'

'I could also say I'm itching to get going. You think it'll be long before we get the klaxon and the all-clear?'

Ruzicki shrugged his shoulders. He did not want to get involved in a long conversation when his eyes had to be everywhere so that he could ensure single-handedly the smooth functioning of the engine room. Other memebers of the raiding party were busy planting the bombs all over the *Lippstadt*.

Ever since Ruzicki had refused to let him arm himself, Bucken knew that, for some reason, he was not a fully trusted member of the gang. He could not waste time figuring out the reasons. His few limited options were all he could think of. It would be mad to try to fight. The risk was greater than death: if he lost control of the yellow box, all would be lost. He could threaten at some point to blow up the ship. If the bluff was called, he would not detonate, and he would be shot. No, it had to be a bluff Ruzicki could not afford to call.

The hip flask ran dry, but the electrician seemed to have hidden supplies everywhere between Swansea and Singapore. He produced a half-bottle of vodka from under a panel of electronic controls. He could not have guessed what was going on, but he sensed an ally in every booze-brother, and Bucken seemed to be one.

'You may call it the seven-year itch,' Bucken scratched himself and joked drunkenly. He had unscrewed the fixing bolt, but he

306

would now need both hands to open the yellow box under his shirt. He looked at the electrician who responded with splendid speed and began to sing and stagger inanely.

'Sit down, for chrissake,' Ruzicki shouted.

The box was open. Bucken had no idea what was inside it. He just clawed, loosened and tore out whatever electronic parts he could. The yellow box was probably dead. Now he had to screw the lid on.

Up on the bridge, Hans was scribbling some calculations of speed and distance travelled. The bombs would soon be in place. The *Lippstadt* would soon reach midway between Port Said and Ismailia, still a reasonably safe distance from the Ballah by-pass – a point that was just about maximum distance from the main stations of firefighting and rescue tugs. Although he knew that the tugs with well-trained crews and modern equipment could answer an alert within minutes, the explosion at Ismailia would delay them, and they would be late for anything except witnessing a major disaster. Whoever was to give Bucken the all-clear klaxon must soon be in touch. Bucken and his box ought to be on the bridge for better reception.

Hans looked out into the darkness of the barren Sinai side. Nothing was moving there. It was too early for Ruzicki's escape helicopter to appear. He turned towards the sporadic lights to the east where two roads, a military and a civilian one, ran along the Canal, behind the screen of high embankment that was peppered with anti-aircraft gun emplacements and Egypt's ill-fated Siegfried line.

A car was catching up with the *Lippstadt*. It flashed its headlights twice, and again after a pause. Hans was pleased. Ruzicki's escape mechanism was working well. Now he could see the vehicle: a Land Rover. Cruising to and fro, it had already passed by the other way. It was waiting for a flare signal that would say that Hans and his men were ready, the bombs were in place. The Land Rover would then slow down to keep abreast with the ship. The second flare would warn the driver: watch out for the mooring boat, we're coming as soon as we've heard the klaxon in Bucken's yellow box.

Hans looked at the captain. He felt sorry for him. Pity that it had to be a German officer. And pity that the decision had gone against wearing masks and allowing the crew to escape. It was Ruzicki's decision, and Hans never argued with the paymaster. But he would keep Ruzicki in his sight from the moment of evacuation – if the escape arrangements came unstuck in any way, Ruzicki would be the first to die. Yes, he must send somebody else to the engine room, and get Bucken and Ruzicki on to the bridge.

The sun was coming up. Km.42, the ideal spot for the completion of the job, could not be far, thought Hans.

The radio officer warned the captain: 'Time for us to call Hamburg, sir.' The captain looked at Hans, seeking his approval.

'Pretend that the satellite link has broken down,' Hans said. 'Send a telex. And no heroics, please. Any unusual word or set of figures or unnecessary mention of the time or other data, and I'll take it that you're transmitting a coded alert about terrorists and things like that. So I won't even ask you to reveal your secret codes, just watch yourself, please.'

Hans poked his submachinegun through the hatch to the radio cabin. The man with the friendly moonface began to tap in his telex call signs. Hans watched his white hands working the keys, his flame-red hair fluttering under the ventilator. His wedding ring was a wide band of old gold. From his parents or grandparents, thought Hans. Red hair? Like a Jew's. It brought back memories. Bitter ones. It's been a long time, but not forgotten, he nodded only to himself as he fired a short burst. His eyes had hardly registered the spurting blood when he spun round to cover people on the bridge.

Neuburg moved, but controlled himself. 'Why?'

'I'm sorry. He was trying to cheat. You shouldn't use Jews in such responsible positions.'

'He wasn't . . . I mean to hell with you. What difference would it make?'

'If you, a German, don't know by instinct, you'll never learn.'

In the engine room, Bucken was sitting at the foot of the main generator, munching a sandwich the electrician had brought him. He behaved so placidly that Ruzicki's alertness seemed to slip now and again. The yellow box ruined, the idea for a bluff that could not be called hit Bucken in a flash. When he had investigated a threat to wipe out London by blowing up a wreck full of wartime bombs in the Thames, the blackmailer had had an ingenious scheme. He had told Bucken that the detonator had been set and needed stopping. Only the villain knew how to halt the timer, so he had to be kept safe. Each stopping would start a new countdown automatically – the man was untouchable. Now if Bucken could apply the same principle . . .

The second engineer, a young man with ping-pong bat-sized hands and thinly-veiled hostility, went about his work as if Ruzicki was not there. He reached under the central control console for something. He was only an arm's length away from one of the bombs placed there. 'Stop!' Ruzicki shouted and raised the Uzzi.

'He wouldn't dare do anything!' Bucken stepped between the young man and the muzzle, mimicking the ill-coordinated gestures of the meth-drinkers he used to know on his beat.

308

The electrician, tools dangling from his belt, moved closer to Ruzicki, and began some tirade of incoherent babble.

Ruzicki felt trapped and stepped back. 'Stop it. All of you.' The screeching buzzer of the phone on the wall also competed for his attention. To make sure that nothing would happen, he loosed off a burst of fire into the ceiling. Some wires shorted and flashed. Two lights went out. He signalled to the electrician to stand next to the engineer, then answered the phone. 'How goes it? . . . Okay, send relief and we'll come up. Okay. Flares ready? . . . Right. Buzz me then.'

He rang off, and faced Bucken with a half-smile of pleasurable anticipation. 'Well, Superintendent, I won't let you suffer from waiting any longer. Oh, I'm sorry, I always forget, was it Chief Superintendent?'

'What are you getting at? Are we ready to move?' Out of the corner of his eye Bucken saw the electrician's hand begin to inch towards a large screwdriver on his belt.

'We? No, it's me who's ready to move. Your game happens to be up. I want that box.'

'What the hell are you talking about?'

'Come on Bucken, you're no fool.' He raised the submachinegun with his right hand, and held out his left palm. 'Come on, just hand it over . . . '

Fear tightened Bucken's stomach muscles. The parts he had removed from the box were lodged firmly under his shirt, but now they slipped under his belt, down the leg of his trousers, and on to his shoe.

Ruzicki never moved his eyes from Bucken's face and hands, but heard the soft thuds on the shoe. It made him laugh heartily. 'No need to shit yourself, Mr. Superintendent!' Laughter shook him. 'If only Papeete could see you now. You should have seen her when she heard what we'd found out about you.'

'How? I mean how did you find out that I'm a policeman?' It was meant more for the electrician and the engineer than Ruzicki.

'It's a long story. You may not live long enough to hear the end of it.'

'Oh well, if that's the way you want it . . . ' He pulled the yellow box slowly out of his shirt. If the bluff failed to come off and he was shot, Ruzicki would take the box and have the shock of his life when eventually he tried to detonate and the box failed to function. He would just sit in the mooring boat and swear and argue with Hans . . . Suddenly, Bucken found himself laughing with Ruzicki.

'What's so funny?'

309

'Only that you think I haven't known for quite a while that you at least suspected me. Why are villains like you always convinced that cops have no brains?'

'You mean you knew?'

'What do you think?'

'Okay. So you knew. You were a fool not to run for it. Now give me the box.'

'You must be joking.' Bucken held up the yellow box. His thumb was pressing on the code button. 'You see? It's primed. If I remove my thumb or if you shoot me and my thumb comes off the detonator, it's all the same. If I die, you and the ship go up with me.'

The phone buzzer screeched again. Ruzicki knew what it meant: the first flare must have gone up. And he was stuck down here in a stalemate.

'You're under arrest, Ruzicki. Pity that we'll never be partners in that casino, but it can't be helped.' He saw Ruzicki's finger twitch on the trigger. 'Don't be a fool. Even if you go to jail for a short while, you'll live. If you shoot, you're dead. We all are. But, if you play ball with me, I'll see what I can do for you. I could help you . . . ' He stepped closer. 'Now why don't you just hand over the Uzzi? Come on . . . nice and easy . . . ' Yes, that's how his training sergeant had once talked a would-be suicide back from the edge of the roof. 'Come on, give it to that drunken gentleman over there.'

The electrician's eyes glittered behind his half-moon spectacles, and Bucken knew it was not the alcohol: the man had the guts to enjoy the scene. Ruzicki looked confused. 'You must be crazy, Bucken.'

'Yes, crazy enough to die for a good cause.' What rubbish! thought Bucken, but he was playing for maximum effect. He raised the box with a Messianic gesture.

'Okay, okay, don't go mad. Now listen . . . let's work out some deal.'

In the Land Rover, moving slowly alongside the *Lippstadt*, Rabbit Schwarzberg tapped the code into his perfect replica of Bucken's yellow box: three, seven, double two, eight – twice. So the detonator was primed. When the second flare went up from the bridge-wing of the *Lippstadt*, Ruzicki and his men would be at their most vulnerable: waiting for the klaxon, preparing to flee. That was when the Rabbit would press button T for timer – and set it for zero seconds. Some fireworks it would be.

If anything, it pleased the Rabbit that nobody on board would survive. Those who were not killed by the explosions would die in the cloud of toxic gases or the flood of lethal chemicals, and those who survived even that would be finished off in the inferno set off by the pile-up. That's what Quincey wanted, and Quincey was a much more generous paymaster than Ruzicki. Besides, the Rabbit had never liked Ruzicki. He did not like criminal parvenus who treated him contemptuously as a mere craftsman and failed to offer him the trust his track record deserved even from the true aristocrats of the international underworld. And Bucken? He would be the icing on the cake.

Waiting for the flare signal, the Rabbit watched the rising sun. Yes, it should be a fine morning, he thought.

Captain Neuburg wished he had a gun, a bow and arrow, just about any weapon with half a chance against machineguns. With Hans's permission, he examined the radio officer, but there was nothing he could do for him. The man was dead. If I survive this, Neuburg thought, I'll recommend him for the highest possible reward for gallantry irrespective of what he did or did not try when sending that telex. Neuburg returned to the bridge and stared down the length of the ship. Near the bow, between the forward tanks, two men were moving. Startled, he turned to Hans: 'What are your men doing up there? Don't they know it's dangerous?'

'Don't worry. We know the risks of war even if you, you left-over Germans are so weak and know nothing but how to get molly-coddled. Our fight for you was a waste.'

'Wish you had thought about it earlier.' Their eyes clashed. Neuburg was ready to have a go at the old Nazi with his bare hands. Then self-discipline got the better of him. He had to stay alive and do what he could for the ship and his crew.

Hans sensed the tension all around. Within minutes, there might be a desperate bid to defy him. He felt like preempting it by mowing down everybody on the bridge, including his own Arab. But his pride in 'duty above all' was overwhelming. The job was to keep the ship going until the klaxon was heard. What the hell was happening down there in the engine room anyway? He picked up the direct phone.

When the buzzer sounded, Ruzicki hesitated. Talking to Bucken about a deal, watching the two men next to the controls, and thinking desperately about a way out of the impasse were already making too great demands on his brain and senses. The ship swayed gently, a shudder ran through the floor, and it must have caught Bucken

311

unawares. The policeman seemed to lose his balance, and his arms with the box flailed helplessly. 'Watch out! Don't drop it!' Ruzicki bellowed and stepped forward to support him with the muzzle of the gun.

That was all the distraction Bucken had been after. The mild-mannered, apparently gone-to-fat electrician was a survivor of many a bar-brawl in Cardiff's Tiger Bay. He lunged and drove the massive screwdriver through Ruzicki's neck. The gun went off aimlessly as Bucken grabbed the muzzle with one hand, hitting Ruzicki in the face with the yellow box. There was a dreadful crunch of broken bones as everybody got sprayed with blood. For a second, they all stood still. Then the pent-up tension of the last hours burst free. Over the death rattle rising from Ruzicki's throat, they were all shouting and screaming at each other.

'Shoot him!' yelled Karl, the young engineer.

Bucken was blindly fumbling to find the safety catch if there was one.

'Don't you know how to use it?'

'I'm a fucking cop not a universal killing machine!' Bucken turned the gun and hit Ruzicki on the head to silence him. Then he found Ruzicki's revolver, and threw the Uzzi to the engineer: 'Figure it out how it works. You'll have to come with me. We must capture the bridge.'

The Welshman looked ready to throw up. He rummaged among tangled wires behind a cover panel, found a half-bottle of rum and made an earnest attempt at downing it in one go. Bucken knocked the bottle out of his hand. 'You stay and find the two bombs they planted down here. You'll see a short metal rod like a cooking thermometer sticking out of a turkey's arse. Pull it out, that's all you have to do. It's the radio trigger.'

'And the detonator?' he stared at the yellow box.

'It's dead.'

The electrician collapsed and chuckled in helpless hysteria.

Wish I was in better nick, Bucken thought, as he raced the engineer four floors up the stairs. Winded by the climb, he stopped outside the door to the bridge. He pocketed the gun. 'I . . . let me go in first . . . give me a minute to cover anyone you can't shoot from the door . . . You know by now how to work that Uzzi?'

'Guess so.'

'Let's hope you're guessing right.'

Bucken walked in – and Hans was on the verge of shooting him. 'Are you crazy?! Why didn't you warn me you were coming?'

'I thought Ruzicki told you.'

'Where is he?'

'Should be here any minute.' Bucken stepped closer to the Arab behind the pilot. 'Are we ready?'

'Has the klaxon sounded?'

'Not yet.'

Rabbit Schwarzberg was fed up with cruising aimlessly through desert and biblical scenes, just waiting for the second flare signal. His orders were to detonate at or about Km.42. The *Lippstadt* was now some four kilometres beyond that. 'Stop here,' he said to his driver at one of the gaps in the embankment through which he could see the Canal. The bow of the ship appeared. His window was covered by a coarse film of sand. He wound it down to get a better view. It was not often that he would actually witness one of his electronic contraptions wreaking havoc: that was both the advantage and disadvantage of being just a specialist on contract to the men of action. But, this time, it should be a rather memorable spectacle. Excitement dried his mouth. He licked his lips nervously. He waited for the *Lippstadt* to pass him just about halfway. Midships – is that what they called it? He studied only those things he had to blow up, and he had never done a ship before. It annoyed him a little that the job was only to cripple her. But who was he to argue with the client?

There . . . there she was. He activated the timer of his yellow box – and pressed down zero delay.

The Rabbit never saw any of the fireworks. On Quincey's orders, one of the bombs that was meant for the *Lippstadt* had been placed under the front passenger seat of the Land Rover. The yellow box detonated all bombs simultaneously.

The explosion shook the ship from stem to stern. Only her strong construction prevented a complete disintegration. Karl, the young engineer, was catapulted down the stairs. He was numbed by agonising pain in his chest and a dislocated shoulder, but struggled to regain his feet: that cop on the bridge was waiting for him, facing submachineguns on his own.

The Arab on the bridge lost his balance like everybody else, and began firing indiscriminately, mostly into the ceiling, but hitting the pilot, too. Bucken fell on his knees. He had not time to fish the gun out of his pocket. He fired through the cloth, missed, rolled over, bounced up and dived to bring down the Arab in a rugger tackle. He heard the man's head crack hard against the back of the radar – and the firing stopped.

Hans had been thrown against the captain, and they tumbled together. Hans was on top. Neuburg kneed him in the face, but because he was lying on the floor the kick was more provocative than damaging. Hans was dazed by shock and blinded by fury – he felt that Ruzicki must have double-crossed him – but all that failed to blunt his killer instinct. He rose, levelled his submachingun with Neuburg's eyes, and paused for a fraction of a second, just long enough to let his victim know that he was about to die. It was no reflection on his efficiency – merely the old routine resurrected by a sadistic streak in his nature. That passive savagery was his undoing. The young engineer came through the door in a single leap and, virtually in a trance, emptied the magazine into the armed man towering over his captain. He was still firing when there was nothing but hunks of raw meat dancing at his feet on the floor.

'Stop! Karl! For chrissake, stop!' Neuburg's cries seemed to take ages to penetrate his ears. He stared down in horror, his left arm hung limply, and he began to shiver.

The pilot was already on his feet, pressing his head against the picture-window of the bridge, and staring at the devastation below, all along the deck. He did not even realise that he was bleeding. He began to pray mutely, then reached for his radio: it was a reflex rather than logical thinking that made him warn the ships behind. 'Slow down everybody, slow down and stop!' he yelled while yet another explosion shook the ship. Two of the huge deck tanks up front just disappeared in flames and smoke. Fires were flaring up everywhere and, gradually, the waters came alight all around and in the wake of the *Lippstadt*.

On the bridge, fire alarms were wailing, lights were flashing, warning klaxons hooted – then everything stopped. The silence and darkness were more menacing than the cacophony. Centuries or a couple of seconds later, all bedlam was loose again. The stand-by generator must have cut in, but that would provide only emergency power for light and communications.

Neuburg's eyes were darting all over the bridge, trying to identify and assess the damage. He had never had training in cataclysm on such a scale: it was impossible to tell if the ship was still moving or sinking or both. Lethal chemicals must be everywhere. His first thought was to evacuate the ship: every man had his individual escape kit. But where were they? Could they get to the suits? Would they just dive in and die? He reached for the Total Emergency button. Nobody needed an alert after all this, but instinct drove him

314

to follow some sort of routine that would give him the reassurance that he was alive and there was something he could still do. Before he could touch the button, he was threatened by a gun.

'Whatever you do, keep this bloody wreck going!'

'You tell me how!' Neuburg's voice was peculiarly nasal.

Only now did Bucken realise that he was screwing the barrel of his gun up the man's nostril. 'I'm sorry,' he apologised with a vicious grimace. 'Just please keep her going!'

Neuburg, still in a state of shock, looked confused. He had seen Bucken with the raiders, he had also seen him attacking the Arab – why wasn't Karl shooting him?

'He's a policeman,' the engineer shouted over the noise.

'And the people who wrecked your ship wanted a huge pile-up disaster in the Canal. Don't give them the pleasure of success.' Bucken heard himself begging. He had to prop up the man somehow. He wished he knew how to take command and what to do. The *Lippstadt* was probably beginning to slow down. Out of control, she might run aground in the shallow part of the Canal beyond the buoys or crash into the shore, turn across and form a road block the tankers behind could not avoid. These thoughts and worse flashed through Neuburg's mind. Ships had no brakes. The convoy could not even hope to stop within several miles. Ships would hit the *Lippstadt* one after another. No, the only chance was to keep going, try to reach the Ballah by-pass, and slip out of the way. If the engines were badly damaged, it would take ages to get there, but the ships behind would also be slowing down. The only question was: had he anything left with which to steer and control his ship?

He stepped to the wheel and had to push a body out of the way. Until now, nobody had noticed that the Korean sailor on wheel duty had been killed. Neuburg was not even sure of his name. He would perhaps mourn him some day. If he lived to see that day. Moving like a sleepwalker, he felt the wheel. It seemed to have no bite when it turned. He reached for the phone to the engine room. Nobody answered the buzzer. From the corner of his eye he saw that Karl was activating the non-automatic fire extinguishers all over the ship. But nobody could tell how many of them were actually working.

'Somebody must check out the engine room and steering,' Neuburg was thinking aloud.

'What do I look for?' Bucken asked.

'You? Do you know anything about ships?' Bucken's pathetic shaking of the head brought a smile on Neuburg's face – and performed a miracle. The captain woke up from the nightmare. 'Karl!'

'Sir?'

'Go down to . . . ' The screeching buzzer stopped him. It was the Chief Engineer, reporting fires and extensive damage in his domain, omitting any mention of deadly fumes and the beating he had taken, wanting to know in an almost casual tone who was playing what sort of silly games. Neuburg could have hugged him for his coolness although he realised that Chiefie might simply be too dumbfounded to be frightened. 'Listen, I'm sending Karl to help you if he can get through. Steering is my main problem. If you can give me *some* power, we'll try bow thrust.'

The pilot staggered by, trailing blood, whispering, 'I can't see out . . . there's no ship there . . . no ship . . . '

'Shut up. No, not you, Chief, you just listen. The main steering gear seems to be gone. You think you can do something manually?'

'Depends. I'll let you know.'

'I can't see,' the pilot kept repeating, 'there's no ship. '

Neuburg looked up: 'Good God.' The slanting window pane seemed to be the end of the world. Dense black smoke was all he could see beyond. Some stray wind made the smoke cloud swirl aside. Two men came running, one with his clothes on fire, along the deck, jumping over pipes and torn metal until flames shot up and forced them to recoil. Bucken recognised the punk muscleman and Franz. They seemed to be trapped. Then they dived into the sea of fire and chemical spillage below. They were as good as dead. Captain Neuburg crossed himself and reeled off a quick prayer. Bucken did not tell him not to bother.

Neuburg tried the wheel again. This time there was some response. The bow seemed to shift from twelve o'clock to one minute past. Or was it just inertia as the dwindling speed kept the ship on her course? Luckily, that was an almost perfectly straight section of the Canal. But if . . . Neuburg could not finish the thought. Impenetrable black smoke rose to curtain off the view. Even if the Chief performed some miracle down there, Neuburg would not see where he was going. He could steer by compass and charts as in fog, but that would be a hazardous performance even with a healthy ship and no risk of malfunctions. He needed a pair of eyes. He looked at Bucken. The policeman read the thought and turned away, wanting to protest, *no, not me, don't count on me, it's crazy*! But all he said was 'Damn you, Captain, what do I do?'

'I can't ask you.'

'You'll have to. Otherwise I might not volunteer.'

'You may never get through.'

'I'd have never guessed.'

It took four long minutes to dress Bucken in a well-sealed firefighting outfit and breathing apparatus. It failed to improve his spirits that Neuburg was rattling off a multitude of warnings. 'You'll be reasonably safe from heat and toxic fumes though some fumes will penetrate your skin. You can only hope for the best. You'll have *some* protection from chemical spillage, but don't, for God's sake don't, wade through or stand in any large puddles. Try to stick to the elevated catwalk in the middle. You'll pass some raised, open platforms with foam guns. Those may help you to clear a path.' Neuburg fastened the double zips and cuffs to seal the heavy garment. 'You'll be safe to run through fires. The trouble is that, if you ever get through, you'll have to remove the visor to work this.' He handed Bucken a large walkie-talkie. 'Let's hope that forward movement and the wind will keep driving the fumes towards me and away from you.'

'It's the nicest send-off I've had for years.'

Neuburg appreciated the tone of self-mocking from a man who might be dead in five minutes. They nodded at each other – it was as good as a warm handshake. The buzzer sounded. Neuburg had to swallow hard before he could speak. 'Go, man, go, I haven't got all day,' and answered the buzzer.

The Chief reported virtually in monosyllables. 'Found three men alive, two usable, electrician badly mauled. Steering gone. Will try to activate the back-up and work rudder manually from steering room.'

Thank God for German company policy to have belt, braces and hands in pocket, however much the accountants complained about the costs that would be unnecessary under the Panamanian flag, thought Neuburg. 'Anything else?'

'Trying to re-start an alternator to give you one engine to run without lubrication. Think we're pumping all lubricating oil into the Canal.'

Who cares? The engine would run to destruction in less than an hour, but might get the *Lippstadt* into the by-pass.

In the steering room, two men had already connected a handpump and were ready to work it, like railway bogies, pumping oil from one cylinder to another. Karl would be on the emergency phone to get the captain's instructions and watch the rudder indicator. Manual power would not be much to fight the water resistance to the turns of the rudder, but five or six degrees could be enough to keep the *Lippstadt* away from the shallow and shore.

Although Chiefie never referred to the heat and the murderous conditions, Neuburg knew what they must be up against. He also knew that his instructions on the emergency phone would be answered as long as somebody was alive in the hell below. If only he

317

answered as long as somebody was alive in the hell below. If only he knew what instructions to give them: without his 'eyes' battling through to the bow, they all were at the mercy of the shifting clouds of smoke.

Under the extra weight of some thirty pounds of breathing apparatus, Bucken ran, stumbled and crawled, sometimes blindly, in the cumbersome protective suit. He reached the first firefighting platform, but could not stop there: the remnants of two-deck tank dragons breathed fire at him from all sides. It filled him with strange elation to melt into an inferno, feel the heat but part the flames, seemingly unscathed. I must be mad, he thought, and in a way he was. That was why nothing could stop him. He heard the splash of some liquid round his boots, and he could only hope that it was not a potent enough chemical to penetrate his flimsy armour and kill him too soon.

The second platform was relatively free of fire and fumes. He took the risk of removing his helmet and visor, and radio Neuburg. 'You're on course – I guess.'

'Try to activate the foam gun!' the captain cried into the walkie-talkie.

'How?'

Neuburg gave terse, step-by-step instructions: every one of his words sounded like swearing at his misfortune to have an ignorant fool for eyes. In return, Bucken's 'thank you' sounded like the rudest 'fuck you, too' he had ever said to anyone. But the instructions were precise – the gun began to spew out foam and help him on his way.

A dazed, badly-burnt figure held up Bucken's final dash for the bow. The man dropped on his knees and tried to kiss the feet emerging like some abstract saviour from an elephantine snow bath. Bucken struggled to free himself and protect his armour. 'Let go and come with me! We've got a ship to steer.'

Schneider looked up in amazement: the Saviour spoke English, not Latin! 'Well, you never know, do you? You learn something every day!' He wobbled after Bucken, he would have followed him through brimstone and hell-fire – he just about did, until he passed out.

The air up the bow was reasonably clear and Bucken could radio the captain his primitive directions that were unlikely to become a standard part of shipping manuals. But, up there, he eventually witnessed the mirage of two firefighting tugs charging out of the Ballah by-pass. He wondered if such insanity was curable.

318

Papeete's flight was the first to land in London on that Thursday morning. The papers had nothing about Suez. That was good news to her. Waiting for her luggage, she telephoned her husband in Rotterdam. Quincey sounded joyfully excited: 'Hang on, honey, news is just coming in about some dreadful accident in Egypt . . . Hang on, I wonder what it could be . . . '

Papeete rang off. She knew she had failed. Ashenbury had failed her. She took a taxi to Sussex. The driver let her listen to the radio. The news was still garbled, too fresh for any clarification, but there was some mention of carnage and a ship called *Lippstadt*.

She had to wait for Ashenbury in the cold library. Eventually, he came to join her. He was unshaven and generally dishevelled in a way she could never have imagined.

'You cheated me.'

'I'm sorry,' he mumbled, too tired to operate even his stiff lower lip. 'We were late . . . It seems I couldn't prevent it.' He closed his eyes: he had not slept more than three hours in three days. He never saw the pearl-handled paper knife Papeete had snatched from the Hepplewhite writing desk. It was not much of a weapon, but she wielded it with ferocious force. Later it would be claimed she would have killed him if Price the butler had not stopped her cutting his face and throat again and again through flesh, veins, sinews and teeth.

The police were utterly disappointed that Ashenbury refused to press any other charges but breaking and entering when there was no evidence offered for any such offences though assault was more than obvious.

By Thursday afternoon, all the world news media were swamped by conflicting details of *Catastrophe* and *Narrowly Averted Disaster* in the Suez Canal. There were stories about *Horrors Afloat*, Libyan, Israeli and Palestinian terrorism, some *Phantom Policeman*, and even the 'Ghost of the Ancient Mariner who had risen to rescue a burning aircraft carrier'. Environmentalists had a field day with free choice to take their pick regarding the form of *Ecological Doomsday*, and attack or praise, according to taste, the careless/careful transport of oil and chemicals, owners' negligence or seaman's skill under flags of convenience, the collaboration between big business and governments producing cautious/conspiratorial silence. The Egyptian government issued only a brief statement of earnest obfuscation, concentrating on the solitary, indisputable fact that the Canal firefighting and rescue tugs had given a magnificent account of themselves. Some oil and chemical spillage remained to be cleared, but convoys would resume operations in a couple of days.

Savas listened to the television news in his Piraeus taverna. After the initial euphoria, he now knew he had been ruined. He tried to telephone Rotterdam, but Quincey must have gone to ground. Selli in Rome was also unobtainable. Savas called London and he was asked to hold on. He overheard Boothy-Graffoe telling his secretary: 'Savas? No, just ask him to write to us if he wants something.' Before the secretary could return to the telephone, Savas rang off. He asked for his bill. The owner of the taverna waved his money away: 'You've spent a fortune here and brought a lot of business to me, Oldman. Let's say you've earned yourself lifelong credit in this establishment.' To refuse his kindness would have been an insult – to accept it was more humiliating than Savas could bear. He always knew that news travelled fast and in mysterious ways through the backstreets of Greek shipping, but that it would spread that fast . . .

He went home, wrote a brief note for Greta, and took a massive overdose of everything he could lay his hands on.

Later that evening, Greta told the consultant that 'it was a sheer fluke that I returned home so early'.

'Let's hope, madam, that your luck continues to hold. We've pumped out his stomach, but most of the drugs had already been absorbed by the body. At the moment he's in a delicate condition, but it would help, most certainly, if you kept talking to him even when he appears to be in a coma.'

So Greta sat on his bed and talked. She sounded quite cheerful, and she was not putting on an act. 'All right, so you have problems. Are you telling me that you have more problems now than any time in the last twenty years? Utter rubbish. You're penniless and free. Free of responsibilities. Money? Who cares? It's chic to belong to the *nouveaux pauvres*. I could take a PR job or something. Yes, why not? If Jackie Onassis could do it, why couldn't I?' She smiled because the thought made her feel terribly important: nobody had actually needed her help ever before.

Bucken slipped into London as quietly as a visiting tax exile. The flat in Bayswater was a mess. It had the cold, fusty and damp air of an air raid shelter overgrown by weeds. As he kicked all the junk mail aside, he saw several notes and glamour-photos from Helen. 'Things going well. I love you.' Then: 'Things going better. Wish I could tell you.' 'Film job! Imagine!' and 'Speaking part! Two whole lines!!! Why aren't you here?' Apparently, she had left a picture or a note every day for several weeks. Bucken was too tired to feel pleased for her, though he was. He found his phone in the chest of drawers. Luckily, it had already been reconnected. He dialled the paper Freemantle worked for. It was a giggly girl on the switchboard.

'Ada? That's not Ada Tansley,' said Bucken with as much innocence as he could muster.

The girl chuckled. 'Oh, you know her.'

'I'm a friend of hers.'

'Ah. Well.' She began to whisper conspiratorially. 'They say that she and John Freemantle are overdue from their holidays. But I think they've eloped. High time, too.'

Bucken called a friend at the Yard, saying that he was phoning from Acapulco because he did not want it to get around that he was back. 'Do us a favour, old son. Anything on record about Freemantle? You know, the reporter.' A few minutes later he was told that Freemantle was missing but, for some reason, it was not to be made public.

Bucken replaced the telephone in the drawer and drank himself into a stupor. He woke up almost twenty-four hours later. He was not sure what day it was, so he phoned Sarah and asked her.

'Are you drunk?' He said nothing, and she understood that it might be a genuine question. There were few things that could surprise her about Bucken. 'It's Monday.'

'Can we meet?'

'What? Now?'

'Yes. It's urgent.'

'No more games, Bucken. I'm expecting Jeff home any minute now.'

'It's about Spire's little girl.'

'Oh, she's a sweetie. Jeff and I are thinking about adopting her if possible.' She waited in vain for him to say something. 'Bucken? Are you there?'

'Yes. I sometimes wish we had a child, you and I.'

'As I said, no more games.'

'Sorry. I didn't really mean it. It's just that there's something I want to do before . . . before I have a few meetings.' He was thinking about the money he still had stashed away in Switzerland. As it was the fruit of his criminal under cover activities, there would be no way of accounting for it. Surely, the Home Office could not accept it under any heading. 'I've had a small windfall . . . well, a small fortune, in fact. I can't just hand it over to the child, but I thought you might be able to handle it.'

'Bucken . . . are you all right?'

321

'Oh, sure. Will you handle it for her? You'll get a notification from Switzerland.'

'Can I do something? I mean for you?'

'No, no, I'm fine. Zurich will be in touch, and I'll see you around.'

He called Ashenbury's office and simply told the secretary that he would be there within fifteen minutes.

'Welcome home.'

The green choppy seas of the two Turners made Bucken feel sick this time. The crystal goblets were filled, once again, with Dom Perignon but Bucken asked for rum, white rum.

'As you wish.' Ashenbury was still the perfect host, only his eyes seemed to have sunk to the bottom of their sockets, and his face and throat were covered with bandages and plaster.

'You ought to consider using electric,' Bucken said.

'Good idea. Wish you'd mentioned it before I had a close shave.'

Bucken gave a brief summary of events.

'You did well,' Ashenbury managed to say, despite the devastating consequences of Bucken's success: he, some friends and the government had gambled heavily on a Suez closure and lost a fortune the moment the *Lippstadt* slipped into the Ballah by-pass. Because the gamble was inadmissible, he could not enjoy even the soothing effect of complaining about it bitterly. But that was not Bucken's fault. Well, not directly. 'Yes, it's most unfortunate, Bucken, that your labours can't have any public recognition, but you'll have the satisfaction of a job well done.'

'Thank you, sir. Most kind of you, sir. There's nothing like a little praise, I suppose, to keep a fool like me going.'

'I understand how you must feel. It's most unfortunate that Freemantle never got through with your message. If only we knew where you were and what you were fighting single-handedly, nothing would have been easier than stopping the *Aloha* and giving you the backing you deserved.'

'Quite. What I don't understand is why it's being kept a secret that Freemantle is missing. I took the liberty of checking with the Yard and . . . '

'That's right, you've got to discuss it with your proper superiors. It must have been a Home Office decision or something. Way above my head. Incidentally, you haven't mentioned what exactly happened to Ruzicki and the mercenaries.'

'He probably bled to death. The others were either killed by the explosions or they died like the two I actually saw diving into the Canal. What the role of the wrecked Land Rover was and who its occupants were, nobody knows as yet. I suspect that something must have gone wrong. The damage was such that a full identification might never be possible. I know that the police were investigating, but I couldn't wait and get involved. I was lucky to get out of Egypt at all with no questions asked when I had entered the country without a visa or any plausible explanation. But we'll have to invent something for the Egyptians when we start prosecutions and extradition procedures.'

'Quite.' Ashenbury sounded aloof, nodded repeatedly, and for a second, Bucken thought he might have fallen asleep. 'It won't be easy.'

'I know. I'll need a great deal of legal advice as well as your help.'

'My help? No, I don't think I can be seen to be involved with this at all. I mean the whole affair must go through the proper channels. You'll report to the Commissioner, I suppose, and the Home Office or even the Foreign Office will advise you what if anything could be done.'

'What do you mean *if*?'

'Well, as you very well know, we're talking about crimes or unethical conduct abroad, by foreigners, against foreign interests.'

'You're not thinking about . . . '

'Heavens, no!' Ashenbury was quick to protest. 'Of course not. But you know best how complicated these things are. They'll need to be given due consideration. The decision will have to be made,' he gestured towards the oak-panelled ceiling, 'at the top.' He noted the disgust on Bucken's face. 'You're very tired right now. We all are. Ever since your disappearance, I've been in conference, trying to locate you, trying to foresee possible events, day and night. We'll need to rest, reflect and then think clearly. I know how you must feel right now.'

'How about the bastards who're British citizens? There's no question of extradition treaties, we could go for them right away.'

'If that is the decision at the top, sure enough. But then, some of our elders may feel that a scandal could be most counter-productive.' He saw that Bucken was closer to throwing up than probably at any time during the storm aboard the *Aloha*. 'Even if we can recover the tape recording from that Spanish mosque or villa or whatever, the evidence you have may or may not be quite strong enough to support all the charges you suggest we bring. However. There're ways and means. Horses for courses. Right?' He tried to conjure up a reassuring half-smile. He failed. 'I mean those, for instance, who're members of Lloyd's or the Baltic Exchange, could be induced, quietly, of course, to resign without any fuss. Quite a blow, wouldn't you say?'

No, Bucken would not say anything. He helped himself to more rum.

'I don't need to tell you, Bucken, you know it as well as I do that there're always some higher political and economic considerations. That's why you volunteered to do this most unconventional job, and that's why it's appreciated. I wouldn't be surprised if you got an OBE or something in due course. Obviously, it would look suspicious if you got it right away in the, let's say, odd circumstances of your long leave of absence, and the dent in . . . in your . . . er . . . '

'Street credibility?'

'Yes. What an interesting expression. I've always felt I could learn a great deal from you.'

'It's been mutual. Sir.' Bucken emptied his glass, poured himself another rum, drank it, and put the glass upside down on the fine mahogany next to the silver tray. He was already at the door when Ashenbury called after him:

'Incidentally, you may be interested to hear that we've got one of the conspirators.'

'We have? Who's that?'

'Papeete . . . Mrs. Quincey, I mean. I believe you two were . . . are . . . friends?'

'What do you mean we've got her?'

'She's . . . ' Ashenbury paused – yes, it was best to tell him because Bucken would find out anyway and it would look less conspicuous if he first heard it here and now. 'She's in jail.'

'How come?'

'Breaking and entering. That's the correct expression I believe.'

'She's no thief.'

'No, probably not. She broke into my country home but didn't take anything. Otherwise, of course, the charge would be more serious.'

'Why . . . I mean why did she go there?'

'Good question, Bucken, very good question.' Ashenbury deemed it best to let him draw his own conclusions. Bucken did just that: at least now he knew why Ashenbury had been so interested in the Quinceys throughout the case: and he thought he knew why Papeete was beyond his reach and probably immune to any other men – she was in love with Ashenbury: she must have run to him for refuge when things around her began to collapse, and he sold her down the drain.

Bucken took a cab to Holloway. The prison governor was a friend of his, so he managed to visit Papeete at that late hour in the evening for a few minutes. She went ash-coloured when she saw him.

324

'Are you well?' She could only nod. 'You know that you can get bail, don't you? . . . Have you tried?'

'No . . . Not yet.'

'Can I do anything for you?'

'No, thanks, not at the moment.'

'You . . . you know by now, don't you, that I'm a policeman? I mean active policeman.'

She hesitated, then nodded. 'Yes, yes I heard it in Marbella.' She fought off the urge to tell him that she had tried to save him, that she had warned Ashenbury who then double-crossed her, both of them, but she knew that it would be pointless. Ashenbury would deny everything, and why should Bucken believe her rather than him? He would think that she was inventing excuses. Or begging for mercy. And he'd never believe her true motive. Or would he? She needed time to think. Perhaps she could tell him next time. If there was a next time. 'I . . . I'm glad,' she said finally.

'That I'm alive?'

'You could put it that way.'

That night, Bucken drank with his rum-brother landlord of his local in Bayswater. After closing time, they were still at it. The landlord tapped his nostril: 'I ask no questions, but I know what I know. You were away for a long, long time . . . Now you're back. I bet you got your villain . . . and I salute you!'

'Villain? I say gimme a thief, poisoner, bank-robber . . . any honest villain any day rather than . . . than . . . well, never mind. Doesn't matter . . . At the end of the day, what matters is that nobody can kill a sergeant of mine and get away with it.'

He found his way home, up the stairs, and stumbled headlong over a body: Helen's. She had come to push yet another picture under his door, felt no resistance inside, guessed he was back, decided to wait for him – and fallen asleep sitting on the top of the stairs. They helped each other through the door and she was making him some coffee when the phone rang.

'Mr. Bucken?'

'Sort of.'

'Beg pardon, sir?'

'Never mind. Forget it. Yes, it's me, me, me!'

'This is Charing Cross Hospital, sir. I wonder if you could help us. You see we have two unidentified people here in a coma. One of them, the male patient, keeps muttering about a Mr. Bucken, and the nurse in charge has just managed to get your phone number out of him. I wonder if . . '

'Tell me which ward and I'm on my way.'

325

Helen drove but they survived the journey. The houseman on duty told Bucken what had happened. 'Last Friday night, these two were fished out of the Thames. They had multiple injuries, and it was sheer luck that a police launch spotted them. The police thought that some would-be murderers must have tried to dump them but were disturbed before they could fit them out with cement shoes or whatever the expression is. They have a chance to pull through. Just. Perhaps you could help to identify them.'

Five hours later, Bucken was still sitting at Freemantle's bedside when the reporter opened his eyes, mumbling faintly: 'Is this hell or heaven, Bucken?'

'It's worse. It's a hospital.'

'You mean we're not dead?' He tried to sit up but Bucken and the nurse held him down. 'Where's Ada?'

'Next door. Don't worry. She'll be all right. I swear. I have it on the highest authority.'

'You mean God?'

Bucken tried to laugh. That was when Freemantle really regained consciousness. 'I'm sorry, Bucken. I'm sorry.' He began to cry and nothing would stop his tears. 'I couldn't do anything. He cut Ada. I had to tell him. I had to.'

'Sure. You had no choice.'

'Don't be so bloody understanding! I betrayed you!'

'At least we're quits, you stupid scribe, 'cause I tricked and cheated you!'

Freemantle stared at him in horror: 'You mean no scoop?'

'That's exactly what I mean. No scoop.'

Freemantle's hands were shaking. The nurse could see the onset of trauma. She reached for a syringe and filled it with sedatives. She signalled to Bucken to leave but he paid no attention to her.

'No scoop because, if you wrote that story, you'd be sued for a billion dollars.'

'That's a lot of dollars, Bucken.' He was sobbing again. The jab went in. 'Lots and lots of dollars.'

'Yeah. But I'll give you the stuff to write it as fiction!'

'You will?' As the injection was taking effect, he began fluffing his words. 'You're a pal . . . Bucken . . . Wish I was a pal to you . . . '

'You are. My pal the author, eh? John Freemantle novelist – how's that? Can you see it? Big shiny book with your name splashed right across it. Yeah, we'll do it. We'll call it something like . . . say, *Tsunami*. Okay? First you sleep a little, then I'll tell you the story.'

'And . . . and you'll also trell . . . t-tell me why you risk your bloody arse . . . '

'Because I'm paid for it. And I sleep better afterwards. Guaranteed.'

But he was wrong. Helen had very different ideas for the rest of the day.

ACKNOWLEDGMENTS

Although in works of fiction it may be unusual to acknowledge all the help the author received in his search for factual background, revealing detail and colour, in this case I must make an exception and thank at least a few of the people who gave me generous advice, guidance and inadmissible information. Several of them, like an American banker and shipping magnate, wished to remain anonymous. They know that I am indebted to them. Although I have taken a certain degree of literary licence, I hope that I have not misused their confidence.

This is to express my gratitude towards:

George Adamson, shipping consultant, member of the Baltic Exchange

Frank Amin, shipping consultant

A. Belsham, former Inspector of the Hongkong police

Capt. J. Bowman, marine superintendent, Sealink

Peter Callitsis, ship manager, broker, Piraeus

Vincent Carratu, international fraud investigator, ex Scotland Yard

Rodney Cook, ship sale broker

Dimitri Cotsakis, ship owner

Chris Doak, chemical tanker safety specialist

Jerry Duffy, port captain, former safety manager of PAL Shipping

Eric Ellen, director, International Maritime Bureau

Norman Elliott, shipping consultant, PAN Corporate Services

Ton Grefe, managing director, Smit International U.K.

Trevor Heayns, bank manager, Piraeus

International Transport Workers' Federation

Laszlo Kovats, barrister, Master Mariner

Lloyd's List and Shipping Index

Robert Lowe, ship manager, broker, Athens

Jim MacNamara, radio officer

Albert Morris, Baltic Exchange

National Union of Seamen
Overseas Containers Ltd., ship owners – and the ship's company
  of the M.V. *Liverpool Bay*
David Owen, marine safety consultant, Sabre, Gas Detection Ltd.
Capt. Ken Owen
Alf Perry of The Salvage Association
Port Authority, Port Said
Fred Saul, secretary of the NUS Eastern Region
Graham Scullion, radio officer
Suez Canal Authority, Ismailia, particularly Capt. Aly Nasr and
  Capt. M.H. Hammouda
Peter Sullivan, specialist in ship chartering
Brian Taylor, chief engineer
Capt. G. Varndell, Freightliner 1
John Wilson, C.B.E., chief investigator, SIS, P. & I. Club, former
  Assistant Commissioner, Scotland Yard